DATE DUE

THE CONCISE
Cuddy

BOOKS BY JEREMIAH HEALY

The John Francis Cuddy Series

Blunt Darts, 1984
The Staked Goat, 1986
So Like Sleep, 1987
Swan Dive, 1988
Yesterday's News, 1989
Right to Die, 1991
Shallow Graves, 1992
Foursome, 1993
Act of God, 1994
Rescue, 1995
Invasion of Privacy, 1996
The Only Good Lawyer, 1998
The Concise Cuddy, A Collection of
    John Francis Cuddy Stories, 1998

Non-Series Novel

The Stalking of Francis Quinn, 1998

THE CONCISE
Cuddy

A Collection of
John Francis Cuddy Stories

Jeremiah Healy

Crippen & Landru Publishers
Norfolk, Virginia
1998

Cover painting by Carol Heyer; cover design by Deborah Miller

Crippen & Landru logo by Eric D. Greene

ISBN: 1-8859941-26-9 (limited edition)
ISBN: 1-885941-27-7 (trade edition)

FIRST EDITION

10 9 8 7 6 5 4 3 2 1

Crippen & Landru Publishers
P. O. Box 9315
Norfolk, VA 23505
USA
Email: CrippenL@Pilot.Infi.Net
Web: http://www.crippenlandru.com

To Jed Mattes, whose first commission as
an independent agent came from
one of these stories

CONTENTS

Introduction   9
Till Tuesday   11
Someone to Turn Out the Lights   23
One Eye Open   35
The Three Musketeers   51
Battered Spouse   65
Bertie's Mom   79
A Soul to Tell   93
Double-Con   109
Crossed Wires   120
The Bagged Man   141
Georgie-Boy   161
The Winfield Trade   187
Summary Judgment   200
Yellow Snow   225
Deputy Down   240
St. Nick   255
Spin-a-Rama   278

INTRODUCTION

I was very pleased when Doug Greene approached me at the St. Paul Bouchercon to ask whether I'd ever considered doing an anthology of my short stories. By that point, I'd written eleven novels, each centering on John Francis Cuddy, a fictional private investigator in Boston. Cuddy is a Vietnam veteran who survives the Tet Offensive in Saigon only to return home and lose his young wife, Beth, to cancer. Through the first few books in the series, he remains faithful to her memory, eventually finding someone he thinks can replace her in his life. I based Cuddy on a combination of my dad and an uncle of mine, updating those World War II veterans to the conflict I knew more about myself, but retaining and—I hope—projecting the sense of honor and duty I observed in those men while growing up around them.

I wrote the first of these stories, "Till Tuesday," in 1987 because Lois Adams, an editor at *Alfred Hitchcock's Mystery Magazine*, was gracious enough to request one from me. Frankly, I'd been putting off doing anything but novel-length stories about Cuddy: in the earlier books, he visits Beth's graveside to have "conversations" with her, and I was concerned that I'd run out of fresh ways to present those scenes in the novels if I used any in a short story. Fortunately, as the series continued, Cuddy's graveside visits became less frequent in a natural way, and I found that I liked writing the short stories as though his period of mourning were not yet over. This "freeze-frame" approach allowed me to write Cuddy more "purely," without constantly having to accommodate the necessary (though often joyful) "baggage" he'd acquired as his life evolved through the novels.

This collection represents about the first half of the Cuddy short stories. I've arranged them in the order they were written rather than the order they were published, on the theory that some followers of style might enjoy looking for linear patterns, if any. (Should you spot one, please let me know.) Similar techniques of craft will appear occasionally; I apologize for this, but I was hoping to burn my own brand onto some of the pieces.

Finally, I'll comment on just three stories in the selection. "Battered Spouse" was nominated for the Private Eye Writers of America Shamus Award in 1991. "The Bagged Man" received the parallel nomination for 1993. And "Crossed Wires" (originally entitled "Martin's Finger") was written after I visited my dad in a nursing home. Given that, I'd like you to think of his contribution to John Francis Cuddy, as I do each time I sit down to write about the character.

Jeremiah Healy
Boston, Massachusetts
December 11, 1997

TILL TUESDAY

One

Cambridge, Massachusetts is home to Harvard University, boutique restaurants, and people who believe that Anthony Lewis editorials really make a difference. The two men sitting across from me lived there, but I pictured them more as *Wall Street Journal* than *New York Times*.

The one on the right was an architect, Michael Atlee. Lanky and angular, his brown hair showed licks of white at the temples. He fit poorly into an expensive blue tweed sports jacket and red Rooster tie over slacks a little too pale to contrast correctly with his coat. Atlee held a pipe by its bowl in his hand, but made no effort to light it.

The man next to him spelled and smelled lawyer through and through. Thayer Lane, Esq., was on his business card, followed by his firm's four named partners and an upscale address. Slim with black hair, Lane wore a charcoal pinstripe uniform of power and a muted, paisley tie.

I guessed both men to be perched on the far side of forty-five. Neither seemed especially comfortable having a conference on the Wednesday after Labor Day in a one-room office with "JOHN FRANCIS CUDDY, CONFIDENTIAL INVESTIGATIONS" on the door.

After the introductions, Lane said, "Mr. Cuddy, we are here on a matter which cannot be discussed with the police. You come highly recommended, especially in the categories of loyalty and discretion."

"Thank you."

"I should say that while Mr. Atlee will be your client in this regard, he is uncomfortable with speaking at length. Hence, he asked me to accompany him here today."

I looked to Atlee. "What seems to be the problem?"

Atlee said, "Thayer?"

Lane took his cue. "Mr. Atlee—Michael, is a designer of buildings. Perhaps you're familiar with some of his works?"

Lane ticked off five recent commercial towers. I recognized two of them. I thought they looked like I-beams wearing Tina Turner dresses, but I kept it to myself. "Is the difficulty related to one of the buildings?"

"No, Mr. Cuddy," said Lane. "Let me try to outline the situation for you."

"Go ahead. And please call me John."

"John." Lane spoke like he might otherwise forget the name. "John, are you married?"

"Widower."

"Ah, sorry. Well . . ." Lane took a deep breath. "Michael is married. However, he has been engaged in an affair for three years with a woman, Gina Fiore. Michael believes that Ms.—Gina, has disappeared, and he would like you to find her."

I looked over to Atlee, who sucked on his unlit pipe and blew imaginary smoke at me. His facial movements masked any emotion.

"How long has she been missing?"

"That's uncertain. Michael last saw her this past Thursday, but couldn't reach her yesterday."

Atlee said, "Tell him all of it."

Lane glanced at Atlee and sighed. "Every Labor Day, Michael hosts a family retreat at his summer home on Parker Pond in Maine. We all go up on Thursday night, scour and spruce the place up with paint and so forth against the elements, then relax and shoot skeet Sunday and Monday."

"You shoot skeet on a lake on Labor Day weekend?"

Atlee said, "I've got ten acres. It's private enough."

I said to Atlee, "So she could be gone for as long as six days."

"Right."

"Or as little as twenty hours."

Lane stuck in, "My point precisely."

Atlee said, "Doesn't matter. She's gone."

"Where does Gina live?"

Atlee nodded to Lane, who took over again. "Gina lives in a condominium on Revere Beach that Michael purchased as an investment. Part of their, ah, arrangement is that she is to be available at all times. By telephone and in person."

Lovely. I said to Lane, "A few minutes ago you said 'we'?"

"I'm sorry?"

"You were talking about the lake thing being a family event but you said 'we all went up to the summer place.' "

"Oh, quite. Michael is a client of my firm, but we're also best friends. Roomed together at Harvard and prepped at Choate before that. My wife and I are like family to Michael and Winnie, and Seth's my godson."

I said to Atlee, "Winnie's your wife and Seth's your son?"

He nodded and bit down on the pipestem.

"Any reason for Gina to take off?"

"None." Decisively.

"Who else knows about your relationship with Gina?"

Lane said, "A woman named Marla—I'm afraid we don't have her last name—lives in the next unit in Gina's building and is aware of, ah . . ."

"Anybody else?"

Atlee fidgeted in his chair, I thought at first from impatience. Then he said, "Seth knows, or suspects. Same damned thing, I guess. Saw us once together a couple of years ago in a bar over there. Slumming with one of his swim-team chums. Damned bad luck, but there it is."

I had the impression I'd been treated to Atlee's longest speech of the decade. "Any point in my talking with him?"

"No." Case closed.

Lane said, "That would be rather difficult anyway, John."

"Why is that?"

"You see, Seth is a junior at Stanford this year, and he always leaves the morning after Labor Day to head out there."

Atlee said, "Damned fool has to drive his jeep 3000 miles. Can't take the plane like a normal person."

"In any case," said Lane, "I had a call from him last night. He was near Pittsburgh and wasn't sure of his next destination."

I said, "He called you?"

Lane seemed affronted. "I *am* his godfather."

"All right. I'll need a photo of Gina and her address over in Revere."

Atlee said, "Don't have a photo."

"I'm sure you understand," said Lane.

Before I could reply, Atlee leaned forward, tapping his pipe on my desk for emphasis. "Just understand this. I really care for that girl. I may not show it, but I do. And I want you to find her."

Two

Revere Beach is an incongruous strip of old clamshacks and new highrise towers along a slightly polluted stretch of sand and ocean about ten miles north of Boston. I flashed the key Atlee had given me at the security guard, who smile deferentially and used his magazine to wave me into the lobby. I took an elevator to the ninth floor.

Unit 9A was at the end of the hall. I had a little trouble with the lock, rattling it and the knob twice before the tumbler would turn. Inside, the apartment was airy, with a striking view of the Atlantic through sliding glass doors to a narrow balcony. Versatile sectional furniture for couch and chairs.

Track lighting overhead, a wall unit with stereo, color TV, and even a few books.

I entered the bedroom and was drawn toward some framed photos on the bureau when I thought I heard the snap and creak of a quick entry at the front door. I managed two steps before a perfectly tanned woman in a European string bikini appeared in the doorway to the living room. She leveled a tiny automatic at me and said, "My boyfriend told me to just keep firing until the guy falls."

I got the hint.

✦ ✦ ✦

"Gina and me watch each other's places, you know?"

"Good system."

"Look, at least I can make you a drink or something, huh?"

She was trying hard, a little too hard, to make up for the gun scene. My investigator's ID had convinced her I wasn't a "real" burglar, and she was pleased to introduce herself as Marla, the girl next door. I'd seen everything except the bedroom closet with nothing to show for it. Now she was watching me rummage through Gina's dresses, slacks, and shoes.

"So Mikey figures Gina's flown on him, huh?"

I liked her using "Mikey." I said over my shoulder, "That the way you see it?"

"Without telling me? And leaving all her stuff like this?" She paused. "Hard to say for sure, though. Gina's been a little restless lately."

I stopped searching and turned around. "Restless?"

"Yeah, well, it's not so easy being somebody's sweet harbor, you know? Waiting for a phone call, planning your life around a lunch here or there and some afternoon delight."

Somehow the phrase sounded sweeter in the song. "Would she have left on her own?"

"Not likely. Gina enjoyed being took care of, even by a creep like Mikey."

"How do you mean?"

"Aw, we double-dated a coupla months ago. Her and Mikey and this guy called himself 'Jim.' We drove up to Swampscott to go sailing, like they was afraid to do the class thing and go all the way to Marblehead, maybe one of their bigshot friends sees them there with two bimbettes from Revere."

"You ever see this Jim again?"

"No, but like I said, that wasn't his real name. Stupid guy, he drives us all up there in this big green Mercedes, like we're too dumb to know how to run a plate at the registry."

"You ran his license plate?"

"Yeah. Turns out he's another Cambridge highroller with, get this, the name 'Thayer Lane.'"

Ah, Mr. Lane. "This Lane seem interested in Gina?"

"Coulda been. I kept him pretty interested that day, I'll tell you. Never did hear back from him, though. Good old 'Jim.' "

"Gina ever mention Atlee's son?"

"Not really. Just that the father and him didn't get along too well."

"Some families are like that."

"Boy, you got that right." Her tone changed. "You got any pressing commitments after this here?"

I stuck my head back into the closet. There were three matching pieces of luggage; the size just up from the smallest seemed to be missing.

"Well, do you?"

"Marla," I said, pointing, "does Gina have a full set of these bags?"

She came over, pressing and rubbing more than my request required. "Uh-huh. Gina uses the other one for day-hops." She was wearing some kind of coconut-scented lotion.

"Meaning not overnight?"

Marla stepped back without answering. She kept going until her calves touched the bed, then sat back and onto her elbows, in one languid motion. She hooded her eyes. "Doesn't have to take all night, sugar."

Walking to the bureau, I picked up one of the photos. A girl about Marla's age, long frosted curls, winking at the lens.

"This Gina?"

She licked her lips. "Uh-huh."

"Recent?"

"Hair's a little shorter now. Let's talk about you. And me."

I think she was laughing as I went through the front door.

✦ ✦ ✦

I stood up, put my hands in my pockets. "Mrs. Feeney told me what they were, but it was some Latin name, and I forget it."

What happened to that elaborate altar boy training?

I looked at the purplish flowers with yellowish petals, then at her stone. Elizabeth Mary Devlin Cuddy. "Won't help me much with this one, Beth."

What's the problem?

I told her.

An architect's mistress. Sordid.

"It's about to get worse."

How?

"Tomorrow I intend to see his wife about their son."

Three

The next morning, I stopped at the office to hoke up a manila file folder and some documents, then took Memorial Drive to Cambridge. The Atlees' home was on one of those short streets off Brattle. An aggressively traditional mini-manse, it was surrounded by an outside fence nearly as tall as the trees behind it. I tapped a button on the intercom at the wrought-iron entrance and a minute later received a metallic, female "Yes?"

"Mrs. Atlee?"

"Yes?"

"My name is John Cuddy. I'm a private investigator, here about your son."

"My son? Is there some kind of problem?"

"No, no, ma'am. It's just that, well, it would be easier if I could show you the file."

Hesitation, then the grating buzz and click that tell you to push on the gate.

◆ ◆ ◆

"And you say my son witnessed an accident?"

"Yes, ma'am." I slid the folder over to her, holding my index finger on the document in the middle of the Acco-clipped bunch till she held the place for herself and began reading it.

She was about Atlee's age, with strawberry-blond hair pulled severely behind her head. A peasant dress heightened the sense of bony strength about her. Striking, not beautiful, she probably sat an English saddle well, given some of the bronzed trophies on shelves in the den. The other statuettes looked like awards for swimming and shooting.

"But this isn't even my son's handwriting."

"No, ma'am. That's the handwriting of our Mr. Green, who's no longer our Mr. Green because he fouled up so much, like here when he took down your son's statement then forgot to have him date or sign it over . . . there."

She shook her head and handed me back the file. "Well, I'm sure if Seth were here he'd be glad to help you, but he left for California on Tuesday."

I let my face fall. "Gee, Mrs. Atlee, this case is coming up for trial and all. Do you have a number where I can reach him?"

"Yes. Well, no. Not for a few more days. You see, he drives there, to return to Stanford, and he rather dawdles really, taking roads that interest him and stopping wherever."

"Does he call you?"

"Sometimes. Other times no. If we hear from him, we could ask him to call you, but it would probably be late at night and perhaps not at all."

"Is there anyone else he might call?"

She considered it. "Yes. His friend Doug Cather. Seth and Doug were on the swim team together at prep school. Doug's at Harvard now."

I looked past her to a photo on the mantle. A family portrait of a younger Atlee and wife behind a seated teenager.

"Is that Seth?"

She twisted around and looked back at me. "Yes." She darkened. "Is there something else?"

"No, no. He looks like a fine boy."

✦ ✦ ✦

Doug Cather lived in Kirkland House, part of the not-quite- quadrangle of more-than-dorms nestled near the Charles River. He was tall, broad-shouldered and completely hairless.

"We shave our heads."

"Why?"

"For swimming. Cuts down on the drag effect in the water."

Anything for dear old Harvard, I guess. Cather accepted my bogus accident story.

"No, I haven't heard from Seth, which is kind of funny."

"You two stay in touch that closely?"

"Not really. It's just that he always calls me when he leaves for school, and I kind of waited around for it yesterday morning. Cut classes and all."

"Wait a minute. I thought Seth left for California on Tuesday. Yesterday was Wednesday."

Cather's face clouded over.

I said, "There's something you're not telling me."

"There's something I don't think is any of your business."

"Something about Seth?"

"Yeah."

"Look, I'm not going to give you a long song and dance about confidentiality. You don't know me at all, so you don't know if you can trust me."

"That's right."

"Okay. Here's my problem. I've got to find your friend. You can help me, or I can do it the hard way. Go see other people, his dad, whoever. That might mean I find out worse things than I need to know. All I can say is if you tell me what's going on, I'll try to keep it to myself."

Cather didn't speak.

"We want Seth as a witness for us on this collision. I'm not about to spread rumors that would make him look bad."

"It's not . . ." He seemed to search inside for a moment. "I want your promise anyway. You won't tell anybody?"

"Promise."

He blew out a breath. "Okay, it's like this. After we graduated Choate, Seth and I bounced around for the summer. One day we decide to go to Revere Beach, kind of scope out the other half, you know? Well, we dare each other to go into this bar. I mean, we're way underage and nobody's ever gonna serve us without ID, but we try it anyway. Right off, I spot Seth's father in one of the booths, with a real tough . . . a really sharp-looking chick, just a couple of years older than us. So I start to say something, and Seth sees them and gets all uptight. He's kind of impulsive anyhow, and he bolts out of there and like won't even talk with me all the way home."

"What's that got to do with his driving to California?"

"Well, it didn't take a genius to see what his dad was doing there, and I guess Seth and him had a real blow-up over it. Anyway, Seth decides not to go out for swimming at Stanford, like to punish his dad, I guess. But every year his family has this Labor Day thing to please his mom. So okay, after Seth gets home from the weekend each year, he goes back up to their summer place."

"Seth goes back?"

"Right. He tells his parents he's leaving for school, and he does, sort of, but first he drives up to Parker Pond and does the swim."

"The swim."

"Yeah. He swims out from their property to this little island and back. It's like a ritual, I guess, to prove he can still go the distance. And maybe to think about when he was younger and he didn't, well, know about his dad."

"Would Seth sleep over in Maine on that Tuesday night?"

"Definitely. It's almost four hours to get there, and he probably wouldn't leave his parents in Cambridge much before lunchtime."

"You ever been to this Parker Pond house?"

"Sure. Lots of times."

"Can you draw me a map?"

Four

Even with Doug Cather's sketch, I had to stop at an inn on the main road for supplemental directions. A turn-off went from paved to gravel to hard-pack dirt. Then I saw rutted tracks curve off the road, a primitive driveway running under a white tollgate. Leaving the car, I walked up to the gate. A single horizontal bar, very freshly painted, was hinged on one of two posts and swung inward freely.

The day was warm, the only sound the wind in the trees and a woodpecker hammering away nearby. I decided to approach more quietly than my old Fiat would allow. I tossed my sports coat into the front seat and switched on the hazard lights. Ducking under the gate bar, I started walking.

The driveway doglegged right to insure privacy and squiggled here and there to avoid particularly substantial pines. Passing the last big tree, I spotted the back of the house.

A black Jeep Wrangler was parked at the mouth of an adjoining shed.

I moved through the underbrush and approached the shed, keeping it between me and the large chalet-style house behind it. I stopped at the side of the shed to listen. No noise from inside.

Edging toward the front, I looked through the webby pane of the shed's door. Paint buckets, rake and lawnmower, gasoline can, etc. The Jeep was stuffed to the roof with the odd-lot cartons and containers students use to return to college.

I circled around the house. Every door and window seemed sealed tight. The wind was really howling lakeside, kicking whitecaps against the shoreline.

At the back door, I knocked, waited, and knocked again louder. Inside I could see the kitchen area. Using a rock to break the glass, I was hit with the stench as I opened the door itself. I gagged and tried to close off my nasal passages with the back of my tongue. Grabbing a dishrag off the rack over the sink, I took it to the shed and doused it with gasoline. I held the rag to my face and went back inside.

He was lying on the floor of the great room, cathedral ceiling above him. A dry pair of swim trunks and a beach towel lay on a chair next to him. At his side, a carefully carved and scrolled double-barreled shotgun, one hand around the trigger mechanism. His face was bloated, the head connected only by the few tendons the blast had left of his neck. Seth Atlee, a marionette past all mending.

Gina was on the open, slatted staircase leading to the upper level. Naked, she'd taken the other barrel between the shoulder blades and would have been dead before her nose struck the tenth step.

The house was twenty degrees hotter than the ambient temperature outside. I didn't think my gasoline filter would let me use a telephone.

I pulled the door closed and walked slowly down the driveway. At the gate, I noticed what seemed to be a grass stain on the house side of the swing bar, stark against the gleaming white. Like someone had scraped the inner edge of the bar against a car.

I started the Fiat and drove to the inn to learn about law enforcement in Maine.

Five

The funeral was scheduled for Saturday afternoon, beginning from a mortuary on Massachusetts Avenue in Cambridge. I got there early and parked a block away. Even announced murder/suicides draw large numbers of sincere mourners these days. I watched the arrivals of Michael and Winnie Atlee, Doug Cather, and Thayer Lane with a woman I took to be his wife.

Forty minutes later, the crowd came back out, repairing to private cars to form the procession. I left the Fiat. Pausing at Lane's Mercedes, I could see the lawyer on the porch of the funeral home, bending slightly at the waist and using both hands to shake gently with a short, elderly woman. I caught his eye. He glared at me. I smiled and beckoned. He excused himself, moving stiff-legged over to me.

"Counsellor."

"Mr. Cuddy, don't you think it a bit tasteless for you to appear here?"

"What I think is that Seth didn't kill Gina or himself."

Lane stopped fussing.

I said, "How long did you figure it'd take before they would have been found?"

"I beg your pardon?"

"The bodies. Buttoned up in the house and all. Seth would be reported missing by his college after a while, but who would think to check the lake place?"

"What in the world kind of question is that?"

"You see, the longer the wait, the tougher to peg time of death. After a couple of weeks, no one would swear to anything shorter than a few, bracketed days."

"Mr. Cuddy, I really must get back."

"You didn't want me searching for Gina so quickly after Atlee couldn't raise her. You double-dated with him, Gina and Marla once. Gina was restless, maybe you caught each other's fancy."

"Preposterous."

"But Atlee's a big client and an old friend. So you needed a safe place to try your luck. None safer than the summer home you helped close up the day before."

"I'm not going to—"

"Listen any more? You've listened too much as it is, Lane. An innocent man would have walked already."

He clenched his teeth. "Finish it then."

"You didn't know about Seth's ritual swim. I'm guessing you were in the sack with Gina when Seth burst in downstairs. He would have seen your car. Did he call out to you? 'Hey, Uncle Thayer, you upstairs?' "

Lane looked clammy, unsteady.

"You jump out of bed, try to pull some clothes on. Seth's in good shape, though, takes the steps two at a time. Sees you in the nearly altogether with the woman he recognizes as his dad's mistress. He goes nuts, runs back downstairs, gets a skeet gun. He loads it and comes back, back to purge the stain from the one place he still thought was family inviolate."

"No, no."

"You try to reason with him in the great room, Gina following you down the stairs. A struggle, the gun wavers toward Seth as somebody hits the trigger. Seth goes down, Gina yells, 'You murdered him!' Or maybe she just starts screaming, screaming till you lock onto her as a target and she—"

"You can't prove a word of this!"

"No?" I gestured toward the hood of his Mercedes. "Those gouge marks. You put them there, when you swung the gate in to leave the place on Tuesday."

He blinked, trying to make the scratches go away. "They. . . they . . ."

"Freshly painted gate, two days before. If you'd taken a piece out of the car driving back Monday, the missus would remember it. The kind of thing that would spoil the whole weekend."

"Seth, he called me . . ."

I shook my head. "Nobody called you Tuesday night, because Seth didn't call his friend Wednesday morning. I'm betting the medical examiner saw the bodies soon enough to place both deaths on Tuesday afternoon. The phone alibi would have been perfect in a few more weeks. Now it's going to hang you."

"Thayer? Thayer!"

We both turned. Michael Atlee was chopping his hand toward the lead limousine. For the godfather.

Lane whispered, "What are you . . ."

"Going to do? I'm going to give you a chance here, Thayer. Mikey there is your best friend, right?"

"I . . . , yes he is, but—"

"Then sometime in the next two days you're going to tell him all about it."

"Money. You want money."

"I don't want money, Thayer. I was hired to find Gina Fiore. I found her and was paid. Now you're going to do your job. You're going to be the first to tell your best friend how his mistress and son really died."

"Thayer!" called Atlee, striding determinedly toward us.

Lane said, "But for God's sake, Cuddy, that's not how it happened! The way you said, it wasn't like that."

"Maybe not. You've got till Tuesday to come up with a better version."

I walked back to my car.

SOMEONE TO TURN OUT THE LIGHTS

One

The O'Dell Law Offices were located in the old Prudential tower, abandoned by the insurer when it decided to close a number of regional centers. I took the elevator to the eleventh floor, then followed the corridor numbers to the O'Dell office door. The common hallway reminded me of the Empire Insurance building where I had worked as head of Boston claims investigation before becoming a private investigator.

The wooden version of O'Dell's letterhead which hung next to the doorframe reflected what I'd expected: In addition to the patriarch Michael who had called me, there were two O'Dell males and one O'Dell female listed as attorneys. Walking in, I was welcomed by a nondescript receptionist and ushered immediately into Michael O'Dell's office.

O'Dell stood awkwardly, though he appeared to be in good physical condition for a man of sixty or so years. He said, "John Francis Cuddy?" and I nodded. O'Dell shook my hand, his palm wet, and asked me to be seated as a way of killing time until the receptionist exited, closing the door behind her.

His bushy, gray eyebrows worked furiously as he opened a manila file on his desk and scanned it. "This isn't going to be easy for me."

On the phone, he'd led me to believe some corporation needed my services. Now it seemed more personal.

"Maybe if you told me something about the client involved?"

O'Dell closed the folder, meshing his hands nervously on top of it. "You ever hear of the Cleary Carpet Cleaning Company?"

"I've seen photo ads. With their founder, right?"

"Right. Edward Cleary. Eddie and I go back to college together, Holy Cross."

"Me, too."

"I know. I found you through another alum who'd used you, vouched for your discretion."

"Cleary have a problem?"

"Yes, but he doesn't know it yet, and I'm damned if I know how to tell him."

"Can you tell me about it?"

"Eddie built the business himself, a truck at a time, eighty, ninety hour weeks. He and the business were my first clients out of law school, when I was operating over a deli in Brighton. Long before this place." He waved his hand around the tasteful office, and I got the impression the unspecified move to the Pru was the brainchild of one of his lawyerly relatives.

"Go on."

"Well the Cleary company's still privately held and one of the best in the area. Oh, they've taken it on the chin from some nationwide competitors, and they're not really geared up for some of the big, cover-your-overhead skyscrapers as customers, but it's a good organization with a loyal staff. And Eddie's damned proud of the fact that he's turned a profit every year since he opened. 'Never a year in the red, Mike,' and so on."

"And now his record's in danger?"

"I think so. Damn, I know so." O'Dell squared his shoulders. "Look, let me stop talking around this thing and give it to you straight, okay?"

"Fine."

O'Dell re-opened the file. "Eddie's on vacation now. Takes a week every quarter. Fishing in the spring and summer, the Caribbean in the fall and winter. His wife died years ago, no kids, and the trips are the one extravagance he allows himself. So, I don't like to disturb him, especially the way he's been looking lately. A little sickly, you know? But I needed some information for a tax matter I'm working on, and their bookkeeper was out, sprained his ankle getting off the bus, for God's sake. So I got the assistant bookkeeper to get me into the computer system, and I didn't like what I saw."

"Somebody's been dipping?"

"That's what I figure it has to be, but I don't have any direct proof of it."

"Sounds like you want an audit, Mr. O'Dell. A CPA, not a private investigator."

O'Dell shook his head. "Let me show you what I've found out so far, and I think you'll see what I mean." He took a breath. "The company has a number of accounts in the fifty thousand dollar range. Eight to be exact. Well, I found a ninth I knew nothing about."

"Is that so unusual?"

"Eddie and I have dinner together once a week, maybe every two weeks. He talks business a lot, how great his employees are, and so on. He would have mentioned this outfit, along with the others, sometime."

"Could it be a new account?"

"No. The computer shows it being in-house for almost three years, thirteen thousand a quarter is the billing."

"And the money arrives while the founder is on his vacations."

"No," said O'Dell.

"No?"

"No, and that's what makes me even more suspicious. Eddie doesn't concentrate on the business like he used to, but his people bring him up to date as soon as he gets back on everything that happened the week he's gone. The money always arrives the Thursday before he takes off."

"So it's probably never part of his return summary."

"So it's programmed not to be, seems to me."

"What's this outfit's name?"

"Plummer Industries."

"Never heard of them. They'd have to be pretty big to need fifty-two thousand of rug cleaning a year, wouldn't they?"

"Not as big as you'd think, though the way things are going, any one of the big accounts represents Cleary's technical profit margin for the year. But Plummer's relative size isn't the issue."

"What is the issue, then?"

"Except for a filing with the Secretary of State's office over on Beacon Hill, and a checking account with the Bank of New England, they don't exist. Period."

I thought about it. "Phony company pays money to Cleary for cleaning carpets they don't have? Doesn't make sense."

"That's what I mean. There's something wrong here, but before I tell Eddie Cleary that one of his people is diddling him, I want to have more proof than I've got. The problem is I can't get close enough to the three people it could be without tipping them that I'm suspicious."

"Why only three?"

"Because I know Eddie's internal set-up well enough to eliminate everybody else." O'Dell handed me a paper. "Only these three have the kind of juice and access to pull off something like this."

The sheet had names, titles, and home addresses typed on it. I read aloud. "Manny Krebs, Director of Services."

"Manny's the guy who actually oversees the carpet cleaning operations. He's the nervous kind, but he could conceivably submit an invoice for work that never got done, then somehow use the trucks for other work that paid him under the table."

I didn't quite see that, but I went on. "Anita Singer, Director of Sales."

"Anita basically brings in new business. It's tough in this line for a woman, but Eddie was impressed by the way she worked her way through school. She's done pretty well, based on the customers I do recognize as new ones, but she'd also be in the best position to create a phony one."

"George Bates, Director of Accounting."

"That's the guy who turned his ankle. George isn't really an accountant in the education sense, but he's been there twenty years, Eddie met him driving somewhere. There's never been a hint of trouble before, but he's obviously in the best position to cook the books."

"You said you checked Plummer's corporate filings. Did you pick up its officers, directors, that sort of thing?"

"Yes. Here."

He handed me a xerox of the cover sheet for the Plummer Industries incorporation. Three men filled all positions: incorporators, officers, even shareholders. The names were James Meeney, Ronald J. Roche, and Derwood Robinson. The company's principal place of business was an address in Somerville past Lechmere Sales. The men's addresses were scattered all over Boston.

"Any of these names mean anything to you?"

"No. I checked the phonebook on the company and all three of them. Nothing listed. I even drove by Plummer's given address. Empty lot."

We resolved retainer and billing, and I stood to go.

O'Dell sighed, a glacier shifting. "Can you help me here?"

"I can try."

Two

"Homicide, Murphy speaking."

"The switchboard warned me I was being recorded. Do you keep the machine going when they transfer my—"

"Cuddy, I don't have time for this jive. You want something, say it straight, all right?"

"All right." I pictured him, a stolid, Black Buddha crushing the receiver in his hand. "I'd like you to run some names for me."

"This got anything to do with something I should know about?"

"Just a simple corporate security check, Lieutenant."

"All right, let's have 'em."

I gave him Edward Cleary, the three company employees, and the three principals of Plummer Industries. Then I threw in Michael O'Dell for good measure. Murphy said he'd leave any information on my tape machine.

✦ ✦ ✦

Manny Krebs lived in a wooden three-decker in East Boston within deafening range of Logan Airport's runways. That evening I watched him dash out of his house, shirttails flapping, and climb into a three-year-old Cadillac in the driveway. He took the most direct route possible to the Wonderland greyhound track, me trailing in my Prelude.

I'm not much of a gambler, but I prefer the horses to the dogs. Krebs loved the puppies enough to jog through traffic from the parking lot to the admissions gate. Staying behind Krebs by three people in the line, I saw an older man approach him. The man grabbed Krebs genially by the arm and mouthed, "Manny, how you doing?" before Krebs urgently broke the grasp and trotted toward a betting window, tout sheet in hand.

I went up to the elderly gent. "That Manny, he's always in a rush to lose his money."

The man chuckled. "Yeah. The guy's here every night, you'd think he'd learn to bet better or walk slower, make his dough last."

"I don't know. I don't do that well myself."

"Pal, you gotta do better than Manny there. I tell him, 'Manny, you might as well throw the money into the street, all the talent you got for picking the fast ones.' "

I smiled and moved after Manny. Lounging against the rail, I watched him agonize over the failure of his chanted number 6 to beat the other anorexic hounds pursuing Swifty the mechanical rabbit. Krebs had a long, sorrowful face, with deepset brown eyes and thinning brown hair.

I moved closer, interrupting his comparison of the entries in the next race. "Don't feel bad. I thought six'd finish in the money, too."

"Yeah," he said, not looking up but using a red flair pen to circle numbers on his sheet.

"Hey, aren't you Mr. Krebs?"

He looked up and at me, then my extended hand. He shook absently. "Yeah, Manny. Manny Krebs. Who are you?"

"John Francis. I'm a friend of Jim Meeney over at Plummer Industries. I think your company does their carpets."

Nothing flashed over his expression. "I don't think so. Where's their offices at?"

"Somerville. Just past Lechmere Sales."

Krebs seemed apologetic. "Jeez, we got a lotta accounts over that way, but I never heard of these Plummer people. Maybe you saw me somewheres else?"

"Maybe. I visit a lot of the operations over there."

Krebs darted his eyes to the toteboard, then back again to his selections. "Look, buddy, I don't mean to be rude or nothing, but I got some picks to make here. Be seeing you."

He hurried off toward the parimutuels. Gambling and embezzling often go hand in hand, but I think Krebs had forgotten about Plummer and me both by the time he took out his wallet.

◆ ◆ ◆

The next morning, I laid the roses across the least green part of the sod, hoping to mask what the sunshine had burned due to the cemetery's erratic watering system.

It's like trying to cover the hole in a sweater, John. Everything you do just makes it more obvious.

"I know." Rising, I looked past Beth's headstone to the harbor below us. A couple of sailboats were tacking across each other's bows, violating what I thought were the right of way rules on the water. "I wish this case were a little more obvious."

What's the trouble with it?

I told her.

Wouldn't there be easier ways of embezzling?

"Probably. But employees who tap the kitty generally think the more complicated it is, the less likely they'll be caught."

Are they right?

"Not usually."

Three

"Thank you, Mr. Francis, but I can't imagine we'd switch from our present system of forms to another, even if you had your samples with you."

"I understand, Ms. Singer."

She put a sympathetic smile on her pretty, thirtyish face, framed by blond, Doris Day hair. "I know it's tough to be turned down cold in sales, but if only you'd called first, I could have saved you the trip."

"That's okay. I was in the area anyway, so I thought I'd give it a try. Ron Roche over at Plummer suggested I see you."

"Ron Roche?"

"Yes."

She pursed her lips, thoughtful, then wagged her head. "I don't think I know him. At Plummer, you said?"

"Plummer Industries. Over past Lechmere Sales. I thought you were the one who signed them up for Cleary here."

Singer shrugged. "Not me. I thought I'd canvassed just about every prospect we didn't already have in-house when I started, but I guess I must have missed that one." She picked up a pen and moved a stick-it pad into place. "Is this Mr. Roche the one I should see?"

"Yes. If he's not in, try Derwood Robinson. Or even James Meeney."

She took them down, asking reasonably for correct spellings and underlining the company name. "Thanks for the tip. I'll try to reciprocate sometime, but right now I've got a lunch date."

I said I could find my own way out and did, waiting in the Prelude at the edge of the parking lot. Singer appeared shortly and hopped into a Toyota Celica. I followed her to the Mass Pike, then west till we got to Wellesley, a toney suburb. She twisted and turned for a while before pulling into a driveway that angled up to a massive, pillared colonial. Singer left the car and walked to the broad entryway, pushing the buzzer. I parked down the road a hundred feet and came back in time to see an attractive, fortyish woman open the front door. Hugging each other, they moved inside.

Five minutes later, the window curtains to an upstairs bedroom were drawn against the cruel afternoon sun and potentially prying eyes. Feeling vaguely disoriented, I returned to my car.

✦ ✦ ✦

George Bates hobbled out his front door on crutches. The house was a modest two-family in Arlington, a solid suburb north and west of the city. Five-foot-four and portly, he wore his sandy hair long and slicked back, fifties style. I expected a dedicated employee like Bates to put in a half day's work. Instead he took the Arlington Heights #77 bus down Massachusetts Avenue into the bowels of the Harvard Square station. I parked illegally and raced down the pedestrian entrance to the subway, just managing to spot him and sprint the twenty yards to the rear door of the Red Line car he'd chosen. A college kid graciously yielded her seat to him, and he got off four stops later at Park Street, in downtown Boston.

Above ground, Bates lurched his way down Tremont Street, resting every block or so. He finally turned harborside and struggled through a revolving door into the gallery offices of a national stock brokerage house. He went up to a man about my age sitting behind a desk. They greeted each other like old friends and then hunched over some documents, smiling and pointing like two codgers admiring photos of their grandchildren.

A heavy woman in a business skirt and blouse swept by me with a file in her hand. I said, "Excuse me?"

She turned. "Oh, sorry."

"No harm done, but I was just wondering. Do you work here?"

"Yes, yes I do. Can I help you with something?" Her manner indicated she hoped not.

I gestured toward Bates and the broker. "The younger fellow talking with the man on crutches. He's a dead ringer for a classmate of mine at Harvard, and I was wondering, is his name Cabot Lithgow? We called him 'Skipper' at school."

She restrained her impatience beautifully. "No, no I'm afraid not. That's Jared Kane. He did go to Harvard, though."

"Oh, thank you. I'm so glad I asked now. You've saved me a bushel of embarrassment."

"Don't mention it," she said, bustling away.

I waited till Bates left Mr. Kane, then found a payphone and called the brokerage house.

"Jared Kane here."

"Mr. Kane, this is John Francis calling. George Bates referred me to you. In fact, he mentioned he was seeing you today. I hope I'm not disturbing anything?"

"Not at all, Mr. Francis. In fact, you just missed George."

Kane seemed too polite to mention that Bates hadn't said a thing about me to him. "Oh, that's too bad. How did he seem on the ankle, by the way?"

"Oh, he tottered a bit, but he's too tough a sort to let it slow him down. How can I help you?"

"Well, George and I were talking about investments, and as I told him, with my aunt passing on and all, I have about as much as he does in relatively liquid assets . . ."

"And?"

I could almost hear Mr. Kane salivating on the other end of the line. "And George has been so pleased by how well you've done by him, he said you were the man to talk to."

"Ah, Mr. Francis—"

"Oh, please, call me John."

"Thank you. And call me Jared. Well, we've certainly done our best for George, but I must confess, he does so much of the research and weighing himself, I daresay he should be the broker and I the client."

We both had a good laugh over that one, and I made an appointment with him for the next week that I had no intention of keeping.

✦ ✦ ✦

The message on my tape machine was simple and direct. Or directive. "Call me at home tonight."

When I reached Murphy, he said, "Ran your names. What's going on here?"

The statute that licenses private investigators says you give information only to your client. The reality is you tell the police what they want to know or they stop telling you what you need to know. I gave him the abridged edition.

"You do get into some weird trashcans, boy."

"What do you have?"

"On Edward Cleary, Michael O'Dell, Manny Krebs, and Anita Singer, nothing. On brothers Meeney, Roche, and Robinson, plenty. About all you need though is their current and permanent address."

"Walpole."

"Commissioner wants us to call it Cedar Junction now, but the bars be as strong and the walls as thick."

"How long?"

"Dinosaurs. Meeney been in the longest, since sixty-two. Roche I got from sixty-three, Robinson sixty-six. All lifers, no possibility of parole."

"What about George Bates?"

"That's the cute one. He's an alum. Did himself a dime for armed robbery."

"When did he hit the streets?"

"Sixty-eight. If the paperwork's righteous, he been clean as a baby's conscience ever since. Help you out?"

"Good question."

Four

George Bates was at work early the next day. His office was an interior one, a fluorescent light shining overhead and a brass gooseneck lamp with a green glass shade arcing incongruously next to the computer terminal Michael O'Dell had described to me two days earlier. Bates swiveled around in his chair as I entered. He bade me sit and asked how he could help me.

"I'd like to talk about Plummer Industries."

"Plummer."

"Yes, and your classmates, too. Meeney, Roche and Robinson, Esquires."

Bates leaned back in his chair, pulling on his nose with the fingers of his left hand. "You wouldn't by any chance be John Francis, too, would you?"

"My first and middle names."

"I thought Jared Kane was nuts when he called to thank me for the referral, but I played along. Have you talked with anybody else about Plummer?"

"Anita Singer and Manny Krebs."

"They don't know anything about it."

"I know. When I mentioned Plummer and the boys to them, neither even flinched."

"You talk with anybody besides Anita and Manny?"

He seemed an innocuous little guy, but he'd spent at least ten years learning bad habits from badder folks, so I resettled myself in the chair, right leg tensed for traction and motion. "Just the police."

"Oh." Bates chewed on his lower lip. "Oh, that's a relief."

"A relief?"

He looked at me, bemused. "Yes, Mr. Cuddy. I'm long past violating parole, though I don't see what I've been doing as criminal anyway. I'm just relieved you haven't talked with Mr. Cleary. Who was it sicced you on me, anyway? Let me guess: Mike O'Dell?"

"That's confidential."

"That makes it O'Dell, all right. He came in here needing something the day I was in the hospital, and he stumbled across the Plummer account, right?"

"Why don't you tell me about it?"

"I guess I'll have to. O'Dell tell you how Mr. Cleary and I met?"

"Like I said, you tell me."

"So very careful, aren't you? Good, I like that. Makes me willing to trust you on this. I met Edward Cleary twenty years, six months and twelve days ago. Know how I can remember that so well?" .

"Probably the day they let you out."

A hardening seeped into his voice. "You're a comer, you are. I was trying to hitch a ride. In the rain. New suit, cardboard suitcase just a little stiffer than the suit, black Corfam shoes. Nobody picked up hitchers along there."

"Except Cleary."

"Right. He was a helluva guy then, my friend. Knew I was fresh out, could see it without me having to tell him, but he gave me a lift and asked what I could do. I told him I studied accounting inside, but I couldn't really see anybody taking a chance on me outside. He said he would, and I started here two days later."

"And?"

"And for seventeen years everything was rosy. Oh, we had some tough times, but Mr. Cleary was a helluva businessman too, and we weathered them. Everybody pulled together, and we cleared a profit every quarter."

"Until three years ago."

"Right. Until then, when the nationals started cutting us out of the big, new jobs. Oh, the old customers stayed loyal, just like the staff here, but we stopped getting the new business you need to stay up there."

"Enter Plummer Industries."

"Yeah. I'd been saving the whole time I was here. Never took more than three days off at a time in twenty years, and I rode the market just right. Got into two-families in Arlington there and rolled some over into twelve-unit brick buildings. Then I got lucky with some commercial land out by 495 that I bought before anybody thought of high tech pushing that far west."

"You're Plummer Industries."

"In a manner of speaking. I borrowed the names for the formal stuff, because I knew Jimmy, Ron and Der weren't likely to be wheeling and dealing much themselves. I set up the corporate shell, established a bank account, and salted it from time to time with my capital gains and whatnot from the other deals."

"But why?"

"Why?"

"Yeah. Why set up Plummer to pay money to Cleary for work Cleary never did?"

Bates picked up a pencil, pointing it at me like a gun barrel. "Because Edward Cleary picked up a con on a crummy day outside Walpole when he didn't have to, then offered the con a job that meant something and trusted the con to do it right. Then said Mr. Cleary started to lose his grip just enough at the wrong time competitionwise, and now Cleary Carpet Cleaning just can't catch up. We can't get back there to profitability no matter how much Anita hustles or Manny scrubs, get me?"

"And thanks to Plummer, Cleary's still never had a year in the red."

"You've got it."

"A hell of a thing to do."

"What?"

"Squandering your own retirement money on a business you know is going down."

Bates snorted. "It's nothing. Weren't for Mr. Cleary, I'd be washing dishes somewhere, not sitting on enough to see me through whatever time's left. Which is more than Mr. Cleary's got, from the look he's had lately."

Bates softened a bit. "No, I'll just limp along for a while, long enough to see Mr. Cleary safe in the ground with his record intact. Besides, after he's gone, they'll need me here for a while to wind things down. Somebody's got to turn out the lights, right?"

I just looked at Bates.

He said, "So, what do you do now?"

"Not me. We. We go see lawyer O'Dell and you tell him what you told me."

I stood while Bates shrugged into his coat and onto his crutches. I reached for the switch on the wall.

"Please," he said, smiling slightly, "let me get that."

ONE EYE OPEN

One

Craig Abbot's office featured blonde oak furniture, an onyx desk set, and a view of Boston's waterfront that a harbormaster would envy. I'd known that he was a domestic relations attorney. It looked as though he was a successful one.

Abbot said, "Please, take a seat, Mr. Cuddy. I really appreciate your coming over on such short notice."

"The meeting may be shorter than the notice. As I told your secretary when she called me, I don't do divorce work."

Abbot grinned affably. Insurance agents and divorce lawyers always grin affably. "When I called my contact on the Boston force, he told me John Francis Cuddy was a reliable private investigator with substantial criminal experience. That's what I need for this case."

"Go ahead."

"I also require discretion and confidentiality."

I said, "What you say to your client is within the attorney-client privilege, right? What I look into and tell you is also within that privilege, since I'm acting as your representative. Or, it's within the investigator-client confidentiality my licensing statute imposes on me."

"Very good." Abbot leaned back in his judge's swivel chair, crossing his legs. Brown wavy hair, around six feet tall, fairly trim. Good-looking in a post-preppy way, he seemed mid-forties, but his out-of-season tan might mask another five years.

"Until recently, I represented Wendy Steinberg in the divorce case brought by her husband Michael."

"He the Steinberg killed in the burglary last month?"

"Correct. Under the antenuptial agreement they signed, Michael was to retain all the property he brought into the marriage, including his family home in Beacon Harbor. He was killed there, apparently by a thief."

"If I remember the news accounts, his sister brought suit, claiming your client was the killer."

"Correct again. Naturally, I believe it an action totally without merit, but Lissa—Michael's sister—found an attorney who disagreed." Abbot used about six syllables to bring out "attorney," as though we were talking about the lowest form of life on the planet. I was thinking about people in glass houses.

"The case having been brought, however, it must be defended and dispelled. That is where you come in. I want you to look into the matter and prove, if you can, that Wendy is innocent."

I considered things for a moment.

Abbot said, "Well, are you interested?"

"What do the cops say?"

"You mean about Wendy's involvement?"

"That's what I mean."

"I suppose it's no secret that the spouse is generally at the top of the list, suspectwise. But here there is an interesting quirk which has them stymied. And which should win the civil suit for us."

"Which is?"

Abbot reached into a desk drawer and pulled out a video-cassette case. He popped it open, showing me the cassette itself, then snapped it closed again. "This is a video deposition I took of Lissa two days ago. It jibes with what Wendy has told me. I'd like you to view it before I taint you any further with facts."

"You want me to hear the other side's version before you tell me yours?"

He slid the black container over to me. "I think you'll see what I mean."

✦ ✦ ✦

Abbot's secretary plunked me in a corner of the library, started the video equipment, and left me. The camera focussed on each person present, which included Lissa Steinberg, her lawyer (a bumbler in a polyester sports coat named Treacy) and Abbot. Wendy Steinberg apparently decided not to attend. After the preliminaries of swearing the witness, we had lawyer-to-lawyer stipulations (including using first names for both female Steinbergs to keep straight who was who) and Lissa's educational background.

Abbot asked the questions, Lissa answered them. She sat tall, slim, and just on the plain side of pretty, with honey-colored hair clipped the way Dorothy Hamill used to wear hers.

"Now Lissa, you met Wendy through Michael, correct?"

"Yes."

"Can you tell us how that came about?"

"I was appearing in a little theater production, Michael brought Wendy to it, and we met at the cast party afterwards."

"Would it be fair to say that you and Wendy became friends?"

Treacy said, "Object to the form of the question."

Abbot said, "What's your objection?"

"You've been leading the witness all over the place here."

Abbot said, "The witness is the adverse party. I can ask her leading questions."

When Treacy didn't reply, Abbot turned back to Lissa. "Again, would it be fair to say that you and Wendy became friends?"

"Yes."

"Close friends?"

Lissa bridled a little. Her large, sharp eyes darted left-right-left in a constant rhythm as she considered the question.

"I'd say we saw each other once a week, maybe twice. Lunch, shopping, that sort of thing."

"Are you still an actress?"

"No. I never was one, really. Not intending to make a career out of it, I mean. I'm in fashion design now. Women's outerwear."

"Calling your attention to the night Michael died, you were at Wendy's apartment in Boston, were you not?"

"Yes."

"At 182 Commonwealth Avenue?"

"Yes."

"How did you come to be there?"

Lissa frowned. "Wendy and Michael were going through a divorce, as you well know. It was civilized, but it was still a divorce. Though I felt obvious loyalty to my brother, I wanted to let Wendy know that I still valued her friendship, that their split-up wasn't the end of us as well."

"Who invited whom?"

"I'm sorry?"

"Did Wendy invite you over?"

"No. No, I was in town anyway, and I just stopped by."

"Without calling first?"

"As I said, we were friends. Then."

"Yes, but I take it from your answer that Wendy couldn't have known you were coming, correct?"

Lissa paused.

Abbot said, "Lissa?"

"No. No, she couldn't."

"And you were having drinks, correct?"

"Yes."

"And a phone call interrupted?"

"Yes."

"And what happened next?"

Lissa squeaked in her chair, as though it were the wrong angle for her to be sitting. "Wendy said something like, 'Oh, Michael, Lissa's here now.' And I said, 'It's Michael?' And Wendy said, 'Yes, do you want to talk with him?' And before I could say anything, Wendy said, 'Michael? Michael, what is it?' "

"Can I interrupt you there?"

"You already have."

"What did Wendy's voice sound like, as she was asking him what was going on?"

Treacy said, "Object to the form of the question. You can answer it if you can."

Lissa looked at Treacy and then said to Abbot, "Wendy sounded concerned."

Abbot said, "What happened next?"

"I went up to the phone, and I heard . . ." Lissa produced a tissue from her lap and dabbed at her nose and eyes. Playing a little too hard to the balcony, she'd have to tone things down before the jury. "I heard Michael's voice say, 'Wait a minute. Wait, I think someone's in the house.' And then, there was this noise, like hands clapping, three or four times. The police said those were the shots. And that's . . . that's the last time I heard his voice."

"Lissa, I realize this is difficult for you, but I need to go further. Would you like to take a break?"

Lissa shook her head. Abbot said, "I'm sorry, but you have to speak as well as gesture."

"Oh, sorry. No. No, I can go on now. Let's finish this."

"That night, what happened next?"

"We waited. We waited for Michael to come back on the phone, but he never did. After maybe five minutes, Wendy finally hung up and called the police."

"In Beacon Harbor?"

"Yes, not the Boston police."

"Lissa, assume for a moment that the telephone company shows Michael's call to Wendy originating at exactly 8:51 p.m. that night. Does that sound right to you?"

Treacy said, "Object to the form. You can answer it if you can."

Lissa said, "I wasn't staring at my watch."

Abbot said, "No, I didn't suppose you had been. I'm just asking if that sounds about right."

"I suppose so."

"Assume with me also that the call from Wendy to the Beacon Harbor Police Department is shown by both telephone and police records to have occurred at 8:54."

Treacy said, "Same objection to all the questions in this line."

Lissa said, "All right."

Abbot said, "It seems to me that what you've told us Wendy and Michael said to each other and the noise of the shots must have occupied some of that 8:51 onward time."

"It did."

"Therefore, it also seems that Wendy's call to the police must have been a lot sooner than five minutes after the shots."

"Well it seemed like five minutes. It seemed like five hours."

"What did you do after Wendy called the police?"

"I ran out of there, got to my car, and drove back to Beacon Harbor."

"To your brother's house."

"To my parents' house. They left it to my brother."

"As they had a perfect right to do?"

Treacy said, "Objection."

Abbot said, "Strike the question. You drove to the Beacon Harbor house and . . ."

"And there were police everywhere. They told me . . . they told me Michael was dead. Shot."

Abbot stopped until Lissa finished using her tissue again. Then he said, "Can you tell us what leads you to believe that Wendy had anything at all to do with your brother's death?"

Lissa became resolute. "She had everything to gain from it. If Michael had lived, the divorce would have gone through, and she'd have gotten almost nothing because of the antenuptial agreement. Since he died, she got half of his estate."

"And you got the other half?"

"Yes."

"Have you any evidence whatsoever that Wendy had anything to do with Michael's death besides the financial aspect?"

"No, not if you mean fingerprints or photographs or something. But it's just so cute, don't you see? She has me as her alibi! She must have set it up that way."

"But you told us that you just dropped in out of the blue. How could Wendy have been planning to have an alibi, much less you as that alibi?"

Lissa hung her head. "I don't know. I just think she did it, that's all."

The deposition tapered off from there. When it was over, I told the secretary I was finished with it. Then I told Abbot I was interested in the case. He said to do whatever I thought appropriate for the rest of the day, but to meet him at an address on Boylston Street the next morning at 9:30.

"Why?"

"Because Wendy is due at Treacy's office for her deposition, and I want you to meet her first."

✦ ✦ ✦

"Joe Patrizzi."

"Sergeant, my name's John Cuddy."

"I know, I know. And drop the 'sergeant,' okay? Makes me feel like I'm still back in uniform, and I don't ever want to be doing that again, in Beacon Harbor or anywheres else."

Patrizzi sat down in his chair, a thin file open in front of him. "You're looking into the Steinberg killing."

"If I wouldn't be stepping on your toes."

"Good start. Around here, we don't get many homicides. Like maybe three in my ten years, anyway. What do you want to know?"

"How come you're not pressing the widow?"

Patrizzi shrugged. "We would if we could. She's got the deceased's sister as an alibi, thirty miles away while the guy's getting shot. Phone records and our log downstairs confirm the time of the calls. Kind of tough to show means and opportunity."

"Witnesses?"

"The house, it's on this nice cul-de-sac, maybe three blocks off the water. Nobody home either side, nobody heard any shots, and this Steinberg, he took three in the chest, close range. Only possible is this lady, out walking her dog, thinks she saw a skinny guy running down the street."

"Running?"

"Yeah, but not like jogging. 'Fleeing,' fleeing was the word she used. Woman only saw him from the back. Hat or cap, broad shoulders, but otherwise skinny. Not much."

"Anything out of the ordinary at the scene?"

"Nah. The staties come in, dusted and fussed like they're supposed to, but nothing you could hang on the widow, even if she didn't have the alibi. Motive, now, motive we got up the ying-yang, but nothing else. Phone off the hook, like this guy Steinberg got interrupted on a call. Glass door to the garden broke in, some footprints in the flowerbeds near the patio. Body in the dining room, drawers—where you'd figure the silver was kept—were pulled open. Pretty typical."

"Of a B&E gone sour."

"That's how I see it. The statie attached to the DA thinks the same. You wanna talk with her, I can give you the number."

"No, thanks."

"Look, I don't mean to say we ain't on top of this here, but we checked the widow's bank accounts, phone records, charge cards, anything she might have used to set up or pay for a hit. Nothing out of the ordinary, everything squares. Even the DA don't wanna hear about it, and this is an election year."

"Thanks again."

"Hey, no problem. Come back in the summertime. We got a great beach, and parking's only five bucks, even on the weekends."

"I'll keep it in mind."

Two

Lawyer Treacy was in a dumpy building on upper Boylston Street. I spotted Craig Abbot in the lobby, looking around vaguely like a man who got off the bus at the wrong stop. Not threatened, just inconvenienced. Next to him stood a frosted blonde in her early thirties wearing very becoming make-up. Her clothing was lifted from a Talbot's catalog. Trenchcoat, a white cotton turtleneck with baby whales in baby blue, and a navy herringbone skirt. She exuded the kind of distance that said, "Don't even bother asking me to dance, buddy."

"Ah, Mr. Cuddy. Wendy Steinberg, John Cuddy."

We shook hands perfunctorily as she said, "And just who are you, Mr. Cuddy?"

Abbot said, "He's a private investigator."

She showed no emotion. "Private investigator?"

"Yes. Mr. Cuddy is an experienced criminal investigator I hired. He'll blow Lissa's case sky high."

"But Craig, I thought you told me Lissa's case had no merit, that she didn't have a shred of evidence."

"I did and she doesn't. Mr. Cuddy's job is to confirm that beyond doubt, so we can terminate this matter, hopefully without wasting much more of our time."

Wendy Steinberg shifted her gaze to me. Cool, appraising. She'd have made a hell of a bargainer at flea markets.

The elevator arrived, and we rode in silence to Treacy's floor.

✦ ✦ ✦

The stenographer swore Wendy Steinberg, and Treacy had no objection to my sitting in. Lissa apparently decided not to attend. Reciprocally ignoring the opposition, maybe. No video equipment, just old-fashioned question and answer, with the stenographer taking things down phonetically on one of those little boxes with cashier's tape and odd keys.

It took all of five minutes to see that Treacy couldn't lay a glove on Wendy Steinberg.

He dragged her over the telephone sequence syllable by syllable. The ice maiden confirmed each material point of Lissa's recollections.

Then Treacy said, "Wendy, you have a brother, right?"

"Yes."

"Name Richard N-M-I Dumars, right?"

"What does 'N-M-I' mean?"

"Uh, sorry. That's 'No Middle Initial.'"

"Then yes, Rick Dumars is my brother."

"Younger brother?"

"Yes."

"Age 28?"

A flicker of a smile crossed Wendy Steinberg's lips. "Yes."

"Now Wendy, I understand that Rick and Michael didn't exactly get along."

Abbot said, "Object to the form of the question, if it is a question. You may answer it, Wendy."

She said, "You objected, but I can answer it?"

"Yes."

"All right. Michael didn't get along with a lot of people. Rick and I were two."

The stenographer said, "Excuse me, is that T-W-O?"

Wendy smiled faintly again. "Yes. Of perhaps two thousand. T-W-O again."

The stenographer smiled back.

Treacy said, "Like I was saying, Rick and Michael didn't get along."

"No."

"Do you have any idea where Rick was the night your husband died?"

Wendy Steinberg almost laughed in his face. "I believe he was performing that night."

"What does he do?"

"He's a guitarist in a band. A rock band."

"Where would he have been performing?"

"One of the student bars in Brighton or Allston. Why don't you ask him?"

Steinberg provided his address, spelling it out for the steno.

Treacy turned over the single, henscratched yellow paper he'd been using as a crib sheet for question topics. "Now Wendy, it's certainly true that you and Michael were having marital problems, isn't that right?"

"I'd concede that his filing for divorce from me is proof of that."

"Right. And isn't it true that Michael was . . . uh, seeing someone else?"

Abbot said, "Objection. Instruct the witness not to answer."

Treacy said, "Why?"

"On the record?"

"Yeah, on the record."

"My client is being sued by your client for wrongful death, Mr. Treacy. No one is suing Michael Steinberg or his estate for divorce anymore, much less on the grounds of adultery. I don't see where any extramarital activities of Mr. Steinberg are relevant here."

"You don't?"

"No, I don't."

Wendy Steinberg said, "That's all right, Craig."

Abbot looked stunned, as though the file cabinet had just asked him to open it.

Wendy Steinberg said to Treacy, "Michael was a louse, Mr. Treacy. His catting around wasn't something he should have been proud of, but I certainly have nothing to be ashamed of, either. Michael's affairee, as you lawyers might call her, is an advertising executive, Edwina Vole."

She then went on to spell the name for the stenographer.

✦ ✦ ✦

Treacy finished up by 11:45. I declined Craig Abbot's lukewarm invitation to join Wendy and him for lunch because I sensed he wanted to scold her for running through his stop sign at the deposition. Besides, I had a few other people I wanted to see.

Three

He came to the door in a pair of striped gym shorts and nothing else. He was angular but wiry, the way guys get when they're two years into a five-year sentence. The eyes were bleary, the skin pallid, the hair unstylishly long. Unstylish for most occupations, anyway.

"Rick Dumars?"

"Yeah. What do you want?"

"It's about your brother-in-law."

"My what?"

"Michael Steinberg."

"Oh, yeah. Right. Just a second."

He closed the front door to his apartment most of the way, leaving me to stand in the hall. Through the crack I heard him in another room say, "Well, where the hell did you leave your bra?"

Two minutes later he opened the door. "Sorry, man. The chick just can't get it together, know what I mean?"

"No problem."

"C'mon in."

Dumars never asked for any identification. He'd pulled on a Benetton sweatshirt over the shorts and ran his hand like a rake through his hair as we took opposite seats on a couch and chair.

"So, what now?"

"I'd like to ask you a few questions about the night Michael Steinberg died."

"I already been over this with you guys, but go ahead."

"You can account for your time between eight and ten p.m.?"

"Yeah. Like I told the other cops, I was doing a gig at the Brown-Nose, over on Harvard Ave. I thought you guys already checked that out?"

"With the bartenders and all?"

"Yeah. The bartender, the doorman, him and me had some . . . coca-cola between sets. Otherwise, I was on stage, setting up or playing from eight, eight-fifteen on."

"Till?"

"Jesus, last call. What, one-thirty, I guess."

"How well did you know Michael?"

"Huh." Dumars swung his head around the room. Grad student quality furniture with undergrad quality clutter. "Michael was real into things, like possessions, man. Him and me weren't exactly golf buddies, you know?"

"Ever been out to his house in Beacon Harbor?"

"Coupla times. My sister— You met Wendy?"

"I have."

"Well, her and me don't look much alike, but we get along okay. She invited me out there around the holidays, like a Thanksgiving coupla years ago. Lissa—that's Michael's sister—she was there, too. That's the worst part of all this."

"What is?"

"The lawsuit and all. I mean, Lissa and Wendy, they were good friends, man, like maybe best friends I'd say."

"Anything happen on Thanksgiving?"

"Huh?"

"The time you were at the house in Beacon Harbor."

"Oh. No, nothing happened, except Michael treated me like I was a crasher or something."

"Gate-crasher?"

"Yeah, like that. Obnoxious dude, Michael. I can see him hearing a burglar, walking in on him all indignant-like, saying 'And just what do you think you're doing in my house?' He was like that. Talked like that, too."

"Anybody you know would kill him?"

"You mean, like if it wasn't a burglar?"

"Right."

"Jesus, I don't know. I mean, Michael was obnoxious, but would it be worth the heat to do him? I don't know, man."

✦ ✦ ✦

Edwina Vole worked in an advertising agency on Newbury Street. If the name sounded dowdy, it didn't fit the image the woman projected.

She stood to greet me in an office decorated in tubular chrome and glass. Perhaps five-seven, she had long, pianist fingers and long, lacquered nails. Her hair was done up in a bun, a few wisps casually but I thought intentionally escaping to tickle her ears. I pegged her at twenty-six, the newer model a guy like Steinberg might have ordered given the mileage he'd put on Wendy.

"Mr. Cuddy, I'm afraid I don't know quite what this is about."

Her accent was delightful, the kind the Upstairs people used on the Downstairs people from Masterpiece Theater. "It's about what I told your receptionist. Michael Steinberg."

"I was acquainted with a Michael Steinberg, actually, but he passed away recently."

"Rather suddenly and violently, actually."

Vole stopped, her lips drawing back into anything but a smile. Not a fan of parody, I suppose.

"What do you want, Mr. Cuddy?"

"Let's save some time, Ms. Vole. Your name came up as the deceased's lover. I'd like to ask you some questions. I'm just a private investigator, but the police may be seeing you shortly, if they haven't already."

"They have. Why on earth should I talk to you as well?"

"If you've nothing to hide, why shouldn't you?"

She arched back in the chair. Somehow, it didn't look comfortable enough to be worth the trouble.

Vole said, "It's about that lawsuit, am I right? The one Michael's sister filed against Wendy."

"Yes."

"Well, since they both despised him, I don't really care which of them prevails."

"You seem to be the only person I've met who liked Brother Michael."

"Michael was a difficult man to like. Exciting, stimulating in certain ways, but likable? No."

"Then why were you seeing him?"

"He was smashing in bed."

When I didn't reply, she studied me and smiled. Sort of. "Why detective, I believe you're blushing. Rather an unusual trait in a man these days. Fascinating, actually."

"You have any other interest in Michael?"

She shook her head. "No, my interest was only physical, Mr. Cuddy. And, I might add, Michael's only interest in me was physical. Michael was in marvelous physical condition, the kind you'd expect to live forever. He also was a man of substantial appetite, if I can phrase it that way without making you blush again. I gathered Wendy was not the most attentive appreciator of his charms in that regard. I was simply an outlet for him, though I expect the time we spent together encouraged him to file for divorce."

"So he could marry you?"

"Marry . . . me? Hah, that would be a good one. No, I'm afraid my dear father would disown me if I were to marry a . . . someone like Michael. We aren't quite as religiously flexible in England as you seem to be over here."

I stood. Vole tapped the eraser of a pencil against her teeth and said, "By the way, you wouldn't happen to be Anglican yourself, would you?"

✦ ✦ ✦

Since I was so close to home, I decided to go there instead of back to the office. The little green message light on my telephone tape machine glowed a fluorescent "1."

As I rewound and replayed, a familiar voice said, "Cuddy, this is Craig Abbot. We settled the case against Wendy this afternoon, so we won't be needing your services after all. Please simply send us a bill through this evening, and call my secretary if you have any questions."

I lay down for a while, thinking about it. Then I dressed in a tattered chamois shirt and a pair of stained, torn khaki pants. The bottom of the closet yielded a crumpled Red Sox cap. In the kitchen, I put a quart of orange juice in a brown paper bag, then folded down the top of the bag so I could drink from it without anyone seeing what was inside.

Wendy Steinberg's apartment at 182 Commonwealth was just around the corner and down a block. I chose a bench on the center boulevard of Commonwealth across from and slightly out-of-town from her building's entrance. I splayed my legs in front of me, wrapping my free hand around the slat at shoulder level and sipping occasionally from my bag. Two dozen people walked by, always giving me a wide berth and finding some aspect of a car or bush to stare at. Nobody ever looks a derelict in the face anymore.

At nine-fifteen, following a fashionably late dinner somewhere, the two of them came strolling down the street, arm in arm. He politely held her handbag while she fished around for her key. Then I watched Craig Abbot and Wendy Steinberg enter the building.

A minute later a light flashed on in the bedroom window of one of the apartments, but it didn't stay lit very long.

Four

Craig Abbot's secretary led me into his office and exited, closing the door behind her.

"Cuddy, I'm a bit pressed this morning, so I can give you only a few minutes."

"It won't take much longer than that."

"If you need your fee immediately, I could have my secretary draw a check, but—"

"It's not the money I'm here about."

Abbot heard something in my voice and settled back in his chair. "Go ahead."

"First, I should have realized there was something funny about you hiring me."

"Funny?"

"Yeah. Why go three hundred a day on an investigator for a case as clearly groundless as the one Lissa had on Wendy?"

"As I said, I wanted—"

"You wanted me to prove Wendy was innocent. But not because you thought you needed help in defending the lawsuit. You could win the case so long as Lissa couldn't prove Wendy'd done anything. You wanted something more than that."

"Such as?"

"Such as proof that the woman you were falling for hadn't killed her husband."

Abbot started to say something, then wet his lips instead. Finally he said, "You don't know what you're saying."

"I was camped on a bench outside 182 Commonwealth last night around nine-twenty. Care to guess what I would have seen?"

Abbot folded his arms and kicked his chair back a foot. "My private life is—"

"I don't want to know about your private life, okay? I'm just here to say my piece, then I'll leave and you won't hear from me again unless you decide you want this in writing."

"Why don't you just say it, then. And quickly, please."

"All right. I see you falling for Wendy when she comes in as a divorce client. It happens. You don't predict much of a return on the divorce because of the antenuptial agreement, but you do fine through your practice, so you can stand that. Wendy, however, can't. And I'm guessing Lissa couldn't either. Those two were good friends, best friends according to Lissa's brother. I think they both saw what they stood to gain from Michael's will as opposed to his continuing good health, and I think they killed him."

"Preposterous."

"Think about it. They both have motive, Wendy for his catting around, Lissa for her parents preferring Michael over her on the family house. The trick is to do it right. Wendy sits at her place in Boston while Lissa drives to Beacon Harbor. Lissa is dressed like a man in an outfit she probably designed for that purpose, with broadened shoulders to make her look less female just in case somebody who knows her walks by. Lissa rings the bell, Michael lets her in, maybe saying 'What in the hell are you decked out for?' Lissa leads him into the dining room, shoots him, then kicks in a French door, stomps around the garden, and yanks out a couple of silver drawers, all to make it look authentic. Then Lissa calls Wendy, at 8:51 p.m., leaving the connection made and the phone dangling. Lissa gets out of the house, drives a distance away, and pulls off the costume. Dressed normally, she waits half an hour, then roars back to Beacon Harbor to play the distraught sister at the murder scene. When asked, Wendy and Lissa give separate, consistent accounts of the contrived telephone call."

"Nonsense. If what you say really happened, why would Lissa *sue* Wendy?"

"That's the nice touch here, counsellor. They've got to see themselves as the police will, prime suspects. So, for appearances sake, they break off the friendship on the surface and go at it in a lawsuit, with each impliedly and defiantly providing an alibi for the other on the night of the murder."

"But that would be stupid, Cuddy. The lawsuit would bring out what they wanted to hide."

"No. Look at who they retained."

Abbot came forward. I cut him off.

"Lissa thinks she has a case against Wendy, but the only way that flies given the timing of the phone calls is if Wendy is in it with a confederate. Does Lissa pledge her half of Michael's estate to hire a big firm, or at least a bright solo, to avenge her brother's memory? She does not. She brings in a hack like Treacy, probably at a low hourly rate. Does Wendy hire a specialist in criminal law or fraud to defend her? She does not. She taps a divorce attorney she knows can be controlled because of his feeling for her."

"You can't believe this."

"I do believe it. Let me ask you something. Did Wendy hire you on a contingency basis, like for a third of whatever she gets, or are you per hour?"

Abbot rubbed a hand over his eyes. "Per hour. But that was just a continuation of our prior fee arrangement on the divorce."

"No, Mr. Abbot. That was so she and Lissa could stay in charge, could settle this thing early on without windfall fees to the lawyers if the first hint of outside trouble arose. Tell me, did each woman just say quits and go home with her respective half of Michael's estate intact?"

Abbot looked at me like a child whose puppy just died. "Those are the parameters of the settlement."

"At her deposition Wendy feeds me her brother and her husband's lover. Why? To keep me occupied for a while on people she knows can't help me. Then you achieve settlement yesterday afternoon when your client a few hours earlier found out that you'd hired an investigator, an 'experienced criminal investigator,' I think you told her?"

Abbot said, "I'd like to be alone for a while."

"Just one last thing."

"You're going to the police."

"No, I'm not. And neither are you. You're bound by the attorney-client privilege, and I'm bound to you, either by the privilege or my licensing statute."

"Then what's the last thing?"

"You'd think about it eventually, if you haven't already. Why did Wendy take up with you? Romantically, I mean."

Abbot just shook his head.

I said, "Here are three possibilities. One, maybe I'm dead wrong about Wendy and Lissa. Maybe it did happen the way they say it did, panicked burglar and all. Two, maybe Wendy and Lissa are more than good friends, and you're just a convenient, temporary cover for their own affair."

"God."

"Three, maybe Wendy and Lissa figure they stumbled onto a magic formula with Michael. One they can repeat with you and your estate."

Abbot slammed the flat of his hand on his desk, making his pen set jump. "Damn it, Cuddy, I'm in love with the woman! What am I supposed to do, stop seeing her?"

I got up to leave. "Either that, or from now on sleep with one eye open."

THE THREE MUSKETEERS

One

The first Monday of February started with a parking ticket for stopping in a snow emergency zone and an irate phonecall from a grandmother in Wiscasset, Maine, who couldn't understand why I hadn't found her runaway grandson, a kid about as traceable in Boston as the smoke from yesterday's cigarettes. I was just hanging up when Vincent Biaggi came into my office, closing "JOHN FRANCIS CUDDY, CONFIDENTIAL INVESTIGA-TIONS" so quietly I barely heard the click.

"Mr. Cuddy?"

"Yes," I said, rising and shaking hands with him. "You're prompt."

"I try to be."

Somewhere in his early thirties, Biaggi was just under six feet, with sharp features. He wore an expensive razored haircut and draped a black cashmere overcoat on his arm. Muted glen plaid Brooks Brothers suit, buttoned-down white shirt, regimental tie. A man who had confidence in his own competence. Once we sat down, however, he fidgeted in my office surplus chair. Biaggi didn't seem used to fidgeting.

"How can I help you, Mr. Biaggi?"

"I'm not sure you can."

"Well, what's the problem?"

He stared at me.

"Domestic? Because I don't—"

"Domestic? Oh, you mean like divorce. No, no. I'm already divorced, and it's nothing like that."

"Business then?"

"No. Well . . ."

I leaned back until my chair touched the windowsill. "Mr. Biaggi, we have to start somewhere."

"Yes, yes you're right. I'm acting in a way I'd never tolerate from one of my team. Indecisive. It's just . . . Well, how much do you charge?"

I thought I saw it. Biaggi had a problem he'd already talked over with another investigator. Calling me earlier for an appointment was his way of window-shopping, to see if he'd been offered a fair price elsewhere.

I said, "Three hundred a day, even if it ends up being just a half day. All expenses, including but not limited to travel, lodging, and meals."

"You sound like an attorney, Mr. Cuddy."

"I had a year of law school. Long time ago."

"Yes, well . . ."

I decided to wait him out.

His mouth resolved into a determined line. "Mr. Cuddy, I'm sorry. I'm wasting your time here. I haven't made up my mind yet, and I'm experienced enough to have known that without coming here. It's just that I'm starting a new project at the office, and this is the only time I could get away during the day."

"Tell you what, Mr. Biaggi." I yanked open the center drawer and spun one of my cards over to him. "You make up your mind, you give me a call and we can talk about it. Whatever it is."

He picked up the card, started to put it away, then pulled out a pen instead. "Can I have your home number?"

"You can reach me here."

"Please. I may have to call you tonight about going forward."

I counted to five silently, then gave him the number, repeating the digits because he seemed nervous writing them down. He took out some sort of calendar, covered in burnished leather but fairly unwieldy, and slipped my card under a paper clip that kept the thing opened to the current week.

Biaggi stood, thanked me, and left.

Mentally I kissed him off, then spent the rest of the day into the evening trying to find Woodrow from Wiscasset. I had prime rib at J.C. Hillary's on Boylston Street, a great saloon about three blocks from the condo I was renting from a doctor off in Chicago on a residency. I got home about ten, my telephone tape showing one message in its green fluorescent window. Replaying it, I was surprised to hear:

"Mr. Cuddy. This is Vincent Biaggi at eight-oh-four on Monday night. I'm sorry I acted so stupidly today, but . . . I'm under some pressure. I need to speak with you, but I'm heading out and I can't call you later. Please call me after two p.m. tomorrow at my office."

He rattled off the number. I wrote it down, then rewound the tape to erase and reset. I read *The New York Times* from that morning about events that happened on Saturday and Sunday, then went to sleep.

Two

Tuesday dawned bright, the first clear day since the January thaw. I laced up my running shoes, pulled on a cotton turtleneck and shorts, and shrugged into the Gore-tex two-piece I'd allowed myself for Christmas. I crossed Storrow on the Fairfield Street footbridge and did a leisurely six miles along the Charles River, the first three into a biting northwest wind. The macadam paths were packed solid with the snow and sleet of the previous week, which made jogging easier rather than harder. Once you got the hang of it.

I followed the run with a workout at the Nautilus facility down the street from the condo. It's a lot more pleasant to shop at the Prudential Star Market in the early morning, so after the workout I stopped to buy the week's staples. When I returned to the condo building about 9:30, there was a brown Ford sedan double-parked in front. It had the kind of antenna the driver doesn't need for easy listening.

A thirtyish, broad-shouldered woman got out from behind the wheel. "Cuddy, don't you ever answer your phone?"

"Cross, I look to you like I've been in to hear it?"

She gave me a sour smile. "You got something in the bag that'll spoil, take it upstairs. Otherwise, the lieutenant wants to see you. Don't take the time to change. I'll sign out another unit while they fumigate this one."

✦ ✦ ✦

Lieutenant Robert Murphy is older, stockier, and gruffer than I am. Given the crap he'd had to swallow back when the department didn't consider blacks executive material, the gruffer part was to be expected.

"Garbageman found a citizen dead in an alley down by Quincy Market this morning. Medical Examiner says multiple stab wounds. The uniforms responding didn't find a wallet or watch, but the guy had this fancy calendar thing in his breast pocket, your name down for yesterday afternoon and your card, with home number in handwriting, under a clip. Tell me about it."

I related everything I could remember about Biaggi coming to see me, focussing on his uncertainty.

"So Biaggi never told you what was bothering him?"

"No. M.E. peg a time of death?"

Murphy shook his head. "Body was in the snow behind a dumpster, but Biaggi was out carousing with a couple of his college friends from seven till almost eleven, so we figure eleven to twelve, maybe one at the outside."

"These friends said Biaggi was with them from seven on?"

"Till eleven, when they split to head home. Why?"

"I got a message on my tape last night. Biaggi's voice, telling me it was eight-oh-four but I wouldn't be able to reach him because he was 'heading out.' "

Murphy turned that around a while. "Could be he meant heading out for another bar. The friends say they were pub crawling, making dinner on the free counter stuff at the places they hit."

"Maybe he called from a good phone booth, but I didn't hear any background music or bar noise on the tape. And from what he said to me, Biaggi seemed like a guy who kept track of things like the time. These friends from work?"

"One. Guy named Michael Doyle. Other guy, Sandor Fried, no."

"Biaggi said something about a 'team.' What'd he do for a living?"

"Project leader, consulting group called Harbor Consulting and Research. Down by Lewis Wharf."

"You been over there?"

"Yeah. They keep cops' hours."

Meaning I didn't. "Any help?"

"No. The dude's secretary went numb when we told her, then started crying like she meant to raise the mean high-water mark."

"Check on the ex-wife?"

"Tara Wheaton. One of Biaggi's friends gave me her address up in Marblehead. She didn't seem too broken up about it. Came to the door in a robe, claims she was on a flight from L.A. last night."

"Business or pleasure?"

"Business. Ms. Wheaton's a stewardess. We're confirming her story, but unless something comes up, this here's going down as a mugging gone rough."

"Mind if I ask around a little?"

"For free?"

"Looks that way."

❖ ❖ ❖

Sandor Fried's office told me he'd left for the day. Murphy had a home address for him in Wellesley. After I showered and changed, I drove out there.

Wellesley is the kind of chic suburb you'd build ten miles west of a city. Fried's house fit right in, a big colonial on two nicely landscaped acres.

The front door was answered by a gaunt woman wearing a black wig that should have had some gray in it if it were intended to appear natural.

"What do you want?"

"Mrs. Fried?"

"Yes. What is it?" She spoke precisely, the way denture wearers do when they're not too sure of the fit.

"My name is John Cuddy." I showed her my identification. "I'm looking into the death of Vincent Biaggi, and Lieutenant Murphy directed me to your husband."

Her mouth moved the way a cow's does chewing cud. "Come in then. Sandy's very upset already. Don't make matters worse, all right?"

She pointed me to a sunken living room while she climbed a half-staircase. The parlor floor was covered by clashing Kerman rugs. Disproportionate modern art loomed from the walls. Couches and chairs in blue leather were attended by tables of glass and brass. Not a place designed for kicking off your shoes.

The mantle had photos of two children, a boy and a girl, at various ages up to young teens. No shots of Fried or his wife.

From an upper level, I heard a man's voice say tiredly, "Sylvia, please," then Mrs. Fried's "You got a choice, Sandy. Either I hear what he says from down there or I hear what he says from up here."

After some clumping on the stairs, a defeated man shambled into the room, followed closely by Mrs. Fried. Thinning black hair combed heroically from above one ear up and over the top of his head. Pinched eyes, a large, open face, and a bearlike physique under sweatshirt and sweatpants.

"You're . . . ?"

"John Cuddy, Mr. Fried. As I explained to your wife—"

"It's about Vinnie, right?"

"Right."

He became agitated. "I already told the police. We didn't see anything."

"By 'we,' you mean Michael Doyle and you?"

"Right, right."

Mrs. Fried said, "You want my opinion, this tragedy doesn't happen if the three of you behaved like responsible adults instead of fraternity feebs."

"Sylvia, it was our one night out, okay?"

"Stupid."

"It was a tradition. We always—"

"Traditions can't be stupid?"

I said, "Mr. Fried, maybe if you just told me what happened last night."

"I'll try. Sit, sit, please."

Sandor Fried and I sat. Mrs. Fried stayed standing, arms folded across her chest, watching for openings.

"Vinnie, Mike and I went to college together. We were real close, bio-sci and all, but afterward, with business pressures, we didn't see that much of each other."

"You said 'bio-sci'?"

"Yeah. We majored in Biological Sciences. I went into pharmaceutical publishing, Mike tried med school, but he . . . that didn't work out. Vinnie got into consulting first, then Mike came into it later."

"Can you tell me about this 'tradition' you had?"

"Sure. We decided to kind of revive something we did in college. Go to the bars to watch Monday Night Football."

Mrs. Fried said, "Except the three musketeers here didn't stop when football stopped. Oh no, it's Monday, they've got to kill brain cells."

"Sylvia, do you mind?" Fried turned back to me. "We went out last night, must have been about seven when I got to HCR—Harbor Consulting, where Vinnie works . . . worked. We went to the Market, hit some bars, then said good-bye . . ." Fried stopped. "God, that's a hard way to think about it. We said good-bye about eleven, maybe a little before."

"You were home eleven thirty-five, smelling like a distillery."

I said, "While you were at the bars, was anyone acting oddly?"

"Oddly?"

"Any other customer. Sizing you up or anything?"

"Oh. No, not that I noticed."

"Can you give me the sequence of bars?"

Closing his eyes, Fried seemed to concentrate. "Michael's Waterfront, because it's right by HCR there, then over to the market area itself. The Lord Bunbury, Donovan's, Lily's—no, no, we went down to the Ames Plow first, then Lily's."

"Anybody overdo it?"

"What, drinking? No, no, nothing like that with us."

"I'll bet," from Mrs. Fried.

"Did Biaggi say where he was going after leaving you?"

"No. Not to me. He's free to . . . he's divorced, you know?"

"Fraternity feebs, all of you."

Deciding that Mr. Fried had taken enough from both Mrs. Fried and me, I thanked them and left.

Three

Tara Wheaton lived in a cluster of duplex condominiums that overlooked a yacht club and the expanse of mansions on Marblehead Neck, across the winter-empty harbor. Her building was halfway up the slope from the water. There were no locks on the entryway doors, so I climbed the stairs to her unit and knocked.

The woman who opened the door was about five foot seven, with lustrous brown hair and hooded green eyes. She smiled and said, "You're John Cuddy?"

"Yes, but without more security downstairs, you might not want to give a stranger the name of a visitor you're expecting."

The smile grew lazy. "I've gotten a lot better at making judgements since I got divorced. Come on in."

The first level contained a combination living room/dining room and a glass wall with sliding door to a balcony offering a teasing peek of the Neck over the condo roofs closer to the waterfront.

She said, "Like the view?"

"Impressive."

"I've always liked the ocean, but we bought this place just after we were married because there was no upkeep, and now you can't touch a single-family along the water." She gestured to the sectional furniture. "Have a seat."

We sat facing each other in the L-shaped arrangement. "I really appreciate your taking the time to see me under the circumstances, Ms. Wheaton."

"Tara."

"Tara."

She rose a little, tucking one leg under the other. "Look, let's not play games for what you might think is my benefit. Vinnie and I were married, Vinnie and I got divorced. I'm sorry he's dead, but I'm not exactly crushed. Okay?"

"Okay."

"So, why did you want to see me?"

"After the divorce, did you and Biaggi stay on good terms?"

"Good terms. I guess so. I mean, we could talk on the phone without screaming at each other. That was part of the problem, actually."

"Talking on the phone?"

"No. No, I mean while we were married. Vinnie just wasn't the . . . most passionate guy around."

As I thought about a next question, Wheaton said, "Actually, I have to take that back. He was passionate enough about his job. And about studying back in school. It's just that work was all he was passionate about."

"You met each other in college?"

"Yeah. Sandy, Mike and Vinnie were together from the beginning. They were seniors when I was a freshman. I met Mike first. He introduced me to Vinnie."

"Mike Doyle."

"Right."

"Did you date Doyle first?"

"Kind of. Well . . ." She played with the cuff of her slacks. "You have to remember, this was back in the mid-seventies. I think Mike expected me to hop into bed with him. He was okay, but not special enough for me. Know what I mean?"

"You and Biaggi married in college?"

"Right after. Stupid thing to do, since I already signed up to see some of the world, but to be honest with you, it worked better that way."

"How do you mean?"

"Well, what Vinnie really wanted was kind of a guaranteed date more than a lifemate. He wanted somebody who was around on a regular basis, but not really a wife. A wife would cut a little too much into his work time. So, with me being gone a lot but here often enough, it was perfect."

"What soured it?"

"Oh, I got tired of flying, so I left the airline to become a house-spouse. Plus, I was pushing thirty, starting to think about having kids. Vinnie wasn't really into that, and with me being home a lot, I started to realize just how little we had. As a couple."

"So you got divorced?"

"Right. Real . . . amicable, as the lawyers said. I got this place, because to tell you the truth, he wanted to be closer in to the job anyway. It's ironic, actually."

"Ironic?"

"Yeah. I mean, that Monday night thing with Sandy and Mike is about the only thing he did for fun, I bet, and it got him killed."

"Anybody you know who might have benefitted from that?"

"Benefitted?"

"Yes."

"You mean, like it if wasn't some mugger?"

"That's what I mean."

"Jesus." She hugged herself and settled deeper into the cushions. "The police . . . they think it might be . . . ?"

"You never know. Anybody come to mind?"

"God, I don't think so. Vinnie was a hard worker, but all his family's gone and . . . Jesus, I don't think he really knew anybody outside work and the guys."

"Sandy and Mike."

"Right."

"What do you know about them?"

"Well, Mike, like I said, was okay but nothing special. He knew it, too."

"How do you mean?"

"He's just the kind of guy . . . He's always going to be a B-plus, never an A, you know? Couldn't hack it in med school, got his job at HCR because Vinnie vouched for him, that kind of thing."

"Private life?"

"We all used to go out sometimes, kind of triple date. Mike would never be with the same girl twice, and she'd always be kind of CBA."

"CBA?"

"Yeah. 'Cheap but alluring.' Nothing upstairs. It was like he went through them to prove something."

"How about Sandy Fried?"

"Sandy? Just a teddy-bear. Great guy who made the mistake of marrying the first girl who was nice to him. Has kids he adores and a wife—you meet Sylvia?"

"Yes."

"Then enough said."

"How about you?"

"Me?"

"Yes. You benefit from Biaggi's death?"

The lazy smile. "You're direct about it, anyway."

I waited her out.

"No, I don't. Just the opposite, in fact. Vinnie agreed to give me alimony, 'rehabilitative' alimony, I think they call it. Since I'd left the airline to make a home for him. I had six months of it left, but the deal with the lawyers was that if Vinnie died, the money stopped, and I can't claim anything from his estate or whatever. So I sure didn't want to see him die."

"I thought you said you were back with the airline?"

"I am. After Vinnie and I split, they took me back."

"But you still got the alimony."

"For a while. It's been a nice cushion, but I'm finding flying as a single woman isn't so bad, really, even with the AIDS scare and all."

"Well," I said, rising, "thanks for your time."

She leaned back in the sectional, uncrossing her arms and tossing her head toward the harbor behind her. "So you like the view, huh?"

"Nice."

"Even nicer from upstairs."

"I'll take your word for it."

Four

The door to Michael Doyle's office was swung half open. I could see the heavy, weathered beams and exposed red brick that had been touched up during the renovation of worthless wharf buildings to pricey office space. I knocked on the jamb.

"Mr. Cuddy! Mike Doyle. Come on in. Pleasure to meet you. Though I wish it were under better circumstances."

Doyle was medium height, with reddish brown hair and agreeable features perpetually arranged in a "can-do" smile. He came across as the kind of guy you'd hope would join the family business.

Doyle said, "What can I help you with here?"

"I've already spoken with Sandor Fried. I wonder if you could tell me what you remember about last night."

"Sure."

Doyle repeated everything about the evening that Fried told me, even the bars in the same order.

"Biaggi have any enemies?"

"Vinnie? Just the opposite. Not the most gregarious guy in the world, maybe, but always helping people out."

"When did he start here?"

"Oh, let's see. Eighty-four sometime."

"You started together?"

"Ah, no. Actually, Vinnie beat me by about a year."

"He help you get your job?"

The perpetual smile seemed to falter a bit. "Yes, he did. Like I said, always helping people out."

"What do you do here, exactly?"

"If you mean HCR itself, lots of things. If you mean me in particular, I consult with and advise bio-tech companies."

"Gene-splicing, that kind of thing?"

"Well, yes, sometimes. But more the marketing and development angles."

"And Biaggi?"

"The same, only different. I don't want to appear evasive, but we have a lot of sensitive matters under our wings, so to speak."

"Then Biaggi did bio-tech, too?"

The smile waggled again. "Yes. We were lab partners back in school, and we did pretty much the same sort of work here."

"But he got here first."

Doyle paused, then, very evenly, said, "Yes."

We were interrupted by an older Japanese woman with a trace of an accent. "Michael, see if you can snap Linda out of her trance. She's got to retrieve Vincent's computer notes so you can get up to speed on this immediately. We're in Conference Room Two."

"Right away, Chieko."

After the woman had left us, I said, "Linda was Vincent's secretary?"

"Right."

"And 'this' is the new project Biaggi was shepherding?"

"Uh-huh. Look, I don't mean to be rude, but . . ."

"I understand. Can you point me out of here?"

"Sure."

Outside his office he was gesturing down and to the right when a young woman with a plain face but striking figure burst upon us from a subsidiary hallway. The face remark may have been unkind, because her make-up was smeared by tears and Kleenex.

She nearly collapsed against Doyle, sobbing. "Oh, Michael, what should I do? What should I do?"

"Hey, Linda, it's going to be a tough time for all of us." Doyle shot me a "What can *I* do look" that contained something more than embarrassment and less than sympathy.

I left him to "snap her out of her trance."

I'd parked a block from HCR. From my car, I could see the main entrance of the wharf building clearly.

Linda came out at 3:30 and flagged down a taxi on Commercial Street. I followed to a small apartment house in the North End. She paid the cabbie and entered the lobby. If she weren't so upset, she could have walked it in ten minutes.

I gave her a half hour to settle in, then went to the mailboxes. There were no "Lindas," the only first initial "L" belonging to an "L. Duran" in Apartment H. I pushed the other buttons till someone unseen negligently buzzed me into the building.

Apartment H was third floor rear. No view, but private. I banged on the door.

Linda Duran's voice came from the other side of a peephole. "Who are you?"

I held up my identification, wondering if the convex lens distorted it beyond reading. "My name's John Cuddy, Ms. Duran. I'm investigating the death of Vincent Biaggi, and I think you want to talk with me. Now."

Five

Doyle was livid, shocking even the HCR receptionist. "Where the hell do you get off pulling me out of a meeting! I saw you yesterday, without an appointment, and answered your questions."

"Mike, I thought it would be easier for you this way. I would have sent Linda, but I'm told she called in sick this morning."

"Would you please just tell me what you want?"

"Sure. It seems you've got another meeting to attend."

"What? What other meeting?"

"With Lieutenant Murphy and Sandy Fried. In Conference Room Number One? I'm sure you know the way."

✦ ✦ ✦

Doyle entered in front of me. By the expression on Fried's face, I guessed Mike was shooting daggers at his college pal.

After we all were seated, Murphy said, "I'd like to get some things straightened out. Just so everybody knows the score, anyone here is free to leave any time they want."

Nobody got up.

The lieutenant tilted his head toward me. "Cuddy here had a little talk with Linda Duran yesterday afternoon."

Fried looked at Doyle. Doyle glared at me.

I said, "Seems that Linda kind of clouds everybody's story."

When neither responded, I went on. "Seems Linda and Sandy have been seeing each other. Only Sandy's married, so it had to be on the sly. Monday nights were a good time."

Fried said, "No. Oh, God, no."

Doyle said, "Shut up, Sandy."

"Yeah, Sandy, listen to your friend, let Cuddy speak his peace."

"Thanks, Lieutenant. Seems Mike and Vinnie kept the tradition alive, though, partly to cover for old Sandy with Sylvia back in Wellesley. Great cover, too. Explains booze on the breath, the scent of perfume in the clothes, and all that kind of stuff. Problem though for Sandy: Vinnie gets killed, and by the time Sandy hears about it, he's already told the wife it was just another boisterous night out with the boys."

Fried said, "Does Sylvia know?"

Murphy said, "Not yet. Now be quiet, listen to the man."

"So Sandy calls Mike, and Mike helpfully squares their stories so that Sandy's still covered. Sure, it'll throw the police off a little on possible time of death, especially since the killer took away not just the wallet but the watch, too, which might have broken and revealed the time of the attack. But hell, it was just another mugging, no witnesses, so the cops were never going to catch the killer anyway. Right, Sandy?"

Doyle said, "Doesn't wash, Cuddy. I was with Vinnie till almost eleven."

"Sorry, Mike. Detective Cross and I spent most of last night running down the Monday night bartenders. Four of them work Tuesdays, too, so it wasn't as tough as it sounds. We caught the last one at his house this morning. And guess what?"

Fried had stopped looking at anything but his hands twisting in his lap. Doyle still glared at me, the big vein pulsing at his temple.

I said, "Turns out you three were pretty well known, not by last name, but as Monday night regulars. The guy at the first bar remembers Mike and Vinnie coming in two nights ago, must have been just after eight because he started his shift then. My guess is Sandy was already at Linda's by seven, while Vinnie didn't leave HCR with Mike until almost 8:00. Vinnie wanted to speak with me about something. A suspicion, maybe?

Nobody else jumped in.

"So, the guy at the second place also remembers just Mike and Vinnie. The woman at the third bar remembers Mike, but not Vinnie. The woman at the fourth place is sure Mike ordered two drinks and paid for them. They guy at the last stop remembers only Mike mentioning that Vinnie was in the men's room. Now how about that?"

Doyle said, "Any of them say I had blood on me? Huh? No. The guy who killed Vinnie'd be covered in his blood. So shove it."

I shook my head. "No, Mike. Shove it's what you did. In the alley. All that biological background, you knew that cold weather widens the brackets for time of death. You also knew where to stick the blade, what parts of the body were vital but wouldn't go off like geysers, especially given the layers of clothes Vinnie would be wearing this time of year."

Murphy said, "We checked with the Medical Examiner, Doyle. All the wounds are consistent with what Cuddy here is saying."

Fried jerked his head up. "What? What're you saying?"

Doyle said, "Shut up."

I engaged Fried. "I'm saying Vinnie preceded Mike to HCR, and Mike resented that, despite or even because Vinnie helped Mike get his job here. I'm saying Vinnie was assigned some juicy new project, and Mike especially resented that. And finally I'm saying that Mike stabbed Vinnie to death so he could succeed him as HCR's leading light in bio-tech consulting."

Fried showed the bewilderment of a refugee. "Mike? Mike, what's this guy trying to sell here?"

"Can it, Sandy. He can't prove a thing."

"Prove? Prove! What's with prove? You just say you didn't do it, right? Just say it, say it to me."

Doyle looked at Fried with something approaching revulsion. Fried said,

"Oh God, Mike. Say it!"

Doyle dipped his head, chin resting on his chest. "I want a lawyer."

It took both Murphy and me to pull Fried off the third musketeer.

BATTERED SPOUSE

One

"I feel a little funny, Mr. Cuddy. I've never hired a private investigator before."

I thought Mona Gage had a right to feel any way she wanted, given she'd lost her husband six days before. "That's all right, Mrs. Gage. It's peculiar for most people. Would it help to call me John?"

Her fortyish face set primly. "No, I don't think so. I think it would be better if we kept things formal."

"As you like. How can I help you?"

Straightening her shoulders, she seemed ready to recite. "As I said on the telephone, Kyle was killed in a hit-and-run accident last Tuesday night. He was jogging along this country road—he always thought it was safer, less traffic—and he was struck and killed."

I recalled the media coverage. "There were witnesses, right?"

"The police took statements from all three men who saw it. They stopped, tried to help . . . I'm very grateful to them, but the police say without a license plate, they can't do much."

That sounded about right. "What makes you think I can do any more?"

"We live . . . I live in Calem, Mr. Cuddy. I remembered your name from the college student who was accused of shooting his girlfriend." She stirred uncomfortably. "The young black man, I believe?"

"Mrs. Gage, during the course of that case, I didn't exactly endear myself to Calem's finest."

"That's all right. In fact, that's better. I want a fresh approach. The officers have all been very polite, but I have the impression that they don't think there's a chance of finding the ones who did this. Maybe with someone they don't like involved for me, they'll work a little harder."

Her sense of police pride was quaint; I didn't want to disabuse her of it. "Have you thought about seeing a lawyer?"

She soured. "I have and did. I saw two, in fact. I mentioned to the first one that Kyle's employer, Daly Sporting Goods, maintained a $25,000 group policy on his life, payable to me. The lawyer said he'd be glad to help, provided I gave him a ten thousand dollar retainer. I didn't tell the second lawyer about the policy. She said she didn't believe there was anything much she could do for me. That's when I thought of you."

I could see why. "A minute ago, you said 'the ones who did this.' There was more than—"

"The witnesses said there were several people in the car, apparently drinking. I want them all brought to justice."

Justice. "Mrs. Gage, I'd be happy to look into this for you, but I have to be honest, there probably isn't much I'll turn up."

The prim set again, then a softening. "Are you married, Mr. Cuddy?"

I paused a moment and thought of Beth before saying, "Widower. A long time ago."

"Then you are the right person to help me. I loved Kyle, I . . ." She postponed tears by fishing in her purse. "I even brought a photo of him, if it would help."

She handed it to me carefully, and I accepted it the same way. It showed a muscular, strikingly handsome guy in his late twenties, wearing a bathing suit and blowing a kiss at the lens.

I said, "If it comes to it, I might need a more recent photo."

Mona Gage said, "I took that last summer."

I felt like apologizing, but caught myself.

"That's all right, Mr. Cuddy, no need to be sorry. Actually Kyle is . . . was nine years younger than I am. That didn't matter to him, or to me now. I just want the irresponsible scum who killed him. I want them to answer for it."

We agreed I'd give it three days, then report back.

✦ ✦ ✦

Paul O'Boy, manila folder tucked under his arm, slid into the booth across from me. "The chief finds out I'm seeing you like this, he'll fry me slow in hot grease."

I smiled at O'Boy, a small-town police detective with a mid-sized city brain. "So how come you showed up?"

He shrugged, the skin on his forehead wrinkling toward the few wisps of hair at the crown. "I figure we owe you one after the foul-up on the black kid there."

The waitress came over, took our orders for lunch, then left us.

I said, "Can I see the file?"

O'Boy niggled it over to me, like a kid pushing pennies. "Not much there. Want a summary?"

I opened the folder. "Uh-huh."

"Gage, Kyle, age 29, is jogging about 10:30 p.m. west along Pond Road.

You picture it?"

"No," I said, flipping through accident scene photos.

"Typical country drive, some curves and hills, good for training, so they tell me. Anyway, according to your client the wife, this Gage runs the road regular, usually late on account he works till nine at the sporting goods store there over in the Westbrook."

"Westbrook Mall?"

"Right, right. Guy named Chuck Daly owns it. Ring a bell?"

"No."

"He was a high school phenom back when I was young. Had try-outs with the Sox and a coupla other teams. Spent maybe two seasons in the high-minors, then crapped out. I talked to him, he said the same thing about the running as the wife."

I started reading the responding officers' Incident Report, taking brief notes. "Three witnesses?"

"Yeah. Surprised me a little, that stretch is pretty deserted so long after rush hour. First guy on the scene's there already as Gage is running along, but on the other side of the road, heading east. Checking his tires, thought he heard one of them hissing."

I read, "Ayckbourn, David?"

"Right. Ayckbourn, he's bending over his tire when he hears this car tear-assing around the curve heading west, same as Gage. Ayckbourn looks up in time to see Gage get smacked and fly through the air, car just keeps on rolling as Gage lands and goes down the slope. Let's see . . . yeah, those two shots in your hand."

I looked at photos of the brush and grass incline, one taken from the road angling down and the other from the bottom angling back up to the road. "Who were the other two witnesses?"

"A guy driving east, the same direction as Ayckbourn there, saw the impact and got a partial look at the guys in the car."

"Donato, Angelo?"

"Right, right. Donato says he was looking more at Gage dribbling down the asphalt, but he said he saw at least two guys in the front seat and one in the back. One in the back might have been a woman, he's not sure. But he's the one made the car."

"Then you did get a registration number?"

"No, no. Happened too quick, and no plate on the front, he says. Donato works in an auto bodyshop, ID'd the car as a Fiat 131S, champagne yellow coupe, '75 or '76."

I thought back to the Fiat 124 I'd owned. "Who was the third guy?"

"Witness, you mean?"

"Yeah."

"Hirsch, Harold. Accountant. He didn't see the impact itself, just the vehicle. Hirsch was proceeding east on Pond, and maybe a mile or two before the scene, a yellow foreign job crosses the center line, nearly forces him off the road. Says he saw what looked like a long-necked liquor bottle changing hands in the front. He don't know from cars, but his headlights flashed over the driver, and he thinks the guy was Hispanic."

The *Boston Herald* had run a series about Hispanic kids boosting cars and switching plates before joyriding, thumbing their noses at being identified. "And you figure?"

O'Boy spread his hands. "I figure this here's another Driving Under tragedy, the Governor can add it to his statistics, you know? The witnesses, I gotta give 'em credit, they even tried to help old Gage down in the gully there. Hirsch said by the time he pulled up, Ayckbourn's car was already on the other side of the road, heading west now, and Donato was running across the road and down hill, too. Hirsch tried to go down, but he ain't too athletic, to look at him, and the other guys told him to call us instead. Time the unit responded, Ayckbourn and Donato had Gage back up the hill. The uniforms said they were covered with his blood, but didn't do no good. DOA at the hospital, but probably dead on impact, you ask me."

I scanned the autopsy report. Abrasions and contusions from the tumble down the slope, more importantly a fractured skull, elbow and knee. "The M.E. here makes it sound like Gage really took a shot to the head."

O'Boy nodded. "Pretty consistent with this type of thing, depending on how the bumper caught and lifted him. No skid marks at the scene. His jogging suit had plenty of paint chips on it. The written report'll be a while coming back from the lab, but I got a preliminary this morning. Looks like car paint, all right, foreign manufacture. We got a print-out of all the Fiats from back then still righteously registered, but I figure we're not gonna have much luck there."

Our food arrived, and I closed the folder, returning it to O'Boy. "Thanks, Paul."

"Don't mention it. You're buying, right?"

◆ ◆ ◆

On television, the hero usually starts with the person who's the most photogenic. In real life, you start with the one who's geographically closest, which after lunch meant Harold Hirsch.

He was an independent CPA, an office in one of the lesser buildings of Calem. A darkly attractive woman about my age greeted me inside his door, and when I mentioned the accident Hirsch witnessed, she shuddered. Clicking an intercom, she said, "Hal, I think you better come out here."

Hirsch came through a closed door, saying "Honey, what's the ... Who are you?"

"My name's John Cuddy, Mr. Hirsch. As I was explaining to your secretary—"

"Hanna's my wife," he said, indignantly. "The secretary's out sick."

"Sorry. I'm looking into the accident you witnessed on Tuesday night."

Hirsch, florid and pudgy, blinked rapidly behind spectacle glasses. "Come in, then. Please, come in. Hanna, hold all my calls."

She didn't reply as I followed him into the inner office.

"Sit, sit down. I'm happy to talk with you, but I already told the police everything I know. I didn't actually see the accident, you know?"

"I've read the reports, Mr. Hirsch. I just wonder if I could ask you a few questions?"

"Well, I don't have much time, but a few? Sure, go ahead."

"Could you tell me, in your own words, what you saw that night?"

"I already used my own words in the statement I gave the officers. What more can you want?"

"Well, where were you coming from or going to?"

"Ah, well, coming from, I was coming from a UJA—that's United Jewish Appeal—meeting. I was driving down Pond Road because it's a lot easier on the eyes than the highway, especially when a movie might be letting out."

"And you were heading?"

"Home. Oh, I was heading home from the meeting."

"And a car going west veered into your lane?"

"Right, that's right."

"Do you think you'd recognize the driver if you saw him again?"

"Recog . . . Oh, no. No, I barely got a look at him. I was really stereotyping, I'm afraid. The officer asked me what he looked like, and I just said, 'Spanish,' you know?"

"How long after that before you came upon the accident scene?"

"I'm not sure. Maybe a mile or so. The car coming at me like that, it shook me up."

"I can imagine. What did you see at the scene itself?"

"Well, just the two cars, one heading west and the other going east, like me, but they didn't look right."

"How do you mean?"

"Well, they looked like they stopped real suddenly, the wrong angle and all to be parked at."

"So you stopped, too?"

"Right, right."

"And you saw Gage's body?"

Hirsch gulped and nodded.

"It must have been a jolt."

"A jolt. Yes, quite a jolt." Hirsch seemed to space out on me. "I . . . I never thought he . . . I mean, I never expected . . . well, that one person had so much blood in him."

"Did you know Mr. Gage?"

"No, no. Why would I know him?"

"Well, he worked over in the Westbrook Mall. That's pretty close to here."

"No, I . . . I rarely shop over there."

"Anything else you can tell me about that night?"

"No, no. Just what I told the police is what happened."

I stood up. "Thanks for seeing me."

As I walked out into the hallway, I made a note of the time. I don't usually make citizens as solid and civic-minded as Hirsch so nervous, and I thought it might be a good idea to check later on whether any billable calls were made by him at 2:42 p.m.

Two

The police report said Angelo Donato worked the four-to-twelve shift at a bodyshop in Somerville but lived in a blue-collar town next to Calem. I figured I could catch him at home before he left.

His house was a modest tract ranch with a bottom-of-the-line Toyota in the driveway. I rang the bell.

The tough-looking face that answered belonged to a woman in her late thirties. She wore a tube top and shorts, her legs and arms in perfect muscle tone. The tough-looking part came from the wrap-around sunglasses that masked her eyes but couldn't quite cover all of the mouse on her left cheek.

"Yeah?"

"Mrs. Donato?"

"Yeah. What do you want?"

"My name's John Cuddy. I'm a private investigator."

She tilted her shades to glance down at my ID. "So what do you want?"

"I'd like to speak with your husband about a traffic accident he witnessed."

She crossed her arms, squeezing each above the elbow as though she were cold. "He's not here. He's at work."

"I'm sorry. I thought he was on the four-to-twelve."

"He changed off."

She shut the door in my face.

◆ ◆ ◆

"There's something wrong here, kid."

How so?

A stiff breeze came up, and I put my palm on Beth's headstone to steady me. In the harbor below, a Coast Guard whaler was pancaking over the chop, scurrying to get in before the storm hit.

"A traffic fatality is a wrenching thing, but usually just for the family and the witnesses. With this one, everybody's nervous."

What are you going to do about it?

"I told Mona Gage I'd give her three days. She's still got two coming."

Raindrops began splattering on my shoes. *You keep standing there, you're going to get soaked.*

I smiled down at her. "I don't mind."

◆ ◆ ◆

The sound of someone ripping metal greeted me the next morning at the doorway to the bodyshop. I stuck my head in.

A young Vietnamese firing up an acetylene torch spotted me and said, "No customers in here. Insurance say no. No, no."

"I need to see Angelo Donato."

He held the torch away and yelled at an old BMW. "Hey, Angelo. Hey you, Angelo?"

A face appeared over the trunk. "What?"

"Guy here want to see you. Outside, okay?"

"Yeah, yeah. Okay."

Donato walked over to me. He was about the same height as his wife, but not in the same shape. Blocky, with grimy hands, thick wrists, and black hair, cropped short.

We went outdoors. He turned around to be sure the Vietnamese was out of sight before saying, "Goddam dinks. You'd think they won the war, the number of 'em come over here."

"You spend any time in-country?"

"Me? Nah, I wanted to go, but I had this back problem, couldn't pass the physical."

Right. "My name's John Cuddy. I'm investigating the death of Kyle Gage, and I'd like to ask you a few questions."

Donato seemed surprised. "Questions? About what?"

"About what you saw."

"I already told the police."

"Well, how about some things that weren't in the report. Where were you coming from?"

"That night?"

"Right."

"I was off Tuesday. I had four-to-twelve last week, but that night I was off, and there was this candlepin tournament over in Worcester there I wanted to see."

"Alone?"

"What do you mean?"

"You went to this tournament by yourself?"

"Yeah. None of the other guys could make it."

"How about your wife?"

"She don't like bowling."

"She seems to be in pretty good shape. What does . . ."

I stopped, because Donato clenched both his face and his fists, as though he were about to swing on me.

I said, "Something wrong?"

"No, no. Nothing's wrong. Where do you know my wife from, the club?"

"The club?"

"Yeah, the aerobics things there. That where you met her?"

"No. I was out at your house yesterday looking for you. She said you'd changed shifts."

"Oh. Oh, right. She musta forgot to mention it. She's like that."

"How about you tell me what happened that night, in your own words."

Donato took a breath. "I'm driving down Pond Road, on the way back from Worcester, like I said. I see this guy, turns out to be Gage, get hit. While he's jogging. The car that hits him goes by me, never even slowed down. A Fiat 131S, '75 or '76, champagne yellow. I know these things, from the shop. There's another guy stopped in front of me, changing a tire or whatever. He gets in his car, wheels around in a U-ey, I pull up on my side of the road and run across. We're both trying to help Gage there, Dave and me. We go down that slope, Christ, the guy's really a mess, blood every-where. We carry him back up to the road. Oh yeah, I forgot. This other guy comes along while we're still at the bottom there, and we send him for the cops. That's about it."

"You said 'Dave.' "

"Huh?"

"A minute ago you said, 'Dave and me.' Is that David Ayckbourn?"

"Ayckbourn. Right, right, the other guy, with the bad tire or whatever."

"You know Ayckbourn before that night?"

Donato seemed furtive. "No, no. Why should I know a bigshot like him?"

"Well, you called him 'Dave.' "

He stuck his hands in his pockets. "The cops, they had us together for a while. You go through something like that with a guy, you call him by his first name, okay?"

"Okay."

"Look, buddy, I gotta get back to work."

Donato turned and strode toward the door.

Three

David Ayckbourn had the face of a man who took himself too seriously. About forty-five, trim and compact, he paraded back and forth in front of me as I sat in a comfortable leather chair. His office occupied a top floor corner in one of Boston's new towers. There was a wall of photos and plaques to the side of his desk rather than behind it. It seemed to me he'd designed it that way, so the display seemed more subtle and yet, at the same time, more impressive.

"Go on, Mr. Cuddy."

"The police report suggested that you had stopped for tire trouble?"

"Yes, but not exactly trouble. As I was leaving the parking garage here, I thought I'd heard a hissing noise. I rode home with the driver's window open, and on Pond Road I thought I heard the noise again, so I stopped. Turned out to be nothing."

"You usually come home so late?"

"Often, I'm afraid. I could give you my full corporate title, but basically I'm a troubleshooter. Something goes haywire anywhere in our farflung operations, I'm the one who's sent. Exciting stuff, but not exactly nine-to-five."

"Usually take Pond Road?"

"Not usually. In fact, it's a bit out of the way. But I had something to think through, a company problem, and I thought the countryside atmosphere would soothe me."

With a potentially leaky tire. "After you stopped, you saw Gage get hit?"

Ayckbourn's brows knitted. "Yes. It was horrible. The car just came around the curve like it was drunk instead of the driver. Wham! Then it sped off."

"You didn't get a look at the driver?"

"No. Nor even the car, really. I was watching poor Gage. He literally bounced. I'd seen men do that in the war from mines and mortars, but . . ."

The telephone rang. "Excuse me." He picked it up, using a controlled but clearly authoritarian voice. "Shirley, I thought I said no calls? Ah . . . No, no you were right to interrupt me. Put him on." Ayckbourn looked at me and said, "Sorry about this."

"I can leave."

Ayckbourn shook his head, waving me toward the window. "I'll just be a minute. Enjoy the view."

I got up as he said into the phone, "Farley, what a pleasant surprise."

While Ayckbourn talked I looked across the Fort Point Channel to the impromptu dump of derelict refrigerators, cars and shopping carts. What a difference a couple of blocks can make. In the distance, jetliners descended toward and ascended from Logan Airport's runways.

On the wall of fame, I examined pictures of the troubleshooter at pivotal stages of his life. Ayckbourn graduating from college, a Yale building in the background as if the diploma next to it weren't disclosive enough. Ayckbourn in Marine boot camp fatigues with a pugil stick in his hands, three combat medals framed against his commission in the adjacent space. Ayckbourn and wife, an attractive woman in an all-white tennis outfit, each holding the handle of a loving cup with "Westover Country Club / Mixed Doubles Champions / 1987" engraved on it. Ayckbourn receiving "Man of the Year" plaque from the Calem Chamber of Commerce. Ayckbourn—

Hanging up.

"Well, now. Sorry about that, as I said. Anything else I can help you with?"

"No. No, I don't think so."

✦ ✦ ✦

"Yessir, Kyle, he was a helluva guy."

"He was."

"And a helluva salesman, too. I've got twenty-two employees out front on the weekends, twenty-two, but he was the best. Don't know how I'm going to replace him, I really don't."

Chuck Daly was frowning ruefully, but I got the impression nothing in life bothered him too much. Tall and balding, he still had the spring if not the waistline of the "phenom" Paul O'Boy had told me about. A little Alabama sugar seeped into his speech from time to time, probably residue from his farm team days.

I said, "You have any reason to think someone would want him dead?"

"Kyle? Kyle Gage? Hell, no! Everybody liked old Kyle. Hell, the ladies especially."

"How so?"

"Well—you never met Kyle, did you?"

"No, I never did."

Daly rotated in the cluttered office area. "Let's see, I think I got a softball team photo of him around . . . somewheres . . ."

"I've seen a photo." I took out the one Mona Gage had given me.

"Yeah . . . Yeah, that's a good one of him. Mona take it?"

"Yes."

"Well, she really, what would you say, 'captured,' him?"

"Meaning?"

"Meaning the guy was like me twenty years ago. He was a killer, all right."

"Lady killer?"

"Right, right." He leaned forward, conspiratorially. "Look, I didn't say nothing to the cops, what'd they ever do for me, you know? Also, I didn't want to hurt Mona none. But old Kyle, he had the eye, get me?"

"Any particular preference?"

Daly squinted. "How'd you know that?"

"A guess. Tell me about it?"

"Tell you? Well . . . man to man?"

Jesus. "Sure, man to man."

Daly working his palms as though he were lathering them. "Kyle, they were all after him, from the teeny-boppers to the blue-hairs. But the ones he went for were like Mona, you know? About forty, still good-looking? He said there was nothing like 'em. 'Ready, able, and grateful,' that was how he put it."

"He'd go to their houses?"

"Sometimes. Other times they'd come in here, looking all business-like. 'Oh, do you have this color in my size,' 'No, no, I wanted the Slazenger,' and like that. But then Kyle, he'd come over to me and ask if he could take lunch now and borrow the keys to my place, and I'd say sure. Rack 'em up while you can, that's my motto. Hell, he'd even wash the sheets and all, you'd never know he'd been there."

My silence must have seemed ominous, because Daly grew a worried expression on his face. "Hey, this all I just told you. This is our secret, right?"

"Our secret," I said.

✦ ✦ ✦

I made three stops, the photo doing the trick at each. Oh, there were varying degrees of initial reaction, but once I explained the pattern that of course none of them knew, each broke down and gave me what I wanted. Returning to Boston, I made three calls, spaced somewhat apart.

Four

Daisy Buchanan's is the kind of bar the Bull & Finch used to be before they turned it into "Cheers." Located in the lower level of an old townhouse on Newbury Street, Daisy's is about two blocks from where I live and nearly deserted during the mid-afternoon. Nearly deserted was exactly what I wanted.

They arrived in the order I called them. First Harold Hirsch, then Angelo Donato, and finally David Ayckbourn. Old David must have really pushed it, because he was coming through the door as Donato was filling a seat across from me and exchanging glances with Hirsch.

When Ayckbourn got to our table, I asked him if he'd like a beer. Still standing, he said, "Just what the hell is this, Cuddy?"

"Like I told you on the phone, I have a witness who saw a car on the westbound side of Pond Road that night. That was the side that Gage was jogging along, but none of you mentioned it. I was wondering why."

Ayckbourn took in Hirsch and Donato. "You didn't say anything about a group meeting."

Donato said, "He didn't tell us either, Dave."

Ayckbourn winced when Donato got to "Dave."

I said, "Tell me, Dave, did you get the idea from looking out your window, from spotting some abandoned car over by Fort Point Channel?"

Ayckbourn stiffened. Hirsch wet his lips, and Donato wiped his hand across his forehead.

"I really think you ought to sit, Dave. This could take a while."

Ayckbourn absently reached for and dragged over a fourth chair.

I said, "I'm just going to ramble for a while. We'll assume that you're all making your denials at the right points, okay?"

Nobody moved or spoke.

"First, Kyle Gage was having an affair with each of your wives. They're the right age for him, and at least two of them could have met him buying athletic equipment or clothing at Chuck Daly's store. My guess is that Dave here was the one to catch on about his own wife first. He tails her one day to the store, sees her leave with Kyle and head home or to Daly's place for a little lunchtime love. I think that gave Dave the idea to kill Gage, but then he got lucky."

"Preposterous," said Ayckbourn.

"You see, Dave was figuring he'd have to kill Gage all by himself. Following Gage around to get his routine down, however, Dave discovers, wonder of wonders, that he isn't the only one wearing horns. So Dave brings you two into it, and sets it up for a dark night on Pond Road when everybody can make it."

Hirsch started to say something; Ayckbourn told him to shut up.

"Dave here is stopped on the shoulder, all right, but heading west, not east, as Gage, also heading west, jogs by. What were you doing, Dave? Fumbling around in the trunk? Or maybe crouched out of sight down behind the engine? No matter. As Gage draws even, you step out and crush his knee."

Donato said, "But he was hit by a car!"

"Yeah. A Fiat 131S, champagne yellow. That was a nice touch, Dave. Not only does Fate hand you two accomplices, you even make use of Angelo's special abilities."

Ayckbourn said, "You're crazy."

"I don't think so. Angelo's an expert on that sort of thing. He gets only a brief look at the car, but he can peg it for sure. Another nice touch was your saying you really didn't focus on the car, and Harold here typing the driver without being able to recognize him again. Good use of personnel to make the stories consistent, yet realistic instead of rehearsed. So Dave, did Angie do double duty? Did he make the thing, too?"

The three stared at me.

"Aw, c'mon. You know, the pugil stick. Only instead of a giant Q-Tip like in the service, this one has a good strong shaft and a quarter panel from a Fiat melded onto one or both ends."

Hirsch said, "Oh my God."

Ayckbourn said, "Shut up, Hirsch. Don't say another word. Cuddy, you can't prove this, not a bit of it."

"I can prove that all three wives were lovers of Gage. That'll be enough for the police to expand the investigation. They ought to like the way you guys managed the revenge against Gage. But I think you'll really impress them with the implicit revenge against each wife. You know, how each woman knew only that her lover was killed in a tragic accident witnessed—'There is a God'—by her husband and two other innocent bystanders. You really thought this through, Dave."

Ayckbourn said icily, "What are you going to do?"

"Well, now that, that's a tough one. The cops don't see it as a murder case right now, but we all know they're wrong there. On the other hand, my client is a nice woman who didn't know her husband was a tomcat, and I'm not sure I want to see her hurt. On the third hand, though, it seems to me you guys owe someone a bundle for wrongful death."

Donato said, "What?"

"You killed her husband, Angie. My guess is Dave here disabled Gage with that first shot, then each of you two battered him to seal the bargain. By the way, Dave, what happened to that stick? You couldn't have tossed it at the scene. Someone might have found it and ruined the cover story. My guess is you put it in your trunk, that it was there the whole time you guys were talking to the cops. That took brass, Dave. Tell me, you hold onto it afterwards, too? So everybody's prints are on it, seal things a little tighter?"

Hirsch said, "My God, Dave, he knows! He—"

Donato said, "Dave, what are we—"

Ayckbourn said, "Shut up! Shut up, both of you. Let me handle this." In a resigned voice, he said to me, "What's your price?"

I shook my head. "That's not how I picture it, Dave. I picture it more that the cops parallel what I've found out, then nail you guys criminally. After that, it's up to a civil jury to award my client damages, assuming you guys take it that far."

Ayckbourn struggled to control himself. "You called us here. You must have had some reason."

"Actually, I just wanted to give you all the same start."

Donato said, "Start? What start?"

"Conspiracy situation, the cops generally go easier on the first guy to talk to them. He rolls over on the others, the police see to it he goes to the kind of prison he might walk out of some day. I don't envision you guys lasting too long in a lot of cellblocks."

Ayckbourn's voice ground like glass. "Money, Cuddy. How much will it take?"

"Not for sale, Dave. The detective on the case is Paul O'Boy." I checked my watch. "I figure it's about thirty-five minutes to the station back in Calem." I smiled at each of them. "Gentlemen, start your engines."

Donato was the first one up, Hirsch a beat behind him. Ayckbourn screamed, "Harold, Angelo! For Christ sakes!"

Old Dave took one last look at me, teeth bared, then bolted out the door after them.

BERTIE'S MOM

One

"Parakeet?"

"Parakeet, Mr. Cuddy. Powder blue chest, gray and black head and wings."

The woman sitting across from me was nudging seventy, with white hair in a bun and the style of tweed suit Boston's Irish call "Yankee Sensible." However, she wore make-up that flattered her features, and the hair was swept up rather than pulled back. There also was a sparkle in her eye that I hoped indicated awareness rather than madness.

"Mrs. Addison, I can't find a parakeet."

"You are a private investigator, are you not?"

"I am."

"Licensed by the Commonwealth of Massachusetts?"

I gestured to the wall behind me. "Just like it says behind the glass."

She squinted to make out the calligraphy on the framed copy of the license. "John . . . Francis . . . Cuddy."

"Correct," I said.

"Then why won't you help me?"

"It's not a matter of won't. It's a matter of can't. Look, you say someone broke into your apartment."

"My townhouse. My late husband and I owned the entire building on Marlborough Street."

"But all they took was the parakeet."

"Yes. I conducted a careful inventory, and nothing else was taken, not even some terribly valuable pieces."

"Why would someone risk a burglary to steal a parakeet?"

"I've no idea. Neither did the idiot policemen who responded to my complaint. They smiled at each other and took perfunctory notes, but they obviously believed me mad as a hatter."

I watched her for a moment. "I don't think you're mad, Mrs. Addison."

She softened. "I know. One's sense of humor doesn't necessarily improve with age. One's sense of being humored does, and you're not doing that with me. What you can't understand is why I'm here at all."

"That's right."

"Are you married, Mr. Cuddy?"

"Like yourself."

An uplifted brow. "Widower?"

"Yes."

"I'm sorry, you seem so young to . . . I'm sorry."

"Please, finish your thought."

Mrs. Addison took a breath and held it. Then, "The police said not to worry. They said, 'These things happen, lady.' Well, that burglar took not only Bertie but also my . . . privacy, my security. Can you understand that?"

"Yes."

"I have no enemies, Mr. Cuddy. It's not that I've outlived them. Emmett and I were both born into money, and we never cheated anyone on anything, so this wasn't some twisted act of vengeance. I admit I quickly grew attached to Bertie, even thought of him as a particularly undemanding child. But more basically I want to know who did this and why. I'm used to paying for indulging myself. I expect your services to be no exception."

I thought about it. "I'll give it two days."

"Thank you."

"You have a photo of the bird and his cage?"

"No. But I can show you the cage."

"I don't get you."

"Whoever it was stole only Bertie, Mr. Cuddy. The cage was left behind."

◆ ◆ ◆

We were enjoying a fine autumn day, bell clear with the bite of the Montreal Express on the front edge of the northwest wind. Her townhouse was between Clarendon and Dartmouth, a twenty-minute stroll across the Common and Public Garden from my office and only a few blocks from where I lived. On the walk over we talked about Wellesley College during the Great Depression, her husband's service in North Africa, and how the absence of children from a marriage can make it stronger.

Marlborough Street is a distinctive part of Back Bay. Tall, black gaslight lamp-posts. Three- and four-story townhomes of variously colored stones with bay windows and tiny front lawns cum flower gardens behind low, wrought iron fences. The sidewalks, free-laid brick rather than poured cement, turn into narrow, mogulled skating rinks once the sleet starts to fall.

Mrs. Addison's front doorway displayed a security company decal. As we went through, I said, "Where was the break-in?"

"A cellar window, around back. I know I should have had them barred or alarmed, especially living here alone. But they were so small, I didn't think I needed to worry."

There was a cramped sitting room on the first floor, the Victorian way of escrowing visitors till the folks above were ready to receive them. Dining room and kitchen lay to the back past the lovely, curving staircase.

Mrs. Addison waved at a mesh mini-elevator. "We can take the lift if you're weary?"

"I can make it."

In the kitchen, she flicked on some lights and opened the cellar door. Following, I passed the assortment of possessions a couple might accumulate over fifty years of living in the same house. I felt warm, at ease.

"There."

I followed her angled arm to the boarded-over space of a smashed casement window. Probably ground level at the alley behind the building, it began nearly six feet above the cellar floor but measured only a foot by two feet at the most.

I said, "We're not looking for a big one, then."

"No. You can see where he landed from the scuffing at the base of the wall there."

I walked over. Not enough to be much help, the tread seemed to be a loafer or oxford rather than an athletic shoe. Odd choice given the climbing and running needs of most B&E artists.

"This dust tracked through the house?"

"Yes. It seems as though he went out this way too."

"Why do you say that?"

"No dust or smudges around either of the doors, and no alarm sounded."

As we climbed back to the first floor, I said, "Where were you when it happened?"

"I don't know."

"I'm sorry?"

"I don't know when it *did* happen, Mr. Cuddy. I'd only bought Bertie last week. On Thursday—when the break-in occurred—I visited an antique dealer, a bookstore, a bakery . . . I was in and out, both morning and afternoon. It could have happened any time prior to four, when I saw that Bertie's cage was empty."

We went up to the second floor, the front room a large parlor overlooking Marlborough Street, the rear room a study with studded leather chairs and floor-to-ceiling bookcases. The parlor contained print loveseats of delicate construction, oriental rugs and end-tables, and a magnificent marble fireplace. The only place in the room I wouldn't be afraid to sit was on the floor.

"That was Bertie's."

In one window of the draped bay stood a tall, bent pole with a large and ornate cage suspended from it. A giant snake lamp grown too big for its desk.

Up close, I inspected the intricate, braided wire work, all of it gold, at least in color. Red velvet lined the outside lower perimeter of the cage. The velvet was cut carefully and fitted with a small drawer. I tugged on the knob.

"The drawer is for the bird's medicine or toys, I imagine. Wonderful craftsmanship. I'm afraid it was the cage rather than Bertie which attracted me in the first place."

I slid the drawer all the way out, turning it over. Three inches wide, five inches long, not even two inches deep. There was some discoloration on the back end of the drawer. Sticky. "Where did you buy it?"

"A pet store near my salon. I'd never gone in there before, but it was raining, and I didn't want to ruin my permanent. The proprietor was so rude I very nearly didn't stay long enough to spot this."

I replaced the drawer. It slid a quarter of an inch too far along its track. I used the knob to ease it flush with the velvet covering around it.

"How did you get it home?"

"I beg your pardon?"

"In the rain and all. How did you get the cage and Bertie home?"

"Oh. As I said, the manager or whatever was terribly rude. I finally was able to persuade him to deliver it."

"You have the receipt?"

"I believe so."

"May I see it?"

I played with the cage door and the perches while she shuffled off to the study. No way Bertie could have gotten out on his own. She returned with a pink slip and handed it to me.

The printing above Mrs. Addison's name and address read "Niles Pet Emporium, for the Discriminating Fancier." The neighborhood was near Beth's hillside.

"I'll be in touch, Mrs. Addison."

✦ ✦ ✦

A parakeet?

"Beth, that's what I said." Straightening up, I watched the wind-surfers, wearing wetsuits, brave the cold and chemicals of Boston harbor below the cemetery. The breeze was fairly stiff, the petals on Mrs. Feeney's roses fluttering like tiny flags.

How do you find a parakeet?

"I don't think I do."

Then what are you going to do?

"Mrs. Addison had the bird for barely a week. Not much time for someone to know she had it. Except for the pet shop, which not only knew she bought it but had her address from the delivery."

Yes, but if there was something valuable about the bird, they wouldn't have sold it to her in the first place, would they?

"You have a better place to start?"

Two

Driving toward Niles Pet Emporium, I passed the new Continental Trailways Bus Terminal. Trailways used to have space over by the Statler Hotel. Then urban renewal erupted, the Statler became the Park Plaza, and out went the terminal, bars like the Hillbilly Ranch, and strip joints like the Mousetrap Cafe. The local color was replaced by the monolithic Massachusetts Transportation Building and its five thousand office workers, not to mention four hundred thousand dollar condos fronting on Boston Common.

The pet store was tucked into a structure near the Boston Tea Party ship. No wonder Mrs. Addison chose it as a refuge from the rain. The puppies and kittens in the windows flanking the entrance rollicked and posed like accomplished actors.

Inside, the floors and counters were clean, the scent only mildly disinfectant. One wall held a bank of aquaria, the other cages of various birds, most of which I'd never seen before. I started toward a doorway in the back of the store that probably led to a stockroom.

"Help you with something?"

A man rose from behind a counter to my left. Medium height and balding, he was pot-bellied in a torn, dirty sweater. His forehead, nose and cheeks were scaly, dandruff of the face.

"Are you Mr. Niles?"

"That's right."

"I'm interested in a bird—"

"Got a hundred of 'em. Look around, let me know if you see one I can help you with."

"A bird you already sold to somebody."

He wet his lips with his tongue, wiping his hands unconsciously on the sweater. "What's this all about?"

I showed him my identification. "Mrs. Emmett Addison. You sold her a parakeet last week. Somebody took it."

"Don't remember that."

"Older woman, around seventy. Stylish, sharp. You'd remember her."

"Like I said, can't help you."

A female voice from the back said, "Mister Niles," but the accent made it sound like "Missah Nile," an accent that yanked me back a lot of years and fourteen thousand miles.

I turned. She was in her twenties somewhere, with the coal black hair and fine features of a high-born Vietnamese urbanite. As she fumbled with some sort of food sack, I saw other familiar marks as well. A livid scar running from ear to neckline, and a stump of wrist where her right hand should have been.

"Damn it, not now, Marie."

The bag, heavy and bulky, fell, splitting apart and cascading pellets, edible rather than appetizing, onto the floor.

"Damn it, girl. Those cost money!"

"Sorry."

"Now we'll have to use it ourselves rather than sell it."

"I clean up."

"That won't do it." He turned to me. "I gotta attend to this mess."

I let him get ten feet before I said, "Anybody ask you for Mrs. Addison's address?"

He faltered when he should have just kept going and waved me off. "I said I can't help you. Jesus, Marie. What's the matter with you?"

She looked up at me, doe eyes questioning. "Sorry."

✦ ✦ ✦

I waited a block away, keeping the entrance to the store in my rear view mirror. I figured that Niles would have her leave before he counted the receipts. He did.

She drew even with me, the end of her right arm thrust into a jacket pocket.

I called quietly through the open passenger's side window. "Marie?"

She didn't seem startled, just looked around to be sure Niles wasn't watching. She opened the door with her left hand and climbed in. "You cop?"

"No. Private investigator."

"You got ID?"

I took it out. "You wanted to talk with me?"

She nodded her head. "Drive."

I started the engine. "Where do you live?"

"Just drive, okay?"

"Okay."

I took us away from downtown, back toward South Boston where there was some beach and less rush hour traffic.

After a while, she said, "Nile a bastard."

"That's how he struck me."

"I work for him three year, he treat me like . . . like he can't get no American help no more."

"Some bosses are like that. Makes it hard."

"You don't have to be nice to me. I tell you anyway."

"All right."

She looked out the window. A couple of kids, a boy and a girl, were playing catch with a tennis ball. The girl was better than the boy and uncorked a hard overhand, a rightie. Marie turned away.

"Nile think I can't get better job, way I look."

I didn't say anything.

"I find that cage in the back."

"The cage Mrs. Addison bought?"

Marie nodded. "That cage all dirty, under table in the back. Nile a pig, couldn't see how nice it was. I clean it up, tell him we put it out front."

"And Mrs. Addison bought it."

"She rich. She have the eye for nice things. I can tell." Marie dropped her tone a notch. "I can remember."

"You delivered it to her?"

"Nile try to tell her, 'Take it with you.' Stupid, woman like that don't take things with her. He come to back, I tell him. He get good dollar for cage. He finally say, 'Okay, we deliver.'"

"How?"

"How we deliver?"

"Yes."

"Company. I call. But that not what you want to know."

"No?"

"No."

We were at the Castle Island parking lot. I pulled in, turned off the engine.

Marie looked up at the massive stonework jutting out toward the harbor entrance. "Military?"

"At one time."

"Me, too. At one time."

There was no joking in her voice. Then, "Thursday, last week. Man come to store. Strange man, not very big. Want cage from Nile. Nile say sold. Man get angry, run around store to back, knock me over to look.

Then go to register, throw around receipts."

"Like the man knew where they were?"

"Yes. Like the man know where we keep receipts. He take one, read it. Curse at Nile, then throw receipt in Nile face and run out to street."

"You said the man was strange?"

"Strange look. Face, hand . . . hands all white. Like fish belly."

"Pale?"

"Like red-hair man, but he have brown hair. Like he never see sun."

"Anything else, Marie?"

"Nile know him."

"How could you tell?"

"Nile call him Ollie."

Reaching for my wallet, I said, "I appreciate your helping me."

"Don't want money. Just drop me T station."

"You don't have to take the subway. Let me at least give you a ride home."

"No." She looked at me, hard. "I don't want people see man like you drive me home." She turned back to look out the window. "They make fun of me."

✦ ✦ ✦

There are lots of ways to find things out. One is to confront a person who lies to you. Like the good Mr. Niles. Sometimes, though, that leads to people who helped you and gets them into trouble. If Ollie knew Niles and also knew where the receipts were kept, chances were he'd been an employee of the pet store sometime before Marie came on three years ago. What I needed were some friends with computers that weren't asleep yet.

Three

A guy from my block back in Southie is a cop on the Capitol Police force. I called him and got the parking space behind the State House reserved for a legislator who's been in the House chambers about as often as Amelia Earhart. I walked down Beacon Hill to the C.F. Hurley Building in Government Center.

Jimmy Somogi was still at his desk in the Division of Employment Security. Jimmy was nearly always still at his desk. If the division could clone him, it would become the KGB of a full employment totalitarian state.

"Jimmy, how's the boy?"

"No Irish glad hand, okay?"

Jimmy's folks were from Hungary originally. He came over after the revolt in 1956. His accent didn't mix that well in our neighborhood, and I pulled a couple of America First types off him in the schoolyard once.

"Jimmy, you cut me to the quick."

"What exactly is it you want this time?"

"Simple rundown. I have a name and a probable employer. I need current whereabouts."

Jimmy looked almost disappointed as he propelled himself to a keyboard and monitor. "Just the name would be faster."

"I think it's only a nickname, Jimmy."

He rolled his eyes. "And the employer's Raytheon, right?"

"No. Niles Pet Emporium, in Boston."

Jimmy started to clack the keys.

I continued anyway. "Name's 'Ollie,' spelled 'O-L-L-I-E,' probably. Maybe short for—"

"Oliver. Oliver Toomey, NMI. Off Niles books as of . . . five . . . no, six years ago."

I looked at the screen. "You are truly frightening, Jimmy."

"Name's odd enough, the no-middle-initial won't be a problem. You want current employer?"

"Right."

More clacking. A frown. More clacking still. A head shake. "No good."

"Meaning?"

"Old Ollie ain't gainfully employed in this commonwealth no longer."

I recalled Marie's description of Niles' visitor. "That's what I thought."

Jimmy cocked his head at me.

✦ ✦ ✦

Detective Cross of Homicide was in a chair, eating a cruller and slurping coffee from a styrofoam cup that didn't seem to be on its maiden voyage from the wrapper.

"Hi."

She looked up from an array of crime scene photos. "Murphy's not here."

"I know. I need to speak to you about something."

"Not interested."

"Please."

She sighed, turning the photos face down so I couldn't see them. "Three minutes."

"I need somebody to run a guy through the computer."

"Why?"

I told her, embroidering a little.

She stared at me. "You're kidding?"

I raised my hand to oath level. "God's truth."

Cross lowered her chin to her chest and stifled a laugh. "You realize what'd happen to your rep, I spread this parakeet quest around?"

"Uh-huh. That's why I wanted to see you."

She raised her head, pursing her lips. "And the old woman, the cleaning lady, she had this bird how long?"

My embroidery. "Almost eight years."

"All right." She reached for a pad. "Guy's name?"

It took fifteen minutes to determine that Oliver NMI Toomey had spent his time since leaving Niles Pet Emporium as a guest of the State of Maine, Corrections Department.

◆ ◆ ◆

Augusta is pretty small for a state capital. Not impressive architecturally, it lies just east of Exit 16 on the Maine Turnpike. The foliage was spectacular on the drive north, but the road into the city itself is lined with motels, fast food franchises, and car dealers.

Parole officer Quentin Causwell was a pleasantly plump young man about five years out of college and a hundred years old from his daily work. Dressed in khaki pants, an L.L. Bean plaid shirt and a solid wool tie, he shook my hand and told me to take a seat.

"What can I do for you?"

I identified myself to his satisfaction. He leaned back in the swivel chair, tapping a pencil on his blotter. "Oliver Toomey, huh?"

"That's right."

"What kind of detail you need?"

"Last known address would be nice."

"Might want to know more than that."

Causwell went to a file cabinet, riffled through some folders and carried one back to his seat. He flipped forward, then back a few times. "Investigating officers might remember more'n this, but it's a fair summary as they go. Seems this Toomey and a confederate stuck themselves up a bank. Toomey was from Boston, the confederate a local boy name of Houle."

Causwell used the French Canadian pronunciation, like "school" without the "sch."

"Cross-reference on Toomey's discharge says Houle died in prison. Cancer. Police caught Houle with his share of the take, found Toomey's telephone number on top of a piece of paper on Houle's bed table at home. Nobody ever said these boys were smart, I guess. Our guys matched up with some of yours down there and busted Toomey at work."

"Pet store?"

"Let me . . . Niles Pet Emporium sound right?"

"It does."

"Well, seems Toomey didn't have the goods on him or at his place down there. Don't see anything to show he cooperated. Wasn't a fortune, just over seventy thousand according to the count the bank did. Houle had thirty-five and change when they got him, so figure Toomey's share'd be about the same."

"Unless there was another confederate."

Causwell looked at me thoughtfully. "Unless."

"How soon after the robbery did the cops nail Toomey down in Boston?"

"Next morning, looks like."

"Can I have that current address now?"

"Sure can. Hope you enjoyed the drive."

"How's that?"

"Seems we let your Mr. Toomey go home to roost."

"Boston?"

Causwell lifted what looked like a reduced Xerox closer to his eyes. "Got a pencil?"

Four

It was a rooming house in Charlestown, the obelisk of the Bunker Hill monument rising like a science fiction special effect in the distance. Given the gentrification of the streets around the Monument Square area, it was only a matter of time before people like Oliver Toomey wouldn't be able to live there anymore.

Letting my car rest after the drive from Maine, I saw a short, wiry man with pasty skin come up the sidewalk holding a grocery sack. He cradled it with both forearms the way a fullback does when his team's leading in the last two minutes and the other guys are trying to strip the ball. Like you might carry something through a prison yard.

He turned into the doorway of the rooming house. I got out of my car and approached.

"Mr. Toomey?"

His head whipped around, jaws working overtime on some gum as he checked for who spoke and how many were with me.

"I'm by myself, Mr. Toomey."

"Who are you?"

I showed him. "Can we talk?"

"About what?"

"About six years ago?"

He muttered something I wasn't meant to hear. Then, "Upstairs."

The steps were warped and the bulb was dim, but I didn't sense he wanted to jump me. I followed him up to his room and into it.

Toomey had a cubbyhole refrigerator, into which he stuffed some of the items from the sack. I took the only chair in the room, a ladderback missing two rungs. He closed the fridge and slumped onto the iron bed, head drooped and hands wringing as though he were waiting outside a maternity ward.

"So talk," he said.

"Six years ago you and a guy name Houle stuck up a bank. You got caught, but without your share of the money. Then you break into a woman's house to steal a parakeet she bought at your old employer's pet shop. Why?"

At first I couldn't place the sound; then I realized it was laughter. That muffled, I'm-in-church hysteria I remembered from being a kid.

"Toomey?"

The muffled sound got louder, but not from laughter anymore. He was crying, crying his heart out.

"Toomey!"

He shouted at the floor. "Sweet Mary, Mother of God! That's what's going to send me back?"

"What're you talking about?"

He raised his head. "Look, I tell you what happened, straight jake exactly what happened, can you cut me a break here? Not violate my parole?"

"I won't know till I hear it."

Toomey lay down, the back of his hand wiping his eyes, then covering them to block the light. I felt like a psychiatrist staring at his couch.

"Marty—Marty Houle—and me met drinking one night, he tells me about this bank back where he's from in Maine there, a pushover. I'm making squat at the pet store, Niles treating me like something a dog puked up, so I call in sick and I go for it. The job goes down clean, nobody hurt, but some girl in the bank recognizes Marty's voice, even behind the mask and all, so the cops up there are on him like a blanket. Only I come down from Maine with my share in this gym bag not knowing any of that. I get in by bus, Trailways had a late one, but I'm not stupid enough to carry the cash with me that time of night, guys you might run into. So I stash the bag in a locker at the terminal there and I go home, thinking I'm rich. I go to work the next day, figuring to act natural. No reason to pick up the bag till that night, see?"

"I see."

"So I'm at work, in the back room just chewing some gum, thinking about what I'm gonna do with the money, and I hear a car pull up through the door to the alley. I figure it's just some delivery. Then I hear somebody out front asking Niles about me, and he says "Police?" just like that. So I look around fast, see this old cage, and take the gum outta my mouth and the locker key outta my pocket and stick the whole works to the back of this little drawer thing in the cage there."

Toomey rolled his head on the pillow. "I couldn't believe that Marty would've sold me, so I figured the cops had squat, I'm back on the streets in a week. Uh-unh. It's back to Maine, no bail, and a lawyer who pleads me before I see his name spelled out on the paperwork, get me? Then six years, I'm like a model prisoner. I get my parole, I con the parole guy into letting me hitch down here fast as I can."

"You went to the shop first."

"Yeah, yeah. I went there. Niles recognized me and remembered the cage right away. I could see in his eyes something was hinky. I near took the head off some slant he had working in the back, but the cage is gone. Sold off."

Toomey levered up on an elbow and stared at me. "You got any idea what it's like, doing a long six, an hour at a time, then you find out you're like two days late to pick up the key?"

"Go on."

"I get the Addison broad's address from Niles. Her house—you seen it?"

"I saw it."

"I get in there, and get the key, no sweat, but when I go to the terminal, to . . . where it was, it . . . it wasn't."

"Just the big brown office building."

"Yeah, yeah. I couldn't believe it. I thought I was dreaming or something, you know? It's gone, all gone. Everything even that was around it. Just gone."

God knew what happened to the money when they were taking apart the lockers. But I had a different question.

"Toomey?"

"Yeah?"

"Why did you take the bird?"

"Huh?"

"The parakeet in the cage. You had the key, you didn't take anything else. Even with the broken window and the tracks you made from the cellar, if nothing was missing she wouldn't have gone past the cops to hire me. Why did you take the bird?"

"I didn't."

"You didn't."

"No. I just took it out of the cage, opened a window there, and let him go."

"What?"

"I just let him go."

"Why?"

"You gotta remember. I was standing there, in her living room, with that key in my hand. I looked at the bird, behind bars like I'd been for six years. I thought about working over in the pet store there, how Niles never let none of the animals run around or nothing, and . . . and I just decided to let him out of his cage, too."

"Jesus."

Toomey worked his mouth a few times. "So how about it, buddy? Can you cut me a break on this B&E thing here?"

"I don't know."

"You don't know?"

"No. It's up to Bertie's mom."

A SOUL TO TELL

One

"May I have your attention, please. The Delta Connection, Business Express Flight Three-five-five-seven, with direct service to Nantucket and continuing service to Martha's Vineyard, is now ready for passengers through Gate Fifteen. All rows may now board the aircraft."

I hefted my duffle bag and joined the line of folks handing little passes to the uniformed smile. An hour before, I'd locked "JOHN FRANCIS CUDDY, CONFIDENTIAL INVESTIGATIONS," and hailed a Boston Cab to Logan Airport. It's cheaper to drive to Cape Cod and take the ferry to Nantucket, but I was on expenses, and the client on the phone had said the sooner the better. She also said I wouldn't be needing a firearm or dress clothes, just a camera and lots of film.

We made our way down a flight of stairs and onto a jitney bus with deep leatherette seats. Gas tankers, Marriott food service trucks, and baggage shuttles made for heavy traffic on the macadam. The bus driver pulled up to our plane, a twin-prop Shorts 360 that looked a lot like our jitney with wings. I heaved my duffel into the open baggage hold near the tail. The maybe thirty of us filled most of the seats in the cabin, the take-off reminding me of walking through a machine shop going full blast. When the pilot reached cruising altitude, the stewardess began pouring soft drinks.

The plastic cups were barely on the trays before we began our descent into Nantucket, the "Faraway Isle" of whalers. Gentle hills and moors, sporting a dozen shades of yellow, brown, and orange in the clear October air. My wife Beth and I used to talk about taking a getaway weekend to the island. Before the cancer took her.

On the ground, a guy wearing sonic earmuffs unloaded the baggage hold onto a cart and wheeled the cart to a glassless service window, through which he passed our luggage. Following the client's suggestion, I signed for a Jeep Cherokee at one of the rental counters and got a map and finger-traced directions to 76 Main Street, the bed and breakfast the client named.

There was only one architectural style on the drive from the airport, even the gas stations done in silver cedar-shake siding. The predominant trim color was white, a few nonconformists daring powder blue and even dull red.

Once in town, however, there was a Federalist-period flavor to things, including a number of brick or clapboard mansions and cottages.

The inn turned out to be one of the white clapboard places, a friendly woman named Shirley registering me and asking what I wanted from my time on the island. When I said I wasn't sure, she rattled off ten or twelve spots I could visit, with brochures on what to look for when I arrived at each. After I was shown to my room and oriented on breakfast the next morning, Shirley wished me a good dinner and a good night.

Unpacking took only until four o'clock. Since the weather was clear and I didn't know what the client had in mind for my time, I decided to walk the town and harbor. Main Street angled downhill past quaint shops, spreading and petering out at wharves which held tiny shacks dolled up as art and crafts galleries. Not too many pleasure craft so late in the season, but still a lot of scallopers and charterboats.

At the sound of a hooting horn, people who had been lounging on benches or curbs suddenly gathered themselves and rushed toward a docking ferry. One couple doggy-walked a sea-kayak on its two-wheeled trailer, him at the bow, her at the stern, smiling tolerantly at the odd looks and snapshots being taken of them.

Leaving the harbor, I criss-crossed the streets, noticing the police station on South Water only by the one black and white Ford patrol car parked in front of it. As the sun set, I joined the rest of the tourists in what seemed to be the major preoccupation: reading menus posted outside restaurants and shaking heads at the high prices listed. I eventually settled on a reasonable place called Obadiah's, an old-fashioned basement dining room on India Street. The wide-board pine benches were lacquered, the clam chowder and swordfish magnificent. I added a bottle of sauvignon blanc to the bill.

Back upstairs, the sidewalks were rolling up. I walked off dinner for twenty minutes or so, appreciating the charm of the town in the afterglow of the wine. Climbing back up Main, I nearly broke my ankle twice on the cobblestoned street, the stones themselves rounded but hummocky above the old cement.

At the inn, an equally friendly man named Mitch welcomed me all over again. After a few minutes of small talk, I went up to my room. In the spirit of the island, I went to sleep with the windows open and the door to the corridor unlocked.

Two

"I'd rather hoped to go deaf first, you see."

Eleanor Ware sat across from me, sipping herb tea from a delicate china cup. The cup was the only delicate thing about her. High forehead, broad nose, strong jaw. A whisper of make-up around the eyes, and black hair generously streaked with gray. The hair was pulled back and caught in a ponytail, as though she did that just once each day and undid it just once at night. The kind of clothes you see in a Talbot's window, all earth colors. Fifty-plus, and not the least bit afraid to show it.

Ware received me on a wicker settee in the solarium of a traditional Cape Cod, a railed, wood deck visible through the sliding glass doors behind her. She already had asked me if I'd enjoyed the inn, and I already had told her that breakfast on the patio there had been great except for the yellowjackets. Apparently, the beautiful weather brought them out, wasps being "a small price to pay for sunshine in October." I'd just managed to get us onto why she wanted to hire me, but I was having trouble understanding her.

"Let me get this straight, Mrs. Ware. You want me to follow your husband around?"

"Yes, yes, but not for some—what do you detectives call it, 'ulterior motive'?"

"Investigator."

"Excuse me?"

"I'm an investigator. Detectives are on police forces."

"Yes, yes. Tell me, Mr. Cuddy. Are you married?"

"Widower."

"Oh. Oh, I am sorry." Her eyes blurred as she set the cup in a matching saucer. "Forgive me, Mr. Cuddy. And please forgive too my joke about going deaf. You see, my husband Mycah has been in real estate ever since he came to the island—his office is just off Main Street. He turns fifty-five next February, and he's always promised to retire then. Mycah certainly deserves it, the man has worked day and night for decades and has always been a fine provider. But, with the boom in housing the last few years, he's scarcely had any time to spend with me. And I'm afraid, frankly, that in maintaining and expanding my own circle of friends . . . I'm just afraid that Mycah and I have rather lost touch with one another, that we won't have much in common once he retires."

"So you want me to follow him around?"

"Yes. To see what he does, how he spends his day. Then report back to me so that I can learn more about his interests and at least have topics of conversation when we begin spending more time together in a few months."

I shifted in my wicker chair. "Couldn't you just sort of ask him about that?"

Ware blushed. "Ask Mycah about what he does, you mean?"

"Yes."

"Oh, no. No, that would be . . . inappropriate. He'd feel that I didn't love him enough to have kept up with him."

I thought about Beth, all the time I spent away from her before knowing she was sick. Eleanor Ware's sentiment was a little corny, but I could understand it.

I said, "You want pictures of him?"

"Pictures?"

"Photographs. All the camera equipment I brought."

"Oh. Oh, I see. No, the island attracts a lot of naturalists, you see. When I suggested camera gear on the phone I meant for it to give you—do detec— sorry, *investigators*, call it 'cover'?"

"Close enough. I follow him around pretending to take pictures of the birds and the bushes."

"Precisely."

"You don't think he'll notice that."

"Mycah? No. No, everyone who visits Nantucket and rents a Jeep is sightseeing, and this is a small island with only so many roads. Even if he saw you more than once, he wouldn't give it a second thought."

"Do you want pictures of any of the people he meets?"

"No. Thank you, but no. Mycah must spend a good deal of his time showing properties to prospective buyers from away. From off-island, that is. I wouldn't be needing to meet or talk to any of them. I just want you to trail after him for oh, say three days? Then report back to me. Would that be satisfactory?"

"Three days at four hundred a day added onto my time to get here and back, plus expenses."

"I assure you that I can afford it."

I looked around at the elaborate furniture, adjoining a living room with a baby grand piano but without a television. People who don't have a TV in their living room usually can afford it.

"What I meant, Mrs. Ware, is that you might not be getting much value for your money."

"I'm a fair judge of value, Mr. Cuddy. And besides, even if this is just a whim, I'd like to know. It will help me be a better helpmate to Mycah during his transition from active professional to retired husband."

"You have a recent picture of him?"

She frowned. "Can't you just—what, 'pick him up' outside the house here?"

I gestured toward the front door. "Your house sits on this little knoll with a meadow in front of it. There's no place for me to conceal the Jeep, and even your husband would wonder about a car that picked him up right outside his driveway."

"Yes. Yes, I see your point."

"It would be a lot easier for me to latch onto him at his real estate office, and that way I could start this afternoon."

"Just a moment."

Ware rose and strode purposefully to the piano. She came back carrying a large photo, holding the frame at northwest and southeast corners like an auctioneer's assistant. "This is a portrait we had done at Bachrach's in Boston." The woman couldn't quite keep the pride from her voice. "I'm told they even had it displayed in their glass case on Boylston Street."

The photo showed Mrs. Ware sitting and a bold, assured man with auburn hair standing halfway behind her. His right hand rested on her shoulder, her left hand bent upward to touch his.

"You make a striking couple."

She blushed again and replaced the frame on the piano. Her sentimentality and strength made an attractive combination, and I found myself envying husband Mycah just a bit.

Resuming her seat, Eleanor Ware asked if there was anything else.

"What kind of car does your husband drive?"

"Cadillac."

"Model and color?"

"Coupe de Ville, rather a burgundy. With all the dirt roads on the island, a Jeep would be more practical, but Mycah always loved his Cadillacs."

"You know anyone on the local police force?"

My question seemed to throw her. "The police?"

"Yes."

"What do they have to do with our arrangement?"

"Hopefully nothing. It's just standard procedure to check in with them when I start working in a new town."

"Is it . . . some kind of law or regulation?"

"No. Just good business practice."

"I see. Well, I have a problem with that."

"What is it?"

"On the telephone, when I called, you said that your licensing statute would keep everything between us confidential."

"That's right."

"Confidential even from the police?"

"I don't read the statute every week, but it just says I might have to reveal to a court, not the cops. Why?"

"Well, you see, I'm an islander. I was raised here, with the chief of police, among others. I would . . . It would be embarrassing to me for them to know that I'd hired you to follow Mycah."

"That's understandable. Tell you what. I'll just let the police know I'm down here on business, not what the business is or who it's for. Would that be all right?"

Ware seemed to think about it. "Yes. Yes, that would be fine." She reached down next to her chair and brought up a handbag from which she coaxed a fat envelope. "I'd like to pay you a retainer in advance."

As she counted fifties from the envelope, I said, "A check would be fine."

Ware stopped counting for a minute, weighing the bills in her palm as though that would somehow be a quality control on her tally. "No. No, I got the cash for this, and frankly, it makes it better."

"Better?"

"This is a small island, Mr. Cuddy. It's hard to have secrets, even harder to share them. That's why I wanted someone from away—someone like you —to help me. Paying you in cash means no snoopy bank teller will know my personal business."

Eleanor Ware finished counting and handed me the bills, being careful I thought not to let our fingers touch.

Three

"Kate Hearn."

"John Cuddy, Sergeant."

"Kate, please."

I released her hand. She sat back down behind a cluttered desk, me taking one of the metal chairs in front of it. The biggish patrol officer who had brought me into her office closed the door as he left.

Hearn said, "Chief's on vacation, off-island."

I thought to myself that Mrs. Ware would be pleased.

Hearn inclined her head toward the door. "Ben said you're a private investigator."

"Yes."

"From Boston?"

"My accent gave me away?"

Hearn laughed, one sharp bray. "No, it's just there aren't so many from the Cape, and I thought I knew most of the operatives from New Bedford and Fall River."

Her hair on the sides and back touched the collar of her shirt. The bangs in front were just past her brow. Any longer and she'd have to blow out a breath to keep them off her eyes, which were blue and steady. "So, what brings you to Nantucket?"

"I'm going to be driving around a lot with a camera, and I thought I ought to check in with you first."

"Uh-huh." The steady eyes never left me. "You're going to be driving around a lot."

"Right."

"Make, model and plate?"

I told her. She wrote them down.

"Where are you staying?"

"76 Main Street."

"Good choice."

"I'm comfortable."

Hearn waited me out, then said, "Am I going to get a real answer to my question about what brought you here?"

"Confidential."

"Confidential."

"Sorry."

Hearn puffed out a breath, flipping the bangs. "Okay. Consider yourself checked in, then. But don't expect any favors without doing some yourself."

When I got up, we shook hands anyway.

✦ ✦ ✦

High noon, but not much happening in downtown Nantucket. Three elderly women were window shopping, pointing politely and nodding at everything each one said. A hard-faced guy in a blue jogging suit was loafing on the hood of his car, arms and ankles crossed. He looked like he'd made his money young. Some kids of college age were camped on a curb, knapsacks as backrests, eating ice cream.

I could see the doorway to Ware Realty through the driver's side mirror. I studied a map of the island and fiddled with my camera like a tourist about to strike off for the afternoon. A burgundy Coupe de Ville occupied a parking space three down from mine. A tweedy middle-aged couple had gone into the realty office about fifteen minutes before, he seeming less enthusiastic than she did.

I was down to counting the number of ponds on my map when Mycah Ware came out holding a clipboard in his right hand. In tow were the middle-aged couple and a stunning redhead in a bottle-green dress that I would bet complemented her eyes. The quartet crossed to the Cadillac, the men taking the front seats, the women the rear, the redhead showing some leg as she climbed in. Even the guy in the jogging suit seemed to sit up straighter. Waiting until Ware passed me, I started up and after them.

I should have had ice cream with the knapsackers.

Ware took his customers to three houses, all indistinguishable to me under weathered shingles and white-picket widow's walks. At each stop, Ware sashayed the woman in the couple all over the grounds, tapping and then holding a pen to the clipboard in his hands. The redhead tagged behind with the man in the couple, seemingly doing the same things with her pen and clipboard. Then everybody went into the house for half an hour or so.

The only change in the routine was the part of the island we visited. First west to the Dionis Beach area, then south to Cisco Beach, then east past the airport toward Low Beach.

While Ware and the redhead hucked, and the couple absorbed, I took photos. Of everything. Kids windsurfing in striped wetsuits, a woman in a straw hat painting a seascape on an easel, tufted grasses at the base of dunes. Double-rung fences of gray split rails, country mailboxes with little red flags, kaleidoscopic fields of wildflowers. Estuaries with small sailboats, moors of pumpkin-hued heather. Small trees bent over from the prevailing wind, briar patches even Br'er Rabbit wouldn't call home. You name it, I shot it, my eyes blearing and my back creaking.

At house number three, a blue Thunderbird with classical music wafting from the radio pulled even with me. Bent over my umpteenth wildflower, I looked up at the driver. Preppy face, short blond hair, the kind of guy who wouldn't look quite thirty until he was well past forty.

He said, "You okay?"

"Fine, thanks."

"Saw your car on my way into town, then saw you still here. Thought you might be broken down."

"No. Just taking pictures. Thanks, though."

"Anytime." He waved and accelerated slowly away.

I wondered if I had just met one of Kate Hearn's officers out of uniform.

The Thunderbird was barely out of sight when Ware and the others left the house and piled into the Caddy. We drove back toward town, stopping at a classy private clubhouse set a hundred feet from its driveway. I stole the spirits from some more flora, trying not to notice the rabbit squashed flat near the entrance or the ravens licking their chops on the power lines. An hour later, the Coupe de Ville pulled back onto the road and went the rest of the way into Nantucket. The fabulous foursome disappeared into the realty office for half an hour more, then reappeared with vigorous handshakes and polite kisses all around. The wife in the couple was clutching a big manila envelope and beaming ecstatically; the husband was missing a shirt pocket with his pen and wearing an expression like he'd just been in a train crash.

Once the couple was out of sight, Ware and the redhead smiled at each other and went to the Cadillac. Off we went, this time toward the east along Milestone Road. There was very little traffic. I checked a couple of times for the Thunderbird, but didn't see it.

When we got to the village of Siasconset, Ware and the redhead started house-hopping again. They'd circle around a place, clipboards in hand, Ware apparently giving her some tips as he pointed at exterior features, then to a form on her clipboard. At each house, they'd go inside for half an hour or so, then come back out. These times I shot a towering, red-banded lighthouse; gray, dumpy hens that looked wild; and larger silver-shake mansions with English hedges and gardens.

After the third house, we again returned to town, dusk and a little fog heavy on the moors along the road. A block from the realty office, Ware came to a stop. The redhead and he shook hands theatrically, a pronounced, "we-did-it" pantomime, then laughed. She got out of the Caddy and into a Mercedes convertible, the only one I'd seen on the island so far. Ware waited until she started up before he put his car in gear.

I followed Ware back to his own house, continuing on as he slewed into his driveway and put the Caddy in the garage via some kind of electronic door-opener. Figuring he was through for the night, I drove back to the inn, thinking over dinner that old Mycah probably turned a tad more than my four hundred for his day's work with the middle-aged couple.

Four

I was getting better at keeping the yellowjackets out of my Wheat Chex.

On the patio in the backyard of 76 Main Street, I read the local newspaper and tossed sugar cubes to the sparrows. Past the overhanging branches, there wasn't a cloud in the sky, temperature at eight a.m. in the low sixties. Sweater weather. Mycah Ware might lead a boring life, but I could see why people would want to live their only one on Nantucket.

Reluctantly, I folded the paper and went around front to the Cherokee.

✦ ✦ ✦

There were two sets of different elderly ladies window-shopping, three male knapsackers who spoke in German or Dutch to each other while they ate croissants and slurped coffee, and the same rough-faced guy in a different jogging outfit. The redhead's Mercedes was already on the street. I didn't see Ware's Cadillac, but I wasn't worried.

Just after nine, the redhead came out of the realty office. She was dressed in a conservative gray suit today, talking and nodding a lot to a short, squat, older woman who appeared to be calling the shots for a taller, younger woman from the same gene pool.

The threesome moved on foot toward my car, the jogging suit guy swiveling around, following the redhead with his eyes and sighing. I realized it might be a daily ritual for him, watching the best-looking woman on the island. As the redhead drew even with my car, she squeezed a smile at me into her nodding at everything the squat woman said. Up close, the redhead's face looked carefully maintained, and I bumped her age up toward forty. The squat woman's voice was raspy and commanding, and I decided I didn't envy the redhead her next few hours.

Hearing a car door slam, I looked back up the street. Mycah Ware, in rose slacks and a teal sweater, was crossing to his office. He went inside, staying maybe fifteen minutes before emerging, going to his Caddy, and taking off. I started up and followed him eastward to the Sankaty Head Golf Club, near the lighthouse from the day before. He pulled into the driveway. I stayed by the edge of the road and got out. I walked until I could see Ware at the trunk of his car, yanking out a bag of golf clubs and waving to a kid who hustled over to help him with it.

For the next six and a half hours, I counted four-wheel drive vehicles (fifty-one, but some of them were doubles), species of birds (seven, with only the sparrows, seagulls, and starlings sure IDs), and finally kinds of flowers (I quit at thirty). I even got cruel, snapping candids of overweight tourists on mopeds. They wore helmets at all the wrong angles and silently screamed through open mouths as they careened down the hill.

The Cadillac finally reappeared at the mouth of the driveway. On the way to town, Ware stopped for a couple of belts at the same private club, then continued home, putting his car to sleep again in the garage.

As I drove back to town, I thought it looked like a long thirty years in front of wife Eleanor.

✦ ✦ ✦

It was just dark when I parked half a block from 76 Main Street. Before I could get out, a tall guy in a Mets baseball cap and sunglasses limped over to my driver's side with a map in his hands.

"I wonder if you can help me?"

My hand on the door handle, I said, "Sorry. I don't know the island too well."

The passenger's side door rocked open and the guy in the jogging suit got in, a Smith & Wesson Bodyguard revolver almost lost in his fist. "That's okay. We do."

The guy with the Mets cap lowered his shades. The preppy blond from the Thunderbird. I didn't like his smile much.

✦ ✦ ✦

"Okay, now pull over against that log there."

We were in the parking area for Dionis Beach. There was a big house with two peaked gables and a couple of smaller ones on the bluff, but all looked closed up for the season.

Jogging Suit said, "Turn off the engine."

I did.

"Put the keys on the dashboard."

Same.

"Now play statue for a minute."

Jogging Suit stayed where he was while Preppy got out from behind me. Preppy pointed a little automatic at my face while Jogging Suit opened the passenger's side and came around. Both leveled on me from ten feet away and at different angles as I got out of the car. Very professional and not a good sign.

"Assume the position on the hood."

I complied. They didn't bother with my wallet. Another bad sign.

Preppy said, "We're going to take a walk on the beach. You go first. Turn when we say. Don't do anything stupid."

I led them up the sandpath and over the cliff, sidewinding to the beach below.

Nobody around.

"Turn right and walk east, up the beach."

I started east, them clumping and squeaking in the sand behind me. It was a lot colder right along the water, the moonlight dancing off the waves. The beach stretched into the distance but was only twenty yards wide before it abutted the cliff. Nowhere to run.

We'd scuffed about a quarter-mile along the bowed lines of flotsam when I asked, "Much farther?"

Jogging Suit's voice said, "Keep walking."

Before long, I heard the clattering of wheels on what must have been a boardwalked path. There was also a high-pitched but muted whine that took me a minute to place.

A man in a motorized wheelchair came onto the beach, the tires doing surprisingly well in the sand. He wore a Kangol cap low over his eyes and a muffler over his throat and under a heavy corduroy Norfolk jacket. The muffler was the same dark color as his sweater. He had what looked like calfskin driving gloves on both hands, one cradling a liquor bottle.

The Kangol Cap didn't speak for a good minute after we were close to him, probably to give me the chance to talk my way out of whatever I'd gotten into. I kept my own counsel.

Finally, he said, "You know me?"

"I can't even see you."

Somebody kicked me behind the right knee. Cramping, I went down.

"View any better from there, Cuddy?"

I looked up and under the cap. Handsome face, youngish but strained from the chair. Something familiar.

"I've seen your picture."

"The name's Branca. Victor Branca."

Branca. A rising wise-guy in the Boston-to-Providence axis. Then a skiing accident, a total accident, if you could believe the papers, and he'd left the slope paralyzed from the waist down. Six, seven years ago.

"Now you know my name, you know you answer my questions straight when I ask them."

I said, "How come you know my name?"

A kick to the right kidney. I sagged onto that side and choked back what was rising in my throat.

Branca said, "I ask, you answer. Got it?"

I tried nodding this time.

Seeming satisfied, Branca said, "You camp outside the real estate office there. We figure, maybe you're tailing my wife. So, we check with the car rental at the airport and run you with some people we know up to Boston. Turns out you're a P.I. Also turns out you look to be on Mycah Ware, not my wife. How come?"

There wasn't any good way to say it. "Sorry. Confidential."

A shot to the other kidney. Felt like a different kind of shoe.

"These guys, they can do this kind of thing till you're just jelly inside. How come you're tailing Ware?"

I shook my head and took a pointed toe just under the left shoulder blade that had me twisting in the sand next to a pink tampon applicator.

Branca said, "This Ware, he's clean. We checked him out quiet but good before I let my wife go to work for him. He don't juggle the books there, he don't even have a partner he could be shorting on the take. So, how come you're on him?"

I didn't bother to shake my head this time. One of the boys grabbed me by the hair and pulled me up to my knees.

Branca motioned toward the sea. "You know, even when it's this cold, them crabs out there like to eat." He waggled a finger at me. "Why're you tailing Ware?"

"No."

Somebody remembered they hadn't whacked me behind the left knee and let fly there.

Branca said, "Only one possibility. His own wife put a tail on him. Only one reason for that, too. She thinks he's stepping out on her."

Through clenched teeth, I said, "No."

"Stepping out with my wife."

I got past the cramp. "That's not it."

"It's not?"

"No. His wife just wanted me to find out what he does."

"Why?"

I tried Mrs. Ware's retirement theory on him. It sounded lame even to me, and Branca didn't buy it. Then nobody said anything for a while.

Branca's voice came back, but different in tone. "When I had my accident, that was one thing that didn't get broken, you know? I thought Cynthia was still happy with me. I wanted to live as far away from a mountain as I could get, and this place suited me just fine. But without her, it wouldn't be so good."

If Branca were trying to sound wistful, he needed a little more practice.

"The people up to Boston there told me you were a stand-up guy, Cuddy. I ain't seen nothing different." Branca tapped the liquor bottle. "Boys?"

I got a whiff of the chloroform before one of them clamped the rag over my mouth and nose, but there wasn't much I could have done about it.

Five

"Hey, Cuddy? Wake up. Come on. Up, up."

A strong arm was tugging on my left side. If I could have gotten to my feet, the smell of scotch would have knocked me back down. I wanted to crawl away from the man's voice with the scotch. I cracked my eyes open. The sunlight hurt, but I realized that the man was in uniform, the officer named Ben from the town police. And I was the one who stank of scotch.

Ben helped me up, snatching the empty Johnny Walker Black bottle from next to where I'd been in the sand. Ben waved to someone on the cliff who waved back. The lady in the straw hat at her easel.

I said, "What time is it?"

"Eleven-fifteen."

My head was pounding as Ben made me start to shuffle up the beach.

✦ ✦ ✦

Kate Hearn blew at her bangs and said, "So you drive out to Dionis Beach last night, tie one on, and sleep it off at the tideline."

"Like I said. I don't remember much."

"You look like you hit the ground without a parachute."

"I haven't slept on the beach for a while. Cold sand takes it out of you."

"So does a liter of scotch. You want more water?"

"Please."

I was handed another paper cup.

"This has been an exciting morning for us, John Cuddy."

"Wish I could say the same."

"Lost one of our stellar citizens to a terrible accident."

Finishing the water just kept me from gagging. "Sorry to hear it."

"Yeah. Mycah Ware, real estate broker. Know him?"

"We never met."

"His office is just a little ways from where you're staying. Or where you had been staying before you decided to bed down on the beach instead. Ben here couldn't find you at 76 Main. Shirley and Mitch were some worried about you. One of the patrol cars spotted your Jeep at Dionis and routined it in to us. That was when we went out looking for you."

"I appreciate it."

"Back to this Ware? Terrible situation. Fell down a flight of stairs this morning at a house he was sizing. Witness, one Cynthia Branca, saw him take the tumble. Frightened her near to death. Broke his neck, he did."

"Tragedy."

"Yeah, sure is. But since the witness is wife to somebody who's no stranger to violence, and since you checked in with me just two days before the accident, I thought you might have something to tell us."

I crumpled the cup. "I don't."

"Nothing at all?"

"Sorry."

"I'm sorry, too. I really am."

Hearn turned away and said, "You're free to go, Cuddy. But not to come back."

✦ ✦ ✦

At the inn, I thanked Shirley for her concern. Cleaned up and changed, I packed my duffel bag, got into the Cherokee, and started out.

There were two other cars in the driveway of the Ware house, so I edged the Jeep into the bushes on the shoulder of the road and walked up to the front door. A solemn woman of about fifty ushered me inside. There were three other similar women looking sympathetic in the living room and two older men looking useless and restless. Eleanor Ware was sitting on the couch, the centerpiece of the tableau.

She rose when she saw me, a handkerchief to her nose and mouth. "Thank you for coming."

"I know this is a difficult time for you, Mrs. Ware, but could I see you for just a few minutes?"

"Certainly." Turning to the others, she engaged each in eye contact. "We'll be on the deck. Please help yourselves to the refrigerator, and thank you again for coming."

Once outside, she slid the glass door shut in its track and joined me at the railing overlooking the moor below the knoll.

I said, "I have something you need to know about your husband's death."

"Go on."

I told her about Branca and the boys, that I thought they killed her husband in front of Cynthia to whipsaw her back into line.

Eleanor Ware let me finish before arching an eyebrow and allowing a twinkle into her eye. "Clever, killing two birds with one stone like that."

I was afraid she was losing her grip.

"Mrs. Ware, I don't think you understand. Branca thought—"

"That I believed my husband was having it on with his wife when they 'inspected' those houses. I may have been—is the word 'adultered,' Mr. Cuddy?—but I'm not stupid. That's exactly what Mycah was doing."

I had to hold onto the railing. "He was seeing Cynthia Branca, and you knew it?"

"Of course. Oh, Mycah was *ever* so discreet. No lipstick on the collar. I assume he stripped before he even touched her each time. But he'd grown so . . . inattentive. A wife really can sense these things."

"Then why did you have me follow him?"

"Now why do you think?"

"Jesus Christ."

A wry smile. "You see, Mr. Cuddy. Mycah wasn't just unfaithful. He wasn't even just inattentive. He was boring. God, I can't begin to tell you how unbearable it is to be on an island you love with a man who bores you to tears. I dreaded his retirement. A few hours a day with Mycah was one thing. But the rest of my waking hours for the rest of my life? Inconceivable."

"You set him up."

"I did not. And neither did you. In any way. I'm sure Mr. Branca's reputation is known to you. I know it wasn't to Mycah, or frankly even to me until I did some rather thorough research. But that research convinced me that Mr. Branca would deal with Mycah because of what Mycah had done to him, not because of what Mycah had done to me. And you and I had virtually no role in that."

"Wait a minute. You flew me down here just to get Branca's attention?"

Ware looked at me. "I researched you, too, Mr. Cuddy. You'd lost your wife young. I thought you'd find my desire to be closer to Mycah in his retirement . . . admirable. I felt it would work. And it did."

"Why not just tell him yourself?"

"Tell Branca? Speak to a mobster and inform on Mycah? Just what sort of woman do you think I am, Mr. Cuddy?"

"The sort who'd pull the switch on her own husband rather than just divorce him."

"Divorce would have been too . . . public. Besides, Mycah made his own bier and shortly will lie on it. I am sorry that you were—is it 'roughed up'?"

"Yeah. I still don't see why you needed me, though. You didn't want to talk to Branca, fine. Send him a note, an anonymous tip."

She looked out over the moor, the breeze ruffling the heather in a wave pattern like an ocean of iced tea. "No. No, you don't see it at all. It's as I said to you when we first met. This is a small island, and therefore secrets are very dear. If I'd done everything myself, I wouldn't dare share it with anyone here." She gestured back at the living room. "With anyone in there."

Mrs. Ware turned to me. "I needed someone bound by confidentiality, but I could hardly hire a lawyer to follow Mycah about. You see, Mr. Cuddy, I needed *you*. Otherwise, I wouldn't have had a soul to tell."

DOUBLE-CON

One

Once you've heard it, there's a sound you'll never mistake for any other. My first time, in Vietnam, I thought crazily that it was the whumping noise my mother used to make with her broom, cleaning a rug over the clothesline. After that, though, I knew what it was. The sound of a high velocity bullet impacting human flesh.

Frank J. Doppinger's hand was wrenched from mine, the slug lifting and dropping him akimbo on the ground at the edge of the old firebreak. I'd arrived at this spot after driving an hour from Boston, after passing through Tutham Center, and after six miles of paved rural lane. Enjoying the foliage, I'd carefully watched for the sign screwed to a little post and saying "Fire Road Number 7." On the fire road, the acorns launched by the front tires of my Prelude had whacked vigorously at the undercarriage of the car, and I'd spooked a pheasant at the first curve. It was shaping up to be a nice fall day in the country.

Until somebody shot my client out of our handshake.

I was cowering behind a rough-cut boulder, probably pushed up and over by the bulldozer that made the firebreak long ago. I wasn't fully conscious of picking it for cover or getting to it. I also couldn't place where the shooter was on the ridge wall across the little valley below the fire road, but from the report of the weapon and the size of the hole in Frank J. Doppinger's green windbreaker, I knew the Smith & Wesson Bodyguard over my right hip was significantly outgunned.

I counted to ten, heard nothing further, and took it up to thirty. Then I crawled and crab-walked from boulder to log and log to stump until I had circled around to the Prelude. I opened the door, climbed up and in, and started the engine. Then I backed out as fast as reverse would take me, the acorns this time sounding like bullets against the chassis and scaring the hell out of me. Again.

I fish-tailed onto the main road and drove head first for Tutham Center six miles away.

Two

They were both in their thirties. Lacy, the guy in uniform, was tall, blond and baby-faced. Perrault, the guy in plainclothes, was short, dark and bearded. Lacy's uniform wasn't particularly well-kept, the "Tutham Police" patch the only part that looked clean much less ironed. Perrault's plainclothes were plain to the point of homespun, a jaunty lumberjack who stumbled into the police station.

Lacy rested his rear end on the edge of the interrogation room table. Perrault turned a folding chair around and sat on it backwards, forearms on the top of the backrest. From the smell of the air, the room probably doubled as a cafeteria.

Perrault handed me back my ID. "So, Mr. John Francis Cuddy, private investigator, you just left him there?"

"That's right."

Lacy snorted. "Glad I ain't a client of yours."

Perrault had a French-Canadian veneer over his English. Lacy came on like a hick. An interesting variation on the Mutt-and-Jeff routine, if I'd been in the mood for it.

"You sending a unit out to find him?"

Perrault smiled. "We're just a wide place in the road, Cuddy. We don't got that many units to spare, send them out on a wild goose chase."

"You won't have to chase this one. He was shot dead."

"And you claim he's from around here."

"He claimed it. He came to see me in Boston last week, but just briefly. Said he might be back in touch. Then I get a call from the guy to come out and see him."

Lacy said, "You drive fifty mile on a phone call?"

"The guy said he couldn't come to Boston again easily."

Perrault ran an index finger along his moustache. "And?"

"And the guy gave me a retainer in Boston."

"How much?"

"Three hundred. In cash."

Perrault and Lacy exchanged knowing glances.

Perrault said, "Cash is always nice."

Lacy said, "So you agree to meet this feller on a fire break."

"He said he didn't have a car, but he could hike to it."

"Why couldn't he just ask you over to the house?"

"He also said he didn't want anybody to know he was seeing me."

Perrault broke in again. "So the guy gives you directions over the phone."

"Yes. He tells me, come to Tutham Center. Take the road west out of town till you see the turn-off for Fire Road Number 7. Then go along it about two hundred yards to a clearing."

"And you agree to see a guy in the woods."

"Yes."

"Without you check him out first?"

"Perrault, he said he didn't want anybody to know he was hiring me. He gave me a retainer. I did check directory assistance, no telephone number registered in the name. Look, have you heard from that unit yet? They should be—"

Lacy said, "Just hold your horses there, boy. You ain't even told us the name of your deceased client yet."

He was right. "Sorry. It was Doppinger, Frank J."

Lacy's eyes got wide. Perrault's arms came off the backrest. Both looked at each other, then back to me.

Perrault said, "Lou, get a unit out there. Fast. And get the Chief."

Lacy got up. "But it's Saturday, Reg. He'll be out tending his vegetables."

Perrault just barely kept the knife out of his voice. "So, you beep him, Lou. That's why he carries the thing."

Lacy left and slammed the door behind him.

I said, "You know this Doppinger, then?"

Perrault tugged on his beard and told me to shut up.

✦ ✦ ✦

Twenty minutes later, Lou Lacy came back in with a hulking guy in his late forties. This one wore blue denim overalls and a chamois shirt, both materials dirt-caked and grass-stained. He had a craggy face, no discernible hairstyle, and a pair of cop's eyes as dead as a plastic doll's.

The introduction consisted of "I'm Chief of Police for Tutham. Let's hear it. From the beginning."

After I caught him up to where I'd left off with Lacy and Reg Perrault, the chief said to Lacy, "Let me know when the unit reports in from Number 7."

Lacy started to say something, then thought better of it. "You bet, Chief."

After Lacy left, the chief tucked his right hand into the strap of his overalls just below the clipped-on beeper. "This Doppinger give you any reason why he didn't want folks to know about him seeing you?"

"Not over the phone. After I met him on the fire road, though, he said it was about his wife."

Perrault took in a breath. The chief glanced at him, but Perrault's face was neutral.

The chief said to me, "What about his wife?"

"I'd told Doppinger when he saw me in Boston that I didn't do domestics, and he'd told me it had nothing to do with that. But then out on the road, he said his wife was fouling up his life, that he could see her filing for divorce pretty soon, and that he didn't want her taking the house he'd worked so long to own."

Perrault started paying attention to the floor.

The chief's eyes never left me. "But you say you'd told him in Boston—"

"Right, right. And I told him that on the road, too. He smiled and said, 'Well, just a misunderstanding, then,' and told me to keep the three hundred."

The chief shook his head, as if to clear it. "The man tells you, 'Keep the money'?"

"Yes." It sounded stupid to me, too, but there it was.

"Then what?"

"Then Doppinger extends his hand to me, and I take it, and somebody on the other side of the valley busts him out of his shoes."

"And you just left the man."

"I've seen the dead before, Chief. Big hole, eyes open, pieces of his lung—"

"I've seen dead people before too, Cuddy. But—"

There was a knock at the door.

"Yeah?"

Lou Lacy stuck his head in, a confused look on his face. The overalls shambled out, closing the door behind him.

A minute inched by. I was pretty sure that Perrault wouldn't tell me anything with or without his boss there, so I just tried to relax.

The chief came back into the room alone, crossing his arms and latching onto both straps of the overalls for lateral support.

"Our people just drove out Fire Road Number 7, Cuddy."

"And?"

"Nobody."

It took a second to register that he meant, "No body."

I said, "What?"

"The unit drove the length of the break. Three times down and back. No corpse, no blood, no nothing."

"Chief . . ." I took a breath, started again. "Chief, there has to be."

"There isn't."

"Look, I was standing there, shaking hands with the guy for Christ's sake. Frank J. Doppinger is dead."

"I don't think so."

"Why, because—"

"Because I'm Frank J. Doppinger."

"Oh."

✦ ✦ ✦

The three of us moved into the chief's office, the nameplate centered on his desk saying, "FRANK J. DOPPINGER" in brass relief. Next to the plate was a stand-up frame, a photo of a woman maybe ten years younger than the chief. Doppinger and Perrault were sipping coffee from styrofoam cups. I hadn't seen Lacy since he stuck his head in the interrogation room.

Reg Perrault said, "Cuddy, why you figure anybody would want to fake a murder?"

"It wasn't fake."

"Your client was."

The chief spoke to the framed photo. "The part about the wife wasn't fake."

Perrault didn't say anything, so I didn't either.

Doppinger said, "Ellen and I have been having . . . problems, Cuddy. She's thinking about getting a divorce. Already went to see a lawyer down to Worcester. Reg, this remind you of anything?"

Perrault acted like he wasn't sure what the chief meant.

Doppinger said, "Sorry, Reg." Then to me, "Detective Perrault and Ellen were in school together." The farmer went back to the lumberjack. "Does Cuddy's story remind you of one of our cases, Reg?"

Perrault said, "The double-con."

I said, "The what?"

The chief said, "Reg?"

Perrault licked his lips. "Four, five years ago—"

Doppinger said, "More like seven or eight."

A nod. "There was this guy out here, running a double-con. Name of Moddicky. Rudolph Moddicky. He impersonated guys who really existed and worked in stocks, bonds, whatever. Then he'd con the elderly with that con, using a real guy's rep to get inside, then ripping them off. We—the chief, caught him."

Doppinger said, "By coincidence. Pure luck."

Perrault made sure the chief was finished. "The guy copped a plea but drew some heavy time anyway. He played his cards close in the joint, got out with a lot of good time credit."

I said, "When?"

Doppinger said, "About two weeks ago. Back when he went away, Moddicky made the usual threats about getting even, so I put a routine request in to the parole office for notification-upon-release. I got a call from his P.O. saying Moddicky was coming out."

I thought about it. "You have a mugshot of him?"

Doppinger picked up his phone and mumbled into it. We waited while somebody just outside his door opened and closed a file cabinet, then came in. Lou Lacy.

Lacy seemed angry as he handed a manila folder to Doppinger, who said, "Thanks, Lou." Doppinger waited until Lacy was out of the room before sliding the file across the desk to me.

Something must have shown on my face, because Doppinger said, "Lou's mama was one of the people Moddicky screwed."

I opened the folder. Stapled to the cover was the front and profile of a slim young man with tailored haircut, wideset eyes, and winning smile. "Not my client. He was pushing fifty and burly, kind of sad-looking."

Doppinger said, "Like me."

I didn't answer.

The chief said, "I think when I talked to that P.O. he said a couple of other guys were released from Moddicky's cellblock right before him. A Shaw, maybe a Bennett and an Olsen, too. Reg, can you run them for me?"

"Got a name for the P.O.?"

"Garcia, I think. Male."

"I'll get on it right away, Chief."

Doppinger stood up. "I think maybe I ought to be heading home."

Perrault was clearly trying to figure out a nice way to ask a difficult question. It came out, "You want some company?"

Doppinger said, "I'm hoping I don't have any company stopping by."

Perrault said, "Chief—"

Doppinger held up a meaty hand. "We don't know there's any connection between the client Cuddy says got shot and Moddicky coming hunting. I'm not about to gather all our wagons around the wrong spot if there is a connection and Moddicky's hunting something else. Reg, whyn't you take Mr. Cuddy here down to the motel and settle him in."

Perrault looked in my direction.

Distracted, Doppinger turned to me. "Sorry. That three hundred buy us your time for the night?"

I said, "Sure, Chief."

Three

Reg Perrault directed me to the only motel in town. I checked in to a stale, dark room with two double beds. The clerk directed me to the only restaurant in town, a fifties diner with chrome counter stools (sporting padded, swivel seats) and formica counter top (sporting dated, jukebox selectors). The diner had a license, so I mixed a little alcohol from a glass with the cholesterol from my plate.

Back at the room, I thought about why the body wasn't where it was supposed to be. When that didn't get me anywhere, I tried the TV. An old *Mannix* episode was in commercial as the first siren screamed by outside. I was opening the door of the Prelude when the second cruiser blew past a minute later.

◆ ◆ ◆

It wasn't that hard to find. Kind of out in the woods and down another country lane, but I just had to follow the noise, then the bubble lights bouncing off the treeline once the drivers pulled to a stop.

A guy wearing a six-inch Colt magnum but no uniform stopped me at the edge of the driveway. I told him who I was and suggested he tell Doppinger, Perrault, or Lacy that I was there. He left me and came back just as an older man parked a four-wheel-drive Subaru behind me. The older man got out slowly, carrying the sort of little black bag doctors used to take on house calls.

The doctor and I followed Magnum up the driveway and around the cruisers toward a beautiful farmhouse. About ten feet from the porch, we reached Lou Lacy, kneeling beside a man lying on his stomach. A Winchester rifle with scope nestled in the grass near the sprawled arms of the man on the ground. He had a tailored haircut and wideset eyes but now broken teeth where he'd kissed a rock falling. He also had an entry wound between his shoulder blades and two exit wounds where his lungs would hang.

The doctor didn't pause, but Lacy looked up and shook his head negatively anyway. He was grinning as he did it.

Inside the front door, Perrault was standing next to the body of a woman lying face-up on the carpet. Given the entry wound at her cheekbone, the exit wound in back would cost you your dinner. The hair color and one eye told me she had been the woman pictured on Doppinger's desk.

Magnum left us. After glancing down at the woman, the doctor continued over to Frank Doppinger. The chief was sitting in an easy chair, still wearing the same shirt and overalls. At his right bicep, blood seeped into the torn sleeve. The palm of his left hand covered everything north of his nose, but I didn't see anything red streaming between the fingers.

I looked at Perrault.

Very quietly, he said, "Chief was in the kitchen. Heard the front door kicked open and then the rifle. By the time he got into the living room, Moddicky out there was on the porch."

Perrault shook his head. "Chief got him once and spun him, then Moddicky got off a grazer and the chief got him twice more, last one in the back as Moddicky was going down."

I watched the doctor talking to Doppinger and cutting at the right sleeve with a pair of small scissors. The chief's left hand was down now, and he looked at me.

I turned and left the house.

✦ ✦ ✦

At first light, I was in the Prelude and slewing onto Fire Road Number 7. Dead quiet as the autumn sun just broke the tops of the trees.

Driving to the end of the break, I couldn't find the spot from the day before. I even got out at the one gathering of boulders that looked close, but not quite right. Other than some recent tire tracks, there was nothing to indicate anyone had been there in weeks.

I drove back out, still dead quiet, finally realizing something was out of kilter. I stopped the car at the main road and thought about it.

Acorns. There were no acorns ricocheting off the undercarriage.

I did a three-pointer and went back up the fire break. The ground was clear, nothing in the ruts. Squirrels, maybe?

Leaving the car, I walked a hundred feet in each direction, studying the foliage pretty carefully. Acorns fall from mighty oaks. No acorns because no oak trees. None.

I went back to the main road and checked the little sign for Fire Break Number 7. There were a couple of fresh scratches in the screws holding the sign to the post.

I continued up the main road to Fire Road Number 8 and tried it. Acorns within fifty feet. The boulders beyond that, exactly where they should be. Double-con, the client masquerading as Frank Doppinger met me on Fire Road Number 8 masquerading as Number 7.

I stopped the Prelude at the boulders and got out. There was some dried blood on one rock, but no pieces of tissue thanks to whatever insects had scoured the area. I found some scuff marks where I remembered crouching for cover and some more where someone had hefted something off the ground. Sidestepping downslope about twenty feet, I saw a disturbed section of earth. Some creatures bigger than insects had dug into the shallow grave.

What was left of a face and throat ended at the collar of the green wind-breaker.

I climbed back up the slope, wiping my hands on my haunches even though I hadn't dirtied them. I sat in my car and thought about it. Tried to think through it. Then I turned the key in the ignition and headed back toward town.

Four

"Cuddy?"

"Chief."

Doppinger looked up at me. His right arm was in a sling, his left hand hanging up the telephone next to the living room chair he'd been sitting in the night before.

I said, "Sorry to be interrupting."

"No. No, just making some—" he waved at the phone "—arrangements. You heading back to Boston?"

"Shortly. Thought I ought to report something to you first."

"What's that?"

"I found a body."

He blinked. "Where?"

"Fire Road Number Eight."

"Eight?"

"Yeah. The killer conned me into thinking I was on seven yesterday by switching the signs."

Doppinger hung his head and shook it. "That Moddicky. Always thinking."

"I also put a phone call in to Garcia."

"Garcia?"

"That parole officer you called about Moddicky and his blockmates."

"Oh. Right."

"He gave me a bunch of names and addresses. Seems you were right. A photo's on its way, but I'm pretty sure the guy I met as Frank J. Doppinger out of the fire road is Joey Benson, one of the other inmates released just before Moddicky."

"Benson, you say?" Doppinger took a breath. "Yeah, figures Moddicky'd use somebody he knew to set up his little game."

"Yeah, it does. But why did Moddicky kill him, do you suppose?"

Doppinger started to shrug, then remembered his sling. "Take out a witness."

"A witness to what?"

Doppinger straightened a little. "To your being approached by the guy."

"You figure that's why Moddicky decided to switch the signs and hide the body, too?"

"Who knows? Moddicky was an odd one, Cuddy. Maybe he got off on burying things."

I waited a moment. "Nobody said anything about the body being buried, Chief."

Doppinger's eyes clouded.

I said, "I think the killer approached the guy I met and paid him to impersonate Frank J. Doppinger and feed me the song and dance that got me out on that fire road. The killer wanted the arrow to point toward Moddicky, but not too clearly too soon. Otherwise, the level of protection you should have mounted at your house yesterday might have been uncomfortably high."

The voice got raspy. "What are you saying?"

"You needed a way out of the marriage, preferably death over divorce so you got to keep this house. It was sharp of you to mention your talk with the parole officer to Perrault and me. Even sharper to admit he'd told you about other blockmates of Moddicky, 'Bennett' instead of 'Benson.' But Garcia also says he gave you names and addresses."

"Moddicky pulled a double-con on you, Cuddy. He's still got you believing it."

"No, Chief. The double-con the killer had in mind couldn't work with Moddicky directly. He knew you and hated you. But it could work with Benson, a blockmate Moddicky could have known but probably never buddied up to, never told how Frank J. Doppinger brought him down. You hired Benson to get me into it. You would have had to snatch Moddicky a couple of days ago, though. To be sure nobody would come forward with an unshakable alibi for him once he was dead. Tell me, Chief, where did you stash him?"

"You're blowing smoke up your own—"

"Anyway, you did stash Moddicky out here someplace, alive. You watched my meeting with Benson, picking him off when you saw us shaking hands, knowing he'd already told me everything you wanted me to hear. Then you waited for me to slink off before burying Benson and switching back the signs. Nice touch, by the way, to tell the boys you'd be in your garden. Made them beep you instead of telephoning and let you show up at the station in soiled overalls, fresh from Benson's hasty grave."

Doppinger's left hand dropped to the outside of his thigh, rubbing it.

"You can't prove any of this, Cuddy."

"Here at the house last night you shot Moddicky with your service revolver and your wife with the Winchester you'd used on Benson. Then you probably fired a round through the rifle with Moddicky's dead hands around it and another through your sleeve with something to catch the powder burns."

The doll's eyes got colder as a snub-nosed revolver appeared from under the seat cushion.

"It won't wash, Chief."

"Sure it will, Cuddy. You came to the station yesterday, claiming this Benson was your client. You were in with him and Moddicky all along."

"I'm not even armed."

"I put a throwaway in your hand, and nobody will know you weren't."

"Perrault and Lacy will know."

"What?"

"They frisked me before I came in here."

"They . . . ?"

From the kitchen door, Perrault's voice said, "Put it down, Chief."

From the porch window, Lacy leveled a shotgun. "Please, Chief."

Doppinger's eyes went around the room, through the walls and around the house. Measuring something. Maybe his losses.

He dropped the snubbie on the floor and used the hand to cover his face instead.

CROSSED WIRES

One

"I used to have a corner office, Mr. Cuddy, but once I went 'Of Counsel,' I was . . . relegated to this broom closet."

A senior lawyer like Stanton Wilcox might think of the twelve-by-fifteen with a pie-slice view of Boston harbor as a broom closet, but it probably beat my private investigator space by twenty square feet. Wilcox himself was pushing eighty, a compact man in a glen plaid suit and hand-done bow tie. Widow's peak of white hair combed straight back, bushy white eyebrows over hawk eyes, pug nose and determined jaw. He looked like a man who believed in precise aggression.

Wilcox had already motioned me to the captain's chair in front of his teak desk, him taking the judge's chair behind it. There was nothing between us on the desk except a layer of lemon-scented polish.

"I'm please to meet you, Mr. Wilcox, but I'd be interested to know how you found me."

"Understandable. Michael O'Dell once worked for this firm. He commended you for your discretion."

I'd done a job for O'Dell involving a small, family-held corporation he represented. Looking to the closed door behind me, I said, "A firm this size doesn't have its own private agency on retainer?"

Wilcox nodded, one sharp dip of the chin. "Michael also mentioned your . . . acumen."

I waited.

The old man came forward in his chair, elbows on the desk like a bouncer getting ready for arm wrestling. "This is personal."

"Personal to you."

"Yes."

I took out a pad and a pen. "Go ahead."

Wilcox closed his eyes, then opened them and seemed not to blink for the next few minutes. "I believe a friend of mine has been murdered."

"Save yourself some money. Dial nine-one-one."

The lawyer's expression said he wasn't used to hearing debate from the chair in front of him. "Let me be more . . . elaborate, then. A friend of mine from the war named Joseph Luntayne died under suspicious circumstances."

"What circumstances?"

"He was in a nursing home and died of an apparent heart attack."

"And you find that suspicious?"

"Joe had a stroke eighteen months ago. He needed a cane, sometimes a wheelchair, but not often. There was nothing wrong with his heart."

"A doctor told you that?"

"His treating physician and the pathologist."

"There was an autopsy, then."

"Yes. I ordered it."

"Ordered it?"

"As Joe's executor. At least for now."

I stopped writing notes. "I don't get you."

Wilcox clapped his hands, resting his chin on them. "Joe and I were in the OSS together. Before your time, but—"

"The Office of Strategic Services."

The sharp nod, which almost cracked his knuckles, then a relaxing of the formal manner. "We were teamed. Dropped into France a few months before D-Day. Worked with the French on German troop locations, resupply points." Wilcox leaned back in his chair, seeming to drift back as well. "Huddled in some broken down manger, manure pile for a table, me watching for gray uniforms while Joe hunched over the radio, transmitting back to . . ."

The commando-spy returned to the present, shaking his head. "In any case, we'd known each other fifty years. After the stroke, Joe had to enter a nursing home. He had plenty of money, but he could see his children eying it, watching it shrink."

"From the nursing home bills."

"Five thousand a month."

"You're kidding?"

"No. And that's just room and board."

"Wife?"

"I beg your pardon?"

"Is your friend's wife still alive, too?"

"Oh. No, Emily passed away ten years ago."

"How old was your friend?"

"Seventy-seven. He died on his birthday."

I took some more notes. "So his children are what, in their forties?"

"Correct. Walter's the oldest, a sort of ne'er-do-well. Descended from high school teacher to insurance agent to postal worker. Anne's the middle one, a veterinarian. And a spinster, too, though I'm not sure she cares.

Philip is the youngest. A pharmacist, which I always thought was a rather alliterative profession for him to pursue."

"And they were all interested in Luntayne's money."

"Yes. Eight months after the stroke, Joe stabilized. It was pretty clear that he was going to survive, probably for a long time."

"Probably till his money ran out."

"That's right. So he had me re-draft his will."

"How?"

"To provide that if any one of his children killed him, none of them would inherit."

I rested my pen. "I thought that if somebody committed murder, he or she couldn't inherit from the decedent?"

"That's right. But this way, Joe insured that his death would be investigated. Joe loved power, Mr. Cuddy. He loved being in control. For example, when we were in France, even though I was the senior man on the team, he would maneuver things so he got to send those messages. That way, he controlled what and how much information our superiors received. Of course, he'd been Signal Corps, so he was better at it than I was."

"What makes you think your friend was killed?"

"It's just too pat. If any one of the children is the killer, none inherit. They all hated Joe, with some justification. He really was quite a miserable man in many ways, and a difficult father at best. They rarely visited him in the home, and the only time they were all there together was his birthday."

"So the only time they all had equal opportunity was the one day he happens to die."

"Correct. Thereby giving each of them the argument of reasonable doubt without any of them being the only one needing an alibi."

"How do you get around the pathologist's saying it was a heart attack?"

"I've spoken to him, and to other doctors I know. They all say it is possible to induce heart attack without much trace using potassium chloride, a relatively available compound."

"You figure they fed it to your friend?"

"No. More likely they injected it. Joe needed a Heparin lock in his arm."

"What's that?"

"I'm not a medical man, but the Heparin is basically a semi-permanent spigot inserted in the arm to receive intravenous solutions. He had one in him that day when I saw him earlier. Someone with a syringe could have simply shot him up through the lock."

"Which would have caused the heart attack."

"Yes. Rather quickly, I'm told."

I thought back to nursing homes I'd visited. "Your friend have a roommate?"

"No. Well, yes, technically but not really."

"Again?"

"Joe's roommate was . . . a vegetable, I'm afraid. A boy who'd been in some accident. Joe didn't like to be around him any more than necessary. In fact, any time I would visit, Joe would insist I walk him down to one of the day rooms or out onto the patio to get away for a while."

"Why didn't your friend just change roommates?"

"Probably because he found it satisfying to be in control one last time. As I told you, Mr. Cuddy, Joe could be a difficult man."

I started flipping back through my notes. "And you want me to look for evidence that one of his children killed him."

"Exactly."

I found a dangling point. "Before you said you were Luntayne's executor 'at least for now.' "

Wilcox pursed his lips. "Yes?"

"What would make you stop being his executor?"

The old lawyer moved his tongue inside his mouth for a moment. "The will provides that if one of the children did kill Joe, I receive the entire estate as alternative beneficiary."

"At which point, another lawyer as executor would look better?"

"Correct."

"Mr. Wilcox, why did Luntayne bother with that?"

"What?"

"Why did he bother with the 'alternative beneficiary' business? You were his friend, you'd have investigated his death anyway, right?"

Stanton Wilcox just stared at me.

Two

The Pineview Nursing Home was just off Interstate 93 north of Boston. From its semicircular drive, it offered a view of maybe three pines, all stunted and surrounded by stones, as though expecting an attack. The home itself was made of yellow bricks and seemed all on one floor. The main entrance announced itself with two Doric pillars and a front door that didn't require a bell to be pushed.

The small lobby was carpeted, a felt bulletin board with plastic numbers and letters scheduling the times for each meal and activities like Reflection

Period, Limbering Up, and Pet Therapy. The meals accounted for half the entries.

In one corner of the lobby was a counter like a cheap hotel. The fat woman behind it seemed weary beyond her tasks. I identified myself to her.

She groaned and said, "Mrs. Hernandez?"

Another woman, not fat, came across the lobby toward us. In her thirties and attractive, she had long black hair drawn over a shoulder and three-inch high heels. In between, her bright print blouse set off her pleated skirt, and her introductory smile suggested that "Mrs. Hernandez" was glad to see me.

Until I told her why I was there.

Hernandez frowned. "Please come into my office."

We walked behind the counter and stopped at another door, this one needing a buzz-through. The office was cheery, with lots of plants and primary colors. A first-stop nursery school rather than a last-stop nursing home.

Hernandez tapped a chair with a long red fingernail, then settled on the edge of her desk. I decided to stay standing instead.

She said, "I really don't see how we can help you, Mr. Cuddy."

"I'm just interested in seeing Mr. Luntayne's room, maybe talking with some of the other patients."

"Residents."

"Sorry?"

"We call our guests 'residents,' Mr. Cuddy. They aren't sick, just old."

"I was under the impression Mr. Luntayne was just old, too, but he died here."

"Of natural causes. A heart attack."

"Should I be calling you 'Dr. Hernandez'?"

That almost brought a smile. "No. But it doesn't take a medical degree to understand that older residents, especially when weakened as Joe was, might die of many things."

Joe. "Do you call all your residents by their first names?"

"We try. It makes them feel a little more with it. And with us." She gestured at her blouse and the walls. "We want to make them see that life doesn't have to turn gray just because their hair has. So we paint the walls and dress up a little and run organized, simple activities to keep their attention and help them pass the time a little more productively."

The nursery school image flashed back. "Mrs. Hernandez, no one is accusing Pineview of anything. You told me your job, let me tell you mine. I look at places and talk to people. I read papers and write things down."

The almost-smile again. "No car chases or gunfights?"

"Just on major holidays."

Hernandez turned something over in her head. "All right. Come with me."

✦ ✦ ✦

The corridor was a good sixty yards in length and straight as an arrow. The lobby carpet was repeated, but the rooms we passed had linoleum floors. Probably easier to clean. As in mop up. Two orderlies in orange shirts were pushing buckets with just long handles visible above the wringers.

Both walls of the corridor had wooden bannisters everywhere but the door openings. A few residents made their way along the bannisters, Arctic explorers in a blizzard holding on to a lifeline. Others were in wheelchairs, scuffing across the rug with one foot, a slow-motion version of the kids on scooters they once must have been. A very tall man in a cardigan sweater had his pant legs rolled up to half-calf. He moved six inches, then repositioned a four-posted walker and moved six inches more, his shoes never leaving the ground.

The public address system clicked on and off several times, a breathless operator paging various people. As we went by the typically open doors, you could hear snatches of conversation. A Caribbean lilt saying "Come now, Louise, come, come. Just a little more eggnog?" An Irish brogue, "Oh and he's adorable. Your grandson, you say?" Next to the nurse's station, a Vietnamese singsong, "Anybody know when Charlie voided last?"

We turned a corner and started down an identical corridor. Passing a large, airy room, I saw eight men and women in wheelchairs, arranged in a quarter-moon formation around a large projection TV. Half of them were watching Phil Donahue interview a transvestite. The others were asleep, heads tilted so far forward they would pitch their frail bodies onto the rug but for the restraint masquerading as lunch tray that held each person in his or her chair.

"Mr. Cuddy?"

"Right. Sorry."

We reached the midway point of the second corridor. A loveseat in a quiet alcove provided a rest stop for the residents and probably a refuge for the visitors.

Hernandez said, "Please sit down for a moment. I want to make sure Martin isn't being looked after."

"Martin?"

"He was Joe's roommate."

My guide disappeared behind a door and started talking to someone in a loudish voice. I dropped into the loveseat. Stiffly-sprung, probably designed for ease of access and egress, not comfort.

Hernandez re-opened the door, beckoning me.

A half-bath was visible in one corner. The double room itself was furnished perfectly symmetrically. The metal-framed beds were side by side, a lowboy bureau at the foot of each and a mirror over each bureau. There were complementary landscapes and seascapes covering the rest of the wall space. What I took to be Luntayne's bed was empty.

Hernandez stood over the other bed, the one nearer the window. The bed was raised at forty-five degrees, the crib bars elevated, I assumed to keep its occupant from falling out.

In the loudish voice, Hernandez said, "Martin, this is Mr. Cuddy." Haloed by the light from the window behind her, she used the back of her right hand to brush the left cheek of the man in the bed.

He was clean-shaven, with the kind of haircut I would have had in the Military Police if I hadn't seen a barber for three weeks and didn't comb it. His eyes were open and seemed focussed, staring into the mirror at the foot of his bed. The mouth was twisted, a crooked half-smile that seemed perpetual, the two front teeth protruding slightly beneath the upper lip. His legs and feet were under the sheets, his arms outside them. The right hand was clenched into a claw, but the left was open, even relaxed, except for his middle finger. That one twitched up and down randomly on the sheet, like a woodpecker rotated ninety degrees and battering the ground instead of a tree trunk.

Hernandez talked to him again. "Mr. Cuddy is here about Joe. You remember Joe, don't you?"

No reaction from Martin that I could see. I said, "Can he hear us?"

Hernandez wagged her head slowly and used a normal tone. "We don't really know, but the experts say it's best to speak to him as though he can. We've tried various stimuli, but nothing has worked over the years."

"Years?"

Hernandez went back to the loud voice, running her fingers through his hair. "Martin has been with us for five years now. Haven't you, Martin?"

"What happened to him?"

She looked at me strangely. "Tragedy happened, Mr. Cuddy. An automobile pile-up while he was riding on 93 with his parents on vacation. They were both killed, and there was nobody back home in Indiana to take him."

"So you did."

"Yes. The state appointed a guardian. The guardian retained an attorney who obtained a handsome settlement from the guilty parties. We have to keep his bed cranked up to allow him to breathe easily, but otherwise the settlement allows us to care for Martin in comfort."

"So far as you know."

The strange look again. "Yes. So far as we know."

In the corridor, a wizened woman in a wheelchair was being pushed at a good clip by a twelve-year-old boy. The woman's skin flapped against her neck chords as she went, "Vroom, Vroooooom."

I said to Hernandez, "This other one was Luntayne's bed?"

She broke contact with Martin. "Yes." Then in the loud voice, "Joe and you were roommates for over a year, right, Martin?"

Nothing but the erratic finger motion.

I moved to the door side of Luntayne's bed. "Which arm had the Heparin lock in it?"

"The Heparin?"

"Yes."

"Well, I don't—"

The public address system interrupted her. "Mrs. Hernandez, Mrs. Hernandez. Please come to Reception. Mrs. Hernandez."

My guide waited until the breathless voice clicked off. "I'm sorry, Mr. Cuddy."

"Is there anyone else I could speak to?"

An orderly went by the room.

Hernandez said, "Delroy. Delroy?"

The orderly came back, head in door.

"This is Mr. Cuddy, Delroy."

He looked at me suspiciously.

Hernandez said, "Delroy was the one who actually found Joe. Delroy, Mr. Cuddy has some questions to ask you."

The man spoke to her. "You want me to stop what I'm doing or he going to ask them while I'm working?"

I had a feeling I already knew the answer to that one.

✦ ✦ ✦

Delroy Briggs unfolded an X-frame of metal dowls. "So ask."

I watched him in the utility room, me sitting on a rigid plastic basket, him stretching and fitting a big yellow trashbag over the metal frame. His slender hands worked quickly, though he must have been near sixty himself, with the almost blue skin that some black men seem to get as they grow older. His eyes were a little rheumy in a sad face, the bones noticeable at the sockets and at the back of the jaw. The hair was short, shot through with white strands that were still rare enough to stand out.

I said, "When did you find him, Mr. Briggs?"

"About eight."

"P.M."

"That's right."

"What did you think?"

Briggs held his answer through the unfolding of another frame. As he fitted another trashbag, he said, "You family?"

"No."

"Ever know the man?"

"Uh-unh."

"Then what I thought was, 'Thank you, God, for finally taking this bastard from us.' "

I laughed a little, Briggs a little more.

"He was hard to be around?"

"No." Briggs reached for another frame. "No, in fairness to the man, he wasn't like one of these old farts who always whines, or wets hisself. He was more bossy, full of hisself, had to keep letting you know who was paying the bills, paying the salaries of folks like me and the food girls and so on."

"He liked to be in control."

"That's it. That's the man. Old Joe, he'd be setting up in his bed and he'd point that cane of his." Briggs raised his arm, like a man giving directions to a tourist. "And he'd say, 'Delroy, I believe you missed a bit of paper towel under the sink there.' And I'd say, 'Why, thank you, Joe, I do believe you're right.' But it wasn't like with some of the other folks, they like to joke around with you. With Old Joe, it was mind-games. Like he did with Martin."

"Martin?"

"His roommate. Poor boy, he ain't probably got laid yet, he's in this car ac-ci-dent. Come out of it like you seen him in there. But every night I'm making my last pass, like around eleven, eleven-thirty, and Old Joe he's in his room with the light on, talking a blue streak to that poor boy."

"Talking to him like Martin could hear?"

"What? Oh, hell, no. No, more like, 'Well, Martin, what do you think of the weather lately?' Or 'Don't you think Janine might be a lot of fun under that little blue dress?' Like that. Then he'd wait a minute, then he'd say something else."

"Like Luntayne was having a conversation with Martin?"

"More like Old Joe was just enjoying hearing his own voice, wanting to wait Martin out before talking some more. Like to ag-gra-vate the poor boy account of he can't talk back. You know what I'm saying?"

"Like controlling Martin by controlling the flow of things."

"Right. Right."

"Mr. Briggs, do you remember which arm had the Heparin lock when you found Luntayne?"

The man paused between frame and bag. "Old Joe, he was just a pincushion, had so many in him while he was here."

"But do you remember which one that night?"

Briggs paused again. "I believe it was the left one."

"So, the door side of the room"

He went back to his job. "Yeah, I guess you could say it that way."

Three

I spotted him outside a three-story townhouse halfway up the block. "Walter Luntayne?"

Shifting the leather strap of the mailbag to a different part of his shoulder, the man turned to me. "Yeah?"

"Mr. Luntayne, my name is John Cuddy. I'm a private investigator."

I handed him my ID folder. Luntayne pushed the parade cap above his forehead to read it. Maybe six feet tall and pudgy, he had reddish hair and a beefy face, a little florid from the weight of the mail he was humping. His legs were painfully pale under the uniform shorts he wore above white socks and black tie shoes.

Luntayne closed the folder and gave it back. "What's this about?"

"I'm looking into the death of your father."

He shifted the strap again. "Why?"

"Any suspicious death gets investigated."

Luntayne started to grin. "Hey, what's suspicious? He was an old guy, and his heart went pop."

I watched him for a moment. "I take it you aren't too upset by his passing."

"Upset? You never knew him, right?"

"Right."

Luntayne let the strap slide off and the bag thump onto the sidewalk. "Well, let me tell you how upset I was. When Anne—she's my sister?—when Anne calls me with the news, I say to her, 'Well, looks like Martin's gonna have to find another roommate.' "

Luntayne laughed at his joke. From the pacing of his words, I had the feeling I wasn't the first person to hear it.

"You weren't crazy about your father then."

"Hey, I don't want to sound like some kind of ingrate, but the fact is, you wanted something from the old man, even as a kid, you didn't have to ask for it, you had to beg for it. He was a miser about everything in his life. Money, attention, you name it. He was so tight, he squeaked."

Another laugh.

I said, "Can you tell me what happened the day your father died?"

"Sure." Luntayne looked at the stoop behind him. "How about I take a load off?"

"Go ahead."

He used a hand to sweep the third step, then settled himself on it. "Well, it was the old man's birthday, which was about the only time any of us were together to see him. Anne got there first, of course."

"Why of course?"

"She was bringing the cake. Then I got there about six, six-fifteen. And right behind me, the pill-pusher rolled in."

"Your brother Philip?"

"Right. So we all spent a rough hour with the guy, trying to make small talk nobody was interested in hearing, then we cut the cake and left."

"No presents?"

"Well, sure. We had presents. It was the guy's birthday."

"What presents?"

"Let's see. I got him a flannel shirt, account of it gets kind of cold in those rooms there, even in the nice weather. Anne bought him some book he said he already read. And Phil, what—oh yeah, Phil brought him an electric shaver. Probably got it wholesale at the place he works."

"The pharmacy?"

"One of those megajoints with fifty aisles and more security guards than cashiers, you know?"

"Did your father appear to be in any discomfort?"

"Just from having us there."

"What do you mean?"

"He liked it better one-on-one. So he could keep things in hand over you without distractions from somebody else."

"When did you leave?"

"We all left about the same time."

Which wasn't the question I asked. "When was that?"

"Maybe seven?"

"So you spend an hour with your dad on his birthday."

"A real long hour. Anything else?"

"I understand you haven't always been a letter carrier."

"That's right."

"I'm wondering what made you leave the other jobs."

"What does that have to do with my father's heart attack?"

"I can always just ask around."

Luntayne mulled that over, then shrugged. "Out of college, I was a high school teacher. Tried it for a while, couldn't stand the yard-apes I got in my classes. After that—"

"What did you teach?"

"Chemistry. After that, I tried insurance for a while, but I didn't like the hustle, you know? Always having to push things. I've been with the service fourteen years, and it suits me."

"Enough so you'll keep at it?"

"Huh?"

"After you get your inheritance?"

A grunt. "My cut of what's left will be maybe, *maybe* a hundred-ten, a hundred-twenty thousand. Not exactly enough to retire on."

"But enough to help out."

"I've had my eye on a place at the Cape, all right? This economy, it'd be a good buy. Can I use the money? Sure I can. So can Anne and Phil there."

"How do you mean?"

"Well, Anne, she wants to pull the old ripcord, head out to the country and be some kind of veterinarian saint, but she hears sick cows don't pay as good as sick poodles. And Phil, he just hates being a pill-pusher so much, he'd probably go around the world or something."

"But not you."

Walter Luntayne stood up. "Hey, Uncle Sugar treats me just fine. Salary, vacation time, bennies. I'm here till I die."

A third laugh.

Four

Standing in the reception area of the veterinary hospital, I could see Anne Luntayne before she could see me. A stocky woman with fluffy hair, reddish like her brother's. She wore a green smock with some stains down the front of it and blue jeans underneath. Luntayne was turning toward a teen-aged boy, also in a green but dirtier smock, handing something to him.

A syringe.

Luntayne heard the receptionist call her name, then point to me. The vet shed her smock, showing a checkered cowboy shirt underneath.

Luntayne walked over. "Can I help you?"

I introduced myself and explained why I was there.

Her eyes, brown, grew wide. "What can there possibly be to investigate?"

"Can we talk somewhere more privately?"

Luntayne looked around, then said, "We have a patio outside?"

"Fine."

She led me through a rabbit warren of doors and small rooms with yapping and yowling and other creature noises I couldn't place. Behind the building, we hit an enclosure with a brick floor ten feet square and one round table with those white resin lawn chairs.

"This is our lunch area in good weather. Please, sit down."

I took one chair, she another. Mine gave a little, but was surprisingly comfortable.

The brown eyes fixed on me. "Why are you looking into my father's death?"

"Because of the way his will is written."

That threw her. Then, "You mean the part about none of us getting the money if one of us . . . killed him?"

"Let's start with that day. When did you all arrive?"

"I don't know. I guess I was first to get there."

"Why?"

"I picked up the cake."

"Why you?"

"Out of a sense of duty, if not affection, Mr. Cuddy. If it were up to either of my brothers, my father would have nothing but a couple of catalog presents he didn't need."

"What time did you get there?"

"I don't know. Six, maybe?"

"Who arrived when?"

"Me first, then Walter, then Philip."

"When did you leave?"

"About seven, I suppose. It wasn't a particularly pleasant time. It never is."

"Why?"

"Mr. Cuddy, my father is . . . *was* not what you would call a good man or a good father. He was a war hero and always thought that put him above everyone else, as if he were a scientist objectively observing us during an experiment. I saw enough of people like that in college and vet school to know what I'm talking about. He was a cold, manipulating man, and if you want to hear any words of regret from me, you'll be in that chair a long, long time."

"Did you and your brothers all leave at the same time?"

"From my father's room, you mean?"

"Yes."

"We did. He—my father—was getting tired. Or faking it, having grown weary of having us standing around him and knowing we weren't enjoying ourselves."

"Could either of your brothers have gone back to the room?"

Luntayne paused. "You mean . . . what? To smother him or something?"

"Or something."

Her lips narrowed. "I suppose so. There aren't any restrictions at the home as to when you get there or when you leave. I suppose one of them could have doubled back without me noticing."

"Would either of your brothers have a reason to do that?"

"Money, hate, the accumulated distaste of a lifetime. Philip would love the money, especially."

"Why especially?"

"He doesn't enjoy being a pharmacist. He never had the brains for med school, but I think he liked the idea of dispensing cure-alls more than the practice of it. He doesn't like people much, that man."

"And you?"

"Me?" She waved a hand at the building behind us. "I've cast my lot for animals, Mr. Cuddy. They are far better patients and far more grateful for any kindness you show them."

"Any thoughts of leaving the hospital?"

"No. Oh, I've toyed with it from time to time. Fantasized about being a real vet out where livestock needs one. But I've grown a little too accustomed to the city life."

"How about Walter?"

"The sloth-bear?"

I just looked at her.

"That's what my father always called him, because he was so big and lazy. I suppose Walter could . . . do something to my father. We none of us care much for the others, the one shared legacy from our father. But I doubt Walter would do anything. He's more the neighborhood slob who can't let go of a joke once he's told it."

Anne Luntayne shook her head. "Do you know what he said when I called him about our father being dead?"

"Let me guess."

Five

The security guard pointed to a gawky man in a white Nehru jacket. Philip Luntayne was standing on a raised platform behind some low glass in the back of the store. I passed down an aisle with everything from potato chips to suppositories. My target stepped from the platform with a vial of pills, handing it to a black woman who asked him a series of questions. Luntayne nodded twice and smiled once, but as soon as the woman turned away, he snarled at her back. Then he noticed me and exchanged the snarl for a "Yes?"

I outlined the situation, which revived the snarl. Around it, Luntayne said, "Perhaps we should step in back."

There was a jail cell of an office with a refrigerator and two cracked vinyl chairs. We sat across from each other, three feet apart, Luntayne having trouble arranging his legs. Everything about him was disproportioned to the long side. Legs, fingers, face, even the gene pool reddish hair, which wasn't so much stylish as neglected.

"I don't know what I could possibly tell you."

"Start with what happened at the nursing home that day."

Philip gave me the same sequence as his siblings.

Then I thought of something I hadn't asked the others. "Did you leave the cake with your father?"

"No. No, he barely touched it, and of course Wally didn't have any, so we gave some of it to one of the orderlies and Anne had to carry most of it home."

"Why didn't Walter have any?"

"He's diabetic."

"Which orderly did you leave the rest of the cake with?"

"Oh, I don't know. Kind of a skinny black man, sort of watery eyes."

"Delroy Briggs?"

"I really couldn't say. What difference does that make?"

"Probably none. Could your brother or sister have doubled back after you all left your father's room?"

Luntayne pulled on his jaw, making his face momentarily longer. "Why would either of them do that?"

"Your father's money was going to Pineview at the rate of five grand a month."

"So. It *was* his money."

"But it, or what was left of it, would be yours."

"One-third mine, so long as no one of us pushed him to the other side.

Don't think I hadn't thought of it, though."

"But it would have been wrong."

"No. Ridding the planet of that terrible man would have been right. It's just that the risk was too great. Besides, I rather liked the thought of him incapacitated enough to become as frustrated as we were growing up."

"How so?"

"Let me count the ways. He was never, *never* satisfied at any accomplishment we might achieve. Wally at least had the excuse of his condition and weight, but Anne and me? Driven to succeed but never rewarded for any accomplishment."

"Is that why you went into pharmacy?"

"No. No, I rather slid into this. Thought it would be an easy life. Instead, it's like being a toll-taker in reverse."

"Or a letter carrier?"

"Wally, Wally. Let me tell you, I think he's finally found his niche in life. No ambition required, though no possibility of getting a leg up on his dreamhouse at the Cape."

"A retirement spot?"

"Yes. As though a government employee would notice the difference between 'working' and 'retiring.' But Anne, now, what she wouldn't give for an extra hundred thousand or so, let her become the James Herriott of *New England.*"

"And you?"

"Me?"

"Like to get out of the 'toll-booth'?"

"Oh, yes. Someday. Soon, even."

"Why soon?"

A smile that would curdle cream. "Now that my hundred or so will be dropped in my lap. And not in quarters, either." Luntayne checked his watch. "Unfortunately, though, I really must get back to the halt and the lame."

"One last question?"

"Certainly."

"You still need a prescription to get a syringe in this state?"

The smile disappeared completely, but Philip Luntayne did nod his head.

Six

I sat in my office and looked out the window at the trees on the Boston Common. Each of Joseph Luntayne's children despised him, and each had a good use for one-third of the estate. If their father died before Pineview got all of his money. Only problem was, I had no evidence to prove which, if any, sibling might have done something about it.

I lowered my eyes to the Park Street subway station. Some homeless people cadged the tourists for spare change. Two past-prime folksingers had a guitar case opened in front of them with some dollar bills fluttering optimistically toward the power of suggestion. A man in a wheelchair with a knob on a stalk near his mouth, briefcase in his lap, motored past all of them without a sideways glance.

I got an idea. It wasn't much of one, but it might be worth a few telephone calls.

✦ ✦ ✦

"Pineview Nursing Home."

It sounded like the fat woman behind the counter in the lobby. "Mrs. Hernandez, please."

"She's not at her desk."

"I'd appreciate your paging her."

A huff, then "Hold on." Two minutes of Muzak followed by a click.

"This is Mrs. Hernandez."

"John Cuddy. I have a couple more questions for you."

"Yes?"

"What's Martin's last name?"

"Martin? You mean Joe's roommate?"

"Yes."

A hesitation. "It's Dallman. Martin Dallman. But why?"

"Any surviving relatives?"

Another full stop. "His parents were killed in the accident. I don't think —No, I'm sure there were no other relatives. But what's this about?"

"Please, Mrs. Hernandez, just bear with me a minute. Where in Indiana was Martin from?"

"I'd have to look that up."

"Would you?"

✦ ✦ ✦

"Police Department, Sergeant Cole."

"I'm speaking to the Prentice, Indiana, police?"

"Sure are."

"Sergeant, my name is John Cuddy. I'm a private investigator in Boston and I'd appreciate some help."

"Sure thing, if I can."

"I'm trying to trace any neighbors of a family named Dallman."

"Dallman, Dallman . . . Family got killed in that auto crash back by you all?"

"Right."

Cole sucked in a breath. "Lordy, that was some time ago. Let me think. I believe Edna Peese might have been living out to them back then."

"Can you spell that last name?"

"Sure thing. Let me dig out her number for you, too."

"Thanks."

"No pro-blame-oh."

✦ ✦ ✦

"Hello?"

"Edna Peese?"

"Hello?"

I repeated the name, a little louder.

"Yes. Yes, this is Edna Peese. Who might you be?"

I told her.

"What could a private investigator from Boston want with me?"

"I'm calling about the Dallman family."

"Oh, what a terrible thing. Just terrible. Five years ago at least, but I still can't bear to picture what happened to those good people."

"I wonder if you knew Martin?"

"Martin? Of course I did. They lived catty-corner to me since he was a pup. Martin used to mow my lawn and trim my hedges. I never saw him after the accident—don't have the kind of money to go back East. But has he . . . improved any?"

"I don't think so."

"Poor boy. Poor, poor boy. Such a nice youngster, always interested in history, too."

History. "What kind of history?"

"The Eighteen Hundreds. Always studying up on cowboys and Indians, Union Pacific and Western Union, buffalo hunts and cattle drives. Not to mention all the hoopla and gadgetry that went with them."

"How about World War Two?"

"World War Two?"

"Yes."

"My, not that I recollect. He was more into the last century than this one. Right to be, too, given what it did to him."

"I'm sorry?"

"That car crash. Would never have happened back in the Old West."

✦ ✦ ✦

Dead end. Hanging up the telephone, I looked back out the window. Same pan-handlers, same singers, even the same man in a wheelchair, this time heading back the other way, using his mouth on the knob to push the stalk back and forth like a throttle, maneuvering around the people or things that didn't yield to him.

I thought about it, then picked up the receiver and dialed my client's number. After a receptionist and secretary, I heard, "Stanton Wilcox."

"Mr. Wilcox, John Cuddy."

"Yes?"

"When I was in your office, you told me that back in the war, you'd stand guard and Joseph Luntayne would work the transmitter, right?"

"That's correct."

"Because he was 'better at it,' you said."

Impatience crept into the lawyer's voice. "Also correct."

"Better at what, Mr. Wilcox?"

Seven

Stanton Wilcox and I got to Joseph Luntayne's old room together. After a while, I called the three siblings and told each that his or her inheritance hinged on being at Pineview within the hour. Philip the pharmacist arrived first, Walter the mailman second. Anne the vet walked in with Mrs. Hernandez ten minutes later. Which made seven of us, including Martin Dallman.

Anne said, "What's going on?"

Philip tugged on his chin. "Stanton and Mr. Cuddy won't tell us."

Mrs. Hernandez crossed her arms. "Well, they'd better tell me."

I asked everybody to sit down. The three Luntaynes did.

I looked from face to face. "I know what happened here on your father's birthday."

Walter said, "What do you mean?"

"All of you told me how much your father enjoyed being in control. It struck me as odd that someone like that would want someone like Martin as his roommate."

I looked over to the other bed. Martin Dallman stared straight ahead at his mirror, the smile still crooked, the finger still twitching.

Mrs. Hernandez said, "It's not so strange. Several of our residents prefer . . . inactive roommates. That way, the sentient roommate can watch television or go to sleep without disturbing or being disturbed by the other."

Anne said, "Dad also told me he liked the fact that Martin couldn't exactly rifle through his stuff."

I nodded. "But wouldn't you think your father would get even more enjoyment from being able to control his roommate, too?"

Walter said, "How could you control Martin?"

"By limiting his means of communication."

Mrs. Hernandez uncrossed her arms, slapping her thighs in the process. "Martin can't . . . communicate."

"Delroy Briggs told me he'd hear Joseph Luntayne talking with Martin."

Anne said, "Who is the world is Delroy Briggs?"

Philip said, "One of the orderlies, according to Mr. Cuddy." The pharmacist turned to me. "But everyone *talks* to Martin. He just can't hear it."

"Yes, he can."

Enough people said, "What?" that I couldn't tell who was first.

I said, "Martin can hear. And see. But a lot of wires got crossed by the accident, so he can't communicate except in one way."

Mrs. Hernandez put a sarcastic edge on her voice. "And what way is that?"

"Briggs told me that Luntayne would pause while talking to Martin, here in the room, with the lights on. Why have the lights on? And why did Luntayne, who seemed to enjoy having Martin around, always make sure Mr. Wilcox was never around him for more than a few seconds on each visit?"

The vet looked at her brothers, but neither seemed forthcoming. "All right. I'll bite. Why?"

"Martin loved the Old West. Studied up on it, including the gadgets from the era. Even learned something along the way."

The pharmacist said, "What?"

"Telegraphy."

The postal worker said, "He can read our minds?"

"Not telepathy, Walter. Telegraphy. Morse code. The one wire the accident didn't cross. Martin's twitching is really tapping. Tapping out messages in Morse code. In his mirror, he saw who doubled back to this room that night, who took out a syringe, probably loaded with potassium chloride. All of you had access to syringes, Anne and Philip through their professions, Walter through his diabetes and insulin prescription. All of you also had access to potassium chloride, a simple enough compound for a vet or a pharmacist or even a former chemistry teacher. But even though only one of you did it, all of you lose out on the inheritance because of it."

Mrs. Hernandez said, "You mean Martin told you somebody killed

Joseph?"

"Once Mr. Wilcox watched Martin's finger long enough, the message was pretty obvious. Martin even told us what the killer said as the injection was flooding into the veins and toward the heart. What was it, Martin?"

Everyone watched the man in the bed as the finger drummed on the sheet.

Stanton Wilcox translated. " 'Well, Martin, it looks like you're going to need a new roommate.' "

The five of us who could turn our heads stared at Walter Luntayne. The mail carrier just stared at Martin's finger.

THE BAGGED MAN

One

Charles Weinstein sat behind his desk and played with a miniature sailing yacht on the blotter. He reminded me of a four-year-old in his bathtub with a rubber duck. There were photos of two prior generations of Weinsteins on the wall to my right, the grandfather who had started the stock brokerage firm of Weinstein, Peck, and the father who had left the firm to Charles. Since Charles was now in his early sixties, he'd been at the helm for a while, the pressures of anticipating the market not very evident in the fine white hair (cut preppy style), or in the unlined, squarish face (with its out-of-season tan), or in the rigorously conservative gray suit (that probably cost more than everything in my closet combined).

Weinstein said to the yacht, "So, Mr. Cuddy, could we start with one of your business cards?"

I rolled my rump in the captain's chair with a Harvard logo on it and fished out my wallet, slipping a "JOHN FRANCIS CUDDY, CONFIDEN-TIAL INVESTIGATIONS" from the slot where Weinstein probably carried Visa and Carte Blanche plastics with holograms on them. Weinstein took the card, flicked at its corners with the fingernail of his thumb, and seemed to be deciding where he'd hang it as a sail on the model in front of him.

I took in the rest of the office, nestled into one of the old wharf buildings that before Boston's renaissance in the bicentennial summer could have been picked up for ten thousand in back taxes. Picture window view of the dormant, winter harbor, the working boats out long before, the pleasure craft berthed till spring. Diplomas from all the right places on the wall with the forebears. Furniture solid cherry and polished and nicely blended with the pattern in the oriental rug beneath us. Weinstein, Peck had the entire floor, and, based on my walk through the large, crowded pit outside his office, Weinstein himself enjoyed the nicest corner of it.

Weinstein decided my card would look better under the border of his blotter than rigged to a mast. "You come highly recommended for your persistence, Mr. Cuddy."

"From whom?"

He seemed to like the "m" I'd put at the end of "who" and reeled off the names of three attorneys I'd helped over the years.

I nodded. "You've done that much homework, maybe you don't need me."

A tired sigh. "Oh, but we do. I'm sorry to say, we do." Weinstein swung in his judge's chair a quarter turn, just enough to appreciate his view. "You've heard of 'The Ain't'?"

Weinstein pronounced the name like a nun would say "turd."

I said, "Who hasn't?"

One disgusted nod. "That is, of course, part of the problem."

Every media outlet imaginable had covered the story in tedious detail. The Ain't had been a homeless man in a blue parka, green fatigue pants, and combat boots. He'd slept at a shelter called "Bed-Down," run by a former Patriots linebacker who had given its endowment for safe investing to Weinstein, Peck. They'd plunged about half of it into junk bonds and other securities I couldn't remember much less explain, none of which did especially well. The Ain't had put a sandwich board over his shoulders and an old-fashioned megaphone to his lips. The sign read something like "Ain't Fair What They Done to the Home" on one side and "Weinstein, Peck Lost Half Our Money" on the other. The megaphone treated passersby to a never-flagging harangue in a southern accent about con men bilking charities and fat cats enjoying three-martini lunches off the sweat of little people. The nickname came from the first word of the sign and the paper bag with eye- and mouth-holes the man always wore over his head, like the New Orleans Saints fans a few years back.

I said, "Why is he still a problem to you?"

Weinstein came back from the view. "You mean because he's dead?"

"Right. He started picketing—what, Monday?"

"Correct."

"Next night he turns up in a vacant lot near the shelter, face in a makeshift campfire. No more picketing, no more problem."

"Except for one." Weinstein opened a drawer, pulled out copies of *The Globe* and *The Herald*, and spread them on his desk. "I take it you've not seen Wednesday's papers?"

"No. I was in New York yesterday."

"They can be easily summarized. The innuendo is that we had the poor wretch killed."

"You're kidding."

The tired sigh again. "Read."

I did. Weinstein was right about the slant of the stories.

He said, "Over the last twenty-four hours, I've received no fewer than ten calls, some of them from clients of forty years standing. Their message was less veiled than those news accounts."

"Meaning they're taking their business elsewhere."

"Unless this matter is resolved quickly, and we are exonerated completely."

"Which is where I come in."

"Precisely."

"Any suggestion on where I should start?"

"The broker involved, Jancy Bickles, is waiting to see you in our conference room. Her brother, Truman, is the man who runs Bed-Down."

"Which is how Weinstein, Peck got the account."

"Correct. You may also want to speak with her supervisor, Joel Comerford."

"I'd rather see her first."

"Probably easier for you in any case. Joel's out with the flu."

"A problem of this magnitude, maybe he could come in sick."

A shake of the head. "No. No, I have a strict rule about that. No one comes in sick or everyone comes down sick. You can see Joel at his condo."

Apparently Weinstein's concern about health didn't extend to independent contractors like me. I got Comerford's address on Beacon Hill and finished up the details of retainer and billing.

I said, "Anything else?"

Weinstein tented his fingers on the desk over the yacht, like he was building it a boathouse with a cathedral ceiling. "How soon before you'll be back to me?"

"Hard to say."

The tired sigh accompanied me out of the office.

Two

"So you're a private investigator."

Jancy Bickles looked up at me, trying to be light rather than flirty. The big brown eyes and broad smile tried hard, but her voice wasn't in it and that tends to mean the heart isn't either. About five-five in business heels and blue suit, her hair was worn short but not scalped, two small hoop earrings piercing each lower lobe. The black face had the kind of sharp features that needed no make-up to bring them out. As soon as she turned off the smile, the features took a sad cast, as though she'd just done her best to cheer the mourners on the receiving line of a funeral.

I sat down on the chair opposite her across the conference table and took out a pad. "B-I-C-K-L-E-S."

"That's right. And 'Jancy' with a 'J,' not an 'N.'"

Bickles had the speaking voice of a network anchorwoman. "I've never seen that spelling before. Where are you from?"

"Alabama, originally, near the Gulf Coast. Just like my brother."

Bickles laid out the last sentence very evenly.

I wrote "ALA" on my pad. "Meaning, how come I'm asking you questions I already know the answers to?"

"For starters."

"Sometimes when I start an interview, lollipop questions get the ball rolling."

The smile came back, a little jaded. "Bull."

I folded up the pad. "Why do I get the feeling you've dropped a syllable since moving north?"

"Mister Cuddy, why don't I just go through everything I know for you. Then you can ask me real questions and save both of us some time."

"Fine."

She waited a moment, then took a deep breath. "First, I had nothing to do with that man's death."

"That's fine, too."

Bickles regarded me a moment before continuing. "Second, neither did my brother."

"Truman."

"Truman."

"Okay."

"Third, that man—have they identified him yet?"

"Not according to the papers."

"Third, that man was vile. I'm not going to pretend I'm sorry he's dead, though burning like that must be a horrible way to die. He was an ignorant and offensive cracker."

I waited, but she seemed to have made the points that mattered to her. "By 'cracker,' do you mean a southerner in general or a Georgian in particular?"

"I mean that old southern attitude, like he was right because he was white, and I wasn't because I'm not."

"How did your brother come to invest with you?"

Bickles regarded me again, a woman who thought about her answers before she gave them. "Same way as everywhere else, Mr. Cuddy. He had money to put to work and a relative in the business."

"Was your brother the only one from the shelter who talked with you?"

"Yes. Oh, he has a board and all. But most of the people on it just like the way it sounds on their résumé, like they're involved with the plight of the homeless. They don't really want to know about things."

"So your brother gave you—what, about two hundred thousand?"

"Two hundred fifteen thousand." The even voice again.

"And you put it where?"

"Into small-company growth stocks and high-yield corporate bonds."

"Fliers and junk."

Bickles bristled. "No, Mr. Cuddy. Growth investments and high-yield income instruments that gave Bed-Down a fighting chance to be able to increase the value of its endowment while maybe, just *maybe*, allowing my brother the chance to earn a living wage running the place."

"Your brother knew what he was putting the shelter's money into?"

"He did. My supervisor and I explained it to Truman in this very room."

"Joel Comerford."

"Yes."

"Do you know anything at all about the dead man?"

"No. All I know is that he parked himself outside our building here on Monday and started parading up and down the sidewalk with those stupid signs and bullhorn—"

"On TV it looked like a megaphone."

Bickles waved her hand. "Whatever. He'd rant and rave and save his best for when he saw me."

"He knew you?"

The jaded smile. "Weinstein, Peck is progressive, Mr. Cuddy. In fact, it's a damned good place to work. But how many black female brokers you figure even a progressive small house has coming in the doors downstairs?"

The accent broke through the polish a little. "What did the man say to you?"

"He went on about how I'd put the shelter's money into uranium mines and the Brooklyn Bridge. About how I should never have taken on so much money so young. About how I should have gotten other people to oversee my work. All the cute little codewords for racism and sexism."

"Did anybody approve your investments?"

The bristling again. "Yes. Joel signed off on all the originals, and I got oral approval of every trade thereafter. You have to understand, Mr. Cuddy, I handled my brother's account more carefully than any other one I service here. I knew we were in some long-shot bets, and I wasn't about to have my neck on the line alone."

"How did your brother take the losses?"

"The losses?"

"On the investments."

"Oh. He understood. He knew things were a little risky, and they still might turn around."

"You said the dead man started picketing on Monday."

"Right. Saw him the first time on Monday morning coming to work."

"He died sometime Tuesday night."

Jaded smile. "So I've heard."

"Mind sharing with me where you were on Tuesday?"

No bristling this time, just the even voice. "My brother came over to my apartment for dinner."

"And where is that?"

"My apartment? Back Bay."

Less than a mile from where the body was found. "When did he arrive?"

"Around seven."

"Just the two of you?"

"Yes."

"When did he leave?"

"He stayed for the ten o'clock news on Channel 56. That's when he saw the story about the man dying."

" 'He saw'?"

"What?"

"You weren't watching television together?"

"No. I was in the kitchen, getting dessert ready. Truman called me into the living room."

"What name did Truman use for the man?"

"Same as everybody."

" 'The Ain't'?"

Still the even voice. "That's right."

"Ms. Bickles, did you tell your brother about The Ain't bothering you?"

"None of your damned business."

Three

I knocked on the door and heard a lilting female voice say, "Just one sec."

Two bolts were thrown, and the wide six-panel swung inward. The woman opening it was kewpie-doll pretty, in her late twenties, with blond hair piled up in a bun on top of her head. She was wearing a sweatshirt and sweatpants and holding a dust rag between manicured fingers.

I said, "I'm sorry. I was looking for Joel Comerford."

"Hey, come on in. I'm just cleaning off some of the stuff from the den."
She closed and bolted the door behind me. "Joel? Hey, Joel?"

She turned back to me. "He's up there now, working on his computer.
How he can stand the smell of that fresh paint, I'll never know. It drives me
out of the place. I'll get him."

The woman turned away and started down the hall, putting on her brakes
almost comically, then spinning and coming back to me like a little girl.
"Gee, where are my manners. I'm Danielle, Joel's wife."

"John Cuddy."

We shook, and off she went again. A woman who got a little less
attractive, but a little nicer, the more you talked with her. I wandered away
from the door, seeing a living room that looked a bit over-furnished. Near
the rear windows, a bunch of newspapers were spread on the floor, and some
Windex and paper towels were sitting on the sill. On the newspapers were
prints and photos and documents in frames.

Danielle came back, the sound of thumping feet on an internal staircase
behind her. She said, "Don't mind the mess, I just hate to lose the chance to
clean everything up right." She went past me and held up one of the frames.
Mounted behind the glass was a diploma. The only words I could make out
were "Duke University" and "Joel D. Comerford."

Danielle said proudly, "The Harvard of the South."

A man's voice behind me said, "Danielle, now put that down and stop
boring the man."

The voice had more than a trace of the South to it. The man it belonged
to looked to be in his mid-forties, wearing khaki slacks, a turtleneck sweater,
and a pair of topsiders. His hair was blond, too, thinning but gamely styled
and combed. He carried a pipe by the bowl in his left hand, and a legal pad
in his right. He shifted the pad to the pipe hand to shake with me.

"Charles said you might be by. If you can stand the smell of paint, we'll
leave Danielle to her spring cleaning and sit up in the den."

"That sounds good."

Comerford sniffled and coughed a little. "Coffee?"

"No, thank you."

"Danielle, the phone rings, how about you let the tape take it, okay?"

"Okay." She still seemed a bit put down about the "boring" remark.

I followed Comerford up a circular staircase for a narrow lighthouse to
a second floor landing with three doors off it. Two were closed, and I guessed
they were to bedroom and bath. The third was open, the doorway filled by
a partial view of the Charles River over the tops of Mary-Poppins town-
houses on the downslope of Beacon Hill.

Comerford said, "Always love that view from the open door."

Containing only a massive desk and two red leather chairs, the den gave the impression of having been stripped for the paint job. The nails were in the walls, masking tape still running along some woodwork and window trim.

I said, "You doing over the whole apartment?"

"No, no." Comerford motioned me to take a seat on one of the chairs while he moved behind the desk and fiddled with some buttons on a computer and modem hook-up on top of it. "I picked up a flu bug, and Charles has a strict rule—almost an obsession—about us coming to work with germs." A soft chuckle. "I'm hoping to sneak in for a few hours this afternoon, but fortunately I can stay hooked to the office with this system and still have time to get to things that need doing." Comerford gestured with his pipe. "And this habit smokes up the walls and ceiling like you wouldn't believe."

I could believe it.

Comerford sank into his chair and sniffled and coughed again. "Charles only reached me as you were coming in the door downstairs. Seems you're going to look into this Ain't character's death for us?"

"That's right."

"How can I help you?"

"When was the first time you saw him?"

"First and only time was Monday. I got in to work early, opened a window to get some air, and heard him from the street. He was out in front of the building, yelling away into that cheerleader thing. I thought he was just your usual garden variety nutcase till I heard what he was saying, then saw him light into Jancy as she arrived for work."

"He was there Tuesday, too, right?"

"Far as I know. He wasn't there when I went home sick on Monday afternoon. I thought he was gone for good, truth to tell. Just a temporary thing, you know? I think he still would have been, it weren't for the media circus."

"You figure the attention brought him back?"

"Sure, why not? Homeless guy, he hasn't got anything better to do. I'm telling you, they hadn't put him on the air, he's gone in another day, maybe two, max. But make him a star, and . . ." Comerford shrugged.

"He make any threats to anybody?"

"Threats? Not that I saw. He did seem pretty rough—crude, I mean."

"How did you come to be involved in the investments Jancy Bickles made for her brother?"

"Same way I always am. Charles assigned her to me when he took Jancy on, us both being from the South and all. Charles, he's a good man, but he kind of figures there's no difference between Alabama and North Carolina, when there's all the difference in the world. But Jancy is sharp as a tack, no 'token' black in any way. She passed everything by me on her brother's portfolio, and I approved all her decisions."

"Does that mean you agreed with them?"

"What, her decisions you mean?"

"Yes."

Comerford thought about it. "Yes, in terms of the kinds of investments. Would I have picked the same identical stocks and bonds? Maybe not, but there wouldn't have been a big difference."

"In what happened to the shelter's nest-egg, you mean?"

Comerford's jaw clenched, then relaxed. "Mister Cuddy, that brother of hers came in with a goal. His goal was to grow his money and pay his bills, all at the same time. Jancy and I explained to him everything we could think of, and he understood it all. Now, I'm not saying he's as sophisticated as Jancy. But he knew it was 'no guts, no glory' time."

"You ever been to the shelter?"

"No, but if you want to go there, I can call Truman, and he can give you directions."

"Don't trouble. One other thing?"

"Sure."

"When the dead man was speaking through the megaphone, could you pick up his accent?"

Comerford worked his jaw again. "You know, I've been thinking on that, figuring the cops or somebody might ask. I'm not sure, now, what with that megaphone distorting things, but I'd have to say . . . L.A.?"

"Los Angeles?"

Comerford shook his head. "Lower Alabama."

We watched each other before I thanked him and he walked me down and out of the condo.

Four

Detective Sergeant Bonnie Cross was lost in the Homicide file in front of her. She was wearing a padded blazer across shoulders wide enough to make her body type "sturdy." Her brown hair was parted in the middle and tied back as though she hadn't had time to wash it that morning.

I said, "Sergeant?"

The look in her eyes wasn't half as telling as the styrofoam cup in her left hand. The tarry dregs at the bottom had dried so thoroughly that there was no leak as she crushed the cup in her fist.

"Cuddy. What do you want?"

"Have I come at a bad time?"

"There hasn't been a good time since my senior prom. What?"

"The Ain't thing."

She started to mouth the words, then nodded. "Right, right. It's one of mine. What's your interest?"

I told her.

"Good luck to you and to them."

"What do you mean?"

"I mean Tuesday about eight p.m. the uniforms get flagged down by an elderly couple walking their dog. The dog's the size of a Shetland pony, which is what gave them the courage to be out in that neighborhood at night. The uniforms respond and find this white male in a vacant lot face down in the campfire, empty bottle of rye next to him. A marshmallow would have looked better."

"Photos?"

"Haven't got them yet."

"No rush on this one?"

"Look, Cuddy, there are three ways the homeless tend to leave us. One, they get drunk and freeze to death in a doorway. Two, they get drunk, fall asleep in that doorway, and slide down so they drive their chin to their chest and close off the windpipe. Three, they get drunk, fall asleep—"

"And burn themselves to death."

"Cigarette, sterno, this guy a campfire."

"Identification?"

"Not yet and not likely."

"What about prints?"

"Hands went in, too."

"How's that?"

"We figure he was sitting over the fire, pitched forward and face and both hands went into the coals."

"Wiping out facial features and fingerprints both."

"Right."

"Seems a little . . . comprehensive, don't you think?"

"Not really. Nobody touched his teeth."

"So if you had an idea of a name, you could maybe check his dental charts."

"Medical examiner said the fillings were old but looked military. Don't ask me how he can know that because I don't like even thinking about dentists, myself."

"Anything at all to trace the body?"

"M.E. found some kind of injury to the left cheekbone and skull in front of the left ear. Thought it might have been shrapnel. Probably disfiguring unless the guy had a lot of cosmetic surgery."

I thought about the paper bag the dead man wore.

Cross said, "That it?"

"How about time of death?"

"The fire and the cold screw that up some, but he was last seen alive leaving that shelter he slept at about five p.m."

"Who saw him?"

"Truman Bickles, guy who runs the place."

"How about his effects?"

"The guy was found in a blue parka, fatigue pants and boots, all right? When we realized he was this Ain't character, I went to the shelter—what's it called?"

"Bed-Down."

"Bed-Down, yeah. Ought to be able to remember that. Anyway, I went through his stuff. Just the signs he wore and this loudspeaker he made out of rolled cardboard and twine."

"That's all?"

"No. No, Cuddy, that wasn't all. There were three pairs of briefs, soiled. There were two pairs of socks, holey. There were a couple of stories from the papers about him and the shelter's money your client lost for them. There was no secret diary or message in milk. Hell, we don't even think the guy was done, unless you've got something more than what I've heard."

"I don't."

"Great. You do, call first. No need to come all the way in next time."

"It's been a pleasure, Cross."

"You'll excuse me, I don't like to start lying so early in the day."

Five

The entryway was in an alley, the reception desk an imposing counter. Next to the counter was a solid, scuffed metal door. Over the counter was a thick Plexiglas shield scratched and stained by God knows what. The immediate impression was that somebody had constructed a blockade, but the man standing behind the counter looked to be blockade enough to me.

At six-two, two-forty, Truman Bickles had been a middle linebacker for the Pats. He'd had a few good seasons before a bad knee made him yesterday's hero. He appeared a bit chunkier than two-forty right now, his gut straining against the Nike training pants and longsleeved tee shirt with penpocket.

I shoved my ID under the glass. Bickles glanced at it, then pushed a button on his side of the counter that caused the door to buzz and let me come through it.

"My name's Truman Bickles."

The voice rumbled around the enclosure. Instead of offering me his hand, Bickles turned and walked me over to some gutsprung chairs around a battered metal desk with a black dial phone. Its receiver looked as though it had been used to drive nails.

We took facing chairs, Bickles' eyebrows arching just a little as he said, "My sister told me you might come calling."

"I thought she might."

"What do you want to be messing around with a dead man for?"

"I don't, especially. I just need to find out why he got that way."

Bickles chewed a minute. "Man broke the pledge, the demon rum did him in."

"You believe that?"

"It's what happened lessen somebody can tell me something different."

"You have a name for this guy?"

"Uh-unh. Man wants to come to my shelter, he don't have to leave no name. He just have to be sober and stay sober."

"You ever know this man to fall off the wagon before?"

Bickles did some more chewing. "No."

"When did he first get here?"

"About two, maybe three weeks back."

"Would your records show it?"

"Uh-unh. I just keep a head count, I don't register the men like they was in a hotel."

"You ever see this guy without the bag on his head?"

Bickles' eyes narrowed. "No."

"Did anybody else?"

The big man squirmed, a real test for the chair he was in. "One time, last week, one of the other men and him got into a tussle."

"Over what?"

"Other man, he pulled The Ain't's bag off. I don't allow no fighting here, but by the time I broke them up, The Ain't had his bag back on and didn't give me no more trouble."

"I'd like to speak to this other man and anybody else who knew The Ain't."

The eyes narrowed some more. "Don't know about that."

"What do you mean?"

"Can't see that this thing's done me no good so far. Don't see it getting no better if I let you poke around the men."

I nodded. "Since this thing hit the fan, how're your contributions holding up?"

Bickles squirmed again. I thought I heard a rivet pop in the chair frame. He said, "Contributions come in irregular. No set pattern to them."

"Fine. Then I just hang around outside, wait for your guys to come in or go out, and offer them twenty to talk with me for a while."

Bickles snorted. "You know what they do with that money."

"I know. I don't like it, and I don't want to be part of it. But either I get my information in here for free or I'll have to give out bottle money to people who don't need it."

"Oh, they need it all right. They just can't take it."

I'd made my argument, so I sat back.

Bickles chewed a little more, and then a little more again before saying, "I opened this place account of I thought a man should have a place to go when things are tough. My sister, she gave me a place to stay when I got waived. That meant something to me, so I give her my business here. Things didn't work out right, somehow. I knew why, I wouldn't have needed her in the first place. But this thing's been bad for the shelter, bad for her, and bad for me. I don't want it to be bad any longer than it has to be."

I bided my time.

Bickles put his hands on the arms of his chair and heaved himself up. "You want to start with his friends or the guy in the tussle?"

"Friends first. One other thing?"

"What?"

"When you spoke with The Ain't, could you tell where he was from?"

"From? You mean like, originally?"

"Yes. Based on his accent, maybe?"

Bickles shook his big head slowly, left to right. "Never been no good at accents."

Six

"Friend?"

"So I've heard, Maury."

"Well, now, son, I'm not certain The Ain't had what you'd call a friend."

Truman Bickles had lent me the use of the cramped office and went looking for people I might want to see. Maury was the first.

He sat across from me, a skinny parody of a Red Skelton sketch. Black formal hat with chunks missing from the brim, a seagull feather like a sore thumb in the band. Three-day growth of beard, mostly white, and a half dozen teeth, mostly yellow. Maury wore gloves, even though it was warm in the room, an unlit cigar stub stuck between index and middle finger on his right hand.

I said, "If you weren't friends, what were you?"

"Acquaintances, at most." Maury gestured with the cigar butt. "Erstwhile roommates. The Ain't enjoyed the bunk nearest the cellar window, you see, and mine was across from his. The Ain't was quite proud of that window, though he spent little enough time in the room."

"Where did he spend his time?"

A sweeping gesture. "The great outdoors, son. Like most of us, The Ain't preferred the wonders of nature to the blunders of man. Except for a dry bed and some hot water, of course."

"You never got a name from him?"

"No. No, but if I had, I'm sure it would have been worthless."

"I don't get you."

"I'm sure any name he would have given me would have been an alias."

"Why?"

Maury stuck the cigar stub in the corner of his mouth. "Well, The Ain't was always holding forth about con men, how some people always conned their way through life, when in fact he himself was running a bit of a game."

"Like wearing a bag over his head?"

"Perhaps. But I mean more his demeanor. When other people were around, he'd come on strong. The good old boy, with sourmash grammar and so forth. Then when we'd converse, he sounded like a college man, and believe me, that you cannot fake, at least not with me."

"The southern accent was a put-on?"

"No, son. No, he had an accent all right, from what part of the South I couldn't guess. But he could speak the King's English when it suited him, and he put on the hillbilly aspect when he wanted."

"Ever talk with you about his past life?"

"No, he didn't. But then, if he had, I would have thought he was exaggerating—wait a minute, now. He did talk about Old Bro."

"His brother?"

"I thought as much, but it was never very specific. Just, 'Old Bro' is running a game on life,' 'Old Bro' isn't playing square.' That sort of thing. Once The Ain't got onto a topic, he never got off it. Stubborn that way."

In Vietnam, 'bro' was what one black soldier might call another. "Could he have meant some friend he called 'bro,' as in 'brother'?"

Maury took the cigar from his mouth and put it in a breast pocket. "As I said, The Ain't really didn't have what you'd call a friend."

✦ ✦ ✦

"What if I don't feel like talking with you so much?"

"Then you're free to leave, Julio."

"Freedom. That's a nice word, you know it? Fighting I done for freedom, look where it leave me."

Julio tried to cross his arms. Barrel-chested and sliding to fat around the beltline, he couldn't quite manage it, the hands not tucking into the elbows. He had a dark beard and a fringe of hair like a tonsured monk that hung long in the back. The burning eyes were the most animated thing about him.

I said, "Was The Ain't in Vietnam, too?"

"Yeah. That's how his face got messed up."

I stopped. "You saw him?"

"I see him every day, man."

"I mean, you saw his face without the bag over it."

"Oh. No, man. What I mean is, he tell me, he's walking point one day in the bush, he hits a tripwire and knows it, so he does a dive, but some of the mine, it catch him in the face, mess it up."

"He ever mention what unit he was with?"

"Just that he was Army."

"Where he was in-country?"

"Never talked about it much. Never talked a whole lot about anything, 'cept for the demons."

"The demons?"

"Yeah. I was here one day, he was sleeping over in his bunk by the window there? Well, he's having this nightmare or something, man, so I go over, shake him some. He come out of it, said thanks, the demons was after me, and they was all wearing blue."

"Blue, the color?"

"I guess so."

I thought about it. In Vietnam, the North Vietnamese regulars wore blue uniforms. "Could he have meant NVA?"

"Don't know, man. Full tour in-country, and I never seen an NVA. Just seen this bro and that, get cut down and blown up."

I stared at him.

Julio said, "Fighting for freedom, you know it?"

✦ ✦ ✦

"He was a son of a bitch."

"How do you mean, Teddy?"

"How do I mean? The hell does 'son of a bitch' mean to you?"

Teddy of the tussle thought he was a tough guy. You could see it in the broken nose and scarred brow and home-inked tattoos on his forearms. The kind of guy who bullied his way through life, whining every step of the way.

I said, "What did you two fight over?"

"Wasn't a real fight. I'd have kicked his ass, Tru hadn't pulled me off him."

"What was the beef?"

"Aw, he was always wearing that stupid bag, like he was some kind of serial killer or something. 'Halloween Five—The Ain't,' get me?"

"Go on."

"Well, I wasn't the only one he pissed off—the son of a bitch was stubborn as a mule—but I was the only one with the guts to yank his bag off."

"And what happened?"

"He went nuts, coming after me. Must have had some time in the army or something, 'cause he knew how to hit. But he didn't have a chance against me."

"You saw his face, then?"

"Yeah, I saw it. All ugly, big piece of it missing on the left side. Kind of threw me at first."

"You notice the color of his eyes?"

"You kidding me or what?"

"How about hair?"

"Dirty, all matted down from being under that bag all the time."

"Color?"

"Looked brown, I suppose."

"He say anything to you?"

"What, about his hair?"

"About anything."

"Just yelling at me, 'What'd you do that for,' get me?"

"You answer him back?"

"Yeah. Yeah, sure I did. I said, 'At least with that face, they won't have any trouble identifying you.' "

I paused. "Did he say anything else?"

"Yeah. He said, 'Charlie taught me how to do that.' "

In Vietnam, we called the NVA "Charles," the Vietcong "Charlie."

Teddy said, "What are you looking at?"

"The Ain't said 'Charlie'?"

"Yeah."

"Not 'Charles.'"

" 'Charles'? The hell knows anybody called 'Charles'?"

I did. The man who hired me.

Seven

As late lunch, I grabbed a take-out pastrami sandwich and went back to my office with its four walls. The two windows overlook the Park Street subway station, the low roofs below me dusted with a fine layer of sooty snow. I sat at my desk and ate my sandwich, the pastrami promising to revisit me in the night. Then I started playing solitaire with pages from my pad, hoping some of the things I'd picked up from the interviews would make some sense.

Charles Weinstein was hoping I could stop the flow of clients away from him due to bad publicity and innuendo. Jancy Bickles was sure The Ain't was racist and sexist and more sure that she'd done right by the shelter's money and that neither she nor her brother Truman had had anything to do with The Ain't's death. Joel Comerford confirmed Jancy on the investments and thought The Ain't might have been from Alabama. Bonnie Cross and her people found no evidence of identity and weren't even sure a homicide had been committed. Truman Bickles seemed to care genuinely about his shelter and the men in it, but could offer no help on identity. Of the other homeless The Ain't knew, Maury thought he was a con man and a college grad, Julio confirmed he'd been in combat in Vietnam, and only Teddy had actually seen his face.

I shook my head and reshuffled the notes, dealing them out randomly this time. No apparent matches. Shuffle, deal. Nothing again. Shuffle, deal. Zip.

The tenth go-round, I got "Cross: Combat boots"; "Julio: Walking point/tripwire"; "Teddy: Identification/Charlie taught me." In Vietnam, the guys sometimes slid one dogtag onto a bootlace so that if they were badly mangled, there'd be two possibilities for identification. A longer shot than Jancy Bickles' junk bonds, but worth a phone call. Cross was out, so I left a message for her to check the boots for any ID.

I went back to shuffling and dealing. I lost count of the number of hands I dealt before I got "Jancy: Southern accent;" "Maury: Con man/Old Bro"; "Julio: Demons/blue." Fainter than smoke, till I remembered a comment I hadn't written down, because I hadn't been interviewing the person at the time.

I ran it through in my head, over and over. Then I dialed a number, eventually got the person I'd asked for, and broke the connection. I lifted the receiver again, calling a different number. Getting the person I wanted right away, I asked if I could come over in fifteen minutes. Then I hung up and called Cross again, reaching her this time.

Based on what she'd found, I asked Cross to join me.

Eight

As he came through the door, Joel Comerford tried to cover the shock in his face, but he couldn't quite pull it off. He said, "Danielle, what's going on?"

Bonnie Cross and I stood up from the couch. Danielle had been serving us afternoon coffee and tea and little biscuits and couldn't quite see the reason for her husband being rude.

"Joel, this is Detective Cross. And you remember Mr. Cuddy."

Comerford clamped down on something rising in his throat and said, "*Detective* Cross?"

Cross said, "Sergeant Detective, actually."

Danielle said, "Oh, I'm sorry."

Cross said, "No need to be."

Danielle turned to her husband. "Was everything all right at the office?"

Comerford worked his mouth a little, then put on a smile. "Danielle, could you excuse us for a minute?"

"But Joel, I'm just—"

"Honey, maybe go upstairs for a while?"

"But that paint smell is still so strong—"

"Then take a walk, okay?"

Danielle stopped dead at the edge in his voice. She got very pale, then said, "Okay," and went out through the front door of the condo.

Comerford waited until the door closed, then said, "What is this?"

Cross read him his rights. Comerford swallowed twice, then said he understood them, taking a wingchair in the living room.

Cross sat back on the couch and turned to me. "Go ahead."

I said, "Your wife was kind enough to show us the photos you had to take down in the den when you repainted it."

Comerford didn't say anything.

"You started the paint job Tuesday afternoon. She said the smell was so strong it drove her out. For dinner and a movie. That gave you time to slip out and go visiting." I held up one of the framed photos, showing Comerford and a very similar other man with blond hair. "Time to go visit your brother Joel who was 'killed' in Vietnam."

Nothing.

"Such terrible luck for you. Twenty years ago, your brother comes back from the war, disfigured, maybe disillusioned. Chucking his college education, Joel goes on the sauce, you lose track of him. Then you decide, 'Hey, that great education he got and I didn't? Why not cash in on it?' So you take his diploma and you take his name."

"You can't prove any of this."

"Because we can't identify the body?"

Comerford started to reply, then shook his head.

I said, "You came north, to avoid most of the Blue Devil alums of Duke, one of whom might notice you're not your brother. You attracted a beautiful wife, got a great job. Everything is coming up roses until that incredible piece of bad luck. Joel ends up at the shelter whose investment account your firm loses money for."

Comerford said, "Those investments were all—"

"—they probably were all good risks. But that's not the point, is it? Some people at the shelter who knew your brother said he was stubborn, that once he got onto something, he stuck with it. Must have been a bad morning for you Monday. A miracle Joel wasn't set up outside to spot you coming to work early. Up in your office, though, you hear his voice through the megaphone. No wonder you got sick. The one man who could destroy your career and your life as a grad of 'the Harvard of the South.' You slipped out somehow, maybe when he was taking a break, then stayed home Tuesday while he kept up the parade, giving no impression of ever leaving. You couldn't very well stay home sick until he got tired of picketing, because you knew he might never get tired."

"Ridiculous."

"So you paint the den on Tuesday to get rid of your wife and to have a reason for no photos on the wall in case the police come by to speak to you. You slip out of the condo after she does. You buy a bottle, maybe as a peace offering to your brother, maybe as just a prop for physical evidence. You went over by Bed-Down, waited till you spotted him coming or going. Maybe you even tried to talk sense to him?"

Comerford flushed.

"Maybe you tried to get him to see things your way. Somehow I don't think he was amenable to an amicable settlement. Somehow I think he liked the idea of being the gadfly for the money you helped lose for his shelter. Maybe he thought of a new slogan on the sandwich board, 'My brother Stole My Name and Our Money.' "

"Stop it!"

I watched Comerford seethe.

"Wish I could stop. I wish you had. But you didn't. When Joel wouldn't see the light of reason, when he refused the bottle, what did you do? Sucker-punch him? Maybe with the bottle? Then you set up the fire, and pushed him into it, dousing him with the booze as an accelerant. To burn off the face that was so like yours, to burn off the fingerprints that would be on file with the Army. Tell me, did he wake up? Did he start to come to and—"

"I told you to stop it! This is my home, I can tell you to get out!"

"You still think we can't make the identification stick?"

"No."

"We can make it stick. We have your brother's dogtag."

Comerford's eyes bulged.

"He kept it in his boot, between the heel and the sole. The tag will let the police access dental records. His teeth will tell us who he is, and your fingerprints won't match the ones of 'Joel D. Comerford' that the Army has."

Comerford stared down at his finger pads. Then he brought his hands to his eyes and began to cry into them.

GEORGIE-BOY

One

The waitress walked as though she were practicing to be fat. Her arms went out to the side eight inches past her hips, the hands flicking back and forth with every other step. Blonde and a little past thirty, she wore a black uniform with white piping and stopped at my booth. An order book appeared from the front pocket in her apron, a cheap ballpoint from over her left ear.

I said, "How are you?"

She smiled a little, the right side of her mouth crooking up, the other side staying flat. "Fine. You?"

"Okay."

The woman gestured with the pen at the empty formica tabletop. "Coffee?"

The place was well air-conditioned, but the thermometer on a savings and loan three doors down had read eighty-eight degrees Fahrenheit. I looked past my waitress to the counter of the coffeeshop, trying to read the little white letters pressed on the black felt boards near the ceiling. "Lemonade, if you have it."

She smiled a little more. "You got it."

I watched her walk back past old-fashioned chrome stools toward the cash register. Another waitress, dark-haired with a ripe body pushing at her uniform, leaned an elbow on the counter, sneaking a look at me. A male voice yelled something from the kitchen, and the other waitress said something back with enough Spanish accent on it that I didn't understand her.

I checked my watch. I was supposed to meet a woman named Cherie Malloy at the coffeeshop ten minutes earlier. When Malloy had called my office in Boston, I'd asked her to come there, but she said she couldn't get off from work for that long and asked if I could come out instead. Malloy said we could talk in private because she knew the place and it wouldn't be busy that time of afternoon on a Wednesday in July. Ordinarily, I wouldn't have gone for it, but the week before had been slow, and the current one slower, so I did.

I looked around the coffeeshop. It was empty enough, but I had the feeling from the Hispanic waitress that I stood out as somebody who wasn't a regular. I didn't think Cherie Malloy was going to enjoy much privacy for our conversation.

If she showed at all.

I figured to give her one lemonade's worth and then chalk it up. My waitress started over with a large soda fountain glass in her hand. The door to the kitchen behind her swung open, a guy with one of those paper short-order caps sticking his head out. Looking exasperated, he yelled, "Cherie?"

My waitress stopped dead, looked at me, and bit her lip. The Hispanic waitress glared at the guy in the cap, who said to her, "What'd I do?"

My waitress continued on to my booth and set the glass of lemonade on a napkin. "You're John Cuddy, right?"

"Right."

"You're a private eye, you must think I'm pretty stupid, huh?"

A sentence long enough for me to finally recognize the voice on the phone. "Can you sit down?"

She looked back toward the counter, where the Hispanic waitress was still laying into the cook. Then Malloy arched her rump a little and slid into the bench on the other side of the booth, the leatherette squeaking under her.

I said, "Why'd you run a game on me?"

Malloy shrugged. "See how you treated people."

I thought about it. "How I treated a waitress in a place I'd never been before."

"Right, right. I figure, you treat me okay in this dive before you think I'm a client, maybe you're a good guy to hire."

"I pass the test?"

Malloy gave me the crooked smile. "Yeah." She looked down at my left hand. "You married?"

"Widower."

"Oh." The smile lingered unconsciously before she realized it was still there. "Oh, Jesus. I'm sorry."

"That's okay. It's been . . . years now." I cleared my throat. "So what's this about?"

"My husband George."

"Divorce case?"

"Kind of."

"Sorry, Ms. Malloy. I could have told you on the phone—"

"No, no. It's not like I want you to follow him or anything. Hell, he's already walked out on me and Trudy."

"Trudy?"

Beneath the formica, she dug into the apron, coming up with a photo.

I turned it around. A girl maybe three years old, a smaller and happier version of Cherie Malloy, looked toward the lens. The little girl was holding an ice cream cone, what might have been strawberry running down the sides of the cone onto her fingers, tongue out trying to catch it. Malloy had the photo in a laminated holder, like a valuable baseball card.

"I keep that with me so's I can remind myself why I'm working here."

I passed back the plastic. "What do you want me to do?"

"Georgie-boy walked out three months ago to the day."

"And you want me to find him."

"Yeah, but not like that. Look, can I sort of just go through it? Then you can tell me if you're interested or not."

"Okay."

"Okay." Malloy set the photo of Trudy down carefully. "Georgie-boy and me, we got married four years ago. He met me maybe six months before that, saying to me, 'It's time I got married, settled down, Cher.' So we did. Then he wanted a baby, so I gave him Trudy. That's how he got his nickname. We was watching that movie, *Georgie-Girl*, with that Redgrave actress does the weight commercials now. When he said he wanted a baby, like the woman in the movie, I started calling him 'Georgie-boy,' and it kind of stuck. Then when he got restless at work, he decided to go into real estate, DeNapoli Agency in town here. Not the greatest timing in the world, but he seemed to do okay at it. Then he wanted this classic Mustang, so he bought that."

I let her go, hoping I'd see a point to it or a way out of it.

Malloy fingered the photo. "Georgie-boy and me rented this little house. Never had the bucks for a down payment." She snorted a laugh. "Like the dentist who never gets his teeth fixed, Georgie-boy the real estate man never bought a house. But we was doing okay, till he met this Southern belle?" Malloy drew out the last two words, lilting them at the end, like she was imitating somebody. "She was a real lady, he told me. Didn't smoke, didn't curse, couldn't even drive a fu . . . car. But he told me he wanted her, because she knew how to keep a house, cook a meal. I ask you, how was I supposed to do all that with Trudy and this place keeping me running?"

"Ms. Malloy—"

"Sorry. No, really. I'm sorry. You don't have to hear all this sh . . . stuff. So, all right, Georgie-boy, he's real upfront about it. All business-like. Comes home one day, tells me, 'Cher, I'm moving out.' Just like that, always so upfront. He packs his clothes and his pipes and his bicycle on the back of that Mustang and drives off. So I go to divorce court on him, and I get something called a temporary order, and Georgie-boy ain't too happy, but what can he do, even the judge tells him it's pay support or the judge puts something on his paycheck at the agency and I get my money that way."

Sensing I was about to say speak, Malloy speeded up. "But Georgie-boy, he paid faithful, every Monday every week till two days ago."

"When he didn't."

"Right. So last night I called Scarlett O'Hara there and asked for him, and she said she ain't seen him since he left for work yesterday morning."

"How about work?"

She shook her head. "I called them, too. They say he never showed up on Tuesday."

"Ms. Malloy, I—"

"What I think is happening here, Georgie-boy is testing me, like I was testing you before. He's trying to see, am I gonna make a stink? Well, I called the cops, and they let me talk for like a minute before they said I oughta wait a while. I called the divorce court, and they said I wasn't on welfare, I had to wait a while too, there was nothing they could do."

"So you want me to do what?"

"Kick over a few cans, find the one he's hiding under. Let him know I'm not going to take this."

"Ms. Malloy, I bill out at—"

She dipped back into the apron. "I don't have a lot of cash, but I figure it's money well spent to let Georgie-boy know he can't get away with this kind of thing. He's gotta pay me what he owes, else Trudy goes without, get me?"

I watched Malloy hold out a small stack of twenties that looked like she'd acquired them one at a time. I looked down at the plastic holder with Trudy's picture in it. Then I took out a pad and said, "I'll run a tab on it. You have a photo of George, too?"

She brought one out, a candid of a slimmer her and a guy in his thirties. Wiry, he was maybe six feet, with a thin mustache under a peak nose and a lock of brown hair across his forehead. He gave the camera the kind of yearbook smile that said nobody would want to talk with him at a high school reunion.

I said, "His last name's Malloy, too?"

My client nodded.

"Description of his car?"

"Mustang, like I said." Malloy's voice dropped into a drone, like she was reciting something she'd heard over and over again. "Red convertible, sixty-seven, with white interior. Mint condition, the 289 engine. He's even got one of those key rings with like a little toy Mustang on it."

"Do you know his plate number?"

"It's what he calls a vanity plate."

"Go ahead."

"It's G-E-O, then a dash and B-O-Y."

Cute. "Where does he live now?"

She gave me an address, one town over.

"And the name of the woman he's with now?"

"Leah Anne something or other. She'll be at the house."

"You know anybody I should speak to at the DeNapoli Agency?"

"Probably Debby DeNapoli. She runs the place. But his best friend there was a guy named Steinfeld. Sam Steinfeld. I never met him, he was kind of Georgie-boy's guy friend, you know? Hit the bars, go to the ballgame, whatever."

"Anybody else you can think of?"

"Who you should see, you mean?"

"Yes."

"Just Rosa."

"Rosa?"

Malloy turned halfway and said, "Rosa."

The Hispanic waitress left the counter and swayed toward us.

Malloy turned back to me. "Rosa lives like across the street from Georgie-boy's new place."

I decided to get out what I'd been wanting to say to her. "Ms. Malloy, a lot of people like your husband just want to . . . take a little time off from things sometimes."

Pocketing the photo of her daughter, Malloy stood up and slid out of the booth. "Believe me, Mr. Cuddy, Georgie-boy, he don't know what he wants. I gave him everything, and it wasn't enough."

Two

Rosa took about thirty seconds settling herself into the bench seat across from me that Cherie Malloy had been warming. Up close, she looked a little older than my client, with red, vivid lipstick and black, lustrous hair drawn back into a mane with metal barrettes. She carried with her a cigarette and one of those tin foil ashtrays. Exhaling, she let the smoke wend out her nostrils, making the coffeeshop feel more like a 1940's nightclub. Rose seemed very aware of her body and very interested in whether I was aware of it too.

"So, you a private eye, eh?"

"John Cuddy."

"I'm Rosa."

"Your last name?"

"Echevarría."

"She pronounced it "Et-chay-varr-*ee*-ah."

"Ms. Echevarría, I understand—"

"Rosa."

"Sorry?"

"Call me Rosa, John. Everybody does."

More smoke, a slow smile with more settling of the body into her seat.

"Rosa, I understand you live across the street from George Malloy's new place?"

"Not exactly across the street. We down a few houses."

"We?"

She paused. "My son and me."

"How long have you been there?"

"Couple years."

"Since before George moved in?"

"Yeah, way before that."

"What can you tell me about him?"

A deep drag on the cigarette. "You got to tell Cherie all I'm gonna tell you?"

"Probably not."

"Her Georgie-boy, he seem to me real interested in his new woman."

"Leah Anne?"

"If that's her name."

"You don't know her?"

"Tried to say *hola* to her a couple times, first when I see her. I think she don't want to know the little spitfire from Guatemala."

Echevarría said "spitfire" with her eyes as well as her mouth, a word she'd heard somebody else use and thought I might like.

"Then you don't know her last name?"

A slow shake of the head.

"What does she look like?"

"Brown hair, okay face, tight . . . figure."

"What makes you think George liked her so much?"

"He was living with her. Pretty good sign, eh?"

"Anything else?"

A shrug. "I'm sitting on my porch, I see them. Sitting on their porch, walking sometimes, mostly in his hot car, the Mustang convertible. They do things together, even go shopping for food. Man, I tell you, Georgie-boy back that little car of his into the driveway, he got so many bags from the grocery store, you think the little car would break. But they unload into the garage like a couple of high school kids on a first date, all joking and . . . "

Echevarría reached across the table to the pen in my right hand and ran her nails down my fingers. Funny, before then I hadn't noticed she'd painted them dark red.

" . . . touching each other all the time, like this."

"So they seemed happy to you."

"In love."

Just then a stringy teenager in jeans and a purple tank top came through the front door. He was burning his eyes into me, watching Rosa turn toward him. The kid walked past Cherie and the cook without speaking or looking at them, coming toward us.

I watched his hands.

The kid stopped just short of my booth, hammering Spanish in a low mutter to Echevarría. She crackled back and waved him away. He retreated to a stool, but only rested his butt on it and crossed his arms.

Rosa brought her hand back to the foil ashtray, fiddling with it a little.

I said, "Your son?"

"Yes."

"What's his name?"

"Miguel."

"Does Miguel know George at all?"

"I don't ever see them together."

"Will he talk to me about George?"

"Not even if I tell him or you beat on him."

I nodded. I had the feeling I wasn't the first man Miguel had seen his mother getting friendly with. "You know George is missing."

"I know Cherie think he is."

"What do you think?"

"I think Georgie-boy the kind of man, he look around a lot, maybe see something."

"What kind of thing?"

"Maybe a new kind of thing he like."

"George ever look at you that way?"

The slow smile. "Wouldn't you?"

Echevarría gave me the address of Malloy's house. As she got up and walked her son out, he kept watching me. I kept watching them, trying not to let Miguel know whether it was his mother or him I was watching.

Three

I drove my old Honda Prelude back into the city, moonroof and both windows open to manufacture a breeze, parking it behind my office. Upstairs, I got on the telephone.

"City Clerk, Parking."

"Cholly?"

"Speaking. Who's this?"

"John Cuddy."

"John. What's the matter, you get towed somewhere?"

"No, Cholly, but thanks for asking."

"You guys, the Vatican was in Boston, you'd leave your wheels in the Pope's personal space."

"Not my car at all."

"What is it, then?"

"I got a plate I'd like you to watch for."

"Watch for. You mean like, run through the computer on the overdues?"

"That, too. But I want you to watch for this one on the lists coming across your desk."

"The lists . . . you mean the current tickets?"

"Yes."

"You out of your mind or what?"

"Cholly—"

"I get a thousand tickets a day coming through in here from all over the city, John. You want me to watch for a plate on one of them?"

"This is a vanity plate, Cholly."

"John, I don't care does it read PIUS XII, how am I— "

"Cholly, this is a fifty-dollar vanity plate we're talking about."

"Oh." I could hear somebody saying something to him in the background. Then in a louder voice Cholly said through the phone, "Let me just get a pen, Captain."

✦ ✦ ✦

"Stolen Car Unit, Pingry."

"Big Earl, how are you?"

"Depends on who's asking."

"John Cuddy, Earl."

"Well, well. Somebody waste their time on that bomb of yours?"

"Not this time. I have a plate I'd like you to watch for."

"See if it turns up where it shouldn't."

"Or anywhere else. I'm not sure it's stolen."

"Meaning?"

"Meaning, the owner might still be driving it, Earl. I'd just like to know if anybody calls it in."

"A little dicey for me to enter it into the databank without a formal request."

"How about if the request comes from a former President?"

"Might depend on how well history regarded the man."

"Ulysses S. Grant?"

"An honor and a privilege to serve him."

◆ ◆ ◆

"Mrs. Feeney said these pink and whites would last a long time, even in this heat."

A good quality in a carnation, John.

I straightened up from the grave, looking down Beth's hillside to the harbor below. A couple of sailboards skittered on the same tack, the working boats long out and not likely back for a while. After I'd finished on the telephone, I figured it wouldn't hurt to make a visit before going out to George Malloy's new house.

Something on your mind, John?

I told her about my client from the coffeeshop.

Thought you'd sworn off divorce cases.

"This is more than a simple trace, Beth."

But if you find him, all he has to do is bolt again, right?

"Right."

So it doesn't seem your client gets much satisfaction for her money.

I looked back at the harbor. "Probably not."

Oh, John. You're not going to charge her, are you?

"Never can tell."

I always could.

I came back to the headstone. "No argument there."

Four

It was about six p.m. when I pulled up in front of George Malloy's address. The houses on both sides of the street were old wooden two-stories, all single-family with detached, one-car garages except the corner buildings. Rose Echevarría's house was easy to spot: Miguel lounged in an old sand chair on the shady porch of the corner house three doors down and across from Malloy's. Miguel gave me the finger as I got out of my car. I smiled at him and went up the empty, short driveway to Malloy's garage.

There was a stout, fairly new padlock on the swinging doors. I used my hand to shadow the webby glass panes at eye level. The Mustang wasn't there, the bicycle Cherie Malloy mentioned silhouetted against a ghostly white background at the far end. There was an assortment of garden tools flush against the side walls, as though they generally had to yield to a car. Given the Mustang's potential collectability value, the padlock probably made a lot of sense.

"Can I help you?"

I turned toward the voice. A woman in her late twenties, medium height, with page-boy brown hair watched me through the screened back door of the house.

"Are you Leah Anne?"

"That might depend on the gentleman doing the asking?"

She ended the sentence with a lilt, but more elaborately polite than flirty. I went toward her, taking my identification holder out from my pocket and extending it long before I reached her.

The woman half-opened the door and took the holder from me, mouthing the words on my ID as the scent of roasting duck wafted through the kitchen behind her. She was wearing an inexpensive dress but nice jewelry, her legs shapely over two-inch heels. I glanced around the backyard. Two of those white resin lawn chairs and a TV tray stood in the grass, as though two people often sat there but never had company over.

She closed my folder and returned it. "What does a private investigator want with me?"

"It's about George."

"Oh?"

"He is missing, right, Ms . . . ?"

"Oh! I'm terribly sorry. It is Leah Anne. Leah Anne Darcelay?"

Another questioning lilt as she gave me her hand. A little dry, very delicate.

I said, "Could we step inside?"

Darcelay looked over her shoulder. "I'm afraid the duck is making the kitchen an oven today. Perhaps the lawn furniture?"

"Sure."

She led me to the little arrangement but didn't sit. "Can I offer you some lemonade?"

My day for citric acid. "Thank you."

"I'll be just a moment."

She walked back to the house with a bounce in her step. As Rosa Echevarría said, Leah Anne had a tight . . . figure.

Darcelay came out in a minute carrying a carved oak tray with a plastic pitcher and two simple tumblers filled with ice. There was a green leaf crushed in the bottom of each glass.

"My mother always put mint in her lemonade, and I've never varied from her good example."

Darcelay poured for both of us, then replaced the pitcher carefully on the tray. "My mother's also."

"I'm sorry?"

"This tray. An heirloom of sorts. I'm told it dates from just after the War Between the States."

She sat down, brown eyes on me. "Now, how can I help you, Mr. Cuddy?"

"When was the last time you saw George Malloy?"

"Tuesday morning. He left for work quite early. Didn't even want me to get up and make his breakfast."

"You saw him leave?"

"From the bedroom window. He pulled out in his car, top down because it was such a fine day, like today. He waved to me as he drove away."

"You seem very calm, Ms. Darcelay."

She took a dainty sip of lemonade. "I am resigned, Mr. Cuddy."

"What do you mean?"

"Well, I don't want to sound fatalistic, but I don't believe George is . . . missing on his own account?"

"You don't."

"Nossir. I believe something happened to George somewhere."

"Why?"

"Because of what he left behind."

"Such as?"

"Me."

Darcelay smiled, very politely.

"Anything else?"

"Yes. His pipe collection in the living room. His bicycle in the garage. His clothes in our bedroom."

"Perhaps he wanted to . . . make a clean break of it."

"Nossir. Nossir, you don't know George. He is a very forthright man. I cannot imagine him leaving me here, but if he decided to do it, he would have fessed up, face to face."

The same thing Cherie Malloy had said about him. "Have you been to the police?"

"I called them Tuesday evening, after George missed dinner. I'd cooked a beef roast, and it was his favorite, and he would never have missed it, even for a big business deal. The police told me I had to wait some further period of time before they could take a report on him."

"How about after that?"

"I called them again after his wife—oh. Oh, my. You must be working for Cherie, then?"

"Go on."

"Well, I called them again after Cherie said he had missed his obligation. George believes very firmly in obligations, Mr. Cuddy."

"Did you call his office?"

"No. No, they called me here. A Miss DeNapoli?"

"Debby DeNapoli?"

"Perhaps. She seemed quite upset about George."

"She tell you why?"

"Why she was upset?"

"Yes."

"I assume because she was worried about him, too."

"George have any good friends at the office?"

"He often spoke about someone named Sam. A Jewish last name, I believe."

Sam Steinfeld, according to Cherie Malloy. "Had George . . . gone off before?"

"Nossir. George was a solid man, Mr. Cuddy. Solid. We were saving toward a down payment on a real . . . on another home, so as to move up to a better neighborhood? He was quite attentive to his work."

"Would you mind if I saw the inside of the house?"

"Why . . . no, no if you believe it would help you."

Darcelay stood and set down her drink. I did the same, then followed her into the kitchen. I could see what she meant about moving up. The room was immaculate, but the cabinets were warped, the stove roasting the duck was an old gas range, and the refrigerator a narrow jobbie like the one in the condo I rented.

We started with the living room. Cheap, mismatched furniture with striking accessories like the old oak tray. Next to the best chair in the room was a rack of pipes and a couple of folded pouches, that thick, cherry flavor of pipe tobacco in the air.

Upstairs was a bedroom with a queen-sized four-poster covered by an elaborate, frilled comforter that looked custom-made. Across the hall was a sewing room/home office with accompanying, tinny furnishings. The clothes in the closets were carefully ironed and hung at one-inch intervals.

Even the bathroom was spotless.

"Basement?"

"Of course."

We went back downstairs and down again. Hot water heater and other guts of the house. A few tools on a pegboard, none of them looking much used except a wrench and a screwdriver. I fingered them.

"George uses those for his bicycle."

"In the garage."

"Yes."

"Anything else out there?"

"More tools, some car things. George keeps it padlocked, on account of the bicycle and the Mustang?"

"You have a key?"

"I did have, but I lost it, and he keeps the only other one with him."

I headed toward the stairs to the first floor. "George ride his bicycle around here?"

Darcelay followed me up. "Nossir. He likes to go over to the river."

"How does he get there?"

"Sometimes he rides it, sometimes he takes it on this metal contraption he straps to the trunk of the car."

Back upstairs, I smelled something burning from the kitchen. Darcelay hurried past me.

She opened the door to the oven, some smoke coming out. "I am afraid this stove is not quite reliable any more."

"Thanks for your time, Ms. Darcelay."

"You'll be going then?"

"Yes."

"Would you like to take some duck with you?"

"No, thanks."

"Even a little singed, it's quite a good recipe. Cooking and keeping a house, that's what I'm best at."

Leah Anne Darcelay gave me a brave little smile. I turned to leave just as the corners of her eyes welled up, maybe from the smoke.

Five

I parked at the curb in front of the DeNapoli Real Estate Agency by nine-thirty Thursday morning. The agency appeared to occupy all of a modest but perfectly restored clapboard colonial, white with green shutters. There didn't seem to be very much going on, just one car in the parking lot that had been paved over the right sideyard of the house. That one car was a beauty, though. A four-door Mercedes, black with tan interior.

Pushing open the heavy entrance door, I saw a woman barely into her twenties behind a reception desk inside the foyer. She had long brown hair drawn back and slightly frizzed over a silk blouse that had to stretch a bit to cross her chest. Her eyes were big and green, but the make-up couldn't quite cover the bags under them nor do much for the bloodshot look in them. There was a small brass plaque on her desk that said "BECCA."

The woman said, "Can I help you?"

"I'd like to see Mr. Steinfeld."

"Sam—uh, Mr. Steinfeld isn't in today." Her hand reached for a pink pad. "Would you like to leave a message?"

"Actually, I'm really looking for George Malloy."

Malloy's name pushed a button inside her. She swallowed with some difficulty and picked up the telephone. "Debby? There's a Mister . . . ?"

Becca looked up sheepishly, like I shouldn't think she was always like this.

I said, "Cuddy. John Cuddy."

Into the phone, Becca said, "There's a Mr. John Cuddy here to see George."

Becca's voice had a little trouble with his first name, but she nodded into the phone and looked back up at me. "Ms. DeNapoli will be right out."

Becca wasn't wrong. If I'd wanted to sit down, I wouldn't have had time before a compact woman in a blue pants suit appeared in a doorway that looked as though it would lead to the biggest room on the floor. She was my age or a little older, with sharp eyes and big earrings and what would have been called a Pixie haircut when the Beatles were on Ed Sullivan.

DeNapoli came forward and extended her hand. "Debby DeNapoli, Mr. Cuddy."

We shook firmly. At that range, she looked awfully tired for the shank of the morning, and I thought about Leah Anne Darcelay telling me how upset DeNapoli had been on the telephone.

George's boss said, "Becca, please hold my calls," and used her head to ask me to follow her back toward the doorway.

DeNapoli's office had a bay window looking out toward the street and French doors on the other side of the room. The doors led onto a flagstone patio, a small marble fountain in the center of it and rose bushes surrounding it. The office itself was done in mahogany and oxblood leather, brass tacks anchoring the seams of three easy chairs that paid homage to the desk like the Magi at the Manger. DeNapoli used her head again, this time to gesture me toward one of the easy chairs as she took the desk chair.

"You're looking for George?"

I sat down. "That's right."

"You're not a client of this office."

DeNapoli said it like she didn't need me to confirm it.

I decided to wait her out.

She watched me, pursing her lips. "Police?"

"No. Private investigator."

"You have any identification?"

I took it out and handed it across the desk. DeNapoli glanced at it, like she'd seen one before, then closed it and tossed it back toward me. Not rudely. More like she just couldn't spare the energy to get up.

"What's this about, Mr. Cuddy?"

"I've been asked to look for George Malloy."

DeNapoli watched me some more.

I said, "Given how you and Becca out there seem to be taking it, though, somehow I think there's more to it than employee absenteeism."

DeNapoli closed her eyes and was so still that for a second I was afraid she'd fallen asleep. Then the eyes came open abruptly. "Do you have any idea where George is?"

"Not yet."

DeNapoli breathed very slowly. "I haven't called the police. The newspapers would . . . it could ruin my business, it gets out."

"What did George do, Ms. DeNapoli?"

This time she huffed out a breath. "I've spent twenty years building this business, Mr. Cuddy. Took it over after my father died. We've been rock solid, all the time he ran the agency, all the time since."

"Until now."

DeNapoli let her chin drop and used the index fingers of both hands to rub her temples. "This was supposed to be my vacation week. Down at the Cape. I take one week a month in the summer. I'm down there, I get a call from Becca on Tuesday, saying the bank is a little concerned about something. I call my banker, guy I've known since high school. He tells me two of my brokers came into a branch of the bank Monday afternoon just after lunch. He tells me one of them's George Malloy. George goes to an assistant manager at this branch, uses his signature authority to get a certified check drawn from our escrow fund there. You know what that is?"

"Where you park other people's money pending closings?"

"Right. We had three sales pending at the time, which is damned good for this market. So, we had one-sixty in the escrow, and George gets a certified for one-fifty of that."

"A hundred-fifty thousand."

"Right. Certifieds, you use them all the time. The assistant manager knows George, doesn't think anything of it."

"But?"

"But there's no closing scheduled on any of those deals right now. Plus, it seems George and the other broker leave that branch, and like an hour later the certified is cashed at another branch."

"Cashed for one-fifty?"

"This market, it happens."

"Do I get to guess whose signature is on the check?"

DeNapoli closed her eyes.

I said, "So it's three o'clock Monday afternoon, and George Malloy has a bagful of cash that isn't his."

"And isn't mine, either, except the agency's responsible for it."

"You have George bonded?"

The eyes opened. "Of course. The surety company, it'll make the money good for the clients. But if this gets out . . . "

"It won't if I can help it, Ms. DeNapoli."

"I don't know who you're working for, but I wouldn't mind you telling me when you find George."

"Any idea at all where he could be?"

DeNapoli pursed her lips again. "Becca wasn't sitting where you came in, crying her eyes out every ten minutes, I'd have said he was with her."

"Office romance?"

"She's just a kid, and George is married—still married to somebody, living with somebody else. I never put my foot down. I mean, it's a free country, and both of them were doing their jobs just fine, but it was hard not to notice them kind of disappearing around lunchtime."

Georgie-boy, Georgie-boy. "The other broker at the bank. Sam Steinfeld?"

"That's right."

"Is he gone, too?"

"Tuesday, after Becca calls me, I drive back from the Cape like a bat out of hell and drag him in here. Sam says he rode to lunch with George and then went into the bank with him after lunch on Monday, but wasn't paying any attention what George was doing. Sam says he didn't have any customers that afternoon, so he decided to call it a day and asked George to just drop him home." DeNapoli shook her head. "That's why I can only take a week at a time. While the cat's away, the mice run wild, you know?"

"So Steinfeld claims he wasn't with Malloy for the check cashing."

"And the guy at the bank that did the cashing says he saw only George."

Which didn't mean the other broker wasn't out in the Mustang, waiting for Malloy to leave the bank. "Where's Steinfeld now?"

"I sent him home Tuesday. Told him to take a couple of vacation days till I could sort this thing out."

"You're thinking either Malloy or Steinfeld took the money Monday and you haven't called the cops yet?"

"They worked for me, both of them. I put bread in their mouths and roofs over their heads, all right? It's a little hard to accept one of them, or both of them, stealing from me."

"I were you, I'd call the surety company on the bond. They have notice of claim requirements."

Close to a smile. "Thanks. I spent most of Tuesday night reading through the policy, then getting my lawyer out of some fishing camp up in Maine there so she could read it, too." DeNapoli's lips went back to the pursed look. "Anything else?"

"Two things. I want to talk with Becca."

"Brace yourself for a flood. What's the other thing?"

"Sam Steinfeld's home address."

Six

"But I didn't know he was gonna steal it! I thought he . . . saved it, you know?"

I waited while Becca used the third Kleenex she'd pulled from the little cellophane packet. We were sitting in the conference room of the DeNapoli agency, door shut, air a little close between Becca's perfume and emotions.

I said, "Where were you and Malloy supposed to run off to?"

A sniffle. "George said, 'Let's just let the road take us where it will.' "

Poetic. "Becca, how did you think George Malloy saved so much money on his commissions?"

"He was just so . . . smooth. He said everything with like, confidence, I dunno. I was in love with him, I wanted to believe in him, too."

"What was the deal?"

A swipe of the Kleenex under her nose. "The deal?"

"How were you going to meet up with him?"

"Oh. He was supposed to pick me up Monday night, and we'd drive through the night till he figured we were far enough away to stop, get a room and some . . . sleep."

"Monday night?"

"Yeah."

Leah Anne Darcelay had said he'd taken off Tuesday morning. "You and George have any back-up plan?"

"Un-unh. It was gonna be simple, see? He packs his stuff Monday night, picks me up, then we take off."

Except his stuff never got packed, and he hung around till Tuesday morning. "He wasn't supposed to give you a call, let you know he'd be to your place in ten minutes or whatever?"

"Un-unh." Becca reached for another Kleenex.

"When he didn't show up on Monday night, what did you do?"

"I waited, and I worried. I couldn't exactly call *him*, you know?"

"Because he'd be at his house."

"With that woman he was with."

Becca said it with a little more bite than I thought her own glass house could tolerate.

"How friendly was George with Sam Steinfeld?"

A shrug. "I dunno. They were friends, did a lot of stuff together after Sam's divorce."

"When was that?"

"I dunno, six, eight months ago. Terrible thing, he had like three kids, teenagers. His wife and the kids moved back to her parents out-of-state somewheres, left Sam with his house all to himself."

And probably a hell of a court-ordered support burden. "Sam have money problems?"

"It's a recession, okay? Everybody's got money problems."

"Except for George Malloy, who 'saved' all that money."

Becca shook her head and reached for the last of the Kleenex.

Seven

Sam Steinfeld's address turned out to be a split-level on a nice block with a manicured lawn and two-car garage, double door up. Inside the garage slumped a four-door Chevy the vintage of my Prelude. The sedan looked like a horse in the barn at the end of a long day on the trail. The other stall had no car but lots of gardening implements and tools spread over it, as though it had been a while since the Chevy had a stablemate. As I walked toward the front door, I heard the sound of an electric drill from the back of the house, so I wound around the garage past some flower beds.

The backyard was a postage stamp, but even its small space was being filled by a partially constructed deck. All the concrete footings were embedded in the ground, small metal shafts projecting above half of them. The other half already had wooden posts mounted on them. A stocky man with curly black hair and a sleeveless sweatshirt was holding a yellow object in his hand like a Flash Gordon ray gun. He unplugged it from the long orange extension cord and walked toward me, stepping over some pressure-treated decking boards that awaited the other wooden posts going in to support them.

"Help you with something?"

"Sam Steinfeld?"

"That's right."

"My name's John Cuddy." I inclined my head toward the deck. "Nice work so far."

Steinfeld ran a burly forearm over his brow, moving some sweat around. "Always liked working with tools. Had a few days coming to me, so I figured, get a jump on the job while the weather's still good."

"Debby DeNapoli already told me why you have a few days off."

Steinfeld gritted his teeth. "I'll sue her. I'll sue her for libel."

"Slander."

"Huh?"

"It's libel if somebody writes it about you, slander if they just say it."

"You a lawyer?"

"Private investigator. I'm trying to find George Malloy."

"Malloy?" Steinfeld turned away to spit, vigorously but politely. "That's what I think of my good friend George Malloy."

"Want to tell me about it?"

"Why should I?"

"Be good practice for when you have to explain things to the police."

Steinfeld considered that. "Okay. But not too long."

"So you can get back to the deck."

"That's right."

"You have any idea Malloy was pulling an embezzlement?"

"Hell, no. Monday, he asks me, do I want to have some lunch, and I say sure. So we do, have a couple of pops at this pub, then he says he has to stop at the bank. I go in with him, kind of talk with this cute teller while he's doing something with one of the manager guys. Then he gives me a lift home here."

"And you start on the deck."

"I go out and figure the materials I need and buy them."

"Malloy never let on what he was going to do?"

"Hell, no. I'm telling you, he set me up."

"Set you up how?"

"He has me go into the bank with him, to get the check, Debby says. I never see it, he never mentions it. Understand?"

"He uses you as cover for what he's doing."

"Right, right. So nobody'll suspect him. All the time, though, he's using me, make me look bad, maybe deflect some attention over to me."

"You knew about him and Becca?"

"Becca? Of course I did. Have to be blind not to. Understand, George is the kind of guy, he sees something he wants, he goes after it."

"Like with the classic car."

"George got that car, I told him, it's not practical, George. The clients, they like to ride around in air-conditioning, plenty of legroom. Well, turns out a lot of clients are like you and me. They remember that car from when they were young, it makes them feel good."

"But that's not why Malloy got it."

"Hell, no. The car, the clothes, the women. Chasing on the side got me divorced. Chasing things, anything, that's what George lives for."

I took in the house. "Big place to rattle around in by yourself."

"Huh. This economy, it's cheaper for me to live in it than try to sell it or rent it. Besides, I got used to having a house for all my tools and stuff. Couldn't get used to an apartment or condo if I tried."

"Still, must be a heavy nut to make each month, carrying this place and supporting the wife and kids someplace else."

Steinfeld squinted at me, clenching his fist. "What does that have to do with George bugging out?"

"You think that's what happened?"

"Think? I know that's what happened. He got a idea of something he wanted, he went after it."

"But left without Becca."

"Who knows. Maybe he had another one besides her on the side."

Something clicked. "Malloy ever mention a woman who lived across the street from him?"

"Just some Hispanic. Said she looked like a hot number but she worked with his ex—"

"His wife, you mean."

"Yeah. I remember him saying he wouldn't mind giving her a try, but she had a problem with his wife being her friend and all."

"She had the problem."

"Right. Georgie-boy, he didn't have what you and I might call scruples, understand?"

I looked down at the concrete footings peeking above the grass line. "How long do you have to let those cure before you can work on them?"

Steinfeld looked at me strangely. "Not that long. They been in a while."

"How long?"

He looked down at his drill. "Since Tuesday afternoon."

Eight

When I got back to my office, there was a message on my answering service to call Earl Pingry at the Stolen Car Unit.

"Pingry."

"Earl, John Cuddy."

"Ah, the man representing Ulysses S. Grant."

"The same, Earl. What've you got?"

"Got your vehicle."

"How?"

"Punk was driving the Mustang around Beacon Hill. Showing off, you can believe it. Punk runs a light on Charles, broadsides a car coming down Beacon Street itself."

"Car wrecked?"

"Not too bad. Just lousy luck for the punk."

"Hurt?"

"Hurt? Oh, no, man. Nothing like that. Though he almost was."

"I don't get you."

"The car he broadsides belongs to an Area A cop, just made the last payment on it this month. My brother officer spread-eagles the punk over the trunk of the Mustang, probably would have busted his skull there weren't twenty witnesses around."

"Where's the punk now?"

"Area A. Want to talk to him?"

"If I can."

"Just go on down there, use my name."

"Thanks, Earl. You have his name?"

"The punk?"

"Right."

"Yeah, hold . . . on . . . just—here it is. Tough one. 'Etcha-*var*-ya, Miguel.' "

I let out a breath. "Earl, I think it's pronounced 'Et-chay-varr-*ee*-ah.'"

❖ ❖ ❖

The interrogation room table at Area A looked as though it had been a training ground for foul-mouthed termites. Miguel Echevarría, dressed in jeans and a Miami Sound Machine tee shirt, scowled up at me from a battered wooden chair. The detective who brought me into the room was named Milano. She stood behind Echevarría, leaning her head against the wall, while a male detective named Quinn sat at the end of the table and smiled at him. I wouldn't have wanted Quinn smiling at me like that.

Milano had cleared me in the hall to speak to Echevarría, who apparently hadn't wanted a lawyer present for any of this because he "didn't do nothing to worry about."

I sat across from Echevarría, Milano still taking up some wall space, Quinn still just smiling.

I said, "Miguel."

"Who say you get to use my first name?"

"I do," said Quinn.

Echevarría didn't like Quinn's smile, either.

I said, "Miguel, how did you get ahold of George Malloy's car?"

"Was sitting in his driveway, man. Waiting for me, like."

"Where was Malloy?"

"How am I supposed to know?"

"Weren't you afraid he'd see you boosting the car and recognize you?"

"Didn't take no time at all, man."

"To pop the ignition and—"

Echevarría came forward in the chair. "Didn't have to, man. Keys were in it. Like I didn't really steal the thing at all, man."

Quinn chuckled, deep in his throat, never breaking the smile. Milano held up a key ring with a miniature Mustang on it, jingling it like a little hand bell.

I said to her, "Can I see those?"

She dropped them into my palm. Besides the car token, it had two car keys, a house key, and a heavier, office-style key. I hefted them, thinking, until Milano asked for them back.

I turned to Echevarría. "The keys were in the car."

"Like I said, man."

"When did you take it?"

"Couple days ago."

"Which day?"

"I don't know, man. Was the day before I seen you hanging around my mother."

"The day before you saw me in the booth at the coffeeshop."

"Right."

"That means you took the car Tuesday."

Echevarría hooded his eyes, got cagey. "You say so."

Quinn said, "Don't you just love him?"

Milano grunted, like it wasn't the first time she'd heard Quinn use the line.

I said, "Why'd you take the car, Miguel?"

"It was there."

"Was it because of the way Malloy looked at your mother?"

Echevarría was up and reaching across for me. Quinn was a beat slow, but Milano had both hands on Echevarría's shoulder from behind, like a dance step they'd practiced. She slammed him back down again hard enough to compact his spine.

Echevarría grimaced and twisted in the chair, but spoke only Spanish to us for a minute. Even Quinn cut him a little slack before saying, "Now in English, braintrust."

I waited for Echevarría to stare him down a minute. Then, "Miguel?"

He looked back at me.

"Miguel, where did you keep the car the last few days?"

"Friend of mine, he's got this old garage. I kept it there."

"Why?"

Echevarría gave me a disgusted look. "Fresh car like that wouldn't last ten minutes on the street, man. I wanted to cruise the wheels for a while, you know?"

I thought about it. There was one way it all made sense, maybe. To the detective, I said, "Either of you see the Mustang at the accident scene?"

Quinn said, "I saw it when they were towing it away."

"Was there a bicycle carrier on the back of it?"

"No."

I turned to Echevarría, who was looking at me wide-eyed. "Miguel, when you took the car, it had a bicycle carrier on the back of it, right?"

The eyes got wider. "How'd you know that, man?"

"So it did."

"Yeah. The mother', he use the rack thing to carry his bike when he go for a ride on it."

"What happened to the carrier?"

"I took it off, man."

"Why?"

Echevarría looked at Quinn and me. "Spoils the image, you know?"

✦ ✦ ✦

Milano told me they'd gotten a call that Echevarría's mother was on her way. I sat in the area just inside the stationhouse door until I saw Rosa and my client bustle in, still wearing their black and white waitress uniforms.

When I stood up, Rosa noticed me and stopped dead. Her face had aged a couple of years in the few days since I'd seen her, and she lost another few months examining mine for news about her son.

"Miguel, is he . . ."

"He's all right, Rosa."

Cherie Malloy said, "What are you doing here?"

I looked at her. "It would help if I could talk to Rosa for a minute in private."

Rosa looked bewildered but eager, Cherie shaking her head but saying, "Sure, sure. Whatever you say."

I drew Rosa off to the side while Cherie Malloy took my seat on the bench.

Echevarría said, "What is happening here?"

"You knew Miguel had George's car."

"Not when I talk with you, I don't."

"But you realized it."

"I see him . . . After you talk to me, I see him with the keys, but I . . ." She looked back over her shoulder at Cherie Malloy. "But I don't tell Cherie because I don't want Miguel to get in trouble for it."

"He is in trouble for it, Rosa."

She spoke quickly. "I know he been going off somewhere, doing things. But he always is doing things."

"Rosa, I'm trying to keep this down to just joy-riding."

"Just . . . " Echevarría paused. "What can I do to help my son?"

"Answer an odd question."

"What is it?"

I lowered my voice. "Back at the coffeeshop, you told me you used to watch George Malloy and Leah Anne unloading the groceries at their garage."

Echevarría looked confused. "Yes?"

"Why did they do that?"

Nine

"Veal chops?"

"Why, yes."

"Go through the duck, already?"

"No. No, there's still plenty left."

"Can I have some?"

"Surely can. Come on in."

I followed Leah Anne Darcelay from the back door into the old kitchen. She busied herself pulling a steak knife from a butcher block holder near the sink and a dinner plate from the cabinet over it. From one drawer came a silver fork, beautifully polished, from another a cloth napkin, beautifully ironed. Darcelay laid the place setting on a woven grass mat at one side of the little kitchen table, then turned to the narrow refrigerator. As she opened the door, I could see each wire shelf inside was chock full of cooked meat, wrapped in plastic or baggies and stacked like a carefully-loaded moving van.

Tugging out the duck, Darcelay suddenly stopped and took a breath. She turned to me, forgetting to close the 'fridge. "Oh, Lordy, you've guessed, haven't you?"

I said, "You might want to shut the door."

"Oh. Oh, yes." She did, then placed the duck package very carefully on the table. "Was it something I said?"

"Three things. One, the timing was off. Why would George hang around till Tuesday morning instead of leaving Monday night?"

Darcelay nodded.

"Second, there was no padlock key for the garage on George's keychain when the police took it off the car thief."

Another nod. "Yes. Yes, I needed that, you see. I'd lost mine, as I told you?"

My turn to stop. A little more slowly, I said, "The third was you saying you watched him drive off Tuesday morning. It didn't fit with what the car thief said."

Darcelay didn't nod. "You would take the word of a car thief over mine?"

"You left the keys in the car."

This time I got the nod. "It was very difficult. I can't drive, and I knew that no one would believe George had disappeared if his car was still here. I was sure that if I left the keys in the Mustang one of the degenerate children in this neighborhood would steal it and leave it somewhere vile."

"At which point the police would try to trace George from wherever the car was found."

"But the body, that was even harder, you see."

"Heavy."

"Oh, my yes. Too heavy to carry him anywhere."

I inclined my head toward the garage. "George went out there to get his bicycle, leaning against the . . . freezer."

"Yes. He was going to take everything he really cared about and run off with that . . . secretary. He told me here, right here in my own kitchen. Then he went off with his keys in hand, opening the padlock on the garage, going inside, taking out the rack, mounting it on the car. All . . . routine, like he was just going for a short bike ride before sitting down to the lovely meal I'd cooked for him."

"And you had to cook quite a few meals after that."

"Oh, my, yes. George barely fit in the freezer, even with all the roasts taken out. And this little refrigerator, it has such a small freezer compartment? I've had to cook up a storm, I'll tell you." Darcelay bit her lower lip. "I'm afraid I'm going to lose the turkey to the heat, though."

Very quietly, I said, "The money?"

"Oh. Oh, that's what really did it, you know? It's in a suitcase upstairs. I tried to put it under the mattress, like you see in the movies. But there was so much of it, the comforter would ride up and look too short for the bed?"

I think I just stared at her.

"I'm not sure what I would have done if I hadn't followed George out to the garage. But he was home so early, really quite early for him. And he marched out there in that forthright manner of his." Darcelay mocked a toy soldier's stiff arm movements. "And I followed him and asked him what he was doing. And he just began explaining how he was leaving and putting that rack on the car with a screwdriver and when he came back into the garage he set down the screwdriver and reached into his pocket and took out this wad of bills and began counting them off and then he tried to give them to me, telling me this would 'tide me over,' pushing them on me like I was some . . . some *whore* he was paying off and so I grabbed the screwdriver and then I . . . I . . ."

Leah Anne Darcelay picked up the steak knife from my place setting and tried to show me.

THE WINFIELD TRADE

One

Venetia Scott said, "Slow down a bit and take this next right."

I looked over to her. "Much farther?"

She shook her head. "Not more than a mile now. I really *do* appreciate your driving me from work, Mr. Cuddy."

My new client said it like she was thanking a waiter for bringing her an extra cocktail napkin. About five-five and mid-thirties, Scott looked trim in a gray herringbone suit with a ruffled white blouse and two-inch heels. Her face was thin, but she had big green eyes and generous lips and auburn hair drawn back into a bun that hinted at shoulder length once loosened.

Scott had called me at my office. A lawyer who represented her bank in major loan deals had recommended me as a private investigator who could be trusted on a confidential matter. I told her I'd call her back, then dialed the lawyer. Venetia Scott had checked out as a recently promoted vice president in charge of computer lease agreements for one of the few Boston financial institutions still taking nourishment without government receivership. I'd picked her up just fifteen minutes ago outside one of the bank's branches, filling up the time more with small talk than business as she gave me directions to her home address.

"Ms. Scott, I take it whatever you want me to work on has to do with your house?"

"It does."

"Just what, exactly?"

My client took a deep breath. "Beginning about a month ago, someone has been staying there while I've been away on weekends."

It was Thursday as we were talking. "How do you know?"

"Little things. And feelings. I'm *very* sensitive that way."

Jesus. "Do you live alone?"

An icy tone. "What difference does that make?"

"What I mean is, could somebody else in the house be responsible?"

"No. Since my divorce, I live alone except for Winfield."

"Winfield?"

"My cat."

I smiled. "Named after Dave?"

"I beg your pardon?"

"Dave Winfield. Yankee outfielder who was unhappy in New York, moved to a couple of other teams since."

The icy tone again. "Winfield is not named after an *athlete*. He is named after Winfield Scott, a general in the Mexican-American War. I'm a traceable descendant."

"Oh."

✦ ✦ ✦

The cat turned out to be a tubby orange tabby with yellow eyes and long whiskers. He was affectionate enough, brushing against my pant cuffs and purring like a snoring lumberjack when I scratched between his ears.

We were in the foyer of Scott's modest Cape Cod, the smallest house in a good neighborhood. A terrific investment in the mid-eighties, it was probably holding its value as well as could be expected now. I'd checked the front door on our way in. No sign of forced entry.

Scott walked me through a living room with colonial furniture, including an old-fashioned slider chair, to a kitchen extended via a deck into the back-yard. The back door lock and jamb looked fine, too.

"You keep your windows locked?"

"Always."

"Security system?"

"No."

I stepped out onto the deck and looked left, then right. Each bordering house was nestled on about an acre, hers only a half-acre by the looks of the landscaping that acted as boundary lines.

"Neighbors?"

Scott pointed left. "That place has been empty for three months. Foreclosure, but not by my bank." She swung right. "The couple on the other side have been in Florida for six weeks. Which is my point, really."

"Your point?"

"Yes. If someone simply wanted to break into a house and occupy it like a *squatter*, there are better choices within easy reach. No, Mr. Cuddy, this is harassment."

"Harassment."

"Yes. Subtle, but clear."

"Could you share some of the subtleties with me?"

A labored sigh. "Toilet paper roll just *slightly* out of kilter."

I looked down at Winfield, who had followed us from room to room. "Maybe the cat, toying with it?"

The icy tone a third time. "Water glasses rinsed and dried, leaving no spots. Forks placed in drawer tines down rather than tines up."

"Forks?"

"I beg your—"

"Forks plural, or just one each time?"

"Just one."

"Same for glasses?"

"Yes."

We moved back into the living room. "You think it's harassment, you must have somebody in mind."

"*Three* somebodies. Do you wish to take notes?"

I sat down in the slider chair. Comfortable and silent.

Scott used her left hand to tick off names on her right, as though she were vigorously polishing her nails. "First, Chris Murphy, my ex-husband. He's a police officer in the next town."

Uh-oh. "He still have a set of keys to this place?"

"No. The locks have been changed twice."

"Twice?"

"Yes. Once after the judge ordered him out during the divorce three years ago, and again five weeks ago."

"Just before you noticed the 'subtle harassment.' "

"Exactly. That brings me to the second—what would you call it, 'suspect'?"

"The second person will do fine."

"Second is Luther Dane, my assistant at the bank. I lost my keys at work, which was the reason I had the locks changed again. Luther would have access to my new key."

"This Dane have any motive?"

"Yes. He would love to see me foul up due to pressure here so that he could get my job."

"Is that realistic?"

"It's how I got *my* promotion."

"By forcing out a boss?"

"Precisely. Which brings us to number three, Irene Presker."

"Your former boss."

A nod. "I'm sure she has it in for me after I nudged her out."

I found myself rooting for Presker but fought it. "She have access to your keys?"

"Not that I know of."

"Who was the locksmith this last time?"

A wave of the hand. "A nice man, got on *famously* with Winfield.

Vietnamese, I think. He came by to change the locks on a Friday just as I was leaving."

"And the next week, the live-in stuff began happening."

"The next weekend."

"Why is it that you go away weekends, Ms. Scott?"

She glanced involuntarily toward a shelf on the wall. I could see a framed photo of Scott in casual clothes, hugging a handsome man of about fifty with gray hair that looked carefully styled even in the breeze that lifted it.

My client said, "I'm seeing a man who's allergic to cat dander, so I spend weekends at his home."

"Name?"

"I don't want you approaching him."

"I'd just like his name in case it comes up."

"Evan Speidel."

I looked at the photo again and took a guess. "Also in banking?"

"Yes. He'll be the next president of Ridgeview Savings and Loan, a *solid* institution."

Scott put more into "solid" than I could have with a hammer.

"Speidel have a key to your house?"

The icy tone got glacial. "I keep a spare at his home."

I glanced down at the cat. "Why not just give Winfield away?"

My client glared at me. "I bought him for Chris originally, but Winfield stayed with me as part of the divorce settlement."

I chewed on that a while.

"If you're thinking that Evan has anything to do with this, forget it."

Actually, I was thinking that Venetia Scott might have been better off with the cop that liked cats than the banker who couldn't, but I kept it to myself.

Two

On Friday morning I got up early and went over the addresses Venetia Scott had given me. Then I drove to the downtown area nearest her house.

The sign over the glass door said "Main Street Locksmith" in tintype. The walls of the six-by-seven shop were lined with brass knobs and sturdy plates and imposing deadbolts. A skinny man with Southeast Asian features sat behind a steel counter with an English-language newspaper open in front of him. His black hair hung over his forehead almost to his eyebrows, and he worked a bony index finger one word at a time through a column that had the phrase "Khmer Rouge" in its headline. Behind him, purple beads, strung vertically on wire, curtained entry to the back of the shop. The beads shimmered a little as I closed the front door.

The man looked up at me, smiled and said, "Can I help, sir?"

I said, "Mister . . ."

"Hun is my name."

I showed him my ID. He looked at it a long time, reading "John Francis Cuddy" as carefully as he had the newspaper.

"What you want?"

I pocketed the leather holder and explained that I was asking questions for Venetia Scott.

Hun's eyes grew wary. "Ms. Scott?"

"Yes."

"What is problem?"

"No problem for you. I'd just like to ask you a few questions."

Hun looked resigned. "Ask."

I pointed at the article he'd been reading. "You're from Cambodia originally?"

"Why that matter?"

"No reason, except you're reading an article about the Khmer Rouge."

Hun's jaw clenched. "I no need to read about Khmer Rouge. I live through Khmer Rouge. In Phnom Penh, then in camp, then in jungle." He stabbed the paper with the tip of his finger. "Newspaper used to say two million people kill by Pol Pot. Now say only one million. How can this be?"

I didn't have an answer for him. "You changed the locks at Ms. Scott's home?"

"Yes, I do that for her."

"Anybody ever ask you for keys to the house?"

Hun's eyes widened. "Ask me?"

"Yes."

"Nobody."

I went through the names I had, including the new boyfriend, Evan Speidel. Hun shook his head no, the eyes stony at each one. I got the feeling that other interrogators hadn't treated him so well in the past.

"Anyone else here I could talk to?"

Hun's eyes went back down to the article. "Is nobody else. Only me."

✦ ✦ ✦

Chris Murphy, about six-two and two hundred pounds, looked like a surfer who was losing his dishwater blond hair. And his temper at me.

"Cuddy, I don't get why you're asking me all these questions."

"I'm hired to ask questions. These are simple ones."

"Simple, huh? Like am I harassing my ex-wife and you won't even tell me what I'm supposed to be doing?"

I'd called Murphy at police headquarters in the neighboring town, then waited for him outside, as he'd asked me to. We were standing next to a dented, five-year-old Corvette that I took to be his car. Murphy had his arms crossed, beefy hands working on the outside of his sportscoat.

"Murphy—"

"I mean, the hell position am I in with the department, I get accused of harassing my ex-, this day and age?"

"So you haven't been in any kind of contact with Venetia Scott."

"No, I told you. Not her, not the bank, not the house. Not since the restraining order way back when."

I hadn't mentioned the house.

Murphy said, "You think I'm nuts or something, a cop violating a restraining order?"

I didn't think he was nuts. I did wonder how he and Venetia Scott ever got together, but I wasn't sure I wanted to find out.

"Seen your cat lately?"

"My—Winfield? Hell, that little bugger still around?"

"How do you mean?"

"Aw, Venny, she never cared much one way or the other for the cat. Just like another pawn in the chess game between her lawyer and me."

"Because you wanted him back?"

Murphy looked exasperated. "Cuddy, she held on to him because I made her *think* I wanted him back."

"Why would you do that?"

"So I could get what *I* wanted, like this car, some other stuff to set myself up in a new place."

"While she got the house."

"Right, right. Hell, it was like a negotiating tactic on my part. What do you think, I'm stupid?"

I let that one pass, too.

✦ ✦ ✦

Irene Presker had answered her own telephone and now answered her own door. The condo complex was a nice one, low and by the sea about eight miles south of Boston. From the parking lot, I'd seen a little skyline through the smog in the distance and a couple of playful sailboats through the mist in the foreground.

Presker, however, did not look playful herself. About five feet tall, she was pushing a hundred fifty, mostly through the hips and thighs. Her hair was curly and too black to be natural, the make-up overdone considering she was apparently working at home that day.

Staring at my ID, Presker said, "Which would be easier for me, to talk with you or call the cops?"

"Calling the cops, definitely."

The hint of a grin. "You're really a private investigator?"

"Really and truly."

"All right, come in."

The living room was a little box without fireplace or harbor view, a small, open kitchen cloistered with it. A corridor ran off in one direction toward two closed doors, I assumed a bedroom and a bath. Presker took one barrel chair, me the other, there not being space enough for couch or even loveseat.

"So, what's this about?"

"A former associate of yours is being harassed. Your name came up."

"I'm supposed to know something about 'a former associate' being harassed?"

"That's what I'm here to find out."

"Hah. You wasted your gas. The only one I could . . ." Presker's eyes did grow playful. "Not Venetia Scott?"

"Yes."

"There is a God. I must thank him."

"Ms. Presker—"

"So, is Venny going nuts?"

Venny. The nickname her ex-husband had used. "You're not even curious about what the harassment is?"

"Not unless it's really awful. I'd rather use my imagination."

"Why so down on Scott?"

"Down. Down, now there's a great word for Venny. Put down, shut down, shot down. Lots of possibilities there."

"Possibilities?"

"For who's harassing her. Let me tell you something about your client, Mr. Cuddy. Venny, basically speaking, is a witch. An absolute witch. She begged me to take her on as my assistant at the bank, and her résumé wasn't in the personnel folder before she was laying the groundwork to replace me. Venny sucked up to people, slept with people, whatever it took. Oh yeah, one other thing, too. She really did master the job."

"Which is?"

"Doing loan papers on complicated computer leases. You know the jargon?"

"None of it."

"Then I'll spare you. Just figure that she can understand complicated relationships, technical and financial, then protect the banks as to them."

"And you taught her?"

"That's right."

"And now she's in your office in a downtown skyscraper and you're working out of your house."

"Oh, but I'm con-*sult*-ing." A thick layer of sarcasm coated Presker's voice. "My own *home* office. It's really much *so* much more meaningful and satisfying than a *mere* salary and stock options."

It took me a minute to appreciate that Presker was lampooning Scott's speech patterns.

"Anything you can tell me about who might be after her?"

Presker laughed, not a pleasant sound. "Try the guy who replaced her. Maybe he's learning at the witch's knee."

✦ ✦ ✦

Luther Dane was a young black man with horn-rimmed glasses. I met him sitting at a desk outside Venetia Scott's office in the skyscraper. He looked studious in a blue suit, white button-down shirt and quiet tie. At least until he started talking. Then he both looked and sounded studious.

"I don't have any idea what could be behind this, Mr. Cuddy."

Scott was at a meeting, so Dane and I had moved into her office, a nice view of the beige and gray airport and a verdant harbor island through a window that I was sure couldn't be opened. Dane had taken Scott's desk chair without seeming to think about it. I tried one of the captain's chairs, my shoulders covering the emblem of a local business school emblazoned on the backrest.

"No reason for anyone you know of to be harassing Ms. Scott?"

"Venetia Scott is a warm and wonderful human being."

Dane's words would have sounded fine to a bug planted in the office. His face and body language told a different story, like a Mideast hostage giving a canned television interview.

"You're not interested in scaring her out of her job?"

"Ms. V. Scott does not scare."

"Rattle her then. Enough so she starts to make mistakes here at work."

"Her mistakes would be looked upon as my mistakes, too."

"Not if you created the record correctly."

Dane smiled. "Law school, Mr. Cuddy?"

"A year, nights. You?"

"Four years, nights. Worked long and hard to get this far. I'm not about to pollute my own well."

"So, if you're not interested in scaring or rattling your boss, how do you plan to get ahead?"

"By outworking her. Her and anybody else I'm competing with."

"And you figure you can outwork Ms. Scott."

"The way she's spending her weekends? You bet."

I hadn't said anything about weekends. "How's that?"

"Her weekends, man. She's spending them somewhere else."

"How do you know?"

Dane spread his hands wide, encompassing Scott's office. "Because I come in every Saturday and half a day on Sunday, Mr. Cuddy. I'm here, and she isn't, and that means she's off somewhere."

"Like at her house?"

"Not when I try to reach her there."

"Why would you try to do that?"

Dane shrugged. "Even on weekends, questions come up that I'm not good enough to answer."

"Yet."

Just a smile.

Three

After speaking with Luther Dane, I didn't wait for Venetia Scott to come back from her meeting. Instead I got my car out of hock at the parking garage next to the bank and drove to the suburban town where Ridgeview Savings and Loan had its offices.

I sat outside the red-bricked and gold-domed building for an hour before being rewarded by the appearance of Evan Speidel. He shook two sets of hands on his way from the main entrance to a black Lincoln Continental. Inside the Lincoln, Speidel drove sedately about three miles to a butcher block and ferns saloon just off a busy mall. I parked three slanting rows away from his car and followed him into the restaurant.

When he shook a few more hands and took a table, I slid onto a stool at the bar, the mirror above the top shelf bottles allowing me to watch Speidel in reflection. After a waiter presented him with a *Wall Street Journal* to skim, a cocktail waitress brought him what looked like a dry Manhattan without his having to order it. He glanced up a couple of times, like a man watching for someone to join him.

Someone did.

Irene Presker swooshed through the place, still made up but now dressed like Venetia Scott had been in bankers' tweeds. Speidel took one of Presker's hands in both of his as greeting. Then they sat down across from each other and began talking. I couldn't see any way of getting out of there without her spotting me, so I sat still and nursed a beer.

They talked through a drink and lunch and were about to order dessert when Presker caught me out of the corner of her eye. She barely paused, covering it with a palm-up gesture to support her chins. Waving off coffee, the consultant waited until Speidel covered the tab by signing for it, then shook good-bye with him as he moved toward the exit and she toward the restrooms.

Presker made sure Speidel was gone before reversing direction and steaming up to the bar. "What's the idea of following me?"

"Maybe I didn't believe everything I heard at your condo."

"Does that mean you have to give me a heart attack in the middle of an interview?"

"Interview?"

"The man who just left is—"

Presker stopped, but I hadn't interrupted her.

I said, "Who is he?"

She tapped a stubby finger on my left arm. "He left before I did, but he was here before I was. I would have noticed you taking this stool if you came in after me. That means you were here before me." Presker looked playful again. "And that means that either you've tapped my phone, in which case you wouldn't have bothered covering this little meeting, or you're following my lunch date. But why?"

I got up before I didn't tell Presker anything else, feeling my client might be a little disappointed in me.

✦ ✦ ✦

I sat in my car until Irene Presker came out. She noticed me, as I'd hoped she would, but just blew me a kiss, which meant I wasn't fooling her at all.

I started up and drove back toward the city, thinking as best I could. Chris Murphy might have intimidated Hun the locksmith into giving him the new key to Venetia Scott's house. Murphy also could have used a skeleton master from his department, but where was his motive three years after the divorce? Luther Dane could have lifted the new key some time at work, had it copied, and returned it before Scott realized it was missing, but he really didn't seem to think he needed to reduce his boss to supplant her. Irene Presker might have gotten the spare key to the house from Evan Speidel, in which case her bluff at the bar was one for the record books.

Speidel might be able to slip away from Scott on one of their weekends at his place, but why go to her place to do, essentially, nothing?

Shaking my head, I focussed on the traffic. At least I knew where that was going.

✦ ✦ ✦

Luther Dane's voice said, "Ms. Scott's office."

I said, "May I speak with her?"

"I'll see, Mr. Cuddy."

Good at recognizing voices, Mr. Dane.

"Venetia Scott."

"Can Dane hear us?"

"No."

"You're positive?"

"Yes. What is it?"

"Given that it's Friday, are you going to Speidel's place?"

"Yes. Why?"

"I have an idea."

✦ ✦ ✦

It was something I'd hoped I could avoid. Solo, you can't really watch a house completely from the street or the back or the sides. Short of a high perch, there are just too many blind spots created by the building itself. But, owner willing, you can cover it pretty thoroughly from one place.

Inside it.

In the dark, I sat on the slider in the living room, Winfield curled up on my lap. I'd paced off the strides to both front and back doors. The slider was almost exactly equidistant from each.

It was barely eight o'clock when I heard something at the back door. Winfield jumped off my lap and did his rotund best to scamper out there. I moved to the wall by the kitchen, hoping I wasn't going to need a weapon. I heard the faint sound of door opening, then closing, then nothing.

I waited five seconds. Then ten. At fifteen, I went into the kitchen.

Nobody. Not even Winfield.

I looked out the windows, but didn't see anything. I went back to the living room and sank into the slider. I thought about it, then thought some more. About what I'd told people, and what I hadn't told them.

And eventually I believed I saw it.

✦ ✦ ✦

I knocked on the door to the mini-mansion a second time. Evan Speidel opened it. He was wearing a silk robe that probably cost more than my rent.

"Yes?" Nice baritone voice, too.

"I need to speak with Venetia Scott."

"At this hour?"

"Tell her it's John Cuddy."

The door closed in my face. Two minutes later, Scott reopened it.

Her robe matched Speidel's, her auburn hair indeed tumbling onto her shoulders. "This had better be important."

I stepped inside the house. "It won't take long. There's bad news and good news."

"What's the bad news?"

"I think we've lost Winfield."

I heard Speidel chuckle from the other room, but Scott's face stayed neutral. "That I can live with, I guess. What's the good news?"

"If you'll trust me to guarantee that it's over, I can end it tonight, nobody getting hurt or in trouble."

The executive in Scott stiffened. "Guaranteed?"

"Absolutely. But I keep everything I've learned to myself."

My client took ten seconds to weigh that. "Do it."

✦ ✦ ✦

This time I kept knocking until a shadow loomed in the weak light behind the purple beads. Hun's head peered out, shook, then came forward slowly with the rest of his body as he let me into the shop.

I said, "Where's the cat?"

He thought about toughing it out, then said, "In the back. Where I live."

"Tied up?"

Hun gave me a derisive look and spat out a word I didn't understand. Winfield came running, slowed only a little by the bead curtain, most of which he could get under. He regarded me but cuddled up to Hun.

✦ ✦ ✦

The locksmith said, "How you know it was me?"

"The other people I talked to, the other names I asked you about, I didn't tell any of them the problem had something to do with Ms. Scott's house."

Hun shook his head. "That is not enough."

"No, but Scott said you really liked the cat. And at her house only the smallest things were disturbed, like someone was visiting, not intimidating."

I stopped, but Hun nodded.

I said, "Only the things you would need to give him food and yourself water and relief."

"I like to give him food. I like to visit him."

"And based on what I told you, you might miss the chance to see him again."

"You tell me problem with house, maybe problem with locks. Maybe Ms. Scott not use me next time to change locks. Maybe I cannot see Winfield again without break in."

"Which you didn't want to do."

"I am locksmith! I do not break in houses!"

"But you'd risk your business to see the cat."

Hun reached down to stroke Winfield's head. "I lose my whole family, Khmer Rouge. This cat only creature all United States nice to me."

"So you were willing to trade your profession for being able to have him."

The stony look. "Yes."

"Ever hear of Dave Winfield?"

"Who?"

"Skip it."

SUMMARY JUDGMENT

One

Steven Rothenberg welcomed me back to his law office. Cluttered and shabby, it hadn't changed for the better since the last time I'd been there. Neither had Rothenberg.

His beard was a little more trimmed, but the black was losing its battle with the gray, and what was left of his hair already had surrendered. A suitcoat hung on a battered clothes tree. His tie was tugged down from an unbuttoned collar, his sleeves rolled up twice, almost to the elbows.

Rothenberg sat behind his desk, me taking the chair in front of it. Sunshine from the May afternoon backlit him, a partial view of the Boston Common visible across Boylston Street.

"I remembered you from the Daniels case, Mr. Cuddy."

"You should."

Rothenberg moved his tongue around inside his mouth. "Can I call you John?"

"Sure."

"John, I've got a capital case here, murder one. I'd like you to help me represent my client on it."

"Private or court-appointed?"

"Appointed, but—"

"Be seeing you."

"Wait, wait a minute."

"Look, Mr. Rothenberg—"

"Steve."

I took a breath. "Steve, you can't feed a canary on what the Commonwealth allots for investigation in a court-appointed. You know it, and I know it."

"Yeah. But this one's different."

"How?"

"This guy actually may not have done it."

✦ ✦ ✦

I closed the file folder. "At least your client had enough sense not to talk to the cops."

"A result of his, ah, prior experiences in that regard."

I slid the folder back to Rothenberg. "So I've read the reports. Let's hear your view of it."

The lawyer came forward in the chair, squaring his shoulders for the first rehearsal of a new play. "My client, Jack Funderberk, is a poor homeless man who saved a dog from drowning in the Charles River."

"Said in there the lagoon next to the Charles."

"The lagoon, whatever. It was still January, and therefore freezing and life-threatening to him."

"To Funderberk."

"Right."

"Go on."

"The sole reason my client goes for the swim is because the rich owner of the dog, one Leah Bland, Miss WASP of 1938, offers him a hundred thousand to save Jeeves' life."

"Jeeves was the dog?"

"Yeah."

"That wasn't in there."

"So I'm telling you. The dog's name was Jeeves."

"Like the butler?"

"Like the butler. Anyway, after my client risks—"

"I didn't think he was your client yet."

"He wasn't. I'm getting to that. After Funderberk drags the dog safely to shore, Miss Bland and her nephew Norbert, who was also there but not as intrepid as my client—"

"Lose 'intrepid,' Steve."

"Not as *brave* as my client. Miss Bland reneges on the contract. Funderberk hires this hack named Theodore Moone to represent him."

"The homeless man hires Moone to sue the old woman for breach of contract?"

"Right, right. I don't know how Moone ever got past high school, much less law school. Those papers—the civil case—aren't in there because it's the result that counts. Moone loses the contract action for Funderberk."

Our courts were awfully backlogged. "How'd they get a trial in only four months?"

"They didn't. Miss Bland was represented by Drysdale, Coppinger and Sewell. Know them?"

"Not socially."

"Very funny. Their head guy, Drysdale, and some female associate blow Moone out of the water on summary judgment because Moone files just an 'information-and-belief' counter-affidavit."

My one year of law school was too long ago. "Slow down, Steve."

Rothenberg spread his hands. "All right, it's like this. Drysdale moves for summary judgment just after the complaint is filed, saying basically Moone hasn't got a case because the affidavits of Miss Bland and the nephew show no contract was ever formed. Moone should have filed his client's affidavit, Funderberk's swearing based on personal knowledge that Miss Bland said what she said that day at the river."

"Lagoon."

"Lagoon. Moone instead files his own counter-affidavit, saying in it that he—Moone—has the following facts on 'information and belief.' "

"And that's not good enough."

"Right, right. Summary judgment is like a substitute for trial, so you have to have the people in the affidavits giving the kind of information that would be admissible as testimony at trial."

"The contract case gets bounced out of court on that?"

"Yeah. It would have been a tough one to win anyway, but at least Funderberk should have had his chance before the jury."

"I take it Funderberk finds out that he's lost his hundred thousand."

"Right. So he gets himself a baseball bat and goes calling on Miss Bland."

"Allegedly."

"No. No, he admits he did that. Went to her townhouse over on Marlborough there and banged around the front door a little."

"Then what?"

"Then he claims he went away, came back again and went to the alley door."

"Behind the house."

"Right, right. He bangs some more with the bat. Miss Bland comes out and gives him what for, and he slams the bat down and stalks off."

"He says."

"Right."

"Then what happens?"

"Maybe an hour later, nephew Norbert finds his aunt bludgeoned to death—"

"Lose 'bludgeoned' too, Steve."

"No. No, that's the word the cops said the nephew used. 'Bludgeoned.' " Maybe a Norbert would. "Sorry, go on."

"That's about it. The M.E. and lab reports all mesh. Funderberk's prints on front and back doors. Death by repeated blows to the head. Bat found at the scene with more of his prints all over it, even a couple of hers."

"How do you figure hers?"

"Defending herself, she tries to grab it away. Who knows? In any case, there were clumps of her hair and bits of—"

I held up my hand. "I read that part, too, Steve. What do you expect me to do?"

Rothenberg clasped his fingers behind his head and leaned back. "Nobody saw him do it, John. All they've got is motive, means and opportunity."

"You don't think that'll be enough?"

"I want you to find some reasonable doubt here, something I can take to the mat. Or at least something to bump down the charge, make the prosecutor think he won't be able to persuade twelve citizens good and true that my client whacked Ms. Bland and Jeeves."

"The dog, too?"

Rothenberg moved his tongue around again. "Afraid so."

"The jury isn't going to like the dog, Steve."

"I know."

Two

Detective Sergeant Bonnie Cross sat at a desk in front of Lieutenant Robert Murphy's enclosure in Homicide. Reading a case file, she was wearing a blue blazer over a gray skirt. Brown hair framed a sincere, open face and fell to shoulders just shy of horsy. Before she talked, you'd get the impression that in college all her classmates went to her for advice.

"What," she said, not as a question.

"Lieutenant in?"

"No."

"Coming back?"

"On the Twelfth of Never."

"Vacation."

Cross turned a page in the folder. "Right."

"It's only May. How can he be off already?"

"Lieutenant's still working on last year's vacation."

I sank into the perp chair next to her desk.

Cross turned another page. "What."

"The Bland killing. I'm in for the defense."

"Bring your magic wand."

"That bad?"

Cross closed the file. "You're working for the lawyer, you've read the reports we gave him. Unit responding finds devoted nephew cradling battered head of beloved aunt in his lap. Blubbers out a story about homeless guy that stands up like Gibraltar. Prints, blood and tissue match on weapon, motive A-1, eyewitness to means and opportunity. You could prosecute this one, Cuddy."

"I got the impression from the lab report that they made the prints before you picked up Funderberk."

"They did. The Mets booked him two weeks prior."

The Metropolitan District Commission Police patrolled the highways and waterways around Boston. "Charge?"

"Your boy beat up another derelict on the river there."

"Funderberk have much of a sheet?"

"You'd need two hands to lift it."

"History of violence?"

"More like a philosophy of violence. If it moved or talked, he hit or kicked it."

"But he saved the old woman's dog from drowning."

"You figure him out, I got an old professor could do an article on it."

"Name of the guy Funderberk supposedly beat up?"

"Shattles, Benny NMI. Mets sent us a copy of the file. Here."

I skimmed it, pausing over the station photos. Both white males, fortyish with brown hair, stringy like they wore hats a lot and didn't wash much. Given the names on the back, Funderberk wore his hair a little longer than Shattles, but you had to compare them side by side. Funderberk's right cheek and lower lip cut, Shattles' left eye closed and nose broken. Glance at them without the bruises, and you might not be able to tell them apart.

"Anybody talked to this Shattles?"

"Cuddy." Cross waved a tired hand over her desk. You couldn't see the top of it for documents and message slips. "We had four killings in the last thirty-six hours. The drug posses and street gangs in Roxbury and Dorchester are renting *Colors* on videotape, just to make sure they do the drivebys right. I think we got this Bland case under control, you know?"

"Appreciate your time."

"Don't hurry back."

Three

The next morning I drove from the condo I was renting downriver to the MDC station near the Museum of Science. I lucked out with a patrol officer who knew Benny Shattles by sight and had seen him half an hour before on the Cambridge side near the Massachusetts Avenue Bridge.

Cruising Memorial Drive in the slow lane, I spotted Shattles along the embankment, picking up soda cans and tossing them into a green leaf bag he dragged behind him. He wore a ski hat and gloves and too many layers of sweater for the sunshine. Even the leaf bag didn't look like it was on its maiden voyage. I found a parking place and walked back to him.

"Shattles?"

His head snapped up, like a man who was in a foreign country and was surprised to hear someone recognize him. "No."

I moved up close to him, and he backed off a step.

"Nobody's going to roust you, Shattles."

He said, "You're already rousting me," a southwest twang still laced through his voice.

"I want to talk with you about Jack Funderberk."

"That jerk? I ain't got no time to talk about jerks."

I took out a five-dollar bill, creasing it longways like a puptent. "I'll buy a hundred cans worth, all right?"

Shattles smiled. Only a front tooth and an incisor on top, the bottom teeth stumpy with gaps between the enamel and gum. The eye was okay, the nose pretty crooked.

Shattles set down the bag, angling a hand wearing an old Army wool-liner toward the bill. I let him take it.

Stuffing the five into his belt, he said, "This won't go that far, you know."

"Far enough. Want to sit down?"

There was a grassy area under a falling tree held up with rubber hoses and wires. I wasn't sorry when Shattles sat downwind.

He tugged on the cuffs of his sweaters. "So talk."

"I understand you and Funderberk had a little disagreement."

"Berk the Jerk? I whipped his butt for him."

"Why?"

"He damned near gets hisself killed swimming after some broad's hound, then thinks a lawyer's gonna get him his money. That's sure a jerk in my book."

"You fought about his lawsuit?"

"Naw, naw. That's just how it got started. I was stretched out here on the river, over by the B.U. bridge. Nice night, river curves so you can see all the lights downtown in the skyscrapers with the working stiffs still in them. I had a bottle, not a big one, just enough for the night. Then Berk comes along, he's down in the dumps. I asks him, how come? He says, his lawyer's gone and booted the money the old lady owes him. I says, how's that? He says, the lawyer screwed up the paperwork somehow, he's not getting a dime. Then I offers him some of my bottle, buck him up some. He gets nasty, like he always does, won't give it back. That's when I whipped his butt."

"When was this?"

"When? I don't know."

"The police hauled you in?"

"Yeah, yeah. Woulda been okay, except somebody heard me whipping him, they called the cops from one of them emergency stands. They hadn't pulled me off him, I woulda killed the guy."

"You figure Berk could have killed the old woman?"

"Berk the Jerk? No way, man. He's just a loser. He went to see a lawyer, for chrissakes."

"Do you remember where you were when you heard about it?"

"Heard about what?"

"The killing."

"Sure, sure. I was here, right here. Policing the area. Some reporter comes up, wants to know if I know Berk. I told her to get lost."

Policing the area. "You ever in the service, Shattles?"

He lost the cockiness. "Yeah. Two tours in-country, first one Khe Sanh. You?"

"Saigon, mostly."

"How about a little extra then?"

"Extra?"

He pointed to his belt. "A little more veteran's benefit, from a rear-echelon type to a grunt in the boonies."

I laid another five on the grass and left him.

Four

Boston's Charles Street Jail has about ten years on the Civil War. The cells are arranged in tiers around a central, open shaft. A giant cage for birds without wings. A federal court order restricted the number of inmates it could hold, and a new jail for pre-trial detainees is supposed to open over by the Registry of Motor Vehicles on Nashua Street. One way or the other, I didn't think Jack Funderberk would ever see it.

A Suffolk County Sheriff's Officer brought Funderberk into the glass-walled room. The officer stepped outside, and Funderberk yanked a chair from the scarred wooden table to sit across from me. The facial bruises were healed, and he'd been shaving regularly. His hair was a little cleaner, too, parted in the center and pulled back behind the ears. His arms and face and neck looked bleached, the skin already taking on the ghost pallor of being inside all day.

I explained to Funderberk why I was there.

He sneered. "Just punching the clock on another loser, huh?"

"Probably."

We waited each other out. Funderberk looked down between his knees. He slapped his hand on the table. The officer on the far side of the glass took a step forward. I motioned him back.

Funderberk looked up at me. "I didn't kill that old broad, man. I should of, but I didn't."

"Tell me about it."

"Won't make no sense unless I start with the stuff from January."

"That's fine."

"All right. I'm at the river, see? I'm just walking. It's a sunny day, only since it's not lunchtime yet, there ain't a lot of people walking around."

"How did you know it wasn't lunchtime?"

"There's like this tower. Across the river, Cambridge side. You can see the clock in it. Wasn't noon yet."

"Go on."

"All right. Like I said, there wasn't much happening. Just this old broad and this kind of short, wimpy-looking guy with her."

"And the dog."

"Right, and the dog. Jesus, man, you'd think somebody like her'd have enough sense not to let the thing run wild, but no, she's got this leash folded up in her hand, dog's off running."

"What kind of dog?"

"Wire-haired terrier. The kind they had in those old Thin Man movies. 'Asta.' "

"How do you know?"

"How do you think? I seen the movies."

"I mean how did you know it was a wire-haired terrier?"

"Oh, I . . . when I was a kid, I worked for a vet after school."

"Okay."

"Okay. So, the dog's running around, and it sees these ducks out on the lagoon. Now, you got to remember, man, it's like the January thaw, the ice on the lagoon is all yellow and you can see open water here and there. Well, the stupid dog goes nuts after the ducks. So what happens?"

"The dog falls through the ice."

"Exactly. Exactly what happens. Only it don't go under. Under the ice, I mean. It's like in the water, trying to get back up on the ice, but it can't and it's really, like—what's the word?"

"Floundering?"

"Yeah, yeah. Floundering. And the old broad, she's pitching a fit on the snow there, and the wimpy guy with her, one look at him and you can tell he's gonna be no good. So I run up to them and I says, "Hey, pinheads, your dog's drowning out there."

"Then what?"

"The old broad starts talking real fast. Not crazy, just real upset. She says, 'Please, please save my dog.' Actually she says, 'Please save my Jeeves,' and I says, 'Who?' and she says, 'Jeeves, Jeeves, my dog.' I look out at the dog, who's maybe going down for the first time, and I says, 'Are you kidding me, lady? I could drown out there.' Then she says, 'You save my dog, I'll give you a hundred thousand dollars.' Just like that. A hundred thousand. The wimp starts screaming at her. 'Auntie Leah, what are you, nuts or something?', like that. So I cuff him one, just to shut him up, and meanwhile this dog's going down for the second time. I says to her, 'Lady, you serious or what?' She says, 'I'm serious, I'm serious. You go save my dog, and the hundred thousand's yours.' I says to her, 'You promise?' and she says, 'Yeah, yeah. I promise, I promise.'"

Funderberk worked his rear deeper into the chair and set his feet harder on the floor. "So I take off my coat there, man, and I pull off some clothes and I jump in. The bottom's all mucky, and I'm losing my balance even before I get twenty feet, and I says to myself, 'Jesus, the hell am I doing this for?' My feet are already numb through the shoes and socks, so I decide to turn back. Then the dog sees me, and the thing starts barking and yowling and trying to get to me. And it's taking a lot of water. So I slog out a little more and I get near it, and I can hear its front claws, scratching on the ice, trying to get up out of the hole of water."

Funderberk swiped the back of his hand across his eyes. "Its paws are bleeding, see? Its paws are bleeding 'cause it's trying so hard to get up on that ice. Well, I finally get to it, and I grab it and kind of half swim back to shore."

Funderberk's face darkened. "I'm so beat I can't hardly stand up, man, but I set that dog on the ground, gentle as a nurse with a baby. Now, what does that old broad say? 'Oh, thank you so much'? 'Oh, where can we send the money'? No way José. She grabs the dog and starts running all stiff-legged, 'cause she was old, see? And the wimp starts after her, but he can't even run as fast as the old broad. And I'm starting to really freeze up, so I yell, 'Hey, hey! I'm going into shock or something here. I need a doctor and a warm bed somewheres.' And they just keep running up that ramp there across Storrow Drive toward the houses. And I'm yelling 'Where's my hundred, lady? Where's my hundred thousand?' And they just keep going, her with the dog and him after her."

I said, "Anybody else see this?"

"No. Nobody, like I said before. Nobody else around. But that's what happened, goddammit! Just like I said."

"What did you do then?"

"I near died, man."

"After that."

"I watched out for them, see? For a week, maybe more. They didn't come back to the river. So I start walking up and down the streets. I spot the wimp guy, carrying some groceries and going into this lah-de-dah doorway on Marlborough. I get the name and address, and I check out the phonebook over to the drugstore and bingo! I got Miss Leah Bland, man. I got her."

"Then what?"

"I go to this lawyer. I'm just walking down the street, trying to figure this thing, and I see his sign in the window there, so I go in. I figure, this is an easy case, right? I mean, everybody and his brother can see the old broad owes me the hundred grand. So I sit down with this guy Moone, and he listens to my story and he takes down the information. He didn't have no secretary or nothing, that should have tipped me right there. But I always had P.D.s before, and they come right to the courtroom or the holding pen, you don't ever see their office, like. Anyway this Moone, he tells me he's gonna bring a lawsuit against them. He says he's gonna bring them to their knees."

"But he doesn't."

"Oh, man. He screws it up. Royally. He gets us tossed out of court because of some kind of paperwork he files or don't file that doesn't have my name on it, I don't know. I get nuts about it, I take it out on this other guy by the river there."

"Benny Shattles."

Funderberk looked surprised. "You know Benny?"

"I read the file. Go on."

"Anyway, I take it out on Benny, then I stew about it some, then I get good and loaded one night and I really feel like crap the next morning. So I go to her house and—"

"With a bat."

"Right, yeah. With this bat. I go—"

"Where did you get the bat?"

"Where?"

"Where."

"Jesus, man, I don't— Wait a minute. Down by the river there. Yeah, by the ballfield over near the tugs, you know? I go down there, watch the softball. Most of the guys use the metal bats now, but they was using one of the wood ones, I guess, and it cracked, so they just left it, and I picked it up."

"And went visiting."

"Right. I wasn't drunk or nothing. But when I go to the front door, the wimp sees me through the curtains and starts yelling for me to go away. The dog, Jeeves, he's at the window, too, front paws up on the glass, barking and wagging what tail he's got, like he's glad to see me. I start banging on the door with the bat, and this other old bag in the next building starts yelling down at me from her window. Saying she was gonna call the cops, I didn't quit. So I go around the block to think about it, then up the alley and start banging on the back door. This time the old broad, Bland herself now, opens up the back door. Jeeves comes out, jumping and licking my hand, like he remembers me and all. The old broad, though, she starts yelling at me and I start yelling at her, and pretty soon the other old bag is leaning out another window, yelling at both of us and saying that's it, she's calling the cops. Well, I slam down the bat and get out of there. I'm mad as hell, but I leave and I don't hurt her, man, I swear it."

"Why'd you bring the bat?"

"Huh?"

"You weren't going to hurt her, why'd you bring the bat?"

"I don't know, man."

"You don't know."

"You don't think of that kind of stuff. You're hung over and feeling screwed and you just have the bat 'cause you picked it up before you thought about going to see her."

"That'll never fly."

"Hey, I don't know what flies and what don't, see? That's why I don't got no job and no house and no money."

"Don't forget no future."

"Real funny. Whose side you on, anyway?"

"I'm going to talk to the nephew and the neighbor who saw you that day. Anybody else you can think of?"

"No. Yeah, talk to Moone, willya? Tell that shyster how he screwed me up."

I stood.

Funderberk used the table to get to his feet. In a different tone, he said, "Hey, man, when you see the wimp nephew, make sure he's feeding Jeeves, all right?"

I looked at Jack Funderberk. "Whoever killed Miss Bland did the dog, too."

Funderberk blinked, dropping his head without closing his eyes. "Aw, no, man. No, no."

I started to feel what Steve Rothenberg had said.

Five

Theodore Moone's office made Rothenberg's look like the Taj Mahal.

I climbed the third flight over the dry-cleaners. I saw the sign in Moone's window from a block away. Up close, it was hand-painted. Probably with the stick Moone had used to stir the paint.

Moone himself told me to step right in. He oozed into a sports jacket that looked like spun Cream of Farina. His shirt was wrinkled from waist to shoulders, the tabs sproinging away from each other. His tie was twice as wide as the one I was wearing. The red toupee was so obvious that the too-high part actually made it look more natural. Flushed face, small eyes, big Irish jowls. I shook a sweaty palm and got the kind of grin that made me want to button the pocket holding my wallet.

"Take a load off and tell me your problems, sir."

I eased into a folding chair with "Wilkie's Funeral Home" stencilled on the back of it. When Moone plopped into a tufted desk chair, some stuffing poofed out like dandelion seeds.

Moone made a ritual of clicking a ballpoint over a yellow legal pad. "If I could just have your name?"

"John Cuddy." I took out my ID and showed it to him.

Putting the pen back into his shirt pocket, Moone exhaled forcefully. "Now what?"

"You represented a man named Jack Funderberk on a case that went sour."

"Sour? I tried to help that bum out, and he commits murder. You got any idea how long it'll be before I live down the bad publicity?"

"Let's talk about the civil case for a minute."

"The Board of Bar Overseers wouldn't like that."

"Why not?"

"Client confidentiality."

"You think the Board would like me telling them you just called your client a murderer?"

Moone puckered his mouth. "What do you want to know?"

"How come the case went sour?"

"Look, I get all kinds in here, all right? All kinds. This Funderberk, he comes in, I wanna open a window. But I hear him out, and what he says makes a little sense. So I call this Miss Bland on the telephone, and she's frosty, she says to call her lawyers. Not her lawyer, her lawyers, plural. Gives me Drysdale, Coppinger—"

"And Sewell."

"Right. That gets me thinking, she's already talked this over with some high-powered people. Maybe Funderberk really has something. So I file a complaint, on this Funderberk's sayso, now, and I get back the telephone book."

"A motion for summary judgment."

"With attached affidavits and exhibits and memorandum in support of this and that. A tidal wave of paper."

"Which amounted to what?"

"Funderberk says she offered him a hundred thousand *before* he went in the water. She and her nephew say she offered Funderberk a hundred bucks *after* he brought the dog back alive."

"Sounds like something a jury should decide."

"Yeah, well it didn't sound that way to the judge. I did the best I could for this Funderberk, but I was buried. This Drysdale and some little superstar in a slit skirt ate my lunch for me. I'm lucky I didn't end up having to pay some of Drysdale's fees."

"Why didn't you file Funderberk's own affidavit?"

Something moved behind Moone's eyes. "You go to law school or what?"

"A year's worth, nights."

"Yeah, well, they don't teach you in law school how you're supposed to reach your client when you need him and he don't have a permanent address or job. I needed him, but he never called me or came to see me. I did what I could."

"What kind of contingency were you on?"

"None of your business."

"I can ask Funderberk about your fee."

"Go ahead. At least now I know where you can find him."

Six

Picture Humpty-Dumpty just before the fall and you'd have a pretty good image of Norbert Bland. He met me at the door to the Marlborough

Street townhouse wearing a brown cardigan sweater over a frayed white shirt and brown pants. Fifty or so, his fingers were short and blunt. Though thinning, the hair and eyebrows were both that glossy black that God gives to wing of crow and Clairol puts in bottle of dye.

As he looked at my ID, a pointy nose appeared to be his most expressive feature. "If we must talk, come in, come in."

The interior door opened onto a hallway, the staircase marching straight to the second floor. Bland led me into a small parlor decorated in Edwardian furnishings. I took one of two straight chairs with oval backs upholstered in faded maroon. Bland took the other.

"I want to be a good citizen, Mr. Cuddy, but I'm not sure how much I should help the man who killed my Auntie."

The last seemed an odd word coming from a man his age. "I appreciate your talking to me at all, Mr. Bland, but I'm really just interested in what you saw that day."

The eyes narrowed. "Which day?"

"Let's start with the incident on the river."

"Oh, really. That's already been resolved by our attorneys."

"Just what you saw and heard, please."

A sigh of resignation. "Auntie and I took Jeeves for a walk. Auntie named him Jeeves because he'd rush to the door like a butler whenever someone rang. Jeeves liked his outings, and Auntie let him off his leash. I'd warned her about that—endlessly, in fact—but to no avail. As luck would have it, Jeeves went bounding after some waterfowl and plunged through the ice, flailing about madly. Well, I don't swim, and Auntie was beside herself, when this homeless fellow approached us and said," Bland scrunched up his face and dropped his tone an octave, " 'Don't worry there, lady, I'll get him for you.' "

"Funderberk."

"As we later discovered."

"He just volunteered?"

"Precisely. I don't doubt his bravery, but after the rescue, naturally Auntie wished to rush Jeeves back here before he caught his death. However, she did pause to offer your Funderberk a hundred dollars for his trouble. A noble gesture, really. Well, the fellow grew nasty, bellowing that he wanted a hundred *thousand* dollars. Can you imagine? So naturally Auntie scooped up Jeeves and began to run while I lingered back a bit, to protect her in case your Funderberk decided to become even nastier. We arrived home safely, and Jeeves made a complete recovery."

"When did you next hear from Funderberk?"

"*I* didn't. Auntie called DeWitt Drysdale. She was always a stickler for advising our attorneys of any potential difficulties, and DeWitt said he would take care of it. Well, thereafter, Auntie got some sort of threatening call from a dreadful man named Moone who presented himself over the telephone as a lawyer, though you would scarcely have guessed it hearing him talk."

"You met him?"

The eyes narrowed again. "Just over the telephone."

"Then what happened?"

"Well, one day this Funderberk fellow came storming up our front steps, brandishing a baseball bat. He was shrieking obscenities and demanding to be admitted to discuss 'what he had coming to him,' I believe was his phrase. Naturally, I refused to open the door. By shouting through the windows, Mrs. Van Nuys—in the next building—and I repelled him."

Repelled. I bet myself that Norbert was going to use "bludgeoned," too. "Did you call the police?"

"No. No, but Auntie may have called DeWitt, because I did hear her use the telephone. I went upstairs to bathe."

"You took a bath?"

"This Funderberk, your client, upset me. I find it relaxing to bathe after I'm upset."

"Go on."

"Well, I was in the tub with the water running and the door closed when . . . when . . ." Bland's voice seemed to catch, and he wet his lips. "When Funderberk returned, to the back door this time. Auntie was always a . . . feisty person, Mr. Cuddy. And I imagine it didn't take much to trigger your client's rage. When I finished my bath, I came out in my robe and started to my room, but I could feel a draft."

"A draft?"

"Yes. As though a door or window were open. Auntie usually kept all the windows closed during the day, you see. Too much soot about for the curtains and draperies. Well, I sensed something was amiss, so I called her name. No reply. I called Jeeves. The same. I went downstairs and Auntie was . . ."

Bland put one of the blunt little hands to his face and spoke through the splayed fingers. "Auntie and Jeeves both were in the back hall, the outside door open. I went to Auntie and tried to pull her up, to get her to a chair, you see. I don't believe I realized she . . . until I saw the blood and the . . . Her head had been bludgeoned, and Jeeves had been smashed almost to pulp. I picked him up—I had to move him to close the door—and that's when I saw the bat, just lying on our patio, drenched in . . . in everything."

"You picked the dog up?"

Bland nodded through the hand.

"Instead of just dragging him away from the door?"

The hand came down. "He was our . . . pet, sir."

"I'm sorry. Anything more?"

"Precious little, I'm afraid. I dialed the police, then tried to . . . I believe that when they arrived, I was sitting on the floor, cradling Auntie's head. I don't . . . I don't really remember much after that."

"Did you happen to see anyone else around?"

"Anyone else?"

"Another derelict, maybe?"

"Derelict? I assure you, sir, one caller like your Mr. Funderberk was quite sufficient contact for this family."

"But you never actually saw Funderberk after he left the first time, out by the front door."

"That is correct. But Mrs. Van Nuys did. Shall I arrange an introduction?"

Seven

"Sit down, young man. Sit, the chair will hold you."

I took a doilied easy chair across from Mrs. Van Nuys, the four-posted walker between us, her gnarled fingers caressing the rubber handgrips like a six-year-old kid with his first two-wheeler. Bluish hair worn in a ponytail and half-glasses on her nose, it had been a while since her first two-wheeler.

"Leah Bland and I debuted together, Mr. Cuddy. My family was from the Hudson Valley originally, not Yankees like the Blands. But we got along famously, just famously."

"So you've known the Blands most of your life?"

"That's right. Leah's father and brother were giants, sir, giants of their times. But I don't expect you've come to hear about them."

"That's right. I believe Norbert Bland explained on the telephone?"

"You must do your duty, sir. And I mine as a citizen. I'm prepared to testify, and I'm certainly not afraid to tell my story more than once."

"I'm listening."

"Well, it was a fine day, the dogwoods and magnolias blooming, the scent of spring in just everything. I'd opened all the windows on this floor—unlike Leah, you see, I enjoyed the fresh air. Furniture be hanged, if you can't live with the soot, get out of the city."

"With the windows open you could hear what happened next door?"

"I could. I condominiumized, if that's the word for it, several years ago at the advice of DeWitt Drysdale, and I must say I haven't regretted it one instant. Fine unit owners around me now, much less upkeep—did you know that all Norbert ever does all day long is clean and maintain that house? Oh, Leah would buy everything for him, the mops and gloves and cleaning fluids and all, but he spends every day keeping that house spotless. I decided to retain the third floor here as my apartment. It has just the nicest bay window in the house and the best sun as well."

"So you heard something that day?"

"I did. I was reading here, thank God for my eyes, still sharp as an eagle's, when I heard this commotion on Leah's front stoop. I made my way to the window, and I could see this disreputable character with a baseball bat, pounding on the door and swearing like a sailor. Well, he seemed quite mad to me, so I advised him that I would summon the police if he didn't go on his way. That seemed to discourage him, and he left."

"Can you describe who you saw?"

"I can. A tramp, approximately forty, I would say. Hair like one of those hippie creatures, brown to black from being filthy. The word 'disheveled' would be generous regarding his clothes, far too many layers for the weather."

"Go on."

"Well, I thought we were quit of him, and never called the police, more's the pity. Then, a short while later, I heard something from the back as well."

"How long after?"

"Oh, minutes."

"Two minutes, ten minutes?"

"Perhaps fifteen or twenty."

"What did you hear then?"

"More shouting. His voice, I was sure. The same man, I mean. I made my way to the rear—I'm surprisingly adept with this contraption." Mrs. Van Nuys almost managed to flex her fingers around the rubber grips. "I thought I would hate having to use it, but quite frankly it's a Godsend. I don't have a nephew like Norbert to look after me."

"When you got to the back, what did you see?"

"The same tramp, ranting at Leah and she giving no ground. That woman was an oak, Mr. Cuddy. Unbending, unyielding. I was just so proud of her, but also concerned for her. I advised the man that I was calling the police, and that seemed to spook him again. He threw the bat down on the ground and strode off, swearing still. I asked Leah if she wanted me to summon the police, and she said no, not to bother. She seemed so . . ."

I waited.

"I'm sorry. She suddenly seemed so distracted . . . uncertain. And that was quite unlike Leah, as I've said. However, I thought that she was probably just reacting from the confrontation, so I left the window . . ." Mrs. Van Nuys bit her lower lip. "If I had called the police that instant, I can't help but think that Leah would be alive today."

"I wouldn't hold yourself responsible for that."

The eyes came over the half-glasses. "I would."

"Mrs. Van Nuys, did you ever see that man come back?"

"Come back?"

"After you saw him drop the bat—"

"*Throw* the bat."

"After you saw him throw the bat down, did you ever see him again?"

"No. As I said, I left the window."

"You never saw him strike Miss Bland?"

"No."

"Did you ever see any other man like this one around the Bland house?"

"Any others? Heavens, no! Do you mean there are more like him?"

Eight

DeWitt Drysdale's office was the Taj Mahal.

Drysdale, Coppinger and Sewell occupied the entire top floor of a fifty-story tower, the kind that's becoming a little hard to rent after the demise of the Massachusetts Miracle. Drysdale himself had a corner office with a sweeping view of Boston Harbor. The mahogany desk matched the mahogany credenza, bookshelves, and chairs. The rugs would have cost the Kublai Khan half his empire, and the paintings were by artists so famous their signatures were illegible.

"Mr. Cuddy, please take a seat. The attorney who sat second chair on the motion for summary judgment, Ms. Talitieri, will join us shortly."

DeWitt Drysdale accentuated the "Ms.," as though he were still getting used to pronouncing the word. In fact, everything about Drysdale was accentuated. Widow's peak of gray hair, brushed stylishly back over his ears. Chiseled chin, complete with cleft. Glasses, the metal frames probably platinum, the faintest tint to the lenses. When we shook hands, I noticed he wore French cuffs under the sleeves of his suit jacket.

I heard the door swish open behind me.

"Ah, Nina, thank you. Nina Talitieri, John Cuddy."

Talitieri was short, even in high heels. Brown eyes, a hint of make-up, curly black hair abruptly chopped off at the neckline. White stockings over the heels, blue two-piece suit, ruffled white blouse. Formidable until she smiled, when you got the feeling she might be a nice person after all.

"Mr. Cuddy."

When we all were settled, Drysdale said, "Just so the ground rules are clear, Mr. Cuddy. I'm not deeply versed in criminal law, but I do know the discovery opportunities for the accused are rather limited. Accordingly, I'm happy to permit you this interview, although all attorney-client communications are obviously out-of-bounds."

"Fair enough."

"Where would you like to begin?"

"Did you ever meet Jack Funderberk?"

"No. Nina?"

"Never."

"Is it typical for you never to even meet the opposing side to a lawsuit?"

Drysdale smiled condescendingly. "I'm not sure there is a 'typical' in our practice, Mr. Cuddy. As you can see, we've done quite well over the years, yet still have time for the unusual case."

"Like *Funderberk v. Bland*."

"Correct."

"You never even tried to depose the guy?"

"Mr. Cuddy, you must understand. There are various devices for disposing of nonsense cases like Mr. Funderberk's. Summary judgment is one of them. As soon as we received the complaint, I was certain it required no formal discovery, such as deposition. Based on the accounts of Leah and Norman Bland as reflected in their affidavits, there was no need to run up the tab, so to speak. After Nina performed some confirmatory research of law, we were prepared to dispatch Mr. Funderberk, and his attorney, rather swiftly."

"Tell me, Mr. Drysdale, if the case had gone to trial and Funderberk won, I take it Miss Bland was good for the hundred thousand?"

A veil slid down over Drysdale's face. "I'm afraid I can't discuss my client's financial position, Mr. Cuddy."

"Leah Bland is dead."

"That makes no difference."

"My guess is you're probating her will up at the courthouse. I can just go read it."

"That you can, Mr. Cuddy. But you can't expect me to be talking to you about it, now can you?"

"Could the Blands have lied to protect their nest egg?"

I tried to watch Talitieri as Drysdale heartily reminded me why the word "guffaw" was coined. The young associate's face gave the impression she was playing poker, and I wondered why she wasn't at least smiling, too.

Drysdale composed himself. "Mr. Cuddy, if that's your best argument, I'm afraid you should be advising your client to bring his toothbrush to court."

I addressed Drysdale but I was pitching to Talitieri. "My client isn't in a position to pop into a drugstore, counsellor. My client is keeping a six-by-nine warm at Charles Street Jail."

Drysdale stiffened. "And with good reason, sir. He brutally murdered a defenseless, elderly woman. And Leah Bland never told a lie in her life, much less one under oath in a formal document like an affidavit."

"Did Leah Bland ever indicate to you any uncertainty about her version of what happened down by the river?"

"Clearly immaterial, sir. And, in any case, within the privilege."

"Did she ever contact you about Funderberk after the summary judgment motion?"

"Same."

"Mr. Drysdale, if my client is innocent, and there's anything you can tell me to establish that, how're you going to feel if you sit on the lid and claim privilege?"

I hoped I wasn't gilding the lily. I felt, rather than saw, Talitieri shift in her chair.

Drysdale tented his fingers over the slate blotter on the polished desk. "An attorney has no choice but to invoke the privilege, Mr. Cuddy. The privilege survives even the grave."

"I wish I was a privilege."

Nine

There was a coffee shop at street level across from Drysdale's skyscraper. I had a hot chocolate and then told the inquiring waitress I'd be happy to pay for five more so long as she didn't have to make them and I didn't have to drink them. That made her happy.

I figured that a law firm like Drysdale's probably expected an associate like Nina Talitieri to work well into the evening. That's why I was pleased to see her coming out of the building's revolving door with a herd of secretarial and other staff people just after five. I'd gotten to her.

Talitieri wore a trenchcoat and carried a leather briefcase. She walked down to the harbor, lost in thought and bumping into at least three people

I noticed. At the water's edge, the young lawyer stood for a while, elbows on the railing, staring past the sloops and yawls dropping their mainsails and furling their jibs and motoring into their slips for the night. I anticipated her direction and took a seat on a stone bench a minute before she started moving again.

As Talitieri drew even with me, I said, "Let's talk about it."

She jumped, but not much. After watching me for a moment, she sat at the far end of the bench, close enough to talk easily, enough apart to give the impression to a passerby that we weren't together.

Talitieri kept her eyes on the sailboats, as though she were trying to learn how to rig one. "You did a good job back there. Drysdale never noticed."

"How'd he get to be where he is? Being dense as a post, I mean."

Almost a smile. "When he was starting out, the road was already paved, you know?"

"By pater and his pater before him?"

A smile and a glance. "Roughly." The smile drifted away. "Whatever I tell you can't be used unless you can figure it out from another source, right?"

"Sounds fair."

"That's what you said to Drysdale back there."

"All right. I promise."

The head swung around, like she was following one of the boats in particular, but her voice sounded surprised. "You mean that. I mean, you really do mean that, don't you?"

"Yes."

Talitieri leaned back, folding her hands on the buckle of her trenchcoat. Only the tips of her toes touched the granite blocks set into the ground. "In law school, I had this professor for Professional Responsibility. That's the ethics course? He used to say, 'Whenever you're representing a client, you have to remember, there are other people around, too.' "

"People like Jack Funderberk."

"His lawyer . . ."

"I've met Moone."

"People in law firms like ours call people like Moone 'hacks.' "

"So would I."

"But this was different. I've only been a lawyer for two years, but Moone . . . Moone gave up too easily, even for a hack."

"What do you mean?"

"All he has to do is file a 'personal knowledge' affidavit in a timely manner and he's all set. He had weeks to find his client and get him to come in."

"Weeks."

"He told the judge, 'I can't find the plaintiff, your Honor. This counter-affidavit is the best I can do.' God, the rule itself says that's not good enough."

"So?"

"So Moone could have fought a little. He could have jumped up and down, filed his own affidavit stating why he couldn't file a personal-knowledge one. That would have gotten him a continuance and bought the time to find his client."

"But he didn't think of it, huh?"

"Aw, the judge even suggested it to him. 'I don't think it'll do any good, your Honor. This guy's a bum.' He actually said that. In open court, the other lawyers waiting their turn, having a good laugh over it."

"Moone gave the case away."

Another quick side glance. "That's how I saw it, anyway."

"What did the Blands tell you about the incident on the river?"

Talitieri shook her head. "No. No, here's what I'm going to tell you about that, and no more. Miss Bland called Drysdale just after it happened, but Norbert is the one who came in to see me. I don't know why. All I know is that Norbert told me the volunteer version that appears in his and Miss Bland's affidavits. I drafted them up that way, sent them out to the Blands for signature, and they came back signed. 'Under the pains and penalties of perjury.' "

"So, not notarized?"

"No. Not necessary. Just the signatures, under oath."

I thought about it. "Were the Blands good for the money if Funderberk won?"

"Sort of."

"What does that mean?"

"Look, you'll have to work that out. Start with the will itself. The Probate and Family Court at Pemberton Square."

I turned it over some more. "Was Miss Bland at the hearing?"

"On summary judgment?"

"Yes."

"No, of course not. Just Drysdale and me."

"Did you ever speak to Miss Bland after the hearing?"

"No. But she did try to call."

"You?"

"No, Drysdale. I overheard his secretary telling him he had a phone message from Miss Bland. The day of the murder. It's the kind of thing you remember."

Talitieri checked her watch. "Look, Mr. Cuddy, I have to go."

"Right. I'll wait here till you're a ways off."

Talitieri stood up, then fussed with her buckle and briefcase enough to say one more thing, out of the corner of her mouth. "Be sure to read that will, now."

Ten

I followed Nina Talitieri's advice. After spending most of the next morning plowing through papers at both the Probate and Superior Courts, I took the subway over to the offices of Theodore Moone, Esquire. I pointed out to him the reasons why he probably wasn't going to be an esquire too much longer. After about half an hour, he told me what he knew. It wasn't much, but I thought it would be enough.

✦ ✦ ✦

The door opened a crack. "Mr. Cuddy, isn't it?"

"That's right."

When I made no effort to move through the door, he said, "Well, what is it?"

"I think we need to talk."

I still hadn't moved, and he seemed to be nervous about it.

"Talk about what?"

"Oh, you know."

He backed away from the door. I caught it with the heel of my hand, and followed Norbert Bland into the parlor.

✦ ✦ ✦

"You really shouldn't have lied about hearing Moone's voice only over the telephone, Norbert."

Bland squirmed in his chair. If he resented my using his first name, it got lost in the wash.

I said, "You were happy as a clam when poor Jeeves went through the ice, weren't you?"

"I don't know what you're talking about."

"I'm talking about the burden that would have lifted from your shoulders."

"If DeWitt Drysdale shared that sort of information with you, I'll—"

"Drysdale didn't say a word, Norbert. I read the will, on file in the Probate Court."

Bland stared at me.

"You were to get the house, and the liquid stuff, so long as you properly attended to old Jeeves. Aggravating, wasn't it, Norbert?"

He fumed.

"You didn't dare poison Jeeves. But, what the hell, Auntie Leah was old, and sooner or later you could manage something. Just one problem, though. The incident at the river really did happen just the way Jack Funderberk said it did. And you were blind scared that if it went to court, to trial that is, your aunt might even back up his version of it."

"She did back it up! She signed her affidavit, just as I did mine."

"No, Norbert. You signed her affidavit just like you did yours. Nobody had to appear before a notary, so you just signed both and sent them back to Drysdale's office. I compared the signature on her affidavit to the signature on her will, Norbert. With no one questioning the signatures in the contract case, you were pretty safe. But if I could spot a problem comparing them, imagine what an expert could do."

"You're bluffing."

"I'm guessing that your aunt really was torn when she thought about what had happened down at the river. I'm guessing you spoke to Drysdale just after the lawsuit was filed. You assured your aunt that you'd taken care of it for her. Then, just after the summary judgment hearing, you told your aunt that Funderberk's case had been thrown out on a technicality. When Funderberk came a-calling, you managed to shoo him away out front. But then he reappeared at the back door, maybe yelling something about her lying in the paperwork. Mrs. Van Nuys says your aunt looked upset after that, and Mr. Drysdale did tell me that Leah Bland never lied. Ever."

Bland's Adam's apple bobbed twice before he spoke. "That's . . . that's . . ."

"You took a bath all right, and overheard your aunt hanging up after she tried to reach Drysdale. It was smart of you to admit that, because the secretary at the law firm would remember that your aunt tried to reach her attorney just after talking with Funderberk at the back door. It was also smart to say you hadn't seen Funderberk hit her. Don't want to make things too neat for the cops. But tell me, Norbert, what did you say to her? 'Auntie, why were you trying to call DeWitt?' "

Bland shuddered, his face like a dam breaking. "Auntie Leah left word for DeWitt to call her back. Something that . . . that hobo said set her off. She confronted me, demanded to know what had happened. I tried to explain it to her, deflect her. But no, she knew what an affidavit was. A statement under oath. She knew she'd never signed one. She called me a liar, that wretched little dog of hers jumping and yapping and snapping at me."

Bland seemed to lose focus. "All it ever did was track dirt into this house, on the rugs, the furniture, everywhere. It was . . ." Norbert came back to me. "I tried to reason with her, I was only trying to protect us from that hobo's insane lawsuit."

"To protect your inheritance, which was why you offered Moone five thousand dollars to take a dive."

"That fool! He responded to DeWitt's motion in order to lose the case but insure a handsome fee for himself. He wanted more, but he took five and was glad for it. Probably more than he makes in a . . . a . . ." Bland seemed to struggle for an appropriate wage period, but he'd been out of the stream too long to be sure.

"So your aunt said she was—"

"Auntie Leah was going to turn me in! For perjury, a crime. She said I'd go to prison for that."

"Where was the bat?"

"Inside the back door. Auntie had picked it up from the patio. She was walking back to the telephone, to call DeWitt again. I didn't know what to do. I grabbed it and I hit her. And her damned dog, too. I crushed him, and then I picked him up and flung him against the door. I didn't know what I was doing."

"You knew enough to wear gloves to avoid leaving your prints on the bat."

"I was already wearing the gloves upstairs, when I heard her on the telephone. Rubber gloves."

"Tidying up a bit?"

"No, no. For my . . . my hair. When I dye it, I wear the gloves. I was just about to when I heard her speaking to DeWitt's office."

"Come on, Norbert. You also knew enough to be sure to move your aunt's body. Getting her blood and brains on you to cover the stains from cracking her skull."

He shook his blunt little index finger at me. "She was going to send me to prison! Her own family. Do you know what happens in jail to men who . . . who can't protect themselves? I couldn't convince her. I had to deal with her immediately, quickly, Don't you understand?"

"Summary judgment."

"What?"

"Never mind."

YELLOW SNOW

One

Jiggy Doyle sat in my client's chair on a cold February day and let his eyes roam around the office. "Nice set-up you've got here, John."

"Thanks."

"I even like the door there. 'JOHN FRANCIS CUDDY, CONFIDENTIAL INVESTIGATIONS.' "

"It kind of came with the office."

"Yeah." Jiggy made the last part of the word a laugh. Jiggy laughed a lot when we were growing up together in South Boston. Now his carrot hair was thinning under a 1986 Red Sox "League Champions" cap, the face fleshy and heavy below the brim. A bulky tweed overcoat I first saw at least a decade ago covered most but not all of the torn sweater under it. His blue jeans were stained and tattered at the cuff, a pair of sneakers nobody would mistake for cross-trainers on his feet. The only concession to currency was the bicyclist's bottle he held in one hand.

I nodded at the bottle. "Still soft for the Gatorade?"

"Never without it. Not since I—well, you know."

I knew. Jiggy had always been a gambler and, until some years ago, a drinker. He drank the way some people talk, which is to say constantly, stopping only to breathe. When his wife Moira finally got him to go into a program, he went over to Gatorade instead of coffee. He said the coffee kept him up but the lime flavor reminded him of a Margarita without the tequila. I didn't think even Moira had been able to control the gambling, though.

"So what's up, Jiggy?"

"I saw you on the tube the other night. About you shooting that guy with the rifle?"

"Mind if we change the subject?"

"Huh? Oh, sure. It's just that I thought to myself, 'Shit, been a long time since I saw old John.' "

I didn't say anything.

Jiggy crossed his right leg over the left, his right sneaker tapping the air rhythmically. His grandmother nicknamed him "Jiggy" for that. To her, it seemed he was dancing a jig with one foot. To me, it seemed he was dancing around something.

"How about you get to it, Jiggy."

He looked down at the bottle, then back up to me. "I need a favor here, John."

"What kind of favor?"

Jiggy blinked, like he hadn't planned on having to explain. "Remember Danny Bennigan?"

I remembered him. Cocky and crude, the closest thing Bennigan had to a character trait was his tendency to call everybody he didn't like "fuck-breath." In the schoolyard, Danny organized two other kids into the first gang I ever saw, shaking the smaller ones down for their milk money. When the gang got around to me, I said no. Jiggy sat on one of Danny's boys while I drew Bennigan and the other. The forces of right won out, though I always wondered if Jiggy pitched in because he was my friend or because he had a bet down on me.

"What's Danny into these days?"

"My pocket. I owe him, John."

"How?"

Jiggy gestured with the bottle. "Danny, he's running this game over a drugstore in Dorchester. Second floor, three tables, two poker and one blackjack. Nice place, good action."

"So?"

"So I'm over there the other night—two, three weeks ago—and I hit this streak, see?"

The way he said it, I didn't think it was a winning streak.

"How much, Jiggy?"

The sneaker bobbed to a faster beat. "Thirteen."

"You're into Danny Bennigan for thirteen hundred dollars?"

The foot stopped, then started again. "Yeah."

"Christ, Jiggy, the hell did you do?"

"I lost, is what I did. Look, I'm over there, see? And I'm at this one table, playing poker, and my luck's not what it might be. So, I notice this guy get up from the other table, and this other guy come in, so I take the chair of the guy that's leaving so the guy coming can have mine."

"To change your luck."

"Right, of course. Change the cards, change the draw, right? Only the stakes at this next table, they're a little steeper than I realize at the time."

"You're betting chips without knowing what they stand for?"

"A sucker mistake, John. Don't you think I know it? But there I am, and before I know it, I'm down altogether thirteen."

I leaned back in my chair, spoke past Jiggy's shoulder. "What did Danny say?"

Jiggy brought his mouth down to the bottle instead of the bottle up to his mouth. He squeezed, tilted his head back, and swallowed. "He said he was gonna go after Moira's house."

Moira had inherited the house in Southie from her mother. It was a three-decker on the wrong side of Broadway, but living shelter-cost-free was probably the only way Moira could have made it with a husband like Jiggy making more withdrawals than deposits.

"He doesn't have any grounds for that, Jiggy."

"Grounds?"

"The house is in her name, not yours, right?"

"Grounds. Tell Danny about grounds, huh? He's got this enforcer drives around in a black Trans Am muscle car with some kind of bug painted on the front of it."

"And?"

"And the enforcer's got blond hair down his collar like a girl plays field hockey."

"I mean, what's Danny going to do about the enforcer?"

"Danny says I'm gonna have a visit from the guy."

"Jiggy. Nobody's going to kill you over thirteen hundred bucks."

The sneaker stopped again. "They start lower and like build to that. I'll make the marker good, but I'm not gonna touch Moira's house to do it, John."

I came forward in the chair. "Okay. Where will the money come from?"

Jiggy's foot hit high gear. "I got a few good tips. They come through, I'm clear."

"And if they don't?"

"That's why I'm here. I was kind of hoping you could go have a talk with the guy."

"The enforcer?"

"Uh-unh. Danny himself. He'll listen to you. He's still afraid of you."

"The schoolyard's a long time ago, Jiggy."

"One thing I learned over the years, John. Life's a schoolyard."

I watched him for a minute, maybe two. I thought about old times and old friends and how you couldn't go back to the one and didn't have many of the other.

Picking up a pencil, I said, "You got an address for Danny?"

Two

The address Jiggy gave me was the poker parlor. That afternoon, I wound down Dorchester Ave, some of the cars at the curb stuck in the snowstorm we'd had the day before. Intersecting the street I wanted, I pulled past the building.

The first floor had a Rexall sign and some used condoms around the edges of a broken window. Otherwise, the "drugstore" was about as lively as a king's grave before the robbers arrive. I checked the other cars on the street. One was a black Trans Am with chrome tailpipes under the bumper and a golden spider painted on the hood.

After a U-turn, I came back halfway, parking my old Honda Prelude in a cleared spot across from the place. Ten minutes later, nothing had appeared at the doorway to the building or in the windows on the second floor. I got out of my car and went up to the entrance. There was a bell that didn't look too far gone, so I pressed it. I didn't hear it ring, so I pressed it again. Still nothing.

I was giving some thought to going through the broken windows of the drugstore when a bolt was thrown on the other side of the door and it opened to the width of a man's face. The guy who stared out at me was about six feet and stringy, left hand on the door and right hand behind him where I couldn't see it. He had brown hair on top in a brushcut and blondish hair fanned out from his neck. The jacket, pants, and shoes matched his car, a little medallion with the spider motif on a gold chain dangling between the lapels. Jiggy must have left out the part about his eyes, though. Hollow and deep and without anything human behind either. A spider's eyes.

"Private club, buddy. Beat it."

"I'd like to see Danny Bennigan."

"Fuck off."

"Tell him it's John Cuddy." I fished a business card form my pocket.

Spider ignored the card. "Danny ain't here."

I still couldn't see his other hand. I had a Smith & Wesson Chief's Special over my right hip, but I wasn't keen on waving it around. "Mind if I see for myself?"

A stiffening. "Believe it."

I swung my left hand, edge up, in an arc, clouting his left on the door. I heard a little crack and Spider cursed, the right hand now coming reflexively forward to cradle the injured one. The Ingram MAC-10 in it didn't quite clear the wood, which gave me the chance to step forward and across the threshold. I caught the right wrist in my left hand, jolting the heel of my right up and into his jaw. Spider went slack but not out, and I took the machine pistol away from him. He slumped back onto the stairs that led to the second floor. I hefted the MAC-10, a hideous little engine of death with a rate of fire like the popcorn maker at a movie house. The welcome wagon tried to get up, my right elbow sending him on to Napland.

I closed and bolted the door, stepping over Spider as I climbed the stairs. The six-panel at the top opened without a key, the room behind it furnished for function. Three round tables and seven chairs to a table. A makeshift wet bar with old porcelain refrigerator. Corduroy drapes over the windows, more for blackout than decoration.

I walked to the tables. Each had a green felt cloth over it, stapled on the underside. There was a dry stain the size of a soccer ball on one of the tables, the stained area lighter than the felt around it.

A short hall ran off the main room with two doors in turn off it. I tried one and found a half-bath that smelled like a plumber's nightmare. I dropped Spider's MAC-10 into the toilet.

The other hall door led to a cramped office with a desk, a telephone, and one chair, standing room only for guests. I rifled the desk. Old magazines, a couple of racing forms, faded gum wrappers. I stopped after I hit the drawer with the used Kleenex.

The desk had a real blotter with leather corners. I tucked my business card under one cowhide triangle and went back out the way I came.

✦ ✦ ✦

I looked down at the gravestone, then to the harbor below. Too nasty for pleasure boats, and the working ones were long gone. A few seagulls struggled to take off into the gusty wind at the foot of Beth's hillside.

What brings you here on a day like this, John?

I came back to her stone, shrugging a little at both the question and the cold. "Jiggy Doyle."

Jiggy, Jiggy. Still drinking?

"I don't think so."

And his other vice?

"Still going strong."

Poor Moira. You certainly had your faults as a husband, John, but thanks be that wasn't one of them.

"No, but it could have been."

A pause. *Meaning, you're going to help him with something.*

"Or try, anyway."

Do everybody a favor.

"What?"

Don't die trying.

✦ ✦ ✦

I drove down the Doyles' street. It was wider than I remembered it. Two teen-agers in a driveway tried to tune the carburetor on an old Ford Mustang, the engine sounding rough and raspy as one came down on the accelerator. Next door, a boy joustled what looked to be his sister as they put the stones in the smile of a snowman. Her ski parka was too long for her, his gloves mismatched. A letter carrier nearly slipped and fell as he came off the stoop of Moira Doyle's house.

I waited until the carrier was three doors down before I walked carefully up the stoop and rang the bell. Moira pulled open the front door with an expectant look that turned to disappointment before she remembered to put on a smile for company.

"John Cuddy? It can't be!"

"It is, Moira. How are you?"

She gave me a hug and tugged me inside the house and toward the kitchen in back. There was the smell of hot chocolate from the stove as she pointed to a chair and went to a cabinet over the sink.

I took in the kitchen. Appliances that looked older than the relic in Bennigan's cardroom. Dingy paint peeling from the ceiling. Both the corners of the linoleum and the corners of the formica veneer on the table curled upward toward the buzzing florescent light, like the petals of a flower toward a dimming sun.

Moira started to pour into a mug before she noticed it was chipped. She dumped the mug into the sink and reached for another in one fluid motion, filling the new one as though each step were a required part of some Japanese tea ritual.

Moira had always been graceful, and more. Half the guys in sixth grade were looking at her before they even understood why. But she had eyes only for Jiggy. Go figure.

They were married as seniors in high school, and it had lasted all the years since, but the milky complexion was a little mottled now and the black hair blowsy. There was also a tightness at the corners of the mouth and in front of the ears, a tension I hadn't seen in her since the days before Jiggy kicked the grape.

Moira set my drink in front of me and tried to settle in with hers, but it didn't work.

"Moira, what's wrong?"

"What's always wrong. Jiggy. You're here, you must know that."

"I was hoping to see him."

"Why?"

"To talk about some things."

"Goddammit, John!" Moira looked away, then bit her lip and looked back. "I'm sorry. I'm—what do they call it, killing the messenger?"

I didn't say anything.

Moira tried some of her chocolate, realized she didn't really want it, and pushed it away, an inch at a time. "I need for somebody to tell me what's going on. If Jiggy won't, I was hoping you would."

"Moira, I can't. When do you expect him back?"

A grunt that would have been a laugh if there were any humor in her. "The twelfth of never."

I stopped. "He's off again?"

"Off? Oh, you mean off the wagon. No. No, he's been faithful to that, John. Once he knew it meant losing me, he's stayed away from the booze. But the gambling, now, that's a different thing entirely."

"Tell me about it."

"What's there to tell you? He gets up, sucks on that Gatorade till he should turn green, then goes to the doggies up in Wonderland or the flats at Rockingham or wherever he can lay down a bet. It's all the man does, but I could take that, John. I have taken it, for twenty-odd—and they have been *odd*—years. But this not . . . knowing, this I can't take."

"Not knowing what?"

Moira thought about something, made up her mind, and left the table. I could hear her rooting around in another room before she returned to the chair.

Moira smoothed out a tightly-folded paper on the plastic tablecloth. "Jiggy had this in a hidey-hole, a place he keeps his winnings the few times he has some to hide. I'm pretty sure he doesn't think I know about the place or this."

She turned the paper so I could read it. A binder for a term life policy. Insured: Raymond—God, I'd forgotten that was his given name—Doyle. Beneficiary: Moira Doyle. Face amount: fifty thousand dollars. Date of issue: two days before.

I checked the name of the insurance company on the binder. I knew somebody there. "Jiggy didn't talk to you about this?"

"John, he hasn't talked to me about anything. Not for almost three weeks. Something must have happened, but . . ."

She left it trailing, hoping I'd pick it up. Instead I said, "You hear from him, let me know?"

It took a minute for the hope to leave her eyes. "I used to get mad at him, John. His answer was always, 'Don't worry, More, I won't touch the house, not ever the house.' Well, three weeks ago, I started worrying about him, but now that's gone, too. Now I'm just scared. I'm just so scared."

Moira Doyle bit her lip again and turned away from me, standing and hugging herself in front of the sink.

Three

Back in the office, I called my friend at the insurance company on Jiggy's binder. The policy checked out. Payment on death so long as cause not suicide.

I hung up the phone, but my hand was still on the receiver when it rang. "John Cuddy."

"Kinda anxious there, Cuddy, picking up so fast. You got a guilty conscience, maybe?"

I hadn't heard the voice for a long time, but it hadn't changed that much. A little deeper, a little more oily.

"Danny boy, your butler wake up yet?"

"Yeah. He didn't appreciate the bath you gave his toy."

"He's lucky only the toy went into the hopper."

"Spider, he'd like for you to come calling again."

"His name's really 'Spider'?"

"Come on over and see."

"I think it's your turn to visit me."

"Might leave kind of a mess afterwards."

"Not where I'm thinking."

✦ ✦ ✦

"Spider, he don't like being this close to cops."

I looked past Danny Bennigan to the blond bomber, sitting sullenly on a pedestrian ramp and watching the parking lot of the Metropolitan District Commission Police on Storrow Drive. The Mets patrol waterways, parks and some major roads in and around Boston.

I'd jogged over from the condo I was renting on Beacon Street. Danny and Spider left the Trans Am out of sight. My guess is that Danny had to drive, given the metal splint on Spider's left ring finger.

Bennigan coughed and spit. He was wearing a blue suit and topcoat, both shining a little in the unkind glare of daylight. His chins covered the knot in his tie and flowed over the shirt almost to the points of his collar.

A fat thumb waggled at the MDC station house. "Lifeguards with guns."

I said, "What?"

"The Mets are always at the beaches there. The Boston cops call them 'lifeguards with guns.' "

"Not to their faces."

Bennigan came back to me, shook his head. "This is about that fuck-breath Doyle, right?"

"You tell me, Danny."

"All right, Cuddy. I'll tell you." The air was cold enough that Bennigan's words came out in puffs of gray, like balloons over the heads of characters in a comic strip. "Doyle comes into my place in Dorchester there and wants to do some business, play a couple hours. I don't particularly like him, I don't know anybody particularly liked him except you back in school. But the fuckbreath, he's got maybe three hundred in twenties on him, so I says, 'Okay. You play at the working table, right?' "

"The working table."

"The poker table for the working stiffs. I call that the working table, account of the stakes are limited. Max bump is five bucks, three-bump max per betting round. The other table's blackjack, so you control your own bet there."

"What about the third table?"

"That's the rollers' table. High rollers. I run a simple, clean establishment. Word gets around to the right people, and they refer me clients."

"And you get a cut of the pots."

Bennigan's eyes narrowed. "You telling this or am I?"

"Go ahead."

He took a breath but didn't seem to get any happier. "So, I'm at my place that night, and I turn my back for a couple, three minutes. Before I know it, your fuckbreath friend's at the rollers' table, drinking his green puke from a big plastic cup and playing this drug baron somebody sent over."

"Local?"

"No. Some fucking South American, he's got this gold cigarette case open on the table next to him, taking a blow once in a while from the snow he's got in there. The baron's also got these bodyguards look like little Indians, you know? I mean, they want to say something to the guy, who looks like maybe he's got some of the blood himself, they walk over to him, cup their hands, like, and whisper in his ear. I had the feeling they was sorry to be in the room, like the poker was taking them away from shrinking heads or something."

"And Jiggy's losing."

"Losing? He's getting creamed. The asshole carries his chips over from the working table and bets them. He knows, he fucking bell-clear knows he ain't supposed to do that with the chips even if he does change tables. Everybody knows that. But he does it and he's losing and the drug baron is getting off on it. Taking the peabrain in the Red Sox hat and the coat like a buffalo blanket. Then Jiggy finally wins a hand, and I'm praying he's gonna have a streak, get even with the board so Spider can throw him the fuck out of the place, when Jiggy, he gets so excited about winning that he spills his drink, the whole fucking cup of it, all over the table."

I tried to picture the light green stain on the felt cloth. "He spills it on the baron's cocaine."

"Right. And his suit. So the baron stands up, and I swear I thought the little Indians were gonna start shooting up the place, and I thank Christ Spider doesn't have his toy out, because I know that would set them off. So I go over to the drug guy and tell him I'm gonna make everything okay. And he says, 'That is correct. You will make up everything.' And I says, 'Wait a minute.' And he says, 'My product, my clothes, my winnings. This man was your guest, and I am your guest. You vouch for him, you make good on his debt.'

"I swear to you, Cuddy, you took one look at this guy and his fucking Indians, you woulda done a strip-tease for him, he asked you."

I could see where this was going. "What did it come to?"

Bennigan knew what I meant. "Thirteen grand."

Jesus.

Danny looked over at his enforcer. "I tell that fuckbreath Doyle, he comes up with the money by yesterday, or I let the Spider loose on him."

"Jiggy doesn't have that kind of money."

"Moira does."

"He won't touch her house."

"I will."

I shifted toward Bennigan just a little. Both he and Spider noticed and perked up.

I tried to keep my voice steady. "I wouldn't touch the house, Danny."

"You wouldn't. We know you fucking wouldn't, Cuddy. But you're not a businessman out thirteen large. Moira? Moira, she's . . ."

Bennigan stopped. For just a minute, he got a faraway look in his eyes, a look that made him seem younger, and thinner, and—

He snapped out of it. "Moira, nobody's gonna touch her from my end, Cuddy. She's had enough heartache living with the fuckbreath. But Jiggy, now. Jiggy's another story. She can take a mortgage on her house there to pay me, or she can take one out to bury her husband, who's living on borrowed time as it is. Either way, I'm gonna see some compensation for my costs here."

Bennigan moved away, the first few steps surprisingly quick, then slower as he realized I wasn't coming after him. As he drew even with Spider and started up the pedestrian ramp, Bennigan said, "Tell Doyle from me, Cuddy. The fuckbreath pays up by tonight, or he's dead by tomorrow."

Spider said, "Believe it," and followed his boss up the ramp.

Four

Two days went by. I didn't hear from Jiggy Doyle or Moira. I didn't want to hear from Danny Bennigan or Spider.

After a long surveillance on another case, I was at home, lying on the couch. I'd been there for maybe an hour when the telephone rang, echoing in the condo.

"Hello?"

"John?"

"Yes."

"It's Moira. Jiggy just called me."

"From where?"

"The Newport Fronton."

"The what?"

"Jai-Alai. Newport, Rhode Island. He was just calling to let me know he was okay."

"Newport."

"Can you . . . ?"

"I'll be waiting for him after the last—what do they call it?"

"Game or match, I think."

◆ ◆ ◆

The Red Sox cap was easy to spot, bobbing just high enough above the heads of most of the patrons coming out the main entrance. As the crowd thinned, Jiggy took a pull from the bicycle bottle and looked around, more for transportation than danger. I let him cross against some traffic and move close enough that I wouldn't have to chase him far if he ran.

"Jiggy?"

He jumped a little, then calmed down, taking another snort from the bottle. "Jesus, John, you scared the shit out of me."

"Gives you an idea of what Moira's been going through."

Jiggy inhaled and let it out. "I got a pretty good idea of that already."

I said, "Let's take a ride."

✦ ✦ ✦

Coming back up Interstate 95, I kept the Prelude in the slow lane, speedometer at fifty-five. For the first ten miles, Jiggy didn't say anything, so I didn't either.

Then, "John?"

"Yeah?"

"You talked with Danny, huh?"

"I did."

"What'd he say?"

"Danny said to tell the little fuckbreath if he doesn't come up with the thirteen large, Spider's going to kill him."

Jiggy closed his eyes.

I said, "Would have been nice to tell me a little more about Spider, Jiggy."

He nodded once.

"And the drug baron at the wrong poker table."

He nodded again.

"And the fact that 'thirteen' had an extra zero after it."

"What difference does it make?"

"The difference is, people do kill you over thirteen thousand."

"No, I mean, what difference does it make, hundreds or thousands, if I don't have it and I won't use the house?"

"Or the life policy?"

The head whipped around to me, the face strobed by the lights of an underpass. "Who told you?"

"Moira. She found the hidey-hole."

Jiggy almost smiled. "I knew she knew about that spot. I figured she wouldn't look there till . . . afterwards."

"After you got yourself killed."

"John, you weren't there. I was having the worst run of cards I ever had. Shit, that I ever even *saw*. Then I realize this guy at the other table—"

"The rollers' table."

"Yeah." A little sheepish. "The rollers' table. Anyway, this South American's got a stack of black chips in front of him like tires at an auto yard. And he doesn't look like he knows shit about poker."

"You see the two guys with him?"

"Danny told you about them, too?"

"He did."

"Well, I wasn't thinking about them. I was just thinking of getting even for a change, maybe even getting a little ahead for once. And I had good hands at that table, John. Good ones."

"It's just that the baron had better ones."

"Right. And then I win that last pot, and it's not a fortune, John, but I jump up a little I guess, and I wasn't using one of these," he gestured with the bicycle bottle, "so everything kind of spilled over everything."

"Including the nose candy."

"Yeah. The Gatorade made it all turn yellow, like snow some dog pissed on, you know? Anyway, I spent two weeks thinking about how to square things with Danny, and I finally came up with something."

"The policy and me."

"You figured it out."

"Tell me anyway."

"I see you on the TV there, I says, 'That's it, John scared Danny off once, he can do it again.' I figure, even if you don't scare him off, you're good with a gun, you'll take that Spider nut off the board. And even if that don't work, the policy will."

"Because I'll make Danny mad enough to kill you."

"Right. Worst case, I'm dead anyway, and this way Moira gets the fifty thousand from the company, which is a hell of a lot bigger stake than I ever brought home for her."

"Moira would really appreciate that."

"Don't go sarcastic on me, huh, John?"

"What you do is, you and Moira take out an equity loan against the house—"

"I won't touch the fucking—"

"—and you figure out a way to pay back the bank, which won't kill you if you can't."

"But will take the house from Moira without paying her any insurance money."

"Worst case, which do you think she'd rather have, you or the house?"

"It ain't what she'd rather have." Jiggy turned to me, an approaching headlight on the lower portion of his face. "It's what's best for her that I care about."

I left it there till we hit Route 128 and swung northeast toward Boston. As I started to talk again, Jiggy said, "I'm sorry I lied to you, John."

"Forget it."

"I won't. But right now I got some thinking to do."

"You want to go home to do it?"

"Yeah." Jiggy closed his eyes again. "Yeah, that'd be nice."

Ten miles later, I turned onto his street. No black Trans Am, but the teenagers were out by their Mustang in peacoats and watchcaps, one holding some wires and the other hooking some up. I pulled to a stop outside the Doyle house.

Jiggy said, "Come in for a minute?"

"Maybe it's something you two should talk about together."

"No. I mean, yeah, we will. But if Moira sees you come in with me, she'll know it's all right. That I'm serious about getting this thing done."

He had a point. "Okay, Jiggy. Let's go."

As we got out, I heard a revving engine, the sound like a strong, full-throated roar. I was thinking that the teenagers had done a good job on the carburetor when brakes squealed and Jiggy knocked me down behind a car.

As I looked up, a bullet hit the Gatorade bottle, making a popping sound and sending a spray of liquid onto the snowbank. More slugs stitched their way across the front of Jiggy's coat, tossing up little clouds of gray threads and red mist and bowling him around like an unbalanced top until he went down onto the sidewalk.

I drew the Chief's Special from behind my right hip and came up over the engine block of the car. I could hear a voice from Moira's house as I levelled on the spinning right rear tire of the Trans Am. Just as I squeezed, the car fishtailed, my shot bursting the right front tire instead. The car pivoted on the wheel, slamming into the line of parked cars on my side of the street, sparks flying and multi-cracked windshield now facing me.

A ball of fire rose from behind Danny Bennigan as he screamed and tried to push the pinned driver's side door of the Trans Am through a parked Plymouth. Spider got out of the passenger's side, having to use his good right hand to work the inside handle. I yelled at him to drop to the ground, but he reached back inside the car and came out with the MAC-10 as Danny tried to climb over the center console.

I yelled once more at Spider. Instead of dropping his weapon, he came at me on full automatic. Instead of running, I dropped him just as the fire got to the gas tank and lifted the Trans Am and what would have been left of Danny Bennigan three feet off the ground.

Five

The cops talked to me in the living room, a badge from the fire department joining them because of the Trans Am. In the kitchen, some neighbors took turns making tea and coffee and putting their arms around Moira's shoulders. By the time everybody in a uniform or suit was finished, gray beams of uncertain light were coming through the window.

I said what I could to Moira, a couple of the neighbors giving me dirty looks as some idea of what had happened became clearer to them. My watch said six-oh-five a.m. when I went out through the front door and down the steps to the sidewalk.

I stopped for a minute at the spot where Jiggy had died. There was very little blood on the concrete, his old tweed coat and internal organs absorbing most of it. Where the Gatorade had sprayed, the snow had leached the lime color to a dull yellow. Or maybe the other way around.

I bent down. As I reached my hand out toward it, a voice behind me said, "Hey, don't do that."

Still on my haunches, I turned my head. The snowman kid from yesterday but without his sister.

He pointed the index finger of one mismatched glove. "My mom says you should never eat yellow—"

"She's right," I said, standing and walking back to my car.

DEPUTY DOWN

One

It was one of William Least Heat Moon's *Blue Highways*, on the way from Boston to Florida. I'd spent two weeks working undercover for a high-tech company afraid a competitor was siphoning off its secrets. Netting enough money for a leisurely, kick-the-leaves ten days, I'd locked the pebbled-glass door with "JOHN FRANCIS CUDDY—CONFIDENTIAL INVESTIGA-TIONS" stencilled on it, packed a suitcase, and headed south.

The road was one lane each way, bordered by mossy trees and undeveloped marshes. A nice change of pace from the company's concrete bunker and the interstate's concrete monolith. I could have told you the state I was in, but not the town or even the county without having watched for the little one-by-three signs along the shoulder.

My silver Prelude, the last year of the first design, had just cleared a small rise. Through the open moonroof, I could see a V-pattern of ducks, pacing me five hundred feet in the air. Then I started gaining on a rusted pick-up in my lane. There was a Chevy compact in the oncoming one, so I eased off the gas. Good thing, too, as I drew even with a sheriff's cruiser, white with green and gold racing stripes on the sides and bubble lights revolving on the roof. The husky deputy was just about at the driver's door of the ten-year-old Buick he'd pulled over, more primer than paint on it.

That's when the deputy jumped backward into the path of the pick-up in front of me, his Smokey the Bear hat coming off as his arms flew diagonally above his shoulders like a man clowning for his balance at the edge of a swimming pool. I registered the report of a shotgun and a black face and hand at the driver's side window of the Buick as the pick-up struck the deputy and sent him twenty feet through the air. The oncoming Chevy compact swerved and missed him but clipped the pick-up, sending it sideways. My left front fender banged into the truck as I slewed right onto the shoulder.

When the dust cleared, the Buick was accelerating down the road. A black hand reached out the window, adjusting the mirror as the driver's head, a baseball cap on it, flicked twice that way, like a nervous bird checking its position. The Buick then wheeled off at the first exit, maybe a quarter of a mile south.

I climbed out of my car, wobbling a bit before my knees got used to walking again. The driver of the Chevy was a woman, sobbing into the chest of the older man driving the pick-up. I heard him use "nigger" a couple of times in snatches. Moving to the cruiser, I opened the door and keyed the handset for the radio.

"Break, break, emergency. Break, break, emergency. We have a deputy down. I say again, we have a deputy down."

Then I had to yell to the older man from the pick-up to find out where the hell we were.

✦ ✦ ✦

"Quarter-mile, you say?"

"However far that first exit is from where the deputy's cruiser was."

"Might's well call him by name. Clint Mesketh."

"I'm sorry for your loss, Sheriff."

The man nodded. African-American, his accent sounded more Philadelphia "O" than Deep South. Fifty or so, his hair was shot through with gray, his eyes deepset under bushy brows. He wore the same khaki uniform as the dead deputy, but the Smokey hat was on a coattree against the wall to the side of his desk, and there was a spare tire of fat lolling above the Sam Brown belt as he sat in the high-backed swivel chair. The county building was old, a wooden-blade ceiling fan turning slowly overhead, but the air-conditioner in the window was an energy-efficient newer model, and modern video-tape, hidden-mike, and crime-scene equipment was ordered neatly on the shelves behind him.

I said, "I didn't catch your name."

"Doone. First name's Chester, so I tend not to use it too much. Born down here in the county, but my daddy moved up to Philly for the defense jobs, and I went on the force there for twenty before coming down here and getting myself elected by kinfolk and their friends."

"Thanks for the biography."

"Autobiography."

There was no smile on Doone's lips, but a little something played at the corner of his eyes. I decided I wouldn't much like being on the wrong end of his attitude.

He said, "This here's my first one's not so obvious."

"Obvious."

"On who did it and why."

My turn to nod.

Doone sat forward in his chair. "Car you got the plate on, the Buick, turned up abandoned in the supermarket lot. Been hot-wired out from the same lot earlier that morning, because the owner didn't notice it missing but sure as hell remembered he didn't park it where we found it. We found the shotgun, too. Double-barrelled piece, sawed down to three inches, serial number filed off. Pretty common weapon otherwise, probably three thousand of them in the county. Side pocket by the driver's seat had a diagram of one of our two banks. Crayon on brown paper, couple words misspelled."

Doone paused.

I said, "Kind of . . . complete."

"Yeah. Tidy, even. Deputy stops potential robber; robber panics and fires; robber ditches car and takes off."

"Mask?"

"No."

"Note for the teller?"

Doone shook his head.

"Any need for the driver to be on that section of highway to go from the supermarket to the bank?"

That little movement at the corner of his eyes. "No. And about every soul in the county knows that stretch you were on is the one Clint most times patrolled."

"Maybe not so complete, then."

"Except for you, Mr. Cuddy."

Uh-oh. "I don't understand, Sheriff."

"We took statements from the man in the pick-up you hit and the lady in the Chevy that hit him. You don't need to know their names. All you need to know is the man sees a black face behind every crime between Miami and New York, and the woman couldn't tell you and me apart at ten feet. That leaves us but one reliable, material witness to this tragedy."

"Sheriff, I just want to get my car fixed and be on my way."

"The boys are arranging for the towing, and Jimmy's is the only garage in the county can handle that Japanese car you're driving."

"Sheriff—"

"Jimmy tends to get backed up some, though. Way I see it, you might's well be a guest of the county for a couple, three days. Maybe walk around a bit with me, talk to folks, see maybe one of them jogs your memory."

I exhaled. "You wouldn't have any particular folks in mind?"

"Some. Feller named Jesse Surpock. Claimed Clint used excessive force bringing him in a month or two back."

"Did he?"

"Jury saw it otherwise. Second, there's a brother and the wife. Clint's brother Luke and Clint's wife Julie, that is. Been some considerable strain in the family lately."

"Why?"

"Clint and Julie's boy Keith drowned last summer."

"Accidentally?"

"Definitely. But Clint came back from Vietnam a little . . . roughed up, and losing his son pushed him a lot further down the same road."

I'd been overseas, mostly Saigon as an MP lieutenant, but there was no reason for Doone to know that. "Sheriff, I still don't see—"

"You will. Fourth one I'm thinking about is another of my deputies, Sedell Warren. Sedell's a man of color, and Clint and him had more than words between them a couple weeks ago."

I turned it over. "And there're going to be a lot of people interested in how you handle the investigation into the killing of a white deputy by what eyewitnesses say was a black."

"One way to put it."

Doone stood up by placing his palms on the blotter and levering his rump out of the chair. "I think you're going to like the local motel. Call it 'La Hacienda.' "

"I can hardly wait."

Two

The less said about La Hacienda, the better. Sheriff Doone got me checked in, room and meals courtesy of the county, drinks and anything dirty on the cable out of my own pocket. Then he took me to see Jimmy, who thought he knew of a "feller down to Columbia" with a yen for old Preludes and a scrap pile of replacement parts to match. Then we drove through town and over the railroad tracks to the proverbial wrong side of them.

Doone said, "Surpock's got a room over here. Done time for about everything the legislature can think to prohibit."

"Including car theft?"

"Take Jesse maybe twenty seconds to hot-wire this vehicle. Ten if he was sober, which he rarely is."

We pulled up in front of the worst house on a block of bad ones. Clapboard, narrow and two-storied, with sagging front porches on both levels, peeling paint, and a couple of scruffy kids playing in the dust with a couple of scruffier dogs.

✦ ✦ ✦

"Jesse, this man saw something happen this morning out on the highway."

The man didn't bother to look up at me. He hadn't bothered to look at me as he answered the door to the rear first-floor room or as he sat down on the bed, either. It was more cot than bed, actually, with a threadbare blanket, dirty top sheet, and mattress pad for fitted bottom sheet, lots of stains on it you'd like to think were from somebody spilling lemonade.

Surpock was forty or so, a sallow white man. Wiry to the point of spindly, cords of muscle stood out from sagging flesh, like rich relatives from poor ones at a wedding. The face had seen its share of fists over the years but not a razor for a couple of days. There was a sour smell to the room, empty bottles of a whiskey I'd never heard of lying on the floor near an old Atlanta Braves baseball cap.

Doone said, "Jesse," a little sharper.

Surpock looked up now, the eyes bloodshot and watery. "You gonna beat on me, too?"

"Nobody's going to beat on you, Jesse."

"Tell that to Mesketh, next time you see him."

"Next time'll be at his services, Jesse. Somebody killed him this morning."

The smile that started to cross Surpock's face seemed genuine, both as to surprise and pleasure, but he stopped it halfway as he remembered he had another uniform standing over him. "Man won't be getting no flowers from me."

"What do you know about it?"

"Nothing."

"Where were you this morning, Jesse?"

"Here."

"This room?"

" 'Course this room."

"Anybody with you?"

Surpock let the smile cross all the way. "Just Michelle Pfeiffer, but I had to throw her out, on account of that Madonna girl, she gets awful mad at me if—"

With the back of his right hand, Sheriff Doone clouted Surpock once across the cheek, knocking him flat on the bed.

The spindly man stayed down. "You said you weren't going to beat on me, Sheriff."

"I lost a deputy today, Jesse. And you go and don't show respect for the dead or my investigation, what am I supposed to do?"

"I didn't have nothing to do with it."

"How do you know, till we tell you about it?"

We did, but Surpock was right. He didn't know anything. Or at least he wasn't saying.

❖ ❖ ❖

The next house on our route was two miles away and two steps up from Surpock's. Also clapboard but only one-story, it had browned-over grass, some untended shrubbery, and an old Ford station wagon in a cracked macadam driveway. There was a hand-lettered sign that said, in different-colored paints, "PLASTIC WORMS," "SMALL ENGINE REPAIR," and "FACTORY OUTLET TOWELS."

Leaving the cruiser, Doone said, "Luke likes to cover the waterfront."

"I guess."

"Most likely find Luke 'round back. The worming goes better in the open air."

There was a pungent odor as soon as we turned the corner of the house. A big cauldron burbled over the wood fire, a barbecue grill next to it. A man in yellow rubber gloves and apron was pouring a steaming red goo from an iron pan into molds laid out on picnic benches. Four picnic benches.

Doone said, "Luke?"

The man turned. My only real look at Clint Mesketh had been his features in death, but I could tell they'd been related. The face in front of me was flushed but haggard, with sandy brown hair worn a little too long for style and big forearms under the gloves.

"Sheriff."

Luke Mesketh looked to me.

Doone said, "This is Mr. Cuddy, John Cuddy. He tried to help Clint at the scene this morning."

Mesketh started toward me, then seemed to remember the steaming pan and went over to the grill. He set the pan down and took off his gloves, returning to extend his hand.

"Much obliged for your trying."

I shook with him. "I'm sorry there wasn't anything I could do."

Mesketh nodded, as though he'd been hearing a lot of that in the last few hours.

Doone said, "Kind of thought you might be with Julie, but this was on our way, so we stopped here first."

"I went over there. Appreciate your calling me, Sheriff. It was mighty . . . kind of you. But after we talked about things some, Julie said there wasn't much to do till the funeral, and she said she couldn't do that 'less you released the body."

"Coroner, actually. But she's right. You keeping busy?"

Mesketh followed Doone's eyes over to the picnic benches. "Might's well. Time like this, it's just easier to do the simple things." He looked to me. "Sorry you have to hear this, but the fact is, Clint and me had our problems, and Clint and Julie more problems still, so Clint's getting killed isn't exactly as . . . emotional as it might be."

I didn't know what to say, so I just nodded.

Doone said, "We're going around, talking to folks. Anybody called you or stopped by with any information?"

Mesketh moved his head slowly, left to right. "No, but if they do, you'll be hearing from me. We might not have been close, Clint and me, but this kind of thing, you just can't let it happen."

Doone said, "That's right, Luke. You can't."

✦ ✦ ✦

Back in the cruiser, I said, "You called Luke about his brother?"

"I did. Knew they weren't close, but I figured it'd be good for Julie to have family there when I arrived to deliver the news in person."

"How far from the shooting on the highway to that supermarket lot?"

"One-point-four miles."

"And from there to Luke Mesketh's house?"

"One-point-eight."

"Time enough."

"More than."

I watched the countryside go by. Some trees I recognized, most I didn't, and the flowers, good luck. "Where are we heading now?"

"The widow's."

✦ ✦ ✦

Julie Mesketh's house was painted a bright red. There were beds of tall, purple blooms around the foundation, and the grass was lush and mowed like a putting green. No bicycles or baseball bats or other signs of toys.

On the way to the front door, Doone said, "Go easy."

The screen swung open before we got to it. A sturdy but attractive woman with auburn hair and green eyes stepped over the threshold. She wore blue jeans, a white blouse, and just enough make-up to tell you she hadn't been crying much recently.

"Sheriff."

She looked to me the way her brother-in-law had.

Doone said, "This is Mr. John Cuddy from Boston. He's the one radioed in to us about Clint."

"Oh." Julie Mesketh said, "I'm sorry if what happened inconvenienced you all."

"Not to worry. I'm—"

But she'd already looked back to Doone. "Sheriff, do you know when I'll be able to schedule the burial?"

He waited a moment before answering, and I guessed that he was thinking the same thing I was. That Julie Mesketh was deep in shock, unhinged generally, or just didn't give damn about her husband getting blown apart that morning.

After he explained about the coroner, Doone said, "Can we come in for just a minute?"

"Sure."

We followed her into a small living room. The furniture was what you'd expect, and we all sat. On shelves and the top of the television, there were photo frames turned face down.

Mesketh caught me noticing the frames. "Family tradition. We always bury the photos of someone who's died for a year after we bury them. Keith's will be getting raised again in just a few months."

She spoke pleasantly but without any feeling in her voice, as though she were passing the time of day on the Sunday bakery line. I said, "Your son drowned?"

"Yes. On a day last July, when his father just couldn't find the time to take him swimming. Clint wanted another child afterwards, but really, how can you have another child with a man like that?"

I looked down at the space between my shoes.

Doone said, "When I was by before, we didn't get much chance to talk, but—"

"To talk? To talk about what? How relieved I am that Clint's finally gone? You think prisoners and other deputies were the only people Clint beat up on?"

Mesketh rubbed one bicep with the index and middle fingers of her other hand.

Doone tried another tack. "I was wondering, has anybody called or— "

"Called? Why? You see anybody here, Sheriff? You know of anybody's sorry to see Clint Mesketh consigned to the graveyard shift permanently? I just want to get that man into the ground as quick as possible so I can get on with what I might be able to have as a rest of my life."

Doone rotated the Smokey hat in his hands. "Look, I—"

"There is something you can do."

"What's that?"

"Come on."

She bounced up and started walking toward the kitchen. The sheriff and I exchanged glances and followed.

Mesketh was halfway down the stairs, looking back up at us. "Down here."

The basement was finished, walls white-washed, older and worn furniture on a rug over the floor. The place had a musty smell to it, and a ping-pong table was folded irregularly and stuck in the far corner.

Mesketh approached a padlocked door. "Clint bought that fool table, then never had time to play with Keith. Why buy the thing if you're not going to use it?"

She opened the padlock and pulled back on the door. I could see into a small, hutch-like area with homemade gun racks mounted on the walls. There must have been twenty sidearms and as many rifles and shotguns, with slots for a half-dozen more of the longer weapons.

Doone didn't say anything.

Mesketh waved her hand at them. "Every time Clint'd bring somebody in, he'd take their guns for his 'private collection.' He never told you that, did he, Sheriff? No, he wouldn't, because he filed the number things off them. Before Keith drowned, Clint and Luke would take him out, show him how to be a man with one of these. That's the kind of game Clint liked to play. Bang-bang, not ping-pong."

Mesketh laughed, a very hollow sound in that space. Or anywhere else, for that matter.

Very quietly, I said, "Can you tell if any of these are missing?"

She looked me straight in the eye. "I'm sure I couldn't say."

Three

"Woman gives me the chills."

I said, "In more ways than one."

Doone turned the cruiser down a shady lane and kicked up his speed. "I didn't know about Clint's private collection."

"I believe you."

Doone looked over at me, then said something other than what I thought he had on his mind. "You getting anything out of all this?"

"You mean about who killed your deputy?"

"That's what I mean."

"No."

"Sedell Warren's on the next shift. Be a little easier on the man, seeing him at the office than driving out to his house. Why don't you have some dinner, I'll come back for you around seven."

"Why don't you join me?"

"Because after the day you had, you deserve a drink, and I don't drink in uniform."

"So, just don't have a drink."

Doone shook his head. "Nossir. If I sit down where there's some, I'll have some. Kind of day I had, too." The hands seemed to relax a little on the wheel. "You overseas, Cuddy?"

"For a while."

"Vietnam's what I meant."

"I figured it was."

He looked at me. "I didn't know Clint before his Army time. I do know that being over there kinked him up but good."

"It did that to some, but not to everybody. Most people got discharged and moved back into their lives."

A head shake. "What I'm saying is, the way he was before his son died was bad, but the way he was after that was . . . Well, you saw his wife. Another year, I'd have had to ease him out of the department."

"I can see that."

"So his being dead is kind of a convenience to me."

"I can see that, too."

"Especially if it was some yahoo bank robber just randomly blew him off."

"Right."

Doone pulled into the lot in front of La Hacienda. "Only problem is, I don't believe that's what happened."

"I didn't think you did."

He shifted into park. "And I'm not going to close the case that way if it didn't."

I opened my door. "I didn't think you would."

✦ ✦ ✦

"How was dinner?"

"I'll live."

Doone smiled with his eyes and accelerated. "La Hacienda's got the best kitchen in town."

"Then they'd better check on what happens to the food while the waitress is carrying it to the tables."

"You're lucky I don't take offense real easy."

"Sheriff, I don't see you doing anything real easy."

✦ ✦ ✦

The black man rising from the chair I'd used in Chester Doone's office could be called "colored" and the call would be accurate. His skin tone was almost honey, with blond streaks in his brown hair. About six-two, his left cheek was still bruised like a rotten spot on a pear, but he was shades lighter than the man in the Buick.

Doone said, "John Cuddy, Sedell Warren."

"Deputy."

"Mr. Cuddy."

Neither of us made any move to shake hands.

The sheriff sank into his chair. "Now that we're all like family here, let's share our day with each other."

Warren didn't think his boss was funny, but otherwise he didn't do anything but sit back down.

Doone said, "They still teach you about hot-wiring a car in the academy, Sedell?"

"They show us how it's done, Sheriff."

A judicious nod from Doone. "Cuddy?"

I said to Warren, "You don't look like the man I saw this morning."

"That's good, because I'm not."

"How do you feel about Mesketh being dead?"

Warren straightened a little. "He was a fellow officer. He died in the line of duty. I respect that."

"But . . . ?"

"But if I was going to kill him, I wouldn't ambush him. I'd call him out and beat him to death."

Nice, even cadence to the voice. "I understand you tried that already."

Doone gave me the eye-smile.

I said, "I understand it didn't work out too well."

Warren straightened a little more. "He sucker-punched me."

"Why?"

"Because he was a coward."

"I mean, why'd you two mix it up at all?"

Warren looked to Doone, who nodded once.

The deputy came back to me. "It was in a restaurant. I was sitting at the bar, Clint and his wife were at a table, having dinner."

"And?"

"And he thought I was looking at her too long."

"Were you?"

"Yes."

"Because she's attractive."

"Because she's too attractive to take his abuse. Everybody knew it, but everybody knew she had to."

"Why is that?"

"If she ever tried to divorce him, or just walked out on him, Clint would of killed her."

"You know about Mesketh's basement?"

That threw him. "What?"

"His private collection of guns."

Warren paused. "I heard him talking about it once. That's all."

"I take it you don't have an alibi for this morning?"

"You can take a lot of things, mister."

Doone said, "Se-dell," the voice lilting a little on the second syllable.

Warren glared at me. "I've been with the department three years, but soon as most folks in the county hear that a black deputy had a fight with a white one, and the white one's dead at a black man's hand, they already got me tried and convicted."

Doone said, "You were, you wouldn't be wearing what you're wearing."

Warren looked down at himself. "What, the uniform? The badge, the gun?"

Doone closed his eyes. "Take your pick."

✦ ✦ ✦

"You mean that about him not looking like the man in the Buick?"

Doone and I were alone in his office. "That's right. The man I saw was a lot . . . blacker."

"That mean you don't think Sedell's the one that did it?"

"Not necessarily. It'd be a great deflection for him, to wear a mask or darken his skin temporarily, throw off any witnesses."

"Seems to me the killer went to some trouble to have witnesses."

"I was thinking the same thing, Sheriff."

Doone pursed his lips. "While you were having dinner, I called the coroner. He's releasing the body to Julie, and she's having the burial tomorrow afternoon."

"No wake?"

"We'd call it a 'viewing' down here, but no."

"Why are you telling me this?"

"I was hoping you might come by, take a look, see if anything—"

"Jogs my memory."

The little tug at the corners of his eyes. "Right."

"No thanks, Sheriff."

"What's the matter, you don't like *sleeping* at La Hacienda, either?"

"While I was waiting for my food, I called Jimmy. He said my car'd be ready first thing tomorrow."

"Jimmy now, he was being a little hasty. I called him, too, a bit after you did. Turned out he was wrong about that part from Columbia. Your car won't be ready till after the funeral."

I looked steadily at Doone. "Thanks."

"For what?"

"For going to the trouble of calling Jimmy like that."

A massive shrug. "Don't mention it."

Four

"So, you take in any sights this morning?"

"Sheriff, I don't have a car, remember?"

"Not a bad town for walking."

"I sat by the pool, reading."

"Well then. That's about what you'd be doing down in Florida, right?"

"About."

We were standing outside a Protestant church in the middle of the town. There were thirty or so uniforms like Doone's and more in slightly different colors and patches and sidearms from all over the eastern seaboard. A lot of the officers looked rushed and fidgetty, like they hadn't had much time to get there and were surprised by the brevity of the ceremony inside and the fact that they outnumbered the civilian mourners three-to-one.

The hearse carrying Clint Mesketh's coffin came around from the back of the church, turning onto the street and slowing to allow the crowd to form a throng behind it. Julie Mesketh and her brother-in-law Luke were at the head of the processional with a minister, just behind the hearse itself. Then the people from the Sheriff's Department, both uniformed and plainclothes, including Sedell Warren. Then civilians, most of the men in light-colored dress suits, Jesse Surpock in a collared shirt and slacks, a dark stain down the right leg. The officers from the other agencies brought up the rear, with Chester Doone and me trailing near the back of the pack. I thought Surpock looked nervous, maybe from all the uniforms walking point and drag around him.

We went slightly uphill, then down again, maybe half a mile before the street ended at a cemetery gate. Everybody filed in after the hearse, arraying themselves around the only open gravesite. Nobody had anything to add to the minister's short reading, and we were drifting back toward the church fifteen minutes later.

Doone said, "Anything?"

"No."

He shook his head. "Can't see holding you from your vacation any more, then. Lift to Jimmy's?"

"That would be nice."

Getting into his cruiser, I said, "You think she'll spring for a headstone?"

Doone looked across the parking lot, then ratcheted the steering wheel into place. "I doubt it."

Next to the church, Luke Mesketh held the passenger's door of his station wagon until his sister-in-law settled into her seat. Then he came around to his side, got in, and rolled down the window. Sticking his arm out, he adjusted the rearview, and then flicked his head twice at it before pulling away.

I said, "Jesus Christ."

✦ ✦ ✦

The smell seemed a little less pungent this time around. Maybe the wind, maybe the materials, maybe just me expecting it. He turned around, kind of sharply, then bent over the molds again. "Saw you at the funeral. It was good of you to stay over for it."

I said, "Was it more that you hated him or more that you lusted after her?"

Luke Mesketh froze.

"Or maybe Keith was the last straw, though you waited kind of a long time to do something about that."

Mesketh turned to me, the gloves and apron and pan giving the scene a surprisingly domestic flavor. "What're you talking about?"

"I'm guessing it was Julie. You wanted her, he had her, he'd never let her go. You knew his routine. You fix small engines, it wouldn't be that hard to hot-wire a car's ignition. You used some of your plastic there, black plastic, to make a mask and gloves, wore a baseball cap to cover the hair line. Good enough to fool somebody from a distance and even your brother up close, at least for a few seconds. But you had to be sure it was him in the cruiser, so you adjusted your outside mirror to see him walking up to the Buick."

Mesketh just stared at me.

"Then you shot him and took off. Where'd you get the gun, Luke? His private collection, or just one you picked up and sawed off?"

"I don't know what you're talking about."

"You saw your brother driving your sister-in-law crazy, especially since your nephew died. You figured the diagram and the gun would look good, and the black disguise a nice deflection. And it was."

"The man wore a mask, how can you know who it was?"

"You've got a habit of flicking your head at the car mirror, Luke. It's like a fingerprint for you."

He wet his lips, looked around his yard. "Why are you saying these things to me?"

"Your little set-up's cost me time and money, Luke. Time and money. I've been stuck here when I could have been unlaxing on a beach somewhere, and I figure to be compensated for my time."

"Compensated?"

"Yeah. If I have to tell the Sheriff what I know, it'll be another couple of days, easy. So I figure, since I was on vacation, I should get double-time, not just regular rate."

"What . . ." Mesketh licked his lips again. "What are we . . . talking here?"

"Let's say twenty-five hundred, round numbers."

"I . . . I can't raise that kind—"

"Luke, Luke. I don't know what the going rate is down here, but if you'd spent just half that in Boston on a competent button man, you wouldn't be where you are now. So some of that three thousand is like tuition, you know? Tuition for the lesson you learned."

"Three . . . ? But you just said twenty-five—"

"Education's expensive, Luke, and higher education's the most expensive of all. Better commit now, before tuition goes up any more."

"Three . . . thousand. All right, fine. But it'll take me—"

"A while. I thought it might. I'll be back, say in a week? I'll stop in on my way up from Florida. That'll give you time, and maybe if I see you and get all that cash, I won't have time to visit with Sheriff Doone. What do you say?"

He didn't say anything.

"That seals it then, Luke. See you in a week."

As I got to the front of the house, I reached under the lapel of my suit jacket and unclipped the hidden mike. "Sheriff, you get all that?"

The muted voice at the back of my collar said, "Loud and clear. I hope you were kidding."

Kidding. "About what?"

"About maybe not having the time to come back and visit with me."

I turned off the mike and climbed into the driver's seat of the Prelude.

ST. NICK

One

"Mr. Cuddy?"

Standing behind my desk, I said, "Yes. Ms. Nucci?"

"Right." She carefully closed the old-fashioned wooden door with the pebbled-glass panel reading "JOHN FRANCIS CUDDY, CONFIDENTIAL INVESTIGATIONS." About five-foot-two in low heels, Bernadette Nucci wore a wool skirt and blazer despite the ninety-degree August heat baking the Boston Common outside my windows. I had the impression she'd dressed in the best outfit she owned. About twenty years old, her somber attitude didn't match her nice tan any more than her clothes did the weather.

I gestured to one of the two client chairs in front of my desk. "Please."

Nucci moved awkwardly to the chair, as though she were more used to working in an office than visiting one. "Like, I really appreciate your seeing me on just a phone call."

I sat back down. "That's usually how people find me. What's on your mind?"

Nucci twisted the strap of her handbag as it lay in her lap. "A friend of mine—well, not exactly a 'friend,' I guess, but this woman I like know at . . . *knew* at work, she got killed last week."

"What happened?"

"Somebody . . . She was on her way home, walking from the trolley and got . . . strangled."

"In Allston?"

"That's right. Mary Kohl."

I'd read about it. Kohl left one of the Green Line commuter trolleys that wend their way westward from downtown toward the more residential sections. Her body had been found in an alley.

I said, "The newspaper story didn't mention any witnesses."

Nucci seemed to focus on the ashtray at her side of my desk, still twisting the strap. "I . . . Like, would it be okay if I smoked?"

"Go ahead."

She opened the clasp on her bag, took out a soft-pack of green and white cellophane, and lit up using a slim lighter. I've never smoked myself, but when you're in a service industry, you're better off making allowances for the clients who do.

A deep drag, then a breath that sounded more relaxed. "St. Nick."

"I'm sorry?"

"St. Nick. Nicotine. That's what we call ourselves. The Society of St. Nick."

"Who's 'we'?"

"The other people at The Pickard Company and me who smoke. You ever heard of Arthur Pickard?"

"No."

"Well, he's the boss, founded the place, and he doesn't allow smoking in the building. Or even in front of it. We all have to like go outside in the back, so nobody has to smell the smoke. Only thing is, it's like a wind tunnel down there, so your cigarette burns faster than you can smoke it."

Which might be what Mr. Pickard had in mind. "I'm not sure I follow why you're here."

Nucci grew even more somber. "I was away on vacation when Mary got killed. I come back, and it like hits me. Maybe she's dead because of the Society."

"Of St. Nick."

"Right, right. I mean, she'd only been working with us for a while, and she turns out to be a smoker, so I tell her to come down with me to the Chapel—that's what we call the wind tunnel?"

"The Chapel of St. Nick."

"Right." Nucci took another puff. "Kind of . . . what's the word?"

"The word?"

"For like calling it a 'chapel' and all."

"Irreverent, maybe?"

"Irreverent, right, right. Irreverent. Look, I don't want to give you the wrong idea or anything. I was brought up Catholic, real strict, the nuns and no boys and everything, even in this day and age."

Nucci had an odd way of mixing phrases from what might have been her grandparents' generation with the universal "like" of her own. "Why do you think Ms. Kohl's death might be related to your smoking group?"

Nucci stubbed out her cigarette in the ashtray, smoke coming up from her nostrils. "I don't. I mean, like, I can't prove anything. That's why I'm coming to you."

"Have you been to the police?"

"No."

"Why not?"

"Since I was on vacation when it happened, they never talked to me, and

I don't really have anything to tell them."

"But you think you have enough to tell me."

"Maybe if you . . . Look, I don't know how this is supposed to work, right? I mean, on TV, the people come to Magnum or Rockford and he like takes it from there. But maybe if you heard me out, you'd be able to tell me."

She seemed sincere, and nice, and I didn't have a hell of a lot else to do. "Okay."

Nucci lit another cigarette. "It's like this. I'm a secretary at Pickard; they distribute fixtures for retail stores—the things you'd hang pocketbooks and stuff from?"

"With you so far."

"Well, we have this big warehouse out in Framingham, but Mr. Pickard, he's always had the office in downtown, so that's where it stays. I've only been with the company like two years, but it didn't take two days to know that what Mr. Pickard wants, Mr. Pickard gets."

"And Mr. Pickard wanted a no-smoking policy."

"Right, right. There were only a few of us who smoked, and a couple of them gave it up. The only ones in the Society are me, Donnell Willups, Cassie Carmody, and Billy Danvers. And, of course, Mary."

"Can you spell those for me?"

Nucci did. "And Mary's last name is . . . was K-O-H-L, not C-O-L-E."

"Got it."

She drew some more smoke into her lungs. "Anyway, Mr. Pickard started the policy at the beginning of the summer, so like three months ago. We ranked on it at first, but to be honest, it worked out kind of cool."

Cool. "What do you mean?"

"Well, the Chapel itself is pretty grungy. I mean, it's just an opening between the buildings that overlooks this alley, and the derelicts sometimes come up and try to bum a cigarette off you. But the policy kind of mixes together people who wouldn't spend time together much, you know?"

"So, you get to know each other better?"

"Right, right. Like, up in the office, it'd be 'Mr. Willups,' because he's the Vice President of Operations. He smokes these horrendous Turkish cigars, maybe on account of being black and having a hard time coming up. I never worked for him or anything, but in the Chapel he can call me 'Berny' and I can call him 'Don' and it's like just . . . natural, that's all."

"How about the others?"

"Cassie's good, too. Kind of tough, but I guess you have to be, you're in sales with this economy and all. Billy, he runs the mailroom. Kind of a space-shot, all the time wearing his Walkman and listening to classic rock."

"But you all got along well together?"

"Yeah. I mean, just in the Chapel. We never like got together outside work. But then Mary started oh, maybe three weeks ago, and something happened."

"What?"

"I don't know. I just know the first day I met her, she asked me about where you could smoke, and I like told her, 'Follow me.' We went down to the Chapel, and the other guys were already there."

"Willups and Danvers."

"And Cassie, too. I was kind of late, actually. Mr. Pickard lets us have ten-fifteen to ten-thirty and three-fifteen to three-thirty, and that's it, except for what you can scoff during your lunch hour sometimes, which is what I'm doing here right now."

"Mary Kohl about your age?"

"Oh, no. She's . . . she *was* almost Don's age, and he's got to be nearly as old as you."

Thanks. "How about Carmody and Danvers?"

"Cassie's maybe thirty. Billy's a year younger than me."

"Which makes him . . . ?"

"Eighteen and a half."

I almost smiled at the last part, Nucci still keeping track of age in less-than-yearly chunks. "Go ahead."

"Well, it's that first day, like I said, and Mary and me are walking up to the other three, and Billy says something funny."

"You mean 'funny' as in odd?"

"Yeah."

"What?"

"I didn't really catch it, exactly. It was something like, 'What do you know, here comes Mary.' "

"And that seemed odd to you?"

"Yeah. On account of he didn't say it just like that. It was weird and I didn't know what to think, then Mary smiled and said, 'It's okay, don't worry about it.' "

"Worry about what?"

"I couldn't tell. And I didn't want to ask her, since it was her first day and all."

"Her first day is when you first met her."

"Right, like I said."

"Then how did Billy Danvers know to call her 'Mary'?"

"She got introduced around before that. It's not so big an operation downtown, maybe thirty, thirty-five of us, tops."

"Ms. Nucci, I still don't see what you want me to do."

"Well, the cops have had it—Mary's case, I mean—for like a week now, and nothing's happening. I didn't know her all that well, but she just went through a divorce and has two lit . . . *had* two little kids, and it doesn't seem right nobody's still trying to find out who killed her."

"The police don't much like it when a private investigator butts into an open homicide."

"Well, if they're not doing anything more about it, then why can't you?"

Nucci had already been convinced by her own reasoning.

I said, "It's not very likely that I'll find out something the police haven't."

"Does that mean you'll try?"

I blew out a breath that moved some of the cigarette smoke around the room. "I don't work for free."

"I didn't think you did. I still live at home, so I've got some money saved I didn't spend on my vacation." The sheepish grin again. "Fact is, my family . . . I like took the vacation with my folks this year. Grandmother, cousins, everybody in this one big house at the beach."

I quoted her half my usual rate. She blinked but opened the handbag again.

As Bernadette Nucci fished out a checkbook, I said, "Have you told anybody else you were coming to see me?"

"No."

"Good. Don't."

"How come?"

"I want to look into things without people knowing you sent me after them."

"So, if I see you at work, I should make out like I never met you before?"

"That would be good, yes."

Two

"My lucky day."

"Lieutenant."

"I can't give you but ten minutes, Cuddy, and I'll be stealing that from a drive-by came in an hour ago."

Robert Murphy closed the folder on his desk, making the little American flag stuck in his pen holder wave a bit from the breeze. I sat down across from him. Husky and black, Murphy was decked out in a long-sleeved white shirt, flowered tie, and collar-stay. Since he never bothers to get up to shake hands, I can't comment on his pants.

I said, "The gang-bangers are shooting each other in broad daylight now?"

"Summertime. Nights are too short for all the killing they want to do."

"What happens when these hi-jinks spread outside Dorchester and Roxbury?"

"Then maybe you white folks'll start paying attention, appropriate less money for the tourists and more for the homeboys."

"You think it'll happen?"

"What, the gangs driving outside the 'hood?"

"That's what I mean."

"Someday. And I hope I'm long-retired by then. What're you here for?"

"Kohl, Mary. Strangled last week."

"Wednesday."

"Anything?"

"Yeah. The motorman on the trolley happened to remember her. She wasn't a fashion model, but attractive enough. He says she got off with five or six others at her stop, nothing unusual-looking, nobody she seemed to know or be talking to. Then probably an hour later, the day-care lady at her house watching the children gets to worrying that Kohl's not home yet, so she calls 911 just about the time a car almost rolls over the body at the head of an alley."

"How far from the house?"

"Two blocks."

"Sexual?"

"No signs."

"Robbery?"

"Money and credit card still in her wallet."

I thought about it. "She's on her way home from work, it's still pretty light out."

"Not even seven o'clock, from the way the motorman fixes her leaving the trolley line."

"How was she done?"

"Cord, maybe electric cable."

"So no blood, no real weapon to ditch or get caught with . . ."

A grim smile. "You're thinking, it's somebody who knew her and we'd look for, right?"

"Not very dramatic for a crazy."

"Wish you wouldn't mention that word. I been praying for a week now we wouldn't find another like your Ms. Kohl."

I said, "Headline: MAD STRANGLER STALKS HUB."

"Please. TV reporter sticking a mike in my face, 'Lieutenant, do you think the average person has anything to fear from this?' "

"So, anybody stand out?"

"From Ms. Kohl's life, you mean?"

"Yes."

Murphy let his eyelids drop to half-mast. "You in it for the insurance?"

"No."

"Good. Looks like it'll be all her kids'll have."

"How much?"

"A hundred thousand. Part of the divorce settlement."

"You talked to the ex-husband."

"Almost."

"You almost talked to him?"

"Uh-unh. 'Almost ex-husband,' on account of they weren't exactly divorced yet."

"Meaning?"

"Meaning Kohl, George, gets by her dying what he lost by their divorcing."

"You wouldn't have an address on him?"

"I may be nodding off here, but I don't recall you saying just who it is you're fronting for."

I told him. "Can I poke around?"

A lumbering sigh. "Given Ms. Nucci's probably the only person the decedent knew with an alibi, be my guest. Truth to tell, there's nothing in our jacket on this but a fond hope, and I don't see how you can tramp on that."

✦ ✦ ✦

"George Kohl?"

"Who wants to know?"

The man in khaki shorts and a sweat-stained tee shirt rested the box on the stoop of the address Murphy had given me. The stoop belonged to the house in Allston that Mary Kohl had gotten as part of the divorce, Murphy telling me that George was moving back in to take care of the children. Kohl was about my age, with thinning brown hair plastered on his head and a gut that pushed the box ahead of him on the stoop.

I took out my ID holder.

He read the information carefully. "Private Investigator. Now what?"

"I'll try not to take up too much of your time."

"My time. My time. I remember when I used to have a real sense of that concept, you know?"

"Sorry."

"I just about get over the idea of the divorce, of seeing my kids on a schedule, of losing everything I ever worked for to Mary and her shyster lawyer Hitchcock. I even just move into my own place, first time since last year of college I'm going to be living alone. Then this happens."

I nodded toward the door. "Your children inside?"

"Naw. I packed them off to Mary's sister. A vacation on the farm. Seems to make sense to wait until I go pick them up to tell them."

I wasn't sure I agreed, but then I've never been a father. "Mr. Kohl—"

"And that's not going to be the worst part, you know. The worst part, that's going to be juggling this house and two kids and a job I've already been away from too much because of the divorce hassle. How am I supposed to do all that, huh?"

I thought, the same way your almost-ex was supposed to. "Mr. Kohl, do you know why your wife went to work at The Pickard Company?"

"Yeah. Mary needed the money. I sure as hell don't make enough. Even the judge saw that."

"But she didn't work during the marriage?"

"Just before the kids came. Then after our daughter—the first one, nine years ago—Mary says to me, 'Let's really raise her right, George, no turn-key stuff.' I say fine. So we buy out here in Allston instead of someplace decent, and rot here through another kid—a boy, this time—and a marriage that's crumbling faster than the old plaster inside. Then she decides it's time to end it."

"End it?"

"Yeah, the marriage. Oh, you thought . . . suicide? Hah, that's a laugh. That's the first good laugh I've had for a week. Mary-Mary-Quite-Contrary committing suicide. Let me tell you, pal, she was the last person I know who'd kill herself."

"Where did your wife work before?"

"This retail store, women's clothes, went out of business a couple, three years ago."

"Which is why she had to go elsewhere."

"Else . . . Oh, you mean Pickard's. Yeah, but let me tell you, even if the other store was still around, they wouldn't have taken her back."

"Why not?"

"You never met Mary-Mary, right?"

"Right."

"Well, let me tell you, she was the kind would climb the ladder of success with a knife in her teeth. That knife went into a lot of backs at the old store."

"Anybody in particular?"

"Not that I'd remember. Why all the questions, anyway?"

"I'm just looking into things. Your new place, you going to have to sell it now?"

"Sell it? I never owned it. After Mary-Mary picked me clean, I was lucky I could afford to rent."

"Lease?"

"No. Month-to-month. The only break I got, seems like."

"Because it's so flexible."

"Huh?"

"Being month-to-month, you could leave the new place . . . whenever."

Kohl bristled. "What're you saying here?"

"I'm saying I think this place bouncing back to you because the divorce wasn't final seems pretty lucky."

"Lucky? Lucky, with God knows what kind of obligations Mary-Mary rang up while she was on the loose? Let me tell you, in this real estate market, a house isn't exactly worth killing for, get me? Especially when it comes equipped with two kids."

I left George Kohl moving back into his house. I didn't envy the children who'd be growing up in it.

✦ ✦ ✦

Hitchcock did not look much like Alfred. His first name was Joseph, and he was tall and thin, with dishwater blond hair parted precisely over horsy features and a seersucker suit that had seen better days. He didn't seem particularly thrilled to find me waiting by his secretary's desk when he returned from a pre-trial conference at the Probate and Family Court.

"Yes?" the eyebrows arching.

The secretary introduced us, and I asked if I could have a little of his time for a former client.

"Which one?"

"Mary Kohl."

The eyebrows dropped as part of a frown. "Yes. Yes, come in."

Hitchcock's office was big enough, but cramped, files and lawbooks piled on chairs and against the wall in teetering stacks. There was one chair empty, and I took that as he moved behind his desk. After flickering through a half-dozen pink message slips, Hitchcock sank into his chair without taking off his suit jacket. "Who is *your* client, Mr. Cuddy?"

"I promised I wouldn't say."

"Then you have me at a disadvantage that I'm not sure I want to expand for you."

I began looking leisurely around the room, like a tourist on a sight-seeing trip.

Hitchcock might have grinned. "I take your point, and I wouldn't care to try throwing you out. What do you want?"

"Any ideas you have on why Mary Kohl was murdered."

A pursing of the lips. "That's easy. None."

"Think about it."

"I have. She was not the most likable person in the world, but . . . Do you understand the attorney-client privilege?"

"Mostly."

"Well, then, as you know the privilege survives the death of the client, but to be frank, there's nothing she told me that could help you. Or the police, who've already spoken to me."

"Robert Murphy."

Another grin. "Are you merely well-informed, or also well-connected?"

"We've known each other a while. You dealt with the husband on the divorce?"

"Yes. Directly, I'm afraid."

"So he wasn't represented."

"Correct. In this economy, you see it fairly frequently, but I had the feeling that George Kohl was using it more for sympathy with the judge than because he just couldn't pay another attorney's fee."

"Beyond your own, you mean."

"Correct again, and perfectly legitimate. The judge ordered him to pay my fee with full disclosure and ample supporting evidence of Mrs. Kohl's circumstances."

"Which were?"

"Out of the workforce for nearly a decade, two children of tender years to nurture, a house to support. I could go on."

"Do you know how she came to get the job at The Pickard Company?"

"Yes."

"Can you tell me?"

Hitchcock played with his tie, a regimental one. "I don't see why not. I knew Arthur—Arthur Pickard—in school, and I called him for her."

"Why?"

"She'd been in retailing, but what with all the mergers and acquisitions and bankruptcies, it's a difficult field to enter. I thought she might have a better chance trading on her experience at the periphery."

"A company that provides fixtures to retail stores."

"Exactly."

"And Pickard himself agreed."

"He agreed to interview Mary. After that, she was on her own."

"Did she ever talk with you about how the job was going?"

Hitchcock seemed to consider something, maybe an aspect of the attorney-client privilege. "Not in so many words. I knew she'd started there, but I didn't get any progress reports."

"From her or from Pickard."

A very precise "From neither."

"How about George Kohl?"

"How about him?"

"Do you think he'd be capable of this kind of violence?"

"Everyone is capable of it, Mr. Cuddy. Take you, for instance. I have the feeling that you've seen and done your share."

"No argument there."

"Ever been married?"

Thinking of Beth, I paused before saying, "Just once."

"Was the divorce amicable?"

"There wasn't one. My wife died."

"Oh." Something crossed Hitchcock's face. "Oh, I'm sorry, I . . . Look, my point was going to be . . . I've been involved in a lot of divorce cases over the years. Would I have been surprised if George Kohl stood up and started throwing things at a settlement conference? No. Would I be surprised to learn he'd lain in wait for his wife and strangled her? Yes. I don't think George ever understood Mary, Mr. Cuddy."

"But you did?"

Attorney Joseph Hitchcock said he had other things to do and would I please leave.

◆ ◆ ◆

Tulips? Where did you find those this time of year?

I laid them on the grave so the blossoms were toward her headstone. "Mrs. Feeney saw them at the market this morning and stocked a couple dozen."

They're beautiful, John.

"Then they're appropriate, too."

You seem troubled.

I looked away from the harbor at the foot of her hillside and toward a ballfield. The same one I'd played on growing up, third base beginning in third grade. "New case, Beth."

Tell me about it.
I did.
I feel badly for the woman, but, Jesus, those poor kids.
"I just hope things don't get any worse for them."
If it's the husband, you mean.
"It's somebody, Beth."
What are you going to do next?
"Well, I don't have much to work with, so I thought I'd start at the top."

Three

The next morning I was led into a high-ceilinged office in a pre-War building near the harbor, the kind of place that gets supplanted by a forty-story glass obelisk every couple of years. Arthur Pickard would have had a nice view of a beautiful sloop if he'd been looking out the window behind him instead of at me taking a seat in front of him.

When the receptionist left us, Pickard said, "I'm seeing you at sufferance, Mr. Cuddy."

Mid-fifties, he was sharp-featured and clear-eyed, the sort who wouldn't be used to backing down and might gnaw off your ankle if you knocked him to the floor. He wore a bow-tie and reminded me of a Yankee version of Ross Perot.

I said, "You got a telephone call."

Pickard folded his hands left-over-right on the blotter. "From Joe Hitchcock. Let's not waste any more of my time than is absolutely necessary."

Which made me wonder why he was letting me waste any of his time at all. "How did Mary Kohl come to work here?"

"Joe said he told you. He called me, I agreed to interview her, and I was sufficiently impressed to offer her a job."

"Why?"

"Why?"

"What impressed you about her?"

Pickard refolded his hands, right-over-left this time. More expressive, maybe. "She seemed ready to work, ready to learn, and ready to do what was necessary."

"Necessary for what?"

"For getting ahead in this world. You have no idea how many young men and women sit in that chair and hand me impressive résumés without clue one as to how they will get things done if hired. Mary Kohl was the opposite of that."

I thought about her husband's knife-in-the-teeth comment.

Pickard said, "And then she betrayed me."

I stared at him. "She what?"

"Betrayed me, Mr. Cuddy. She . . . smoked."

He was so serious, you couldn't laugh. "No."

"Yes. There were no nicotine stains on her fingers or her teeth, no smell of it about her, but there it is. Kohl smoked, and I found out about it her first day on the job."

"Is that grounds for firing someone?"

"Not yet. I won't tolerate abuse of drugs or alcohol, nor anything else that could affect the health or well-being of myself or my workers. But I've not yet gone that far with tobacco. As a result of Kohl's betrayal, however, I have instituted a policy of not hiring anyone new who does smoke."

"So, you never asked her during the interview if she did."

A sour face and a refolding of hands again. "No. As I said, there was no . . . objective evidence to cue me on it."

"Where did Ms. Kohl work?"

"Where? I started her in the secretarial pool, just so she would learn the systems faster. She took that positively, agreeing with me that it was better to first have the fundamentals in hand than her nameplate on a desk. Kohl was someone who could take direction, and in fact Donnell asked me to transfer her to his office."

To protect Bernadette Nucci, I played dumb. "Donnell?"

"Donnell Willups. He served with my son in Vietnam. With distinction. He's worked for me ever since they mustered him out."

"And your son?"

Pickard stopped cold. "My son?"

"Does he work here, too?"

"My son is dead, Mr. Cuddy. He died twenty-two years ago this month, in a tunnel below his basecamp near a place called Cu Chi."

The tunnels of Cu Chi, where the Vietcong dug themselves under, around, and through the American troops on the surface. Some of our men, calling themselves "tunnel rats," went down after them. "I'm sorry."

"You're about the right age. Were you there?"

"Not exactly, but near enough. Mostly Saigon."

"You fellows were treated badly, even disgracefully. I hired Donnell more because of that than his being a minority for the stat sheets."

I'm sure Willups would be reassured to hear that. "How long had Mary Kohl been working for him?"

"Less than a week before she died."

"Why did he want her transferred to his office?"

"Ask him. I assume because Donnell saw in her the same things I did, perhaps because they . . . smoked together downstairs. And he needed help."

"Help?"

Pickard paused. "Operations has been . . . slowing down some, with Cassie—Cassie Carmody—doing her job as well as she has. She's throwing more work at Donnell than he can handle."

"You're impressed by Ms. Carmody, too, then?"

"I'm impressed by anyone who can make me money, Mr. Cuddy."

"Does Billy Danvers make you much?"

"Billy performs a necessary task in a competent manner. He can read, he almost knows how to spell, and he occasionally arrives on time. For a worker his age, those attributes amount to a dream come true."

"You seem to know your employees well, Mr. Pickard."

"It's a small company, Mr. Cuddy. But not so small that you should have known about Billy Danvers without my telling you his name."

"Someone else mentioned him."

"It also seems odd to me that you're here about Mary Kohl, one of the 'Smoking Club' or whatever the hell they call it; that I mentioned two others, Donnell and Cassie; and that you mentioned a fourth without my prompting it. Tell me, does it strike you as even odder that neither of us has mentioned the fifth, Bernadette Nucci?"

Pickard's eyes glittered as he refolded his hands one more time.

I said, "What can you tell me about her?"

He smiled, not a very warming sight. "Why don't you waste Bernadette's time instead of mine? They'll all be down there puffing their brains—or lungs —out in a few minutes."

"You keep track of when your employees do that?"

"I keep track of many things, Mr. Cuddy. Many things. You'd do well to bear that in mind. Good day."

✦ ✦ ✦

The back of the building was in the shade, the wind nearly howling through the narrow canyon made by the surrounding structures. It wasn't hard to spot the Society of St. Nick.

As I walked toward them, the medium-build black man I took to be Donnell Willups was just reaching into his coat. Bernadette Nucci had already fired up, holding the lighter for a skinny kid with narrow metal head-phones in his ears. A striking woman who was the right age to be Cassie Carmody was halfway through a hundred-millimeter filtered job.

I said, "Mr. Pickard told me it would be all right with him if I talked to you all."

Nucci said innocently, "Who are you?"

I showed her my ID first, then the others in turn. The hundred-mil woman said, "Cassie Carmody. Start with me."

A dazzling, if slightly predatory, smile.

I looked away from it toward two homeless men sitting against the stone wall of a neighboring building, squabbling over something tall in a dirty, brown paper bag. The wind was whipping the dust around and onto them just as the air currents were taking the smoke up and away from the cigarettes.

I said, "It might be a little easier if I could interview each of you alone."

Willups rolled his lower lip under his upper teeth. "What's this about?"

"The death of Mary Kohl."

Billy Danvers said, "Awesome tragedy, man."

The others gave him a collective harsh look, but he just shrugged.

I said, "Any suggestions?"

Carmody said, "Tell you what. Take Donnell first, because he's going to be worrying about it until he talks to you."

Willups said, "Now Cassie, what are you saying that for?"

Carmody ignored him. "Take Billy second. In fact, buy him some lunch, he needs filling out. I've got a sales call to make by car, so we can ride there together and back if you need more time with me. Berny here can see you after that. Okay?"

I could see why Arthur Pickard was impressed by Carmody, and I wondered how much like her Mary Kohl had been. "Sounds fine to me. Everybody else?"

Just nods, no smiles except for Billy Danvers, who had his eyes closed, "grooving" or whatever they call it nowadays.

✦ ✦ ✦

Donnell Willups seemed nervous in his office, maybe because he never got his smoke outside. The office itself wasn't much, just a twelve-by-twelve with desk, chairs, and computer hutch. Computer print-outs covered every horizontal surface, and more were tacked to every vertical one.

He said, "Excuse the mess."

"Forget it."

"Mary, she was just starting to wade through all this, then . . ."

Willups didn't finish the sentence. About forty-five, he had a face creased with lines and a pock-marked nose almost as wide as his mouth. His hair was military-short, but his sports jacket was wrinkled and the slacks didn't go well with it or the tie. The fingers on his right hand kept drumming the desktop, the portrait of a harried executive.

I said, "She'd been working with you for just a few days?"

"Yeah. I think she would have been good, though. She was only here a week, ten days, she asked me if I was free for a drink. I said sure, and we talked for maybe an hour, hour and a half about what she wanted to learn and do here. She'd already picked up a lot, just sitting in the pool with Berny —that's the young girl downstairs, Bernadette—and playing on the word processor."

"Her experience from the old days wasn't rusty?"

"I don't know, could she type fast or what. I do know she could picture the job, the task at hand, you know what I'm saying?"

"I think so. So you asked Mr. Pickard to have her work with you."

"Yeah." He swept his hand around the room. "You can see why. Cassie's burying me in paperwork."

"Mary Kohl talk about anything that was bothering her?"

"Bothering her? Not to me."

"Maybe to Bernadette—I'm sorry, her last name?"

"Nucci."

" 'Nucci,' thanks."

"That it?"

I wanted to ask him about Billy Danvers' comment on "Here comes Mary," but I couldn't see a way to do that without tipping that somebody, Bernadette Nucci, had told me about it.

I said, "Yes, thanks for your time."

As I moved toward the door, Willups said, "What unit?"

I stopped and turned to him. "We both have the look, don't we."

"You get it, you never lose it."

"Not after what we went through getting it."

Willups took a breath. "So, what unit?"

"MPs as a branch. Saigon, mostly. You?"

"Americal Division, in and around Cu Chi."

"Mostly under it, the way I heard."

"Then you heard it better than I lived it. I was too big to be a tunnel rat, but Mr. Pickard's boy, that's what he did. A good one, too, till the night he ran out of luck."

"Happens to all of us someday."

Donnell Willups shook his head. "Hope it's not for a while yet, myself."

Four

"You call this taking me out for lunch, dude?"

I handed Billy Danvers his hot dog. "Think of me as running a low-budget operation."

"Aw, man, but this is like weak, *mongo* weak."

I paid the vendor under the umbrella for the two hot dogs and matching colas and steered Danvers toward a bench without too much pigeon guano on it. A lot of people were following our example, but sitting on blankets and towels, makeshift office picnics.

Danvers was skinny as a rail, the shock of reddish hair thatch-cut on his head and white sidewalls two inches up from the ears all the way around. Wearing a tee shirt with Mick Jagger's lips prominently caricatured and black jeans that billowed on his legs, Danvers sat at one end of the bench and studiously laid his lunch on one of the slats. As he popped his soda can with one hand and took off the headphones with the other, I thought I heard "Turn, Turn, Turn" coming over the earpieces.

I said, "The Byrds?"

Danvers interrupted a gulp of cola, almost choking. "Oh, too cool, dude. You recognize the sounds?"

"I remember them."

"Sweet music, sweet as burning icing. Your gen' had all the breaks, man. Safe sex, weed to smoke, and the best music the galaxy has ever seen."

Or heard. "Billy—"

"I mean, what's my gen' like contributed to the world, huh? I shall tell you. Mountain biking and bungee-jumping. I perceive a cultural gap there, right?"

"Billy, how well did you know Mary Kohl?"

A shrug. "Just through the Chapel, you know?"

"Where you all smoke."

"Right. She was okay, smoked Berny's brand so they could like double-up when necessary."

"Double-up?"

"Light one and both of them smoke it. The wind in the chapel, man, it does *mongo* bad things to the life span of your chosen brand."

"So both Kohl and Nucci would smoke the same cigarette to make it last longer?"

"Not. To get St. Nick from it faster because the butt would last shorter in the wind, dig?"

Dig. "You talk with Mary Kohl much?"

"Just in the Chapel. Aside from the habit, we didn't have like a lot of common ground, you know?"

"The first time you met her, I hear you said something about her."

Danvers turned to the hot dog for the first time, buying time, I thought. Around chewing, he said, "Don't follow that, dude."

"I heard the first time Kohl came down to the Chapel, you said something about her."

"Oh." Elaborate facial expression. "Yeah, yeah, I remember it well. I said like, 'Hey, what do you know. H-e-e-e-r-e's Mary.' Get it?"

"Modeled on 'Here's Johnny'?"

"*Exacta-mundo*. Like for J.C. when The Tonight Show was totally boss."

"Why?"

Another bite. "Why?"

"Yes. Why'd you say that about Kohl?"

"Just like occurred to me, man."

I looked into Billy Danvers' face and didn't believe him but couldn't see how or why he'd be lying to me about it. "You ever meet her before that day?"

"Not during this incarnation, man." Danvers pantomimed looking at a wristwatch he wasn't wearing. "Oh, so sorry. Got to get back to the mineshaft."

As he adjusted the headphones, I caught a few bars of The Association's "Cherish." Danvers ate the rest of the hot dog on the stroll, seeming to gargle more than drink the cola.

✦ ✦ ✦

"So, how was lunch with Billy?"

"A movie. I'm just not sure which one."

"Try *Wayne's World*. He couldn't help you, huh?"

I looked at Cassie Carmody. We were driving in a Ford Taurus around Leverett Circle toward the Galleria Mall in Cambridge. I would have thought that public transportation, specifically the Lechmere branch of the Green Line, would have been easier, but maybe she had heavy samples of fixtures in the trunk. Carmody herself was on the college side of thirty, athletic without being muscular. She wore her chestnut hair in a flaring, shingled cut, not much jewelry and too much perfume, even with the windows down. Her yellow suit looked like raw silk over a powder-blue blouse, and her eyes even at the wheel had a sideways tendency to keep you in view when you didn't think she'd be watching.

We made the turn toward Lechmere. "So, I've never talked with a private investigator before."

"Not many of us in retail."

"Oh, you'd be surprised. A lot of the store security guys will come over and try to hit on me, but they never seemed . . . real, if you know what I mean."

"Some of them are the real thing, retired cops or military. Others are wannabes, spend a lot of money on gun catalogs and a lot of time doing Robert DeNiro in their bedroom mirrors."

"I thought he was supposed to be a taxi driver?"

"That's the idea."

Carmody frowned, then nodded as though she'd gotten it. "So, which are you?"

"Me?"

"Real or wannabe?"

"Decide for yourself."

A saucy smile this time. "I'd say real."

"What was Mary Kohl?"

"Mary? I didn't know her that well, but she was a wannabe who used to be real."

"How do you mean?"

A shrug. "She had the job, then fell into the trap, hubby and kiddies, then wanted out and back to where she was before."

"Pretty comprehensive."

Carmody frowned again. "For her?"

"For you. Not knowing her that well and all."

"You knew her five minutes—no, five sentences—and you could tell she was a Queen Bee."

"And room in the Pickard hive for only one?"

The saucy smile. "Maybe. I've earned it."

We started passing through the strong smell of skunk. I said, "Don't you want to put the windows up?"

"Why?"

"The skunk."

"What . . . Oh, is there a bad smell?"

"You don't notice it?"

"Uh-unh. Had an accident when I was a kid. I can't give you all the medical mumbo-jumbo, but it took my sense of smell. Makes food kind of boring, since most of that is smell, not tastebuds, but the upside is I care less about eating and more about staying in shape. Or hadn't *you* noticed?"

I looked over at Carmody. "I noticed."

"You going to do anything about it?"

I thought of a hillside across town with stones sticking out of the ground. "Probably not."

Neither a smile nor a frown this time. "Your loss."

"Did you know Mary Kohl before she started at The Pickard Company?"

"Never saw her before."

Mechanical, no personality to the answer.

I said, "Do you know if anybody else did?"

"No."

"When Bernadette Nucci first brought Mary Kohl down to the Chapel, Billy Danvers made a remark, right?"

Carmody looked over at me squarely. "What?"

"Danvers said something about her, using her name."

"Oh, right. I forget what."

"Can you try to remember?"

"The exact words, you mean?"

"Yes."

"Oh, wow, that was what, a month ago?"

"Try."

"Try. Okay. Billy said something like 'Oh, boy. Here comes Mary, dudes.'"

"What'd he mean?"

Carmody turned her head squarely to me again. "I don't know. I didn't get it."

We entered the parking garage for the Galleria. Carmody slid the Taurus into a parking space and said I should wait.

I did. I also watched her walk to the store entrance off the garage. Fetching, but she never stopped at the trunk for any samples.

Once Carmody was gone three minutes, I reached over to the little lever near the driver's door and released the trunk lid. I got out and checked. Full of fancy wood dowls and metal clamps and security cables, all of which added up to retail fixtures and not much else I could see. I closed the trunk and got back in a full five minutes before Cassie Carmody returned, smiling and striding a little to show off her good shape.

◆ ◆ ◆

"And she didn't tell you anything on the way back either?"

"Just small talk. Intentionally so."

Bernadette Nucci rubbed her chin as we let the rush-hour traffic go by outside a coffeeshop. "Like, what do you think? You're wasting your time?"

"Maybe. Maybe there was nothing to Billy Danvers' comment, either, but I'm pretty sure he was lying to me at lunch, and I can't see why."

"I wish I could remember exactly what he said that day."

"Cassie Carmody told me it was 'Oh, boy. Here comes Mary, dudes.'"

"No. I mean, that's close, but . . ." A bleak smile. "Sorry."

"Billy said it was more 'H-e-e-e-e-r-e's Mary.'"

"What, like they used to do on Johnny Carson?"

"Right."

"No. No, then that's definitely wrong. It wasn't like that at all."

"Like what?"

"Like some announcer. It was more like . . . I don't know, like Billy was singing it?"

I just looked at her.

Five

Back in my office, I flipped through the notes I'd taken, trying to read the entries in a different order than I'd written them. Nothing seemed to make sense until I lined up three things I'd been told, one by Bernadette Nucci, another by Cassie Carmody, and a third by Arthur Pickard. Then I thought of something else, something I'd heard but never thought to write down.

It was thin, but I thought I could prove it one way or the other.

✦ ✦ ✦

The next day at ten o'clock, I was in the alley behind the Chapel, paying two guys in torn clothing who looked dirty and smelled worse ten bucks each to sit and be quiet with me since I was dressed the same way. I pulled an old Boston Red Sox bill-cap down over my eyes.

The Society of St. Nick came out and gathered about ten feet above and twenty feet away from me. The smokers talked about how Mr. Pickard had ranted and raved at them about the private investigator the day before. The wind was pretty steady, but it died once, and the pocket of calm brought that sweet smell of burning icing down to me. I took a deep breath, and shook my head for being right, because I didn't really want to be.

✦ ✦ ✦

"Hey, man, you are not supposed to be in here."

"Pickard give the repel-all-boarders command?"

"What are you talking about?"

I sat down in front of Donnell Willups. "I know, Donnell."

His face gave it up, some blinking, then almost a smile. "I knew it. I knew it when Billy came to see me yesterday, after you bought him the hot dog."

"He told you what I asked about?"

"Yeah. He didn't want me getting into trouble, so he said he turned it around some so you'd never get the drift of it. But you did, huh?"

"It took me a while. Bernadette, who's led a pretty sheltered life, told me you smoked these "horrendous" Turkish cigars. Cassie told me she had no sense of smell. Billy loves sixties' rock, and Bernadette said he nearly sang the words when she brought Mary Kohl along with her. The refrain to The Association's 'Along Comes Mary.' "

Willups nodded at his desk top, then took out the case with his "cigars" in them. "'Mary' short for marijuana. Billy saying, 'What do you know, Along Comes Mary.' "

"With Pickard's attitude on drugs, he would have pitched you out."

"In a heartbeat, son's memory or no son's memory. I was floundering here, Cuddy, buried in all this paperwork, but it's the only job I know. Hell, it's the only real job I ever had."

"Then Mary Kohl comes to the Chapel with Nucci, and Kohl realizes what you're smoking there."

"It was the pressure, man. I mean, if I'd been a guy who drinks it would have been martinis for lunch, you know what I'm saying? But back in the 'Nam, I developed a taste for the weed, and it helped me cope. Back then and now."

"Mary Kohl forced you to get her the transfer."

"I thought that might be it, might be enough. Hell, Billy didn't care what I smoked, and so she was the only threat. But I could see what she was doing. Just two days in my office and Mary was taking over my job. Taking it out from under me, man." Willups looked up. "Tunneling under me."

I thought of Cu Chi and nodded.

Willups opened the case, took out a rolled one and stuck it in his mouth, then started patting pockets for matches. "She was fixing to eat me up. I followed her from work once, my car along the trolley tracks. I figured Mary was the type to go home the same, direct way every day, and I was right. I waited for her that night, and . . ."

He seemed to just stall out, like a tired engine on a hill.

I said, "You'd have had to kill both Billy and me, you know."

Slowly, "I know. Billy, he never thought anything about me maybe being the one, but eventually he would. And once you were on to me, I . . ."

Another stall, except for the hand that found some matches. Willups had a match going when he suddenly stopped, the flame just inches from the tip of the paper. With the other hand, he took the "cigar" out of his mouth and looked at it.

I said, "Pickard's policy?"

The Vice President of Operations stared at me.

I let out a breath. "Go ahead. It doesn't make any difference now."

Donnell Willups stuck the thing back in his mouth and lit up.

SPIN-A-RAMA

One

The campaign headquarters for Riley Concannon was a storefront on the main street of the district's largest town. There were catchy posters taped in the windows and pleated buntings draped over them, the buntings flapping a little in the October breeze. I parked my old Honda Prelude at the curb and walked toward the door.

Inside the storefront, the colors red, white, and blue figured heavily in the decor. Volunteers staffed telephones that seemed hastily installed, the cables tied in bunches with those toothy plastic things that come with garbage bags. There were maps on the wall and coffee stains on the floor and card tables buckling under the weight of issue flyers that just had to be printed on recycled paper. The volunteers tended toward the young, with a sprinkling of cheery retired folks, mostly female.

A spry woman in her seventies bounded up from behind a counter where she'd been stuffing envelopes. The nametag over her left breast read "Doris" in curly, Palmer-style handwriting.

She said, "Can I help you?"

"I'm here to see Riley Concannon."

"Can I tell him your name?"

"Better not."

Doris looked at me, then decided against asking her next question. "One minute, please."

She walked toward the back of the space, touching the cardigan sleeve of a burly old gent in a Boston Bruins cap who was using a sponge to wet and seal envelopes. Doris leaned down and probably whispered something to him, because he nodded grimly and stopped with the envelopes and watched me until she reappeared.

The woman with Doris was about forty, five-five and a medium build under a gray suit. She had sharp features and a wary smile. Her reddish hair was thick and ripply, pulled back behind her head with the hanks bowing a little as they went past her ears.

The smile stayed wary as she thanked Doris and came up to me alone. In a low voice, she said, "Can I help you?"

"Riley Concannon called and asked me to come here."

The smile widened, but the voice stayed low. "John Francis Cuddy?"

I nodded.

Her hand came up to shake mine brusquely. "Nona Shapiro. I'm Riley's campaign manager. We appreciate your discretion."

"We won't look discreet much longer out here in the boiler-room."

Her turn to nod.

As we moved toward the back of the building, I could feel the eyes of Doris and her burly friend on me, but there wasn't much I could do about it. Shapiro took me down a corridor and pulled open an old six-paneled door that led to an office best described as cluttered. A broad-shouldered man about my age rose from behind the desk cramped into the corner. He had the buy-you-a-drink? grin and a nose to go with it, the cartilage broken honestly, the capillaries probably a little less so. His hair was sandy and professionally styled, the tie tugged down and the shirt sleeves rolled up eight inches before the elbow. He stayed behind the desk, so I can't say much about his trousers.

The hand extended itself on its own before he said, "Riley Concannon."

The firm shake of a man who wishes he could spend more time with you. "Mr. Concannon, John Cuddy."

"I don't know much about how the private investigator business works, but we really appreciate your coming up on such short notice."

I felt twice as appreciated as I had before. "Only a twenty-mile drive, and you sounded pretty urgent on the phone."

Concannon tilted his head, gauging something. "So why don't we cut short the preliminaries?"

"Since I'm on an hourly basis, it might make sense."

The bar grin again. "I like a man who gets down to business. Have a seat. Nona?"

Concannon resettled into his desk chair, Shapiro tapping a visitor's chair for me while taking one to my right.

She said, "What do you know about Riley, Mr. Cuddy?"

I said, "If we're going to call him Riley, you can call me John."

Shapiro didn't move her head to gauge you the way Concannon had. She just bored in with her eyes. "Meaning?"

"Meaning if it's his problem, why doesn't he tell me about it?"

Concannon said, "Nona's just looking out for the candidate, John."

I glanced from her to him. "I don't know anything."

Concannon's face clouded a little. "What?"

"I'm answering her original question. I don't know anything about you."

Shapiro said, "Riley was the best Democratic selectman the town of

Beacon Harbor ever had. When the Republican incumbent for the state senate seat from this district decided to step aside to accept a judgeship, our party nominated Riley in a heartbeat to run against the Republican challenger, Thomas Whiting."

Her last sentence sounded practiced, like she'd polished it for a press release. "Isn't Whiting a state rep now?"

Concannon said, "That's right, John. I know him pretty well. Hell, we both live in Beacon Harbor, our kids even go to the same school. He's represented this area for almost six years at the statehouse."

"Sounds like he's got a head start on you."

Shapiro said, "In more ways than one. This district's heavily suburban with some real old money, including Whiting's. It's voted Republican since Lincoln was inaugurated."

"So far your kind of problem doesn't sound like my kind of problem."

Concannon sighed and used a key to open a drawer in his desk. He rummaged under something, then came out with an envelope that was too short to be from a business and too narrow to hold a greeting card.

Shapiro said, "We have to be sure that what we're about to show you goes no further than this room."

"There's a confidentiality statute in Massachusetts that prevents me from revealing anything to anybody except a judge under the right compulsion. I'm not a lawyer, so I'm not sure what 'the right compulsion' would have to be, but as far as I know, there've been no cases interpreting that."

Concannon fanned himself absently with the envelope. "Thought you said you weren't a lawyer?"

I shifted in my chair. "Look, you want a private investigator, you could have your pick. I happen to know who referred you to me, because that lawyer called me about two minutes before you did this morning. You asked him whether he could recommend me, he told you he could because I kept my mouth shut after a very bad case went sour for him. You can rely on me, or you can rely on the confidentiality statute and somebody else. Your choice."

Concannon said, "Nona?"

She looked to him.

He said, "I'm persuaded."

Shapiro looked back to me. "I am, too. Show it to him."

Concannon flipped the envelope toward my side of the desk as though he were dealing poker. "Read it to yourself, okay? I'm pretty sick of it."

The return address was embossed in brown, raised ink. Just three initials, "E.O.P.," with periods after them, but an address of "Olde Marsh Lane," no street number, in Beacon Harbor. I opened the flap and took out a parchment piece of notepaper embossed in the same ink with the full name "Evelyn Otis Poole" at the top. It didn't take long to read the note:

Dear Mr. Concannon,

You may recall our meeting at the Friends of the Library breakfast last month. While I was pleased to be introduced to your son, I am afraid I bear rather disturbing news about him.

Last Wednesday, while shopping in Boston, I was shocked to see your son in the company of a disreputable boy. I observed them for only a few moments, but it was evident that the second boy was what I believe is called a 'street hustler,' and they then entered an alley together off Boylston Street. Obviously, I did not remain to see them emerge. However, I do feel it my duty to alert you to this appalling situation and provide you the opportunity to correct it, if possible.

Very truly yours,

Evelyn Otis Poole

I re-read the letter. The handwriting was crabbed, but had a few flourishes that compared to Doris's nametag. Then I folded the notepaper, put it back in the envelope, and returned the package to Concannon. "Well, you have a problem."

He locked the thing in his drawer. "Kevin's the one with the problem."

"Is that your son's name?"

"Yes."

I said, "Being gay isn't the problem. If Kevin's hanging out with the sparrows on lower Boylston, though, he's running one hell of a health risk."

Concannon started to say something, then bit it back and shook his head.

Shapiro filled in for him. "You see, John, Tom Whiting is an upstanding, family-values kind of candidate."

Concannon said, "And I'm not?"

She looked at him. "Riley, please?"

He shook his head some more, but shut up.

Shapiro came back to me. "If this Poole woman ever approaches Whiting or one of his people with her story, there's no way I can run it through the spin-a-rama."

"The what?"

"The spin-a-rama. You know, put a spin on the story that would sell through to the voters."

I said, "Any chance this is a set-up by the other camp?"

"I don't think so. That Friends of the Library event was on the level."

Concannon said, "Family thing, everybody gets to meet the candidates and the spouses and all."

Shapiro seemed to hold her breath, as though she were relieved that's all he had to say on the subject. "After we got her letter, I called Poole on the phone."

I said, "Something like this, you didn't see her personally?"

Shapiro said, "I remembered her from the breakfast. One of the staunch types, the kind who'd send back her eggs if they were a little runny. Besides, I—we weren't sure how seriously to take this."

"And?"

"And Miss Poole—she made a real point of that, by the way, 'Miss,' not 'Miz'—was sure she wasn't mistaken."

I turned to Concannon. "Have you asked your son about it?"

He swallowed hard. "It's not the kind of thing I usually bring up with him, no."

"I meant, maybe there's a reasonable explanation."

Shapiro said, "We've gone through and over this, Riley and I. What we'd like you to do is try to find a reasonable explanation."

"I don't get you."

Concannon said, "We want you to follow Kevin. Not for a week, like spying on him or anything. Just try to figure out whether what Poole says is true."

"And if it is?"

Shapiro cut in. "Then we want a couple of photographs, enough evidence so Riley knows he'd be quitting a lost race instead of dropping out of just a tough one too early."

"Photos? Why not simply take my word for it?"

Concannon's voice cracked with emotion. "Because I want to have something in my pocket if I have to talk to my son about this, John. I want him to know that we—his mother and I—are concerned about his health, both medical and mental. If you find out Poole's right, and Kevin denies it, I want to be able to confront him with some proof without you having to be there. I want to force him to seek help."

"I don't think that's the way to do it."

"It'd be my way, and I'm his father."

Shapiro said, "Will you help us?"

I thought about it. If I passed on the job, somebody else would still do it, maybe somebody who'd try to sell the results both ways. Or somebody who'd tell Concannon, "Hey, no problem," then shake down the kid for as many years as it took him to get out of the house.

I said, "What do you have in mind?"

She glanced to Concannon. "Riley, check me on this. I think all you need to do, John, is follow Kevin this Wednesday."

Concannon said, "Kevin gets out of school at one on Wednesdays."

"Following somebody by car isn't as easy as it looks on TV."

Shapiro shook her head. "No, no. Kevin doesn't drive yet. If he did go to Boston, it would be by train."

I said, "Not many commuters that time of day. I could probably just meet his train at North Station in Boston, pick him out as he left the platform."

Concannon said, "That makes sense."

"You have a picture of him?"

The candidate didn't have to dip into the drawer. He spun a photo toward me. It showed a dozen teen-agers posed standing and kneeling under a banner that said, "Civics Club." Two of the boys had sandy hair and a hint of Concannon's shoulders, but there was no caption. "Which one is he?"

Concannon said, "Kevin's on the far right. I thought this shot would show you how he looks in relation to other boys his age."

I studied the photo. The boy had an anxious smile, like he was afraid the flash would go off before he was ready. "Can I take this?"

"I'd rather you didn't. I had to borrow it from a teacher at Kevin's school."

Okay. I returned it to him. "When do you want to hear back from me?"

Shapiro said, "Yesterday."

Two

"Hey, John Cuddy! I thought you'd be coming up last summer?"

"For the beach, you mean?"

"Yeah, I told you, Beacon Harbor's got the nicest sand on the north shore, and the parking's still just five bucks, even—"

"On the weekends. I remember, Sergeant."

"You remember that, you also got to remember that I don't like the 'sergeant' stuff. I'm outta uniforms to stay. Sit down."

I took the chair next to Joe Patrizzi's desk on the second floor of the police station. There was a nice view of an autumn-dotted hillside out the window. A benny you tended not to get in the city.

Patrizzi slurped some coffee from a mug with "DAD IS THE GREATEST" baked into the side of it. "So, what can I do you for?"

"Nothing this trip. Just a courtesy call, let you know I'm poking around a little up here."

He ran his tongue around the inside of his mouth. "The killing we had last spring?"

"No, I'm finished with that, far as I know."

"This poking you're doing, you figure it'll draw some blood?"

"Not the way it looks right now."

Patrizzi nodded judiciously. "You do me a favor, huh? Its looks start to change any, you pick up the phone, let me know."

"If I can."

"If. That don't sound too courteous to me, Cuddy."

✦ ✦ ✦

The narrow macadam skirted the harbor and a rocky bluff before straightening out into a country lane. I finally saw a converted cottage overlooking about five acres of salt marsh. If you can call a sprawling twelve or fifteen rooms a "cottage." That's what the sign on Olde Marsh Lane called it, though. "The Poole Cottage." The only building in sight on Olde Marsh Lane, too. Probably the way Miss Poole wanted it.

I walked up the flagstone path to the weathered-shingle porch and forest-green door, crickets chirping from the meadow grass. Riley Concannon wouldn't be too keen on my seeing his pen pal, but I wanted to get a look at her from a credibility standpoint before I cooled my heels in a train station for an hour or so on Wednesday.

The woman who answered my knock was pushing sixty and dressed rustically, like an advertisement from L.L. Bean before it got fashionable. Her brown-and-gray hair was short all around, barely touching her collar in the back. "Yes?"

"Miss Poole?"

"Yes."

"My name's John Francis. I'm investigating the situation you described in a letter to Mr. Concannon."

"Investigating? Oh, my word, do come in."

You have money long enough, maybe other people stop trying to take it from you and you grow to trust them. She led me into a comfortable living room with antique furniture so good it probably never would look old. Poole asked if I'd like tea, and I declined, because it was obvious that the woman really wanted to talk with me.

After we sat down, she said, "I was hoping someone would take my note seriously."

"We do, Ma'am. But because of the delicacy of the matter, I have to ask you to promise not to reveal anything we discuss to anyone."

"Oh, of course."

"I wonder, can you elaborate on what you said in the letter?"

"Well, yes, at least a bit. I'd taken the ten-oh-four into Boston to do some shopping. I cabbed from North Station to Copley Place, but it's just so tourist-oriented, I tend never to stay for very long."

"I agree completely."

"I visited Lord & Taylor's as well, and then had an exquisite lunch at DuBarry's on Newbury. There are so few good French restaurants left to us given all that yuppie nonsense."

"Do you recall when you finished lunch?"

"Oh, I had no need to look at my watch, but I went from there to Shreve, Crump & Low on Boylston. One always must stop at Shreve's, even with the financial . . . embarrassments of their recent past."

"When did you see Mr. Concannon's son?"

"Coming out of Shreve's. I distinctly remember looking at my watch, because I wanted to be sure to make the two-forty-two from North Station. Any later than that, and it becomes nearly impossible to obtain a decent seat for reading."

"And what time was it?"

"What . . . ? Oh, when I looked at my watch? Two-twenty-three, exactly. I saw the Concannon boy halfway up the block. He approached this . . . urchin, I suppose would be the polite phrase, though I was a bit more direct in my note. I didn't see any money change hands, but from the way the other boy was dressed, it was quite obvious what the purpose of the transaction was."

"You're sure it was Kevin?"

"Kevin? Is that his name? I met him only the once at the Friends breakfast, but I'm certain it was he."

"Miss Poole, you said you were half a block away."

"Yes, but he is quite distinctive, you know."

"Distinctive?"

"Yes. His . . . tic I suppose you might call it. Or perhaps it's more like a . . . flinch?"

Poole flicked her head to the right, mimicking a punch-drunk boxer. I thought about Kevin Concannon's anxious smile for the photographer, the boy maybe concerned about moving involuntarily at the wrong moment.

I said, "Anything else?"

"Well, I watched them walk toward me and around the block to an alley. One might say a 'convenient' alley. Obviously, I did not remain any longer than that."

"Well, I appreciate your time, Miss Poole."

"I just do hope your Mister Concannon does the responsible thing."

"I'm sorry?"

"Withdraw from the race, before a scandal like this smears him forever."

✦ ✦ ✦

The view from her hillside isn't like the ones Patrizzi and Poole enjoy. There's only the green of the lawn gone brownish from night frosts and the engine noises from commercial boats coming into Boston harbor. The roses I laid diagonally to her headstone riffled in the breeze off the water.

Roses. What's the occasion?

"A case, Beth. One I feel a little guilty taking."

Why?

I explained it to her.

Sad that the father can't talk outright to the son.

Beth and I had never had any kids. Never wanted them, really, but I knew what she meant. "Well, maybe this'll be a step in the right direction."

I hope so, but don't let it get you down if it's not.

As I nodded, the wind came up a tad stronger, forcing me to realign the flowers so the petals wouldn't be blown off the stems.

Three

North Station is a quirky kind of place. It's located in the rear end of Boston Garden, where Orr used to skate and Bird used to shoot. On a game night, it's a zoo, fourteen thousand people jamming up the ramps to find their seats. But on a Wednesday afternoon in October, the station is a quiet place of suburban shoppers waiting for irregular trains, homeless people waiting to be rousted, and tourists from countries where train-travel is a more accepted way of sight-seeing.

Sitting on a scarred wooden bench, I checked the schedule in my right hand. The train that left Beacon Harbor half an hour after Kevin Concannon got out of school would be arriving in about ten minutes. I was decked out in a ski sweater, khaki slacks, and running shoes as walking shoes. I also had a 35-millimeter camera, an unfolded map of Boston, and the stupidest hat I could find. The hat was a baseball cap, the crown over its bill sporting a cartoon lobster wearing a bib. Since I'd have to have a camera around my neck, I decided the cap would help me blend in as a tourist because nobody in Boston has ever seen anyone from Boston with a lobster-anything on them.

The Beacon Harbor train arrived, and I spotted Kevin Concannon right away. He had a gangly, rolling gait, and the head flicked to the right erratically just the way Miss Poole had demonstrated. He wore pressed wool trousers and a calf's wool sweater himself, no hat stupid or otherwise.

Concannon passed my bench. I waited ten strides, then rose and started after him. Outside the station, he crossed Causeway Street and hopped a Green Line trolley like he'd done it all his life. I got on the next car and edged my way to the front of it, watching Kevin through the windshield as both trolleys jounced up and down on the rails. He stayed on past Park Street station, not getting off until Arlington. I followed him up the stairs to the first block of Boylston Street.

It didn't take long.

Concannon made eye contact with a scraggly kid who might have been twenty trying very hard to look sixteen. He wore a bandanna around his neck and tight hiking shorts on a day way too cold for them. The kid smiled at Kevin, talked and joshed a little with him, then inclined his head toward the corner. I snapped off three shots of the boys before they turned and began walking. I got to the head of the alley just as they were choosing a dumpster to go behind. I took two more shots and kept walking past the alley.

Twenty minutes later the kid with the bandanna came out, Concannon trailing him by a minute. Kevin walked back to Boylston, then crossed it, taking an outside table at Au Bon Pain and having a pastry and a styrofoam cup of something that steamed into the fall air.

After about fifteen minutes, a boy walking past the tables lingered a little. This one wore a turquoise body shirt and studded black jeans over cowboy boots, doing his lingering to hitch up one of the boots. Concannon left his table and joined him, the two of them making their way to the same alley. I took basically the same establishing shots again.

This time it was twenty-five minutes, but Kevin came out first, checking his watch and starting to hoof it a little. He flagged a cab, and the taxi took off down Boylston, making the turn at Charles toward North Station and, I guessed, home.

Four

On Thursday morning, Riley Concannon and Nona Shapiro gave me the impression I was their first priority conference of the day. I hoped so.

I laid the manila envelope on the cluttered desk. Concannon's hands twitched, like they didn't really want to open it.

Shapiro said, "Bad?"

"About what Miss Poole described. Two different hustlers within the span of an hour."

Concannon said, "Jesus, Mary, and Joseph."

Shapiro's eyes bored into me. "You can trust the place that developed these?"

"Completely."

She nodded. "Look, John, I know this hasn't been easy for you, either. I thank you for making it a little easier for us."

"Can I see you outside for a minute?"

Shapiro glanced over at Concannon, who was still just staring at the manila envelope. "Okay, but just a minute."

The corridor beyond the six-paneled door was empty, the volunteers, even Doris, not yet on the job.

Shapiro closed the door gently behind her. "If it's the money—"

"What we agreed to is fine. And will be fine. This isn't a shakedown, just a suggestion."

"What is it?"

"Before Riley pulls the plug on the campaign, be sure he talks to Kevin first."

"That's kind of his business as the boy's parent, don't you think?"

"I think that if Kevin hears the plug got pulled before he and Riley work things out, a lot more'll be lost besides a seat in the Massachusetts senate."

Shapiro pursed her lips. "Thank you, John. Thank you for caring."

✦ ✦ ✦

I'm not particularly political, but I found myself scanning the Metro section of the Globe each day, watching to see what would happen to Concannon's campaign. It took almost a week, till the following Monday, but the story made the front page. I felt my stomach turning as I read the headline.

It said, "CANDIDATE WITHDRAWS IN SHOCK OVER DEATH OF SON." The article reported that the boy fell from a rocky promontory near Olde Marsh Lane in Beacon Harbor. I pictured it from my visit to Miss Poole's cottage. The last paragraph told me that the candidate was withdrawing from the race to mourn the loss, the family expected to be in seclusion for several days.

That much was understandable. The part that wasn't included the photographs and the captions underneath them.

One photo showed a stern-looking man with cotton balls of gray gracing his temples. The caption under him read, "Thomas Whiting." The other shot showed the boy I'd followed and photographed. It wasn't the yearbook club display, but there was no mistaking the anxious smile.

The caption under him read, "David Whiting."

I tried out my voice to make sure it was working, then picked up the telephone.

✦ ✦ ✦

"Police, Patrizzi."

"This is John Cuddy calling."

"Cuddy! Look, ordinarily I'd be happy to kibitz a while, but we had kind of a tragedy here yesterday, you know what I'm saying?"

"I read about it. The politician's son?"

"Yeah."

"Tough thing."

"Maybe tougher than you think."

"How do you mean?"

"Well, I don't know, is it ever gonna come out, but it does, you didn't hear it from me first, right?"

"Right."

"Okay." Patrizzi lowered his voice a little. "We got a maybe eye-witness."

"A 'maybe' eye-witness?"

"Yeah. Woman driving her kid to the sitter's, using that part of the harbor road that winds around the bluff. She says she only got a little glimpse like of the Whiting boy, but she's pretty sure he didn't fall."

"No?"

"God's truth. She says he jumped."

✦ ✦ ✦

"Miss Poole?"

"Yes?"

"Miss Poole, this is John Francis calling. We spoke last week at your cottage."

"Oh, my word, yes. I must say, I feel just terrible about this."

"We all do."

"I just hope my confusing which boy was which at the Friends breakfast didn't have anything to do with . . . well, to do with what happened."

"I'm sure it didn't, Miss Poole."

"Well, I'm certainly relieved to hear that."

"I do have a question I forgot to ask you, though."

"Another question?"

"Yes. Just to round out my report."

"What is it?"

I told her, and she told me.

Five

I hung back at campaign headquarters, catching the tail end of the press conference with a couple of dozen rubber-neckers packed just inside the door. The television kliegs made everything seem hot and close, Riley Concannon in what I took to be his trademark tie-tugged-down, sleeves-rolled-up posture behind the impromptu podium, Nona Shapiro just out of camera range on the right, surveying the crowd, not noticing me. Doris and her burly friend stood respectfully in a clatch of volunteers on the other side of the podium. The candidate managed to twist the last question into seeming to fit the perfect, sound-bite answer he gave that had everybody in the room nodding.

After Concannon and Shapiro repaired to the rear corridor, I waited until the camera crews had broken down and the print reporters had rewound and listened to their audiotapes. Then I sidled through the waning crowd without Doris or her friend seeing me.

When I got to the six-paneled door, I didn't bother knocking. Shapiro and Concannon were just breaking a hug in front of his desk. Not passionate, just the sort of spontaneity you jump to when the home team comes from behind to score the winning touchdown.

I said, "A little early to be celebrating, don't you think?"

Shapiro recovered while Concannon's mouth was still open. "John. I was hoping you'd be by."

"I doubt it, Nona, I really do."

Concannon started to say something, but Shapiro put her palm on his chest, and he stopped.

I said, "Good advice, Nona. Hear what I've got first, right?"

Shapiro said, "Would you like to sit down?"

"Thanks, no. I'm not sure I trust even the furniture in this room."

Concannon said, "Now just a—"

"Can it, you sanctimonious son of a bitch. You get me up here, show me Miss Poole's letter and that club photo—"

Shapiro rode over me. "We realized what happened there, John. You see, as you were looking at it, Riley said Kevin was the boy on the far right, but he was thinking *his*—Riley's—right, not yours."

"Nice try, but I'm afraid it just doesn't wash."

Concannon said, "It was an understandable mistake. I was upset, concerned about Kevin."

"When you first got Poole's letter, sure. But after Nona here made her ever-so-obtuse phone call to the woman, you realized exactly what had fallen into your lap."

Shapiro said, "I don't know what you're—"

"On the telephone, Nona. Miss Poole tells me that she mentioned to you about 'Kevin's' tic or flinch or whatever the poor Whiting boy had."

Concannon said, "You weren't supposed to see Poole. We told you—"

"So after that call, Riley, you and Nona knew it was Whiting's son Miss Poole saw in Boston, and you had to figure just what to do with it. Only it had to be obtuse, like Nona's phone call. A set-up that preserved deniability, which is what you're doing now. That's where I came in. Right, Nona?"

Shapiro crossed her arms and rested her rump on the desk. "It's your pipe dream, John. You tell it."

"More than a pipe dream, Nona. You got me to acknowledge the confidentiality statute to you, keeping me from going to anybody after you or Riley or more likely some go-between gave Thomas Whiting those photos I took. How did you phrase it, a 'kindness'? Did your message read something like, 'Tom, despite our respective positions on the issues, the enclosed is something I think any parent deserves to know'?"

Concannon began to speak again, but Shapiro said, "He can't do anything with this, Riley. Don't you see it? That's why he's here ragging us. Cuddy tells anybody about this, about what he even thinks we did, and he loses his license for violating a client's confidence."

I said, "Did you ever even think about what a candidate who's as four-square on 'family values' as Whiting would do? How he'd broach it to his son? What the kid might do after that?"

Concannon got resolute. "I think we've said all we're going to say, Cuddy."

"Not quite, Riley."

He stared at me, but I addressed Shapiro. "Here's the new program, Nona. I'm so overcome by grief that I can't sleep. I go to Whiting, apologize to him and—"

Shapiro said, "We'd have your license in an—"

"Interrupt me again, and I'll belt you." It seemed to sink in. "I'm guessing the board that registers me would understand. Guilt and grief are strong emotions, Nona. They make you do impulsive things. Like withdraw from the race."

Neither said anything.

I held up my hand, index and middle fingers extended. "Your choices are two. Number One, you can withdraw now, I don't talk to anybody, and nobody goes after my license. You don't get sued by Whiting's family and so tarred from the litigation you never run for anything again. Number Two, you can stonewall it, have me go to Whiting while you come after my license. His lawyers will hound you, and Whiting or any warm, breathing body the Republicans put up will blow you away at the polls. Number One or Number Two, but either way, you're out of this race."

Concannon said, "Time. You have to give us—"

"Tomorrow morning, boyo."

Shapiro said, "Tomor—"

"Tomorrow morning, Nona. I don't hear a bulletin about Riley pulling out by then, my grief and guilt will compel me to follow Number Two."

Concannon said, "But that doesn't give us a chance to—"

"What? Put my new program through the old 'spin-a-rama'? You're right, folks, it doesn't."

I managed not to slam the six-panel, but I found the optimism in the boiler-room so thick I nearly gagged walking to my car.

THE CONCISE CUDDY

The Concise Cuddy, A Collection of John Francis Cuddy Stories by Jeremiah Healy is printed on 50-pound Glatfelter Supple Opaque recycled acid-free paper, from 11-point Garamond. The cover painting is by Carol Heyer, and the design by Deborah Miller. The first edition is comprised of approximately one thousand, two hundred copies in trade softcover, and two hundred fifty copies sewn in cloth, signed and numbered by the author. Each of the clothbound copies includes a separate pamphlet, *City Life*, by Jeremiah Healy. *The Concise Cuddy* was printed and bound by Thomson-Shore, Inc., Dexter, Michigan, and published in December 1998 by Crippen & Landru Publishers, Norfolk, Virginia.

CRIPPEN & LANDRU, PUBLISHERS
P. O. Box 9315
Norfolk, VA 23505

Crippen & Landru publishes first editions of important works by detective and mystery writers, specializing in short-story collections. Most books are published both in trade softcover and in signed, limited cloth-bound with either a typescript page from the author's files or an additional story in a separate pamphlet.

Speak of the Devil by John Dickson Carr. Eight-part impossible crime mystery broadcast on BBC radio. Introduction by Tony Medawar; cover design by Deborah Miller. Softcover, Out of Print

The McCone Files by Marcia Muller. Fifteen Sharon McCone short stories by the creator of the modern female private eye, including two written especially for the collection. Winner of the Anthony Award for Best Short Story collection. Introduction by the author; cover painting by Carol Heyer.
Signed, limited edition, Out of Print
Softcover, third printing, $15.00

The Darings of the Red Rose by Margery Allingham. Eight stories about a female Robin Hood, written in 1930. Introduction by B. A. Pike; cover design by Deborah Miller. Softcover, Out of Print

Diagnosis: Impossible, The Problems of Dr. Sam Hawthorne by Edward D. Hoch. Twelve stories about the country doctor who solves "miracle problems," written by today's expert on the challenge-to-the-reader story. Introduction by the author; chronology by Marvin Lachman; cover painting by Carol Heyer. Signed, limited edition, Out of Print
Softcover, Out of Stock

Spadework: A Collection of "Nameless Detective" Stories by Bill Pronzini. Fifteen stories, including two written for the collection, by a Grandmaster of the Private Eye tale. Introduction by Marcia Muller; afterword by the author; cover painting by Carol Heyer. Signed, limited edition, $40.00
Softcover, $16.00

Who Killed Father Christmas? And Other Unseasonable Demises by Patricia Moyes. Twenty-one stories ranging from holiday homicides to village villainies to Caribbean crimes. Introduction by the author; cover design by Deborah Miller. Signed, limited edition, $40.00
Softcover, $16.00

My Mother, The Detective: The Complete "Mom" Short Stories, by James Yaffe. Eight stories about the Bronx armchair maven who solves crimes between the chicken soup and the *schnecken*. Introduction by the author; cover painting by Carol Heyer. Signed, limited edition, Out of Print
Softcover, $15.00

In Kensington Gardens Once . . . by H. R. F. Keating. Ten crime and mystery stories taking place in London's famous park, including two written for this collection, by the recipient of the Cartier Diamond Dagger for Lifetime Achievement. Illustrations and cover by Gwen Mandley.
Signed, limited edition, $35.00
Softcover, $12.00

Shoveling Smoke: Selected Mystery Stories by Margaret Maron. Twenty-two stories by the Edgar-award winning author, including all the short cases of Sigrid Harald and Deborah Knott, one of which was written for this collection. Introduction and prefaces to each story by the author; cover painting by Victoria Russell. Signed, limited edition, Out of Print
Softcover, second printing, $16.00

The Man Who Hated Banks and Other Mysteries by Michael Gilbert. Eighteen detective stories by the recipient of the Mystery Writers of America's Grandmaster Award. Introduction by the author; cover painting by Deborah Miller. Signed, limited edition, Out of Print
Softcover, second printing, $16.00

The Ripper of Storyville and Other Ben Snow Tales by Edward D. Hoch. The first fourteen historical detective stories about the gunslinger who is often confused with Billy the Kid. Introduction by the author; Ben Snow chronology by Marvin Lachman; cover painting by Barbara Mitchell.
Signed, limited edition, Out of Print
Softcover, $16.00

Do Not Exceed the Stated Dose by Peter Lovesey. Fifteen crime and mystery stories, including two featuring Peter Diamond and two featuring Bertie, Prince of Wales. Preface by the author; cover painting by Carol Heyer.
Signed, limited edition, Out of Print
Softcover, $16.00

Renowned Be Thy Grave; Or, The Murderous Miss Mooney by P. M. Carlson. Ten stories about Bridget Mooney, the Victorian actress who becomes involved in important historical events. Introduction by the author; cover design by Deborah Miller. Signed, limited edition, $40.00
Softcover, $16.00

Carpenter and Quincannon, Professional Detective Services by Bill Pronzini. Nine detective stories, including one written for this volume, set in San Francisco during the 1890's. Introduction by the author; cover painting by Carol Heyer. Signed, limited edition, $40.00
Softcover, $16.00

Not Safe After Dark and Other Stories by Peter Robinson. Thirteen stories, including one written for this volume, about Inspector Banks and others. Introduction and prefaces to each story by the author; cover painting by Victoria Russell. Signed, limited edition, $40.00
Softcover, $16.00

The Concise Cuddy, A Collection of John Francis Cuddy Stories, by Jeremiah Healy. Seventeen stories about the Boston private eye by the Shamus Award winner. Introduction by the author; cover painting by Carol Heyer.
Signed, limited edition, $42.00
Softcover, $17.00

The following short-story collections are forthcoming:

One Night Stands by Lawrence Block.
All Creatures Dark and Dangerous: The Dr. David Westbrook Stories by Doug Allyn.
Silent Prayers by Ed Gorman.
Fortune's Fortunes: Dan Fortune's Casebook by Michael Collins.
The Tragedy of Errors and Others: The Lost Stories of Ellery Queen.
McCone and Friends by Marcia Muller.
Challenge the Widow Maker and Others by Clark Howard.
The Velvet Touch by Edward D. Hoch.
The Spotted Cat and Other Mysteries: The Casebook of Inspector Cockrill by Christianna Brand.
Tales Out of School by Carolyn Wheat.
The Adventure of the Murdered Moths and Other Radio Mysteries by Ellery Queen.

Crippen & Landru offers discounts to individuals and institutions who place Standing Order Subscriptions for its forthcoming publications. Please write for details.